HIRED TO
KILL

WITHDRAWN

ALSO BY ANDREW PETERSON

HIRED TO KILL

A **NATHAN MCBRIDE** NOVEL

ANDREW PETERSON

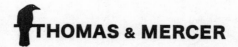THOMAS & MERCER

Text copyright © 2018 by Andrew Peterson
All rights reserved.

No part of this book may be reproduced, or stored in a retrieval system, or transmitted in any form or by any means, electronic, mechanical, photocopying, recording, or otherwise, without express written permission of the publisher.

Published by Thomas & Mercer, Seattle

www.apub.com

Amazon, the Amazon logo, and Thomas & Mercer are trademarks of Amazon.com, Inc., or its affiliates.

ISBN-13: 9781503949300
ISBN-10: 1503949303

Cover design by Ray Lundgren

Printed in the United States of America

This book is dedicated to my uncle,
Glenhall E. Taylor (1925–2016).
A hero in every sense of the word, he served with
distinction and bravery in the US Army's
Eighty-Seventh Infantry Division under
General Patton during the Battle of the Bulge.
A Purple Heart recipient, he is survived by my cousins,
Myrica, Glen, Jamie, and Bill, along with nine
grandchildren and five great-grandchildren.
The Taylor family line is alive and well!

CHAPTER 1

Driving to the twenty-four-hour grocery store, Nathan McBride couldn't shake his dark mood. Every so often, a black curtain descended onto the stage of his life, separating contentment from anguish. It used to trouble him. A lot. But over the years, he'd learned to ride it out. This morning would be no different. Time tended to heal wounds, and Nathan had some deep ones. He'd been reliving his stint in the cage, suspended above the jungle floor, suffering a slow death by starvation. A cruel end to three weeks of interrogation and torture. You'd think twenty-six years would be enough time to move on, but memories hurt more than physical scars. Scars could be hidden. Memories? Not so much.

The saving grace to his life? Harvey's friendship. Nathan's relationship with Holly Simpson was special, albeit long distance, but his bond with Harv went beyond understanding. Harv had risked everything returning to the Nicaraguan jungle to rescue him. Nathan wouldn't have lasted another day. Thank goodness he couldn't remember being carried. He'd spent the two-mile trek unconscious, sparing himself the agony of multiple broken bones, dislocated joints, and severely lacerated skin. His tormentor had been quite thorough.

Stop dwelling. It happened. It's over.

Move on . . .

Like it or not, he'd fallen into another solitary pattern. If it weren't for his live-in housekeeper and his dogs, he wouldn't have any personal contact with other warm-blooded beings for days at a time. Not all was lost. He called his parents regularly, exchanged a few texts with Holly on a daily basis, and took walks and jogs around his Mount Soledad neighborhood.

He wished he could spend more time with Harv, but by trying to help his business partner with the day-to-day operations of their security company, he only got in the way. Harv did everything and, quite frankly, didn't need his "help."

At least Nathan recognized the signs of his own isolation and made an effort to correct his behavior. *Right . . . like shopping for groceries at four in the morning?*

From his Clairemont home, the store was less than a ten-minute drive, especially with no traffic. Downtown San Diego didn't mirror Times Square. This city rolled up its sidewalks well before midnight.

He pulled into the underground garage and scanned his surroundings before getting out. The clunk of his Mustang's door echoed for several seconds. Four other cars sat dormant against the far side of this concrete crypt, probably the employees' rides. Nathan could handle most ruffians, drunks, and two-bit meth heads, but it didn't hurt to be cautious. Better to avoid a fight in the first place. Given his six-foot-five frame, the long scars marking his face, and eyes the color of glacial ice, bullies rarely tested him. More often than not, Nathan found trouble, not the reverse.

The elevator dumped him inside the store, and he again checked his immediate area. All quiet. During these predawn visits, he'd usually encounter a stocker, maintenance worker, or someone checking inventory, but he rarely saw a shopper.

He didn't note anything except for the obnoxious security camera—an intrusive construct of plastic, metal, processor chips, and glass. Despite its antiseptic appearance, the black polyp in the ceiling felt threatening, like the motionless glare of a predator. He really despised what it represented—the annihilation of privacy. The prying eyes of Big Brother were everywhere. If not the government, then private industry. Vegas casinos were the worst.

He'd love to end its electronic life with a two iron.

Oh, man, that would feel good right about now.

He felt hypocrisy at the silly thought. His private security company routinely installed cameras for its clients.

Nathan wondered what the fear of cameras was called. There were official names for every phobia imaginable. He was tempted to pull his phone and look it up but thought, *Screw it.* The world's already infested with a billion and a half cell phone addicts who can't last more than a few minutes without their artificial companions.

Walking past the florist's station, he thought of Holly and made a mental note to have some flowers delivered to her office in the J. Edgar Hoover Building. It seemed hard to believe they'd been together for six years. Ever since her promotion to the FBI's chief of staff, they hadn't seen each other enough.

He offered a forced smile to the cashier. She waved back and quickly resumed staring at her phone. He wondered how many hours she stole from her employer.

Blown away by all the food choices, he rolled his cart down the crackers-and-snacks aisle. No matter how many times he saw this, it still dumbfounded him. What would a starving child from Sumatra think of this obscene display? Thankfully, this stuff didn't get tossed like dairy, produce, and meat. He'd once heard a shocking statistic: every year in the United States, one-third of all the food it produces gets thrown away. *One-third!* Could that be true? Something on the order of 150 billion pounds. He knew it was pointless to think about it, but damn, that was a crazy number.

Nathan never took food for granted. He had, after all, been literally starving to death at one point. Wastefulness didn't anger him as it once had, but—well—okay, yeah, it still pissed him off. A bunch, actually. He'd written his congressman and received a rubber-stamped form letter thanking him for voicing his opinion and doing his civic duty as a concerned citizen. Blah, blah, blah. Typical career politician . . . *like my father?* He knew it wasn't fair to malign his dad or politicians in general. Someone had to do it, right? So why not the great Stone McBride? A perfect fit.

He turned right at the Oreo cookies endcap and worked his way toward the meat counter, currently closed. At the household-needs aisle, he glanced right and saw a mixed Hispanic and white family. Presumably they were a family. These days, you never knew.

What happened next pissed him off worse than seventy-five million tons of wasted food.

Just before he moved out of their line of sight, he saw the man's arm swing in a wide arc toward the woman. He didn't see the impact, but he heard it.

A hard, meaty slap.

He pivoted his cart 180 degrees and returned to the mouth of the aisle.

Holding her cheek, the woman cried softly. The guy looked at Nathan and made an exaggerated "mind your own business" gesture. Firmly hugging her mom's leg, the child had her back to the man.

Don't do it, Nate. Don't you dare . . .

Too late. He'd already started down the aisle.

There were three surefire ways to press Nathan McBride's buttons. Strike a woman. Hurt a child. Or kick a dog.

This jerk probably did all three on a regular basis.

Approaching, he smelled the stench of alcohol.

Not beer or wine. Hard stuff.

Dressed in blue jeans, a white T-shirt, and a smeared ball cap, the guy was pasty white, big—maybe six two—and noticeably overweight. Cheap tats marred his arms. His wife or girlfriend stood a foot shorter. The little girl looked five or six with skin darker than the man's and lighter than the woman's.

Most people would've been intimidated by the guy's size, unless they stood three inches taller, weighed the same, and had a BMI of less than 15 percent—which happened to be Nathan's build.

It's not too late to turn back. You know this isn't going to end well. For who? Or is it whom? Probably whom.

With a smug expression, the man squared up and made no attempt to hide his revulsion at the sight of Nathan's scarred face. A southern drawl declared, "This ain't your concern, Frankenstein. Mind your own business."

Frankenstein? What a dumb ass . . . although technically the monster's name was Adam Frankenstein. Not that this joker had any clue.

Oddly, the guy's speech wasn't the least bit slurred—apparently, he had a high tolerance for corn whiskey.

The man possessed high Slavic cheekbones but lacked the requisite chin structure. Clearly his family tree didn't have enough branches. Six days of stubble made him look like a bad facsimile of Fred Flintstone. When the little girl looked at Nathan, he saw a trace of dried blood under her nose, and her left arm displayed a bruise above the elbow. Her clothes and shoes were scuffed and dirty.

"Are you deaf? I said mind your own business."

Nathan ignored the question and appraised the woman. In her mid-twenties, she wore an inexpensive skirt and buttoned shirt. Black hair hung in a single long braid. Fine cheekbones. Dark brown eyes.

Her most noticeable characteristic: a lifeless expression. Not fear, only hopelessness.

Nathan locked eyes with her and nodded toward the man. "Habla él español?" *Does he speak Spanish?*

She shook her head but didn't say anything.

"Está usted casada?" *Are you married?*

Another no.

"Hey, asshole, what're you saying?"

Without taking his eyes from the woman, Nathan pointed at the man's face, snapped his finger, and said, "Please watch your language."

The woman clutched her daughter tighter when the guy lashed out with the f-bomb.

Nathan ignored it. "Quiere usted que llame a la policía?" *Do you want me to call the police?*

She looked down and said, "No."

At hearing the word *policía*, the man glanced up and down the aisle.

The woman's cheek had turned red, and a trickle of blood ran from her nose. She wiped it with the back of her hand but didn't look. *She's no stranger to being battered.*

Not expecting an answer, he asked anyway, "Usted está aquí ilegal?"

The woman offered a barely perceptible nod.

He now understood why she didn't want the police involved. The child probably allowed her to remain in America, but the price of admission was high. To ease her tension, he told her he wasn't law enforcement.

"Hey, asshole, quit speaking Spanish and get lost."

"I said watch your language."

"Yeah, I heard . . . and if I don't?"

"Then I'll have to wash your mouth out with soap." Nathan motioned toward the right. "The detergent aisle's over there. Would you prefer scented or unscented?"

The girl stole a look from behind her mom. Nathan winked, and she turned away.

Flintstone took a step forward. "Think you're tough, huh?"

Right-footed, Nathan noted. He'd also used his right hand to slap the woman. He tried English with the girl. "Don't turn around, okay? Keep facing the shelves. Your dad and I are going to have a discussion."

"He's not my dad."

"Hey!" said Flintstone. "You don't talk to the kid. You talk to me."

Nathan scanned the far end of the aisle for cameras and didn't see any. He looked over his shoulder in the opposite direction and got the same result.

What happened next made Flintstone smile.

Two more men, slightly shorter, appeared at the end of the aisle. Nathan saw the family resemblance right away. Same cheeks and chins. They also had the same noses, eyes, and hair color: swamp-water brown.

"Hey, Tommy, this asshole just threatened me."

The two men hurried down the aisle. Both right-footed. Cell phones in right front pockets. One had an average build, heavy work boots, filthy jeans, and a black tank top. The other wore cargo shorts, a tie-dyed T-shirt, and flip-flops on the verge of falling apart. He looked like a homeless surfer—scrawny and lean from not eating. All the signs of a meth head. When they arrived, the stench of alcohol tripled.

Before Flip-Flops spoke, his tongue whipped across a missing front tooth. "Who's your friend?"

The little girl held perfectly still.

Nathan made a final sweep of the aisle with his eyes.

Flintstone took a step forward. "Well, tough guy, now what?"

Nathan held his ground. "Here's the deal. I'm placing you under arrest for assault."

"Is this some kinda joke? What're you, a cop?"

In his 5.11 Tactical clothing, he did have the look. "Nope, just a citizen."

"Then you can't arrest me."

"I absolutely can. Now turn around and put your hands behind your back."

Flintstone offered a laugh. "I don't see no handcuffs."

Nathan pointed to the rolls of duct tape. "Works fine."

Flip-Flops whipped his head back and forth, checking the aisle.

"We still alone?" Flintstone asked his brother.

"Yeah, man, but this dude's nuts. Maybe I should get the manager."

"Nah, we can handle him."

The man in the black tank top didn't say anything, but his expression held malevolence. Nathan put his money on the first move coming from that direction.

"Last warning," he said evenly. "Turn around and place your hands behind your back."

He readied himself. Ninety-nine percent of Earth's brawlers will use their right fist and try to strike their opponent's face. Some will charge, but most muscle heads opt for the haymaker.

Tank Top made the first move. His fist shot forward in a blurred flash.

Nathan jerked his head to the left, and his opponent's knuckles found only air.

Off-balance from missing his jab, Tank tried to steady himself, but Nathan was already in motion. He drove his left elbow into the man's jaw, making solid contact. Before Tank fell to his knees, Nathan yanked a twelve-inch frying pan from its hanger. It felt a little light, but it would do.

Tank's momentum took him headfirst into the batteries on the opposite side of the aisle. Packs of Ds, Cs, and AAs rained down on him like large hail.

Flip-Flops said, "Whoa!" and backed up a step.

Nathan gave it low odds the tweaker would join the fight unless it took a positive turn for the inbreds.

Holding the girl tightly, the woman looked frightened, but she hadn't run.

"It'll be okay," he told her in Spanish. "You're safe with me."

Nathan stepped back to widen the gap between himself and Flintstone, which also generated some separation from the woman and the child.

Tank cursed, wiped his lip, and looked at the blood. Nathan could've made it much worse, but brain-damaging blows weren't required yet. That changed when Flintstone grabbed a meat cleaver and pulled the protective sleeve from its blade.

Game on.

Nathan looked him in the eye and asked, "Are you sure?"

In the right hands, a frying pan becomes a miniature Roman shield. And that's how Nathan planned to use it, at least initially.

When Tank tried to gain his feet again, Nathan stomped the guy's forearm, felt the two bones snap clean, then issued a side kick, catching the man squarely on the chin. If the man's jaw hadn't been initially broken, it was now. The blow sent him into the cooking utensils. Freed from their shelves and hooks, all kinds of items pelted the guy. Spatulas. Flippers. Thermometers. Measuring cups and spoons. Basters. Tongs. Skewers. Cheese slicers and potato peelers. But perhaps most appropriately? Meat tenderizers.

The guy waved his good arm at the falling kitchen products as if fighting off a swarm of bees. If it hadn't been such a serious situation, it might've looked comical. When the falling barrage stopped, Tank plopped to his side and lay still.

Nathan turned his attention to Flintstone. "If you attack me with that, I *will* hurt you."

The man froze in indecision. His eyes flicked between his injured brother and Nathan. Blood now flowed from Tank's nose and mouth, and his eyes were closed. The guy had a grade-three concussion for sure.

Nathan kept his expression neutral. "Don't worry. Your brother will be okay, but he'll be eating with a straw for the next eight weeks or so."

"Come on, Bobby," Flops said. "He ain't worth it."

"He's gotta pay for what he just done to Tommy."

"And how will you pay for what you *just done* to the woman?" asked Nathan.

"Why do you care? She ain't shit to you."

"She's a human being, not a punching bag."

"You ain't arresting me."

"Then you'll have to fight. I strongly suggest you drop the cleaver first."

"And if I don't?"

"Then I'll beat you senseless with this frying pan and make myself an omelet."

Flops took another step back. "This dude's gone, man. Look at his eyes. Ain't nobody home."

"This psycho ain't arresting me!"

Nathan winked at the little girl again and offered her a warm smile, then made one more effort at diplomacy. "There's no need for further violence. When the cops arrive to take you into custody, you can walk out of here—looking like you do right now—or you can be wheeled out on a gurney looking like you've been run over by a motor grader. I'm okay either way."

"Come on, man. Let's go!" Flops said.

"I ain't runnin' from this freak."

"Then make your move. I'm done talking."

Flops sounded desperate. "Don't do it, man . . . You seen how easily he whupped on Tommy."

Nathan saw Flintstone's grip tighten. *Okay, have it your way. I gave you a chance . . .*

The overhead fluorescents flashed off the blade when the cleaver arced through the air. Like a swordsman, Nathan brought the frying pan up and parried the man's arm. Before Flintstone could take another swipe, Nathan swung the pan and hammered the guy's knuckles hard enough to pulverize bones.

The aluminum produced a musical *bong* sound. Freed from the man's grip, the cleaver skipped across the floor.

"You son of a bitch!" Flintstone lowered his head and charged.

Nathan shifted laterally toward the guy's busted-hand side.

Like a clumsy oaf, Flintstone grabbed air with both arms. Had this been a bullfight, the crowd would've shouted, "Olé!"

Nathan swung the pan and smacked it on the back of Flintstone's head.

Flintstone kept going, tripping over his brother.

The tweaker bolted, his feet coming out of his flip-flops. Nathan could've hurled the skillet at the fleeing man's head but decided he no longer posed a threat.

He allowed Flintstone to get up. "Are you ready to place your hands behind your back now?"

The bludgeoned man felt the back of his head and snarled at seeing blood.

It's been said the definition of *insanity* is attempting the same failed behavior over and over and expecting a different result. Well, Flintstone roared like a madman and charged again.

Nathan feinted to the left, pretending to repeat the same maneuver.

It worked.

The man shifted his momentum to his broken-hand side. At the last second, Nathan thrust himself to the right and swung the frying pan.

Lionel Richie's ex-wife would be proud.

A third tone rang out as aluminum cracked cranium again.

Amazingly, the man didn't go down.

The guy looked up with his eyes, as though he could somehow see the damaged portion of his scalp. A single word escaped his mouth: "Ouch."

Nathan waited; he'd seen this before. It seemed a good time to Mirandize Mr. Flintstone. "You have the right to remain silent. Anything you say can and will be used against you in a court of law. You have the right to an attorney. If you cannot afford—" He didn't finish.

Flintstone's eyes leveled out, then became unfocused. When his jaw went slack, Nathan stepped forward, grabbed the guy's shirt, and kept him from hitting his head when he collapsed. *Man, this guy weighs a ton.*

Flops was gone from sight, but a quick glance toward the front of the store revealed the cashier with a hand over her mouth, the other hand holding her phone at her side. At least she hadn't videoed the fight. The last thing he needed was a viral YouTube post.

So much for grocery shopping.

Time to go.

He called out to the cashier, "Please call 911 and request an ambulance." When the cashier didn't move, he added, "Now would be a good time." That got through, and she pecked at her phone.

The Hispanic woman's expression hadn't changed.

She's tough, all right. "Do you speak English?" he asked.

"A little."

He'd stick with her native language. "The police are coming. Do you have any ID to show them?"

"No."

"Do you live with him?"

She slowly nodded.

"Is there someplace you can go? Anyone you can stay with?"

She shook her head. Despite a lifeless expression, she had kind eyes.

He wasn't sure if he could trust this woman, but he felt responsible for her predicament. *Predicament?* He'd just knocked her boyfriend into unconsciousness, not to mention fracturing four of the guy's fingers. If Flintstone needed both hands to work, he'd be filing for disability.

"What's your name?"

"Rosa."

"I'm Nathan. Is she your daughter?"

"My niece."

He wanted to ask where the girl's mother was, but the answer might not be a happy one.

"Listen, Rosa, I'm sorry about all of this, but when I saw him hit you, I couldn't let it go."

"It's okay."

"Can I trust you?"

She looked confused. "What do you mean?"

"In order for me to help you, I have to trust you. And you'll have to trust me. Do you think we can do that?"

She didn't say anything, but from her expression, he knew her answer was yes, probably figuring she didn't have anything to lose. On the other hand, she had to be worried he could be a creep and just wanted her—or her niece—for sex. *Now there's a nice cheery thought, Nate.* If she'd been smuggled across the border by coyotes, she might already be a victim of sexual assault, something all too common in the human-smuggling business.

One thing was certain: these two had no chance against a bully like Flintstone. He did whatever he wanted, whenever he wanted. It sickened Nathan thinking about it. How many women, or men for that matter, were stuck in hopeless situations, with no place to go, no one to help them, and no one who cared? Putting himself in her shoes, he knew she also had to worry about being detained and possibly reported to ICE. Nathan thought it unlikely she'd be deported, but with no place to go but a homeless shelter, she'd probably end up back with Flintstone.

"I'll pay for a motel room. You'll be safe there."

She said thank you and followed him to the elevator.

"Does your niece speak Spanish?" He already knew she spoke English.

"Only a little. I've been teaching her."

"How did you get here?" Realizing how that sounded, he added, "To the store, I mean."

"Bobby's car."

"He's parked on the street?" Nathan hadn't seen any other vehicles near the elevator down below. If Bobby had driven into the garage, his car should've been near the elevator.

She nodded.

"How far is it to your house?"

"About two miles. It's an apartment."

"Who else lives there? Any of his brothers?"

She said the one with the black tank top lived there. He worked nights at a strip club and brought women into the house. She also said Tank Top traded drugs for sex with the women. Cocaine and painkillers.

Great, thought Nathan. A fine example for the young girl. He asked how long she'd been with the Flintstones.

"Four months. I moved down here from Gonzales when I lost my job."

"You mean the Gonzales along the 101 Freeway in the Salinas Valley?"

"Yes."

Nathan pressed the elevator button and didn't try to conceal his face from the camera. Too late anyway, it had captured him on the way in. To avoid a paper trail he didn't want, he might have to call in a favor to sidestep being questioned by the police. *Another* favor, he corrected himself. Sooner or later, he'd run out of them.

"Why San Diego?"

"My sister lived here. She got deported last month."

Nathan waited.

"She was a dancer at the same strip club and got caught selling drugs."

"Was your niece born here?"

Rosa nodded.

Well, there it was. A US citizen, the child became a "cut the line" ticket to America, but Rosa's sister had blown it on the lure of easy money. Apparently, exotic dancing for peanut-eating drunks was a fair trade to stay in the land of milk and honey. He instantly regretted the impulsive thought. *Stop being judgmental, McBride. You don't know her sister's story.* The true victim in this ugly mess was Rosa's niece.

The elevator jolted and began to hum. Since there weren't any cameras in here, Nathan pulled his wallet and offered Rosa all the twenties and fifties he had. "Here, take this until you figure things out." He usually carried around two grand at any given time, but he hadn't replenished lately. There might be $1,500 in his hand. A lot of money, but he could afford it.

"No! I can't."

"It's an act of kindness," he said in Spanish. "Nothing more." He extended it toward her.

She murmured a thank-you and tucked the money into her cloth purse.

Despite what he'd said, she probably assumed he wanted sex. Nothing could be further from the truth, but he understood her reluctance. Before meeting Holly, Nathan had paid for sex on a regular basis.

A dark time in his life, but he wasn't that person anymore, and he didn't beat himself up over it.

He made eye contact with the little girl. "What's your name?"

She turned away and hugged Rosa's leg tighter.

"She's shy, sorry. Her name's Lida."

"That's a pretty name. I'm Nathan."

Although it felt awkward, he shook hands with Rosa.

"Does your boyfriend hit her?"

Rosa's reaction said yes.

"Anything else?"

She shook her head quickly.

The elevator door slid open, revealing a quiet garage. Nothing had changed. He told her to wait while he checked the blind corners to his left and right. He doubted Flops was still around, but he needed to be sure.

He took a knee in front of Lida. "Don't be afraid of me. The scars on my face don't make me a bad person." He gave her the best smile he could muster.

Her lips curved up, slightly, then went flat again.

Internally, he made a decision. "I'm going to help your aunt, okay?"

"Okay."

For Rosa, he translated what he'd just said into Spanish.

Trust involved risk, for all concerned. Nathan could be opening himself up to a world of trouble. He knew nothing about this woman. She might self-destruct. Some people can't be helped. Homeless shelters were full of people who, no matter how much aid they received, were going to end up back in the shelter. He thought it noble she'd taken on the responsibility for the care of Lida—no small task by any means.

"Rosa, I only have one request, but it's a big one. If you accept my help, I need your word you'll never contact your boyfriend again. Ever. You'll have to abandon your old life and start a new one."

"What about my sister?"

"I can't tell you what to do about her. It's possible you may never see her again, or it could be a long time. For Lida's sake, you'll have to be the best mom you can. I have friends who can get you a permanent-resident green card and speed up your process for citizenship. Do you want to become a US citizen?"

She nodded.

"Look, you don't have to decide anything right now. I'll take you to your apartment and wait at the curb. Gather whatever you need and come back out. You'll never be going back there, so make sure you get everything."

"We don't have much. Just clothes and my Bible."

Just clothes and my Bible. Thinking about his own possessions, Nathan felt a pang of guilt. *I need to give more to charity.*

"Do you need anything from his car?"

She said no.

"When I drop you off at your apartment, I'll wait three minutes. If you don't come back out, I'll leave. I'm offering you a fresh start. A life free from fear and pain. Think about your niece, the kind of life she'll have if you stay with that man. The police will definitely show up at your house later this morning. If you don't want my help, now is the time to tell me. No matter what you decide, the money's yours. No strings attached."

They reached his GT, and she seemed to hesitate.

The moment of truth had arrived. *Either she'll get in or not.*

Figuring it might be awkward, he didn't open her door. Part of him hoped she wouldn't do it, but leaving them marooned in this parking garage wouldn't sit well.

It boiled down to instinct and trust. What did Rosa's gut tell her about the man she was about to entrust her life to? Not only her life, but Lida's as well. He gave it fifty-fifty odds she'd actually get in.

Perhaps her fear of knowing the police were coming became the deciding factor. She opened the door, slid in, and asked Lida to sit on her lap.

He turned the volume down to zero, then decided some music wouldn't be a bad thing. Driving up the ramp, he tuned in a symphonic channel on satellite radio. She didn't react to "Air on the G String" by J. S. Bach, but he sensed she liked it. He also detected no trace of alcohol on her breath, a good sign.

Hearing the safety belt warning chime, he said, "You should probably fasten your seat belt, but don't put it across Lida."

At the top of the ramp, he rolled his window down to listen for any approaching sirens. Maybe three or four minutes had passed since his initial contact with Flintstone. The fight had been over in less than a minute, and they'd spent another minute or two getting down to the garage.

He heard the first siren when he reached Front Street.

When he asked for directions, she told him to get on the Five south.

He glanced at his passengers as he followed her directions. Rosa seemed so small and vulnerable. She couldn't be more than five feet tall. He wondered what their lives would look like in twenty years. Lida'd be in her prime, maybe with kids of her own. Sometimes Nathan appreciated how random and unpredictable life could be. The chain of events leading up to his confrontation with Flintstone couldn't have been scripted. He knew such things weren't meant for human understanding. If he'd left his house ten seconds later—assuming nothing would've changed during his drive—he wouldn't have been at the household-utensils aisle at the moment Flintstone slapped Rosa. But leaving ten seconds earlier created its own set of variables. He could've been delayed by a red traffic light or stopped to help a stray dog—which he always did. Suppose he'd driven one mile per hour faster or slower on the freeway. What if the elevator hadn't been on the garage level when he'd pressed the button, and he'd had to wait for it to come down? Another near miss, in all likelihood. The variables on Rosa's side of the equation were equally multifaceted.

An uncomfortable silence ensued. Under different circumstances, he wouldn't say anything to fill the void, but their situation was anything but normal. As it turned out, Rosa spoke first.

"Thank you for helping us."

"You're welcome." It was all he could think of to say. This woman's life was about to be inverted, in a good way. She just didn't know it yet. A complete stranger had fought for her, shown her respect, and given her money. She had to be thinking it was too good to be true.

He knew how to ease her thoughts. Using the hands-free feature, he called Angelica, his live-in housekeeper at his La Jolla home, a big place where he spent less time than in his smaller home in Clairemont.

Angelica sounded half-asleep when she picked up.

"I'm sorry to call so early," he said in Spanish, "but I have an emergency."

"Oh no. What's wrong?"

He gave her a quick summary, and Angelica was more than willing to help. Although he trusted the woman sitting next to him, that trust wasn't absolute. He wouldn't bring her into either of his homes, but he could arrange a nice motel room. Once Rosa and Lida went into their apartment to get their belongings, he'd call Angelica again and explain the situation more thoroughly, something he didn't feel comfortable doing in front of his guests. He'd ask his housekeeper to spend a few days with his—refugees?—no, that wasn't the right word. *Victims.* They were victims of violence, battered people who needed a safe haven. Angelica wouldn't ask for anything, but he'd offer her a healthy bonus to stay with them in the motel for a few days. If all went well, and this woman didn't have any crippling emotional issues, she'd be on a path to a much better life with Lida.

She guided him through a graffiti-ridden area east of downtown. Piled like small snowdrifts, trash dominated sidewalks, gutters, and fences. It sickened him. There was no excuse for this. Litter and poverty weren't synonymous.

He pulled to the curb in front of a run-down two-story apartment, got out, and opened her door.

She looked confused.

"It's what gentlemen do."

She offered a thin smile.

"Three minutes, Rosa."

CHAPTER 2

Ten Days Ago

Aside from the air vent's whisper, the clicks from General Hahn's spit-shined boots were the only sounds in the corridor. *Fitting,* he thought. Jong Doo was the most secret military complex in the world. Not even the arrogant Americans could boast of such an accomplishment. It took engineers and tunneling crews twenty-five months to hollow out this mountainside and another twenty-two to build the infrastructure—350,000 square feet of passages, chambers, laboratories, lodging, and food storage. It also housed medical bays, a fully staffed and stocked surgical suite, a water reclamation plant, atmosphere production, and a huge ammo depot. Jong Doo's nuclear-powered reactor and reserve supplies could sustain its occupants for up to three years, longer if certain steps were taken, such as the liquidation of all nonessential personnel. This facility also doubled as the Supreme Leader's primary bunker in the event of a nuclear attack from America.

There was no denying it—the demons of American civilization remained a scourge upon the earth. The near-constant protesting, rioting, and political strife sickened him. Such disgraceful dissidence wasn't tolerated in his country. The sheer number of disloyal whiners and malcontents in America never ceased to amaze him. And all of it on national television? Shameful. If the streets of North Korea ever became a freak show, it certainly wouldn't be televised for the whole world to see. The protesters would be arrested, interrogated, and thrown into prison labor camps—where they belonged.

The facility's primary entrance sat inside a large nondescript warehouse, its helipad irregularly shaped and unmarked. Even the wind sock was retractable. Once a helicopter arrived, it quickly taxied into the warehouse to avoid being seen from space. To the eyes of the West, Jong Doo looked like an open pit mine—complete with earthmovers, excavators, and a waste-rock processing plant. All part of the cover. The heavy equipment was real but dated. It could be moved around to simulate a mining operation but little else.

A few years ago, Jong Doo had nearly been exposed, but the Chinese American spy had been caught before she'd been able to report finding a series of suspicious checkpoints and security measures along the remote canyon road serving the facility. Needless to say, she'd died a protracted death.

A few meters ahead, a vaultlike door prevented deeper penetration into the labs. He thought the biological hazard symbol above the door looked ridiculous, but it served its purpose.

He punched an eight-digit code into the keypad, and the door hissed as it opened. A second door, identical to the first, loomed at the opposite end of the antechamber. He turned around to watch the first door close. There was no going back at this point; he'd either continue farther into the mountain or be killed where he stood. No other options were possible.

He stared at the camera, waiting for the pleasant female voice.

"Identification please."

"General Hahn, ID number eight seven blue two three five yellow."

He found the metallic voice of the computer strangely sexy. Perhaps the inherent danger added an air of excitement and exhilaration that would end abruptly if he misspoke a single portion of the code. He'd be allowed a second attempt. Failing that, the system would suck all of the air out of the chamber. Death from sudden decompression would be painful and grotesque as his blood turned into red foam. Still, there were worse ways to die; he had, after all, been responsible for many of them.

The central computer identified his voiceprint, and the first of three green lights stopped blinking.

"Please place your hand on the capacitance scanner."

"No problem, Mae Lee. How's your day going?"

"My day is going quite well. Thank you, General. How is yours?"

This pleasant exchange always reminded him of Hal from the American movie *2001: A Space Odyssey*. Who would've ever thought that level of technology would actually exist in his lifetime? A testament to the superior genetics of his Korean ancestry.

"My day couldn't be better. I'm looking forward to the demonstration." In reality, he wasn't.

"Yes, of course you are."

Slightly nervous, he watched the middle light stop blinking, its steady glow a welcome sight.

"How are your wife and children?"

"They're doing well, Mae Lee. Thank you for asking."

"Of course, General."

He was tempted to use a non sequitur, say something along the lines of *orange elephants swim upside down in bathtubs*, but this wasn't the place to be a smartass. Mae Lee literally held his life in "her" hands.

He waited for the last security measure.

"Please blow into the Breathalyzer."

A small hatch opened in the keypad, and a rubber tube extended several inches into the chamber. He took a deep breath and complied. If he failed this test, he wouldn't be summarily executed. He'd be trapped in the corridor until security arrived to escort him through the inner door. After that, he'd be placed in handcuffs and marched out of the complex. But it wouldn't end there. A black mark would be placed in his file, despite his rank. How many black marks could you get inside Jong Doo and still keep your job? Exactly zero.

Everyone working here knew the rules, and so far, in its five-year history, not a single individual had ever been kicked out for failing a Breathalyzer test. There were some things you just didn't do. Liquor wasn't allowed anywhere inside the mountain. Period. Except, of course, for the Supreme Leader and his trusted entourage.

"Thank you, General. You are cleared to proceed."

Confirming Mae Lee's statement, the third LED stopped blinking. Another hiss signaled the opening of the inner door. He left the small antechamber and stopped at the security checkpoint.

The second phase of his screening always went much easier. He'd need to undergo a body scan followed by an examination with an RFD wand to make sure he had no transmitters, wires, cameras, microphones, or other electronic devices. The final touch? A thorough pat down.

At last count, Hahn had more than three hundred people working in this facility. But only twenty of them worked in the biochem labs.

After being scanned, he offered the female guard a polite smile and held his arms straight out while she waved the wand. After finishing with the wand, she ran her hands over every square centimeter of his body. He knew this particular security officer and appreciated her diligence. Everyone received the same treatment. Men frisked women as well. Gender played no role here.

"Thank you, General Hahn. You're cleared to proceed."

She sat down at her desk and worked the keyboard. A door to his left clicked and hissed as the internal mechanism released. He stepped through and was greeted by Dr. Soon, a small-framed man with rectangular, black-rimmed glasses. He'd always wanted to tell Soon the nerdy look didn't project intelligence. In fact, it conveyed the opposite. He and Soon were about the same age, mid-fifties, but the doctor looked ten years younger—a result of minimal exposure to the elements.

"Good morning, General."

"Doctor."

"This way, please."

Hahn wondered why scientists' lab coats were always white. Why couldn't they be blue or green? Tradition, he supposed. He'd never cared enough to inquire.

They walked across a short corridor lined with flat-screen televisions displaying the surrounding forest at its current time of day—sunrise. Working in an underground facility like Jong Doo produced a certain type of stress that could be lessened with simulated day and night conditions. As artificial as the TVs were, he liked the ambience they created.

The complex contained nearly a thousand such "windows," and all of them showed the correct perspective of the outside world because the screens were being fed by live cameras. Every so often, they displayed a different landscape from another part of the world. He liked Zhangjiajie National Forest Park the best. Someday, he hoped to go there. The monitors also doubled as general announcement screens, site layout maps, and emergency procedure displays.

They stepped through another sealed door and entered an open common area. Tables and chairs occupied the center of the room. Along one wall, vending machines flanked the entrances to the restrooms. The common area acted like the focal point of a spoked wheel, with each perimeter door leading to a different laboratory complex.

Every section of the bio-development lab remained isolated from its counterparts. If a contagion or compound managed to get loose, it would be contained within its sector.

As a safeguard, the default computer response to a malfunction, cyberattack, or unauthorized entry into the mountain resulted in a lockdown, and General Hahn didn't possess the codes required to release it. A lockdown had to be overridden from Pyongyang via a fractal-encrypted data link. To be sure the system worked properly, it was tested regularly and randomly.

Dr. Soon didn't care for small talk, so Hahn didn't bother. There were only so many times you could ask how the family was without sounding phony. They were both here for a specific purpose, a test of the newest chemical agent in the phase-eight series. Phases six and seven had yielded satisfactory results, but he hoped this newest version would be a home run—a clichéd American expression to be sure, but appropriate nevertheless. In his opinion, baseball was the one good thing America had ever contributed to the world.

Besides baseball, every aspect of his life involved clandestine military operations. Hahn was a secret man, working in a secret world, and he absolutely loved it. It took a toll, though, mostly in the form of troubling dreams. There were many times when he'd awaken in the middle of the night panicked that the facility had been exposed, or worse, closed down and abandoned. They reminded him of the dreams he used to have in college, where he hadn't studied for a test or hadn't done any homework for a class.

He and Soon passed through another environmentally sealed door and walked down a brightly lit hall dominated by doors and lots of security cameras. No simulated windows here. Knowing his every move was being recorded, he kept his expression neutral.

Dr. Soon opened the last door on the right, and Hahn followed him inside. Facing a large ballistic glass window, eight chairs were arranged in two rows of stadium seating. On the other side of the glass, a small white room held three men and one woman, all seated around a metal table. All four lingered on the edge of starvation. In baggy jumpsuits with their wrists manacled to rings protruding from the table, they looked terrified. They obviously knew they weren't here for a gourmet meal. As with the previous test subjects, each of their jumpsuits was numbered from one to four. The room's door had no knob or handle.

Once closed, it couldn't be opened from the inside—something the prisoners had to be acutely aware of. Looking like a ship's porthole, a small glass hatch sat in the middle of the door.

Simultaneously, the prisoners looked at the door. Normally there'd be sound piped into the viewing room, but Hahn didn't like hearing the demos. Besides, everything was being recorded. No need to listen live. Once had been enough . . .

A few seconds later, the door opened, and two armed guards entered the chamber and stood at either side of the table. A third guard came in and barked some orders. The first two guards leveled their weapons at the prisoners, who didn't move as their handcuffs were removed. Then, as quickly as they'd arrived, the guards left.

To Hahn, it felt like watching a silent movie. Above the viewing window, six monitors showed the quartet from various angles. The large digital timer was currently dark.

"How is it delivered this time?" Hahn asked.

"Grenade," Soon said. "Same as the last time."

Hahn found himself holding his breath. No matter how many times he watched these demos, they never got easier to stomach. He gave the cleaning crew credit. Not a trace of what had happened last time was evident.

In the corner above the door, a red beacon began turning, making the room pulsate in crimson flashes. Hahn suddenly felt nauseated. Waiting was the worst part. He understood the purpose of the beacon. If anyone was in the room who shouldn't be, they'd better use the intercom right away.

The flashing stopped.

Hahn adjusted his weight and stared at the hatch.

It opened.

A grenade came through.

It closed.

Hahn counted down from three.

Startled, the test subjects looked at the small cylinder but didn't initially react. In their defense, it didn't look like a fragmentation grenade. It looked more like a small can of spray paint: same shape and size.

The grenade jumped, then began spinning as one end acted like a miniature jet engine. The digital timer began, its bright red numbers announcing each passing second.

"Tell me what you notice," Dr. Soon said.

"The gas element. It's harder to see." The last time he'd witnessed this, the deadly vapor had looked like fog.

"Correct," Dr. Soon said. "It's more effective if people can't easily see the agent. It allows the maximum amount of contamination before anyone realizes they've been compromised."

Hahn nodded. "How long will this variant take?"

"Two to three minutes."

The digital clock passed the eight-second mark.

Hahn asked, "It's also spraying microdrops of the compound like last time?"

"Yes."

"Same dispersion?"

"Yes, but most of the casualties will still result from inhalation. In a crowded area, we estimate a grenade of this size will yield two hundred and fifty to three hundred deaths. I think we can count on the same amount of nonlethal exposures resulting in brain damage, comas, or vegetative states. A few will get very ill but suffer no long-term complications."

Hahn watched as the test subjects acted restless and annoyed.

At twenty-five seconds, three of them began rubbing their hands over their faces as if trying to brush off ants.

Soon spoke calmly. "As with the previous agents, this one also produces an irritating effect on their exposed skin."

At thirty seconds, all of them were desperately rubbing their faces and eyes.

One of the men jumped up from the table and charged the door, beating on the porthole with both fists.

Showing a mouthful of rotten teeth, the smallest prisoner turned toward the viewing window and snarled. Hahn leaned back in his seat as the man charged the one-way glass and pounded with his fists. The subject then turned away, grabbed a chair, and hurled it with all his strength. The ballistic glass made a muted thumplike sound as the chair harmlessly bounced off its surface.

Abandoning the effort against her face, the woman began tearing at her jumpsuit.

"The compound has entered their bloodstream, and it's now affecting the entirety of their skin. More aggressive behavior will kick in momentarily." Soon sounded remarkably calm, as if ordering *galbi-tang* from the cafeteria.

At sixty seconds, their behavior became purely violent and belligerent. No longer concerned about escaping, they snarled and yelled at each other like enraged primates.

The youngest man acted the most aggressively. Hahn glanced away as the man bit into the woman's forearm. The woman fought back by continuously slugging the back of her attacker's head. Oblivious to the blows, he kept his jaw locked on the woman's flesh. With strength Hahn didn't think she should have, she whipped her arm in a wide arc and slammed the man against the far wall. A third subject joined the fray, biting the woman's other arm. With two biters to fight, she lost her balance and fell to the floor. The trio rolled and twisted, leaving smears of blood.

Things got worse from there.

A lot worse.

Dr. Soon spoke again. "We wish we knew how it worked, but it's a mystery. All we know . . ."

Soon's voice seemed to fade into the background as Hahn watched the subjects devolve. He couldn't imagine this chemical agent being deployed in a crowded shopping mall or sporting event. It looked like a slaughterhouse in there. Blood fouled every surface, running down the window in rivulets. The man who'd hurled the chair joined the fight, ripping one of the woman's attackers free.

". . . is that the hallucinogenic element seems to adversely target the prefrontal cortex, but we don't know why. We can see the affected area with functional MRI scans on tightly restrained subjects, but how it works isn't known. It's fair to say we've reached a good balance with compound B82-1. If we add too much of the destabilizing hallucino-genic element, we sacrifice the neurotoxin's effective range and lethality. If we add too much of the neurotoxin, death occurs too quickly, and we lose the chaotic effect we've been tasked to create. It's relatively simple to produce a deadly toxin that kills quickly. Delaying the process is much more difficult to achieve, given all the variables: wind, proximity, objects available as impromptu weapons. It all has to be factored in. We should begin to see the neurotoxin's deadly effect within the next thirty seconds or so."

Hahn wanted to say, *It can't happen soon enough,* but didn't. Appearing weak wasn't an option. As disgusting and vile as he found these test trials, he wouldn't dare express his personal feelings. Life was cheap in DPRK. Human rights? Forget it. And due process didn't exist. Anyone could be arrested for any crime. At any time. Without any reason.

He wondered how these test subjects who were clearly enfeebled by starvation could possess such strength. It defied understanding. Hahn knew drugs like PCP, meth, and other amphetamines impaired percep-tion, but this was something else.

The man who'd hurled the chair at the glass went downhill rapidly. He fell to his hands and knees, then curled into a fetal position, sucking in air like a fish on the deck of a boat. The psychotropic element now took a back seat to the toxin.

Hahn averted his eyes as the man with terrible teeth opened his mouth.

Yes, the room had been insulated from sound, but not totally.

The inhuman shriek penetrated the ballistic glass.

"As you can see," Dr. Soon said, "the toxin affects individuals at different rates of absorption. Not all of them are going down yet."

Hahn felt thankful for the dark viewing room. This was the most violent demo to date. He couldn't imagine a scene like this amplified by a factor of one thousand.

At times like this, he began to wonder if this project had gone too far. It was one thing to slaughter a large amount of people with a weaponized toxin, but making them go berserk first? How could this ever be justified? Would the Supreme Leader ever use this against the Americans? Could it somehow be traced back to him? Would he someday face war crimes like the Nazi scientists had? So many questions . . . but one thing wasn't in question. If Hahn voiced any doubt or challenged this project's validity, he'd find himself on the wrong side of the glass.

"I think we've seen enough," he said. "There's no need to stay longer."

"Are you okay, General?"

Of course, he thought. *Why wouldn't I be okay? I just witnessed the most heinous display of human savagery and mayhem imaginable. Why don't we discuss it further over cookies and tea?*

"I'm fine," he said. "The results are clear. And commendable."

Soon nodded his thanks. "I think we can conclude the compound is ready at this point. I don't see the need for any further refinements or tests."

Like Hahn, Dr. Soon knew the next test would be a large-scale event a few miles away at the Sangyong Reeducation Camp. The Supreme Leader wanted absolute proof the compound worked outside of their controlled laboratories. Such a demonstration wasn't necessary, but neither of them was willing to question the decision.

"I agree. I'll file the report. I'll mention how well you've done, Doctor, and how important you've been to this project."

"Thank you, General. It's not easy to fine-tune these compounds. It's taken eighteen months to achieve this level of effectiveness."

And how many lives? Hahn wanted to ask. Actually, he knew the exact number. The ashes of 487 people fertilized this mountainside. The maintenance garage for the dated mining equipment held a crematorium.

All four subjects were coughing blood, their bodies violently shuddering on the floor.

Four words invaded Hahn's thoughts.

What have we created?

CHAPTER 3

Denise Tabor finished her eyeliner, turned her head from side to side, and pursed her lips. It would have to do. Despite her best efforts, forty-five years of gravity and a lack of adequate exercise had taken a toll. Stomach. Hips. Chest. Not as . . . favorable . . . as they used to be. Her long brunette hair didn't need a significant amount of plucking yet; she had that much going for her. Fortunately, the man she worked for was low maintenance. She couldn't have asked for a better boss, one of the reasons she didn't mind a Tuesday-through-Saturday workweek. Too bad he was married.

She'd been divorced for a little more than two years, and the breakup had been ugly at times. At times? It was pretty much ugly the *entire* time. Denise didn't have a vindictive cell in her body, but the man she'd given her life to had attempted to discard her by refusing to pay any support at all. Nothing. *Seriously?* During their eighteen-year marriage, she'd cooked twenty thousand meals from scratch, washed and folded seventy-five thousand pieces of clothing, and driven 150,000 miles for every need of their kids. And none of that had any value?

When she'd confronted him about his greed, he'd claimed her private sleuthing caused the divorce, and had she not spied on him, everything would've worked out fine because he'd been planning to end the affair and tell her about it. A perfectly reasonable excuse.

It wasn't *his* fault he got caught cheating. It was *her* fault.

He didn't owe *her* an apology. She owed *him* one.

Ultimately, with the help of a lawyer, she'd won a fair alimony schedule, attorney's fees, and a seven-digit cash payment, but it had come at a needless emotional cost.

Had she been angry? Absolutely. And rightfully so. Had it not been for her Bible study group, she'd still be bitter. No matter how bad things seemed, there were always people in much worse situations.

Her two boys—six and eight—and her ten-year-old daughter couldn't possibly understand why Daddy had moved out, not at their ages. If they ever pressed the issue and wanted an explanation, she'd tell them the truth with compassion and kindness. The children loved him, and that was that. She'd never poison their minds, no matter how much he deserved it.

Still, the scars felt fresh. What was his lover's name? Leslie something? She'd met the woman at the firm's Christmas party. Leslie had smiled, shaken her hand, and said, *"It's very nice to meet you."*

She forced the memory aside, wiped a tear, and tried to compose herself before leaving the bathroom. Carmen would have the kids fed and dressed by now, and she didn't want to look like she'd been crying. Besides, she'd shed a lifetime's worth of tears over the last twenty-four months.

It sounded oddly quiet downstairs. Her children were always chattering about this or that. They rarely ran out of things to say.

"Carmen?"

No answer. Maybe they were in the backyard with Miss Kitty. They really loved playing with her.

"Carmen, are you in the house?"

Denise descended the stairs, heading for the sliding glass door to the backyard.

At the threshold to the living room, she glimpsed something and turned her head for a better look.

Her mind screamed in protest, *No, this can't be real!*

What she saw looked so frightening, her mind simply couldn't process it.

A strong pair of hands grabbed her from behind. Agonizing pain erupted in her shoulder as her right arm was torqued upward behind her back.

The scene finally registered.

On the carpet in front of the sofa, her two sons and daughter were bound together and forced to sit back-to-back. Their wrists were secured to the legs of the heavy coffee table with duct tape. Strips of tape also covered their mouths. Red and wet from crying, their eyes reflected raw terror.

Oh, please no!

Carmen lay in front of them, a huge bloodstain under her face. Lifeless eyes stared at the red pool, as if wishing the liquid back.

Oh, dear Lord . . . her neck . . .

Denise reached overload.

Had she not been forcibly held from behind, she would've collapsed.

A smiling Hispanic man sat on the couch. His left hand held a black pistol with a long silencer. Below a plain red ball cap, dark glasses concealed his eyes. A thick mustache and goatee made him look cruel and cold. Even scarier, an oversized scorpion tattoo covered the back of his gun hand.

She'd never been in the presence of evil before, but felt it now.

The room lost focus. Somewhere in the growing haze, Denise understood why. The man restraining her had covered her mouth and pinched her nose.

On the verge of blacking out, her vision faded, followed by sound. She was vaguely aware of a high-pitched whine and realized it was the muffled screaming of her children.

If only she had gotten a bigger breath of air, she might have been able to stay conscious for a few more seconds. The sickening sensation of being suffocated triggered panic. She began struggling to free herself from the man's grasp, which only made things worse. Fighting against primal instinct, she forced herself to relax. She couldn't win this battle; she had neither the strength nor the leverage to fight.

The man on the couch barked something, and the restraining hand—with its sickening lotion smell—fell away. She sucked in deep breaths of air, and the room returned.

No sooner had she regained her senses when the hand closed over her nose and mouth again. The feeling of panic returned, but this time her brain shut down immediately.

Time drifted . . .

Where was she? Who was shaking her?

When Denise opened her eyes, the nightmare hadn't changed, but her children looked more terrified than ever.

The revolting hand still covered her mouth, but she could breathe through her nose.

Why was this happening? Who were these men? Had her husband hired them? She glanced at Carmen, dead on the floor.

No, he couldn't have.

The man on the couch spoke at last. "I trust your situation is clear. If you scream or try to fight, you will witness horrible acts." He nodded to her children. "Need I say more?"

The hand fell away from her mouth.

"Please don't hurt them!"

"Answer my question."

"Please, I'll do anything you ask." She hoped these men didn't intend to rape her, but she'd willingly sacrifice herself to save her children.

The man's expression changed to disappointment; then he nodded.

The hand closed over her nose and mouth again. Reality blurred into a sensation of being submerged in mud. She sensed her children shrieking under the tape, but it could have been her own desperate wailing.

When the hand let go, she nearly vomited.

"I'll rephrase. Do you understand what will happen if you don't cooperate?"

"Y-yes. Please don't hurt them."

"That depends entirely on you."

There was something horribly calm about the man's tone, and she now understood he was no stranger to this situation. He'd slain Carmen as proof of his dominance. What she said next was for herself as much as her children.

"It's okay, babies. Mommy's here. Everything's going to be okay."

"You have a strong instinct to protect them. Admirable. I have two young sons of my own."

If true, she wanted to ask how he could be so cruel, but her gaze kept returning to Carmen's gray face and the yawning wound under her chin.

Movement made her look toward the sliding glass door where Miss Kitty pawed at the glass.

The man on the sofa looked at the cat, then said, "Stay focused on me. The sooner you answer my questions truthfully, the sooner this will be over. Would you like to sit down?"

She nodded and used her free hand to wipe tears.

"Do I need to use the duct tape?"

"You have my children."

He pointed the pistol at Chad's head, and she felt her stomach tighten. *No!*

"Answer my question with yes or no."

Question? What question? Her mouth opened, but nothing came out.

"I asked if I need to use the duct tape on you."

"No."

He returned the pistol to his lap. Unfortunately, Denise was nothing like her boss; she didn't have his Marine training or mental toughness. She hated herself for being so weak and helpless. The man holding her arm forced her into the sofa chair. She pulled her skirt down and pressed her knees together.

"You are Vincent Beaumont's personal secretary. Is that correct?"

"Yes." Her eyes flicked toward the cat again. Miss Kitty's clawing had become more desperate.

"And you've been in that position for how long?"

The man narrowed his eyes as if daring her to lie. She didn't know how much he already knew. If she lied, she had no doubt this creep would hurt her children. She would do everything she could to protect Vince, but she'd have to tell this man everything. There was no way she'd be able to watch her babies being tortured. And she didn't want them to see her get brutalized either.

"Twelve years."

The man crossed his legs as if engaging in casual conversation. He was dressed in expensive clothes. She tried to memorize as much as she could. In his forties and powerfully built, he had a lean face and narrow nose. His black hair sat in a man bun, a look she loathed. The image of this guy drooling all over her made her skin tighten.

"So it's fair to assume that you know a great deal about Mr. Beaumont's private life. Yes?"

She nodded.

"I'm also assuming that you have his home address, telephone numbers, et cetera."

She didn't respond because he hadn't asked a question.

He issued a barely perceptible nod.

The man standing over her slapped the back of her head, jarring her vision.

"I'm aware I didn't ask you a question, but you should respond to everything I say."

"I'm sorry." Her eyes found Miss Kitty again.

Without warning he twisted toward the door, aimed his pistol, and fired.

She covered her mouth, stifling a yelp of fear. The sound had been much louder than she'd expected.

The glass fragmented into thousands of pieces. Larger chunks fell to the carpet and patio. Miss Kitty darted away.

Her kids began squirming and crying harder. The couch blocked them from seeing the back porch, but they knew he'd fired at their cat.

"I didn't kill it. But I trust my point has been made. I would like your undivided attention." He waited with a raised brow.

"I'm sorry."

"In addition to being an expert at interrogation, my colleague is quite skilled at breaking into computer systems." He offered her a grim smile. "He's going to ask you some questions, and you will answer them truthfully. From this point on, *your* job is to make *his* job easier. If at any point we feel you're not being honest, or we suspect you're stalling, this will be the result."

He snapped a finger, pointed at her children, and said, "I don't care which one."

The man stepped out from behind her. Short, bald, and covered in tattoos, the guy looked like solid muscle. In black ink, a huge number four dominated his right forearm. The guy reached down, grabbed Chad's thumb, and looked at the man on the couch.

A nod was issued.

Chad screamed under the tape and began writhing in agony when the man wrenched his thumb the wrong direction. She heard a sickening pop of cartilage.

"Chad!" She jumped out of her chair, intending to claw out the monster's eyes, but the man with the gun was faster. Moving more quickly than she thought possible, he lunged from the couch and shoved her in the chest hard enough to empty her lungs. Gasping for air, she landed back in the chair. Pain flared in her left breast from the blow, which had popped several of her blouse's buttons.

"Chad! It's okay, baby. I'm so sorry. Why did you hurt him? I said I'd tell you everything!"

"Are you yelling at me, Ms. Tabor?"

"No! I'm sorry! I didn't mean to—"

"This is very difficult, but it's important you understand the price of deception. There are twenty-nine more fingers at risk. When those are finished, my colleague will move on to their toes. After that, things will get much, much worse."

Chad's whimpering had softened a little, but she knew how horrible a sprained thumb felt. He was trying to be brave for his mother, but right now she needed to be brave for him. She instinctively knew she needed to keep these monsters focused on her.

How could this be happening? Her world had gone from a normal morning to the worst nightmare imaginable, her children being tortured in front of her while their babysitter lay dead on the carpet. Her ex-husband used to say shit happens; she'd never really understood the depth of that phrase until now. She'd been a good mom and a good person; she didn't deserve this, and her children certainly didn't. They were innocent victims of something they couldn't possibly understand.

"Please don't hurt them again."

The guy snapped his finger again, and the tattooed man returned to his position behind her. "Please tend to her shirt."

She held perfectly still while her blouse was pulled closed, but not before the creep's hands purposely brushed across her breasts. It made her feel sick to her stomach. Although he wasn't much taller than she was, he had to possess five times her strength. She reminded herself this could get a whole lot worse, and probably would. She prayed they wouldn't do it to her in front of her children. Trying to fight these men would be useless. And even if by some miracle she did manage to get the upper hand, the man on the couch had a gun. No, her best course of action was to do everything they asked and keep their attention away from her children.

"We were talking about Vincent Beaumont. Whatever you think you know about him is wrong. He's a war criminal and a murderer." The man paused, and she quickly realized he was waiting for a response.

"He's been good to me."

The creep glanced at her chest and said, "I'm sure he has."

"It's not like that."

"No, of course not. He's a perfect gentleman."

She wanted to lash out, tell him what an asshole he was for the insinuation. Vincent Beaumont was a decent and honorable man. He'd never mistreated her, yelled at her, or made any kind of inappropriate comments or advances. By all accounts, he *was* a perfect gentleman and a good boss. All of her coworkers felt the same way.

Remembering a response was required, she nodded, hoping that would be enough.

"My colleague is going to escort you into your office, where you will give him full access to your computer and any passwords he asks for. I'm assuming you can log in to the BSI computer system?"

"Yes, but I can't look at everything."

"I'm aware of that. If we like what we find, you and your children will not be harmed. If, on the other hand, you do not fully cooperate, we will dislocate all their fingers and toes, then educate them on a subject beyond their years. Is my meaning clear?"

"Yes. I'll tell you whatever you want. You don't need to hurt them."

He simply stared at her. "We don't have unlimited time. If my colleague suspects you're stalling, we will start the process. You'll get no warnings."

"I won't stall."

"Let's hope not . . ." That crappy smile returned, and he reached out and ruffled Chad's hair. "For their sakes."

The tattooed monster poked her. "On your feet, *muchacha*."

She was half dragged down the hall to her office and ordered to take a seat at her desk.

Denise Tabor didn't know if she'd survive the next five minutes or five hours, but she'd do everything within her power to save her children's lives.

Although she hated doing it, she was able to log in to Vincent's computer remotely. When you're someone's personal secretary for a dozen years, a high level of trust develops. She couldn't access all his files, but there were plenty she could.

He ordered her to search for the key words *George Beaumont, Yuma,* and *Marine Corps.*

It didn't take long to realize what this man was after. She did, after all, transcribe Vincent's personal journal on a regular basis. It seemed her captors were interested in a relatively recent incident that had been written off as a narcotics raid. In reality, it had been much more than that.

The monster ordered her to print Vincent's journal entries related to the incident in Yuma.

What he asked for next made her want to vomit.

CHAPTER 4

Situated across the street from the Torrey Pines Golf Course, the headquarters of Beaumont Specialists Incorporated occupied an entire custom-built eighty-thousand-square-foot, three-story building. The largest private military company in the world, BSI had active contracts in over thirty countries, something Vincent Beaumont took great pride in.

The security gate leading into the underground parking garage swung open. After receiving a friendly wave from the guard manning the entrance, Vincent cruised down the ramp and began searching for an empty spot. There was no reserved parking down here; he didn't believe in it. Haughtiness undermined morale. The CEO of the company shouldn't be above taking a slightly longer walk to the elevator.

He found a spot on lower level two and pulled in. As usual, he checked his surroundings for anything that looked out of the ordinary, like an unfamiliar van or a plastic bag or cardboard box. Bombs come in every size and shape imaginable. *Never assume anything,* he reminded himself.

He slid out of his Navigator and retrieved his briefcase from the back seat. Despite having two artificial shoulder joints, he kept his five-foot-ten-inch frame in decent shape. Several days ago, he'd celebrated his forty-ninth birthday. Dark hair with gray invading at the temples looked kinda clichéd, but at least his hair was still there. Thinning, but still there. He'd inherited greenish-blue eyes from his mother's side of the equation.

He wasn't one of life's lottery winners; he was one of life's hard-work winners. Yes, his father, George Beaumont, had founded the company, but he'd been involved in every aspect of BSI since his teenage years. After graduating from college, he'd followed in his dad's footsteps and joined the Marines, the best move he'd ever made. As an officer, he learned leadership skills, dedication, and discipline. Like his father who'd fought in the Korean War, Vincent used the knowledge he'd acquired in the Marines—including several combat tours in Iraq and Afghanistan—to become a better businessman and entrepreneur.

Most people don't understand the concept of turning combat experience into something positive, but Vincent was living proof it could be done, and done successfully. Companies don't run themselves; people run them. And a company is only as good as the ownership and management behind it.

Vincent Beaumont's mettle as a human being had been tested and confirmed. Was he still bothered by the savagery he'd seen in Fallujah? Absolutely. It would always be an integral part of his life. To abandon the memory would dishonor his fallen Marine brothers, something he'd never do. In Afghanistan, he'd witnessed extreme carnage firsthand—Marines disfigured and killed by roadside explosions. Marines with spouses and children.

Enough, Vincent told himself. He wasn't going to start his day like this.

In the break room, he poured some coffee and grabbed an apple from the bowl.

He said good morning to several execs and their assistants before stepping into his office. Every morning he had ten to twelve phone messages sitting on his desk, today being no exception. Vincent preferred the old-fashioned method of reviewing handwritten slips of paper. Imagine that—people using pens, pencils, and pieces of paper to communicate. In his business, low-tech was often better. Even though his server systems were guarded by multilayered security measures, it was always possible they could be hacked. And sadly, the biggest threat to corporate security usually came from within.

Because BSI had satellite offices all over the world, his headquarters received calls at all hours of the day and night. Vincent glanced at the row of clocks above his door before picking up the message slips.

Local time was 10:32 a.m.

Since he'd had a rare free morning, he'd decided to play half a round of golf before coming into work.

He began rifling through the slips. Anything requiring the head honcho's attention landed on his desk; anything else had better not be here. One thing his secretary was very good at: filtering out the garbage. Denise had an incredible knack for cutting through the BS and determining what the real issue was and whether it deserved Vincent's attention.

When he saw the message about Denise calling in sick, he was immediately concerned. She never got sick. Thinking back, he couldn't recall if she'd ever taken a single sick day in the twelve years she'd worked for him. He supposed it had happened; he just couldn't remember when. Almost certainly, if she'd called in sick, she *was* sick.

He took the stairs down to BSI's spacious lobby. Granite floors, a large fountain, and wood-paneled walls gave the foyer an expensive look. Poster-size photos of mine-resistant ambush-protected vehicles offered a hint of what this building was all about.

BSI owned more than fifty MRAPs—several of them Israeli built. Most of them were deployed in the Middle East. The vast majority of BSI's overseas contracts involved VIP-escort services. Wealthy people were often targets of kidnappers and terrorists. Same with diplomats. BSI's MRAPs accompanied VIP caravans on a regular basis.

Vincent's arrival into the lobby didn't go unnoticed. More than one hundred cameras monitored every square inch of the main entry, internal halls, common areas, and parking garage. No one got into BSI's headquarters without being captured on camera. Even the roof employed cameras.

The man seated at the semicircular desk turned to greet him.

Vincent smiled. "Good morning, Karl."

"Morning, sir. How are you?"

"I could be better. I'm worried about Denise."

"She said she's feeling under the weather with a chest cold that came on suddenly."

"She seemed okay yesterday. Did she look out of sorts to you?" He realized how that sounded and backpedaled. "Don't worry. I'm not checking up on her. I'm just concerned because I can't remember the last time she called in sick. Can you?"

"No, sir. I know it's been at least five years because that's how long I've been here."

"Did she say anything else?"

"Something about her pet."

That sounded odd. "Pull up the call. Time stamp oh-six-forty-five or so."

"Retrieving it now, sir." Karl worked his computer, and a few seconds later, the speaker on his phone console came to life:

Good morning, Beaumont Specialists Incorporated.

Hi, Karl.

Hi, Denise, what's up?

I'm feeling terrible today. I've got a really nasty chest cold, and I don't think I should come into work. It came on suddenly.

I'm sorry to hear that. I'll—

I've got to go. Mr. Paws is scratching at the glass door.

I'll give Mr. Beaumont the message, and I hope you feel better soon.

Thanks, Karl, me too.

"Is Mr. Paws her dog?" Karl asked.

"She doesn't have a dog; she has a cat, and its name isn't Mr. Paws. It's Miss Kitty. Get her on the phone. Try her home first."

"Aye, sir."

Vincent liked Karl's response. Like himself, Karl was a retired Marine. Vincent offered all of BSI's jobs to US veterans first.

Karl covered the receiver, said he'd gotten voice mail, and asked if he should leave a message.

Vincent shook his head. "Try her cell."

Thirty seconds later, Karl asked the same question.

He reached across the counter, and Karl gave him the handset.

"Denise, it's Vince. I hope you're feeling okay. Give me a call as soon as you get this message." He nodded to Karl to end the call, handed the phone back, and said if she called back, he wanted her put through immediately. "If I'm in a meeting or on the phone, I want to be interrupted."

"Aye, sir."

"Try her cell every thirty minutes until she answers."

Climbing the stairs to his office, he thought about the name she'd used for her cat. Something didn't smell right. He knew Denise had endured a nasty divorce, but as far as Vincent knew, her husband wasn't dangerous, and he'd never made any threats.

Back in his office, he pulled his cell and called First Security, Nathan McBride and Harvey Fontana's company. Many of BSI's employees used First Security's mobile-friendly alarm systems in their homes.

Like his own company, First Security had an excellent receptionist. No doubt her computer showed his caller ID because she called him by name.

"Good morning, Mr. Beaumont. What can First Security do for you today?"

"Good morning. I need you to check my secretary's home system."

"Sure, no problem. What's a phone number associated with Denise's account?"

Again, Vincent was impressed. "Give me a sec. I need to find her home number. Is that the number you need?"

"Any number associated with her account will work."

"Okay, try this." He recited her cell number from memory.

There was a brief pause. "May I place you on hold while we look into Ms. Tabor's system?"

"Sure, no problem."

"This won't take long. Your call will come back to me if no one picks up within thirty seconds."

Soft jazz music began to play in the background.

We need to adopt the same thirty-second rule, he thought. *No one likes waiting on hold.*

To his surprise, Nathan McBride came on the line.

"Vince, it's Nate. What's going on?"

"I'm not sure. It's probably nothing." He told Nate about Denise referring to her cat by the wrong name.

"Yeah, that's odd, all right, but we're showing green lights at her place. The only activity we have today is her alarm was turned off at six thirty-nine this morning. So far, it hasn't been rearmed."

"Anything else?"

"No, it's all quiet."

"I'm going over there. Call me a paranoid Marine, but I don't have a good feeling about this."

"You're not a paranoid Marine. You're the CEO of the nation's largest private military company. You need to be cautious, all the time. Where does Denise live?"

"Rancho Peñasquitos." He gave Nathan the address.

"You at your Torrey Pines HQ?"

"Yes."

"I'll meet you there."

"Listen, Nathan, you don't need to disrupt your day. I've got this."

"My schedule's light, nothing that can't be shuffled."

"Are you sure?"

"Absolutely."

"Call my cell when you're two minutes out," Vincent said. "I'll do the same if I get there first."

"I think we should be packing for this. I'll have a 226 in my waist pack. You?"

"I'm a Glock man. I'll bring my 17."

"See you in about fifteen minutes."

Heading for the elevator, Vincent used his cell to update Karl. "And by the way," he added, "you're my secretary today, so chop-chop."

***

Nathan meant what he said. In his experience, Vincent Beaumont wasn't being paranoid. He'd come to know Vince pretty well, and he wasn't one to overreact. If one of First Security's secretaries had made the same kind of sick call, he'd have reacted the same way.

Nathan didn't come into the office often, but today was an exception. He'd planned to attend a meeting later this morning with a client who wanted to purchase three of their armored SUVs. Not a huge contract, but not small either. Each SUV's price tag was a cool $785,000. First Security's armored limos weren't just rolling Kevlar shells. They were fully contained environmental, communication, and survival mechanisms. They could withstand being submerged in shallow water for up to an hour, repel chemical attacks, survive fifty-caliber BMG rounds, and take on a bulldozer and win. Well, that was a bit of an exaggeration, but they could take a tremendous pounding and keep going. What made them highly desirable was their patented Roll-Right System, RRS, which employed high-speed hydraulic pistons that returned the vehicle upright from either of its sides or even its roof. Strategically placed pistons fired in a precise sequence, essentially flipping the vehicle back onto its solid rubber tires. It worked perfectly, and First Security Inc. was in the process of licensing its RRS to other armored-vehicle companies, including General Motors, the prestigious manufacturer of "the Beast," the presidential limo series.

Nathan left his office and headed for the Bat Cave, First Security's high-tech garage, where its clients' vehicles were swept for bugs and tracking devices. Countermeasures were a good chunk of First Security's business.

Walking over to his car, he waved goodbye to his head gizmo guy, Lewey. The RRS was Lewey's brainchild. He'd come up with the concept and asked permission to build a prototype. After $3 million and two years of hard work, First Security's RRS-equipped SUVs had hit the streets to universal acclaim.

Driving east on Mira Mesa Boulevard, Nathan thought about Denise's cat, how she'd misstated its name. It had to be deliberate. A clever ploy, almost surely born of desperation.

He found himself pressing the gas pedal a little harder and calling Vince.

Great minds think alike because his phone rang at the same instant he was about to connect.

"Are you thinking what I'm thinking?" Vince asked.

"I think so. I was just calling you. Let's break some laws getting there. My nav says ten minutes, but I think I can get there faster."

"You'll likely beat me. I'm caught in a little bit of traffic on the Five. I'm going to use the shoulder."

"Turn on your flashers," Nathan said. "You never know when some model citizen might decide to block your path."

"Good idea."

"If I get there first, I'll stage a few blocks away until you arrive. You do the same."

"I really hope it's a false alarm."

"Yeah, me too. See you in a few minutes."

CHAPTER 5

Nathan figured he'd better call Harv, or there'd be hell to pay. They'd become instant friends when they first met in the Marines. Not only had Nathan commanded a force-recon unit, but he'd been its primary sniper, with Harv as his spotter. Not many officers became shooters, but his natural-born ability couldn't be overlooked. Not one in ten thousand people had the mindset and physical skills needed for precision marksmanship. Unfortunately, his specialty also created inner turmoil and conflict. How were you supposed to feel good about killing people for a living, especially when you were really good at it? He and Harv had talked about it many times, and they always ended with the same conclusion: someone had to do it.

Evil needed to be confronted and defeated, and all too often, the price was high.

Nathan shook his head. He and Harv had lost many Marine brothers in the Beirut airport bombing. They hadn't yet been Marines at the time, but they went on to serve in the 1st Battalion, 8th Marines. The one-eight had a long and proud history dating back to World War II.

He dialed his friend.

"Hey, Nate, what's up?"

He gave a brief recap.

"I don't think you and Vince are being paranoid at all. If it were my assistant, I'd be doing the same thing. I'm several miles away from my house right now, out jogging. Realistically, I can't get there in under forty-five minutes. You and Vince will have to handle it. Hopefully it's nothing."

"Does it sound like nothing?" he asked.

"Not really, but I don't know Vince's secretary all that well. I trust his gut. May I assume you guys won't take any unnecessary risks if something heavy's going down? I like my world with you in it."

"You've always liked saying that."

"Does it bother you?"

"Not at all. I like being in your world too."

Harv grunted a thank-you.

"I had an interesting experience this morning I need to tell you about."

"Who did you beat up?"

"That's not funny."

"Well?"

"Couldn't you ask me whose cat I rescued from a tree? Good grief, not every interesting experience I have involves violence . . . Damn it, Harv, you can't know that."

"I know *you*. Tell me later; you need to concentrate on your driving. Call me once you know what's going on."

"Will do."

"Check six, old friend. Assume nothing."

Nathan ended the call.

Check six was police and military terminology for *watch your back*. Considering the unknowns they'd be facing, not bad advice.

***

Half a mile out, Nathan took Vince's call and said, "I'm less than a minute away."

"You'll see my Navigator once you turn on Sagebrush."

"Do we have a plan?"

"Well, I thought we'd start by knocking on her door."

Nathan discounted the sarcasm, didn't take it personally. "Is it possible she got a second cat?"

"Yeah, it's possible, but she tends to tell me everything about her personal life."

"Got you. I'm pulling in behind."

"We aren't there yet. It's another quarter mile. Just follow my lead and park behind me when I stop."

"Will do."

Nathan evaluated the neighborhood. It looked like hundreds of other planned residential areas of San Diego's North County. Curbs. Gutters. Sidewalks. Underground utilities. And nice yards. Most of the homes were two-story and shared common side-yard fences. He guessed each one was probably around twenty-five hundred to three thousand square feet with price tags in the $750,000 range. The People's Republic of California continued to get more and more expensive with each passing year.

"We might catch a break here," Vince said. "It looks like Denise's neighbor is watering his grass. I'm gonna pull over and check him out. It's ah . . . probably better if I go alone. I'll give you a signal when I'm ready for you. The fence separating their yards should screen me from Denise's house."

He watched Vince hurry down the sidewalk, then cut across the neighbor's grass.

Upon seeing a complete stranger approach, the man released the trigger on his nozzle. It almost looked like the guy got caught taking a piss and stopped midstream.

While Vince spoke, Denise's neighbor held perfectly still, clearly evaluating if what he heard was a bunch of BS. After thirty seconds or so, Vince showed the man a business card and they shook hands, a good sign.

Vince turned and gave Nathan a nod to join them.

As usual, the introduction was a little awkward because Denise's neighbor spent a little too long looking at Nathan's face. They followed the man through a wooden gate on the far side of the property, away from Denise's place. Their new ally took them through a nicely landscaped area into a backyard containing a swimming pool, hot tub, and a permanent barbecue setup.

I need a barbecue like this, Nathan thought. "Is there a place we can take a look into her backyard without being seen?" he asked, already knowing the answer.

"My spare bedroom upstairs overlooks her rear yard. You want me to go take a look?"

"Yes. Just let us know if anything looks out of place."

"I'll be right back." The guy cursed under his breath when he found the sliding glass door locked. "I have to go around."

Once the man left, Vince said, "I was surprised when you picked up at the office."

"I'm not normally there, but when I heard you were on the line, I took the call."

"I'm flattered."

"You deserve it. Your surveillance team did a knock-up job for us in Santa Monica last year."

"Thanks for saying so. Those guys were ISAF vets. Embedded covert stuff with the CIA."

Vincent wouldn't say more, and Nathan wouldn't ask. Nearly all of BSI's missions during Operation Enduring Freedom in Afghanistan were classified.

"So what's our plan here?"

Vince shrugged. "If no one answers the door and it's locked, I say we bust in."

"I'm okay with that."

"If it's all a false alarm, I'll pay for the damage and give her a raise."

Nathan tilted his head. "Our friend is back."

The man stopped at the sliding glass door, unlocked it, reached down, and pulled the dowel. He waved to them to come inside. From the look on his face, something was wrong.

"What did you see?" Vincent asked.

"Her sliding glass door is shattered."

Nathan exchanged a glance with Vince and asked, "Was it like that yesterday?"

"I don't know."

"Is the glass still in place?"

"Most of it, but some has fallen out."

"Didn't she say her cat was scratching at the glass?" Nathan asked.

"Yeah," Vince said. "And unless it's an African lion, it didn't do that. Do you know if Denise has more than one cat?"

"She just has the one calico, Miss Kitty. She's super friendly and comes over here a lot. I feed her when they're on vacation."

"Have you ever heard Denise call it any other name? Mr. Paws? Anything like that?"

"No, they call it Miss Kitty. Or MK."

"Do you mind if we take a quick look at her backyard from your spare bedroom first?"

"Not at all."

When the man didn't move, Vince said, "Can we do that right away?"

"Oh, yeah, sure. Follow me."

The guy's house was immaculate, and Vince paid him a compliment. He said thanks and quickly led them up the stairs. The spare bedroom offered a good look at Denise's backyard. Similar in size and shape, it lacked a pool but had a nice expanse of grass and a hot tub. A fairly open trellis covered the concrete patio, which was flanked by low hedges. They both saw it right away. The sliding glass door had turned opaque from thousands of small cracked pieces. Countless shards littered the patio. There was no way they'd be able to get inside the house through that door without being heard.

Like the one they were in, Denise's house had a second floor. All of the windows were closed and screened by blinds.

Nathan said, "Take a look at the concrete about four feet out from the door. See it?"

"Yeah, it's a skip mark, all right. Probably medium caliber."

"That's my call too. Good thing there's only a canyon beyond her fence."

"We'd better get over there."

"Skip mark?" the man said. "You mean from a bullet? Shouldn't I call the police?"

Vince shook his head. "Not yet. Give us a chance to assess the situation."

"I don't know . . . I think I should call the cops."

They hurried down the stairs. "We can't stop you," Vince said, "but please give us two minutes first."

"Who are you guys?"

"Let's just say we have more experience than the police at this sort of thing."

Denise's neighbor was on their heels. "That's not much of an answer."

"It's the best we can do. We're using your front door to leave."

The windows along the front of Denise's house were also screened by closed blinds. Nathan knew someone could be peering through the slats, and if that were the case, things were going to escalate in a big hurry. They were in plain sight as they sprinted across her grass.

"If we're going to get shot this morning, now seems like a good time."

"You're such an optimist, Nathan."

They made it to her entry alcove unscathed. "Think he'll wait to call the police?"

"Not for a second," Vince said.

"Shock and awe?"

"Yep. We bust in and shoot anyone who looks threatening. She has three small children and a babysitter, so we can't shoot through any walls. If we don't have center-mass shots or clear backgrounds, we hold fire."

"Let's try not to nail Denise either."

Vince said, "Yeah, that's the general idea."

"I'll take the lead and the right side on entry. Once we're both inside and clear, we'll leapfrog deeper. Three-meter intervals."

At times like these, hesitation led to doubt. Nathan knew the longer they stood here talking, the less confident they'd become.

They both pulled their pistols from their waist packs and nodded to each other.

Vince reared back and kicked the door with all his strength.

Even dead bolted, it was no match for physics. More energy was delivered than it could withstand. Wood splintered, and the door slammed the inside wall with enough force to rattle the windows.

In one fluid movement, they were inside.

Nathan focused on the right side and crouched behind some kind of potted fern.

The living room stood empty, but strange, high-pitched sounds emanated from somewhere ahead and to the right. Directly in front of them, a stairwell to the second floor lay deserted and dark.

Vince advanced to a hallway past his position and looked around the corner at waist level.

So far, no one had shot at them. Vince made eye contact, pointed to his eyes, then pointed to the opening beyond the stairs to the left. Nathan believed it led to the kitchen and garage beyond.

Still using the leapfrog technique, he moved past Vince's position and crouched at the entry to the kitchen. Off to his right, he saw Denise's children.

And something else.

A pool of blood.

CHAPTER 6

In the television room, three terrified kids sat shoulder to shoulder with their wrists duct-taped behind their backs to the legs of a heavy coffee table. Their mouths were taped shut as well. Several feet away, a woman's gray face stared at him, her throat laid open, the only source of the bloodstain.

Nathan brought a forefinger up to his mouth.

It didn't work.

The children continued to tremble and cry.

He wanted to help them, but the intruders could still be in the house.

For now, the children had to wait.

He rushed past them and looked behind the sofa. Nothing but carpet. That left the kitchen, where someone could be hiding behind the counters. In a whisper, he told the kids he was here to help, which seemed to settle them down a little.

He made a warbling whistle to get Vince's attention, then made a gesture to indicate he wanted to clear the kitchen. Vince nodded his understanding and took up a position near the landing of the stairs.

From there, Vince could cover the ground-floor hallway and the door to the garage, but he couldn't yet see Denise's children.

In an aggressive move, Nathan gathered some speed and hopped the countertop as if sliding across the hood of a car. He landed on his feet with his weapon pointed toward the refrigerator and oven. Again nothing. An empty kitchen greeted him.

He diverted to the door leading to the garage and tried the knob. Locked.

Nathan thought it unlikely anyone would be hiding in the garage—with a key—but not taking any chances, he grabbed the dish towel and tied one end of it to the garage door's knob and the other end around the base of a glass tumbler. Since the door opened into the garage, he put the tumbler on the edge of the counter. If anyone opened the door, it would pull the tumbler off the counter, shattering it on the floor.

Satisfied with his trip-wire-like contraption, he hurried over to Vince's position and whispered, "Her kids are scared, but they look okay."

"Where are they?"

"Middle of the family room floor. They're duct-taped to a coffee table. There's a dead woman on the carpet, Latina-looking."

"Carmen," Vince said softly.

Nathan felt it best not to mention her slit throat. He didn't want Vince further distracted. Vince was sharp, but his movements weren't as crisp as Harv's would be in this situation. "We'll have to clear this hallway before we go upstairs. I'll take point on the lineup."

"Uh-uh. It's my turn, Nate."

"There're three doors. One of them will probably be a bathroom. I'll take the right side in each room."

"Let's get this done."

He gave Vince's shoulder a gentle nudge, the signal he was ready to go. Moving as one, with Vince in the lead, they eased down the hall and stopped short of the first open door. As suspected, they found an empty bathroom, and Nathan used its mirror to clear the glass shower stall. The second door on the opposite side of the hall sat closed. Vince pointed to himself, then made an opening-door gesture. He nodded his acknowledgment and eased forward to Vince's left shoulder. Seeing it would open inward, he moved to the far side of the door.

Vince crouched, slowly turned the knob, and mouthed the words *on three.*

Nathan did the countdown with his free hand. When Vince pushed the door, Nathan pivoted to face the room.

And came face-to-face with an empty coat closet.

One door left, also closed.

It also opened inward, so they repeated the same process.

Vince cranked the knob and pushed.

In a fluid motion, he was in the room.

What Nathan saw tugged at his ability to remain calm.

He'd met Denise once or twice, but the woman bound to the chair bore little resemblance to that beautiful woman. The swelling and blood caked around her face and neck were a testament to what she'd endured.

"Cover our six," Nathan said tightly.

Vince didn't move.

"Vince. Cover six!"

He saw Vince move to the door and line up on the hallway leading back to the kitchen and TV room.

Denise's breathing sounded shallow and slow.

"Denise. We've got you."

The woman could only open one eye. The other was swollen shut.

Barely conscious, she whispered, "My babies . . ."

"They're okay. Not hurt."

Even with all this woman had gone through, she still managed a smile. "Who are you?"

"Nathan McBride. Vince is here too. An ambulance is on the way."

"Vince?"

"Yeah, Denise. I'm here."

She tried to look up, but her head didn't make it.

"She's drifting in and out," Nathan said.

"Denise, we have to clear the rest of the house."

"Heard them . . . leave."

"We have to make sure. We'll be right back. I promise."

No response.

"Denise? Denise, can you hear me? She's out again," he said. "She's concussed for sure, maybe worse. You'd better call 911 just in case her neighbor didn't."

"Good idea."

Nathan took a defensive position at the door while Vince made the call, reporting a home invasion with a critically injured victim and one fatality. After providing the address, he told the 911 operator he was in the process of clearing the house.

"No, I'm not going to vacate the premises," Vince said in an irritated whisper. "Just get an ambulance going now!"

At least he's not yelling, Nathan thought.

His friend cursed under his breath and cut the call short.

Looking at Denise, Nathan knew whoever had beaten her enjoyed doing it. He'd seen enough of this to know the difference. She hadn't been struck once or twice; she'd been pummeled into unconsciousness. He doubted Denise had offered much resistance, assuming all the intruders wanted was information. As dark as the thought was, if they'd been sexual predators, Denise's children wouldn't have been spared.

They left the room and started toward the stairwell landing. Keeping his voice low, Vince said, "Heads are going to roll for this. There's going to be some serious fucking payback."

"You can count on me and Harv. We're going to find whoever did this and bury them."

"I want a few hours with them first."

"I'm sure that can be arranged." Nathan needed to direct their attention back to the task at hand. "I'll take the lead going up the stairs, and we'll clear the rooms just like we did down here."

It took less than a minute to check the second floor. Denise was right: the intruders were no longer here.

They hurried downstairs and approached her kids. Still terrified, they clearly didn't trust their rescuers. An understandable reaction, given Nathan's unusual-looking face and everything else these children had undergone this morning.

Nathan had torn duct tape from skin many times, but never from anyone this young. He wasn't sure if the tape would take their skin with it. Being cautious, he started peeling from one corner slowly.

He asked Vince to keep an eye on the front and back doors while he tended to the kids.

"An ambulance is coming. Your mom's okay."

The younger of the two boys didn't say anything, but the older one asked why this had happened.

"I don't know," Nathan said. "But you're all safe now. I'm a friend of your mom, and I'm here with her boss, Vince. I want you to stay right here with your brother and sister, okay? Promise you'll do that?"

"What happened to your face?" the girl asked. "Did the bad men hurt you too?"

If only you knew. "I had an accident a long time ago. Your mom's in her office. She's okay, but they roughed her up a little."

"You mean like a bully?" asked one of the boys.

"Yeah, like that," he said. No doubt they'd heard what their mother had gone through. He repeated his command gently. "I want all of you to stay right here. Okay?"

They all nodded.

The older boy said one of the men hurt his thumb. Nathan saw the swelling right away. The fat part of his thumb was twice its normal size.

What kind of an animal hurts a small kid like this? Vince had it exactly right. Some serious payback loomed on the horizon.

After he had the three kids settled on the sofa, he asked Vince to stay with them while he tended to Denise. He glanced at his watch, wondering how much time he had before the police arrived. Given some of the activities he'd engaged in over the years, he preferred to keep under the radar when it came to the police.

Vince must've read his mind because he said, "I don't mind being on the police report, but you probably shouldn't be."

"How much time do we have?"

"A few minutes at best. I wouldn't be surprised if the CHP also responds. Especially if a cruiser's on the freeway nearby. I'd say you need to be outta here within the next two minutes."

Nathan hurried back to the office. Denise hadn't moved. If anything, her head was slumped farther down. When she didn't respond to her name, he gave her a slight nudge, and she moaned.

"I'm going to get you out of this chair. Sorry, but it's going to hurt." He cut the tape binding her wrists and ankles to the chair's legs and eased her down to the carpet. Her blouse opened in the process; several buttons were missing. When he saw an area of bruised skin, he unfastened the rest of the buttons and clenched his teeth at the sight. Her entire torso, from neck to belt line, looked like it had been used as a speed bag. Literally every square inch of her chest, ribs, and stomach was bruised and swollen. Making matters worse, the underwire part of her bra was pinched across her breasts. He left it in place, reached underneath her back, and tried to unhook it. After fumbling with it for several seconds, he gave up, pulled his Predator knife from its ankle sheath, and cut the bra where it stretched under her arm.

You assholes are going to pay for this.

She stirred but didn't open her eyes.

"Denise."

Nothing.

He said her name louder.

Again, no response.

Hating himself for doing it, he gave her a firm nudge. He needed to know what the intruders wanted. He seriously doubted this was a random break-in.

Still nothing, except for her raspy breathing.

He hustled out of the office and found Vince standing near the base of the stairwell.

"What's going on?" Vince asked.

"I need something from the kitchen."

Passing by the TV room, he again told the children their mom was okay and that help was on the way.

In the kitchen, he opened the cabinet doors under the sink and began looking through the contents. He couldn't find what he wanted but located a good substitute—a can of Comet cleaner. After removing a bowl from the cabinet, he shook out an ounce of bluish-white powder. Next, he added some water and stirred the abrasive cleaner into a soupy mix.

Acutely aware of time, he hurried back to the office, tried to rouse Denise, and got the same result. Nothing. He held the bowl under her nose.

The chemical smell did the trick. She stirred to consciousness, and her good eye opened.

"Nathan?"

"Yeah, it's me. Vince got your cat message."

"My babies . . ."

"They're okay."

"They killed . . . Carmen."

He hoped they hadn't murdered the woman in front of her children. "An ambulance is on the way. You're going to be okay. Who were they? What did they want?"

"I told them . . . things."

"About Vince?"

She nodded.

There couldn't be much about Vince's personal life she didn't know. "It's okay."

"No . . . it's not okay." Her head slumped forward.

"Denise." He gave her a nudge. "What did they want?"

No response. He used the chemicals again, and she opened her eyes.

"What did you tell them?"

Her lips barely moved when she spoke. "Charlene . . ."

Vince's wife. "What about her? Denise! What did they want to know?"

"Her . . . schedule."

CHAPTER 7

Eight Days Ago

The Air Force duty officer picked up her ringing phone with some trepidation. It had been a slow night inside Cheyenne Mountain. Slow was good. Boring was good.

The female voice on the other end spoke calmly and softly. "Colonel Landon, Pave Fire Three just picked up a thermal over DPRK. Check that. I've now got five hot spots."

Landon tapped her knowledge of the Pave Fire satellites. Ultra-high-res camera suites. Thermal imaging overlay capability. Low Earth orbits. They were used primarily for spying on the rogue nation of North Korea.

"Missile launches?" she asked.

"Negative, ma'am. They're stationary."

"Location?"

"GPS coordinates are coming in now . . . It's . . . the Jong Doo underground facility."

"I'll be right there." She picked up her coffee mug and stepped into the adjoining situation room, where half a dozen fifty-inch TV screens flanked a huge central monitor. Like a smaller version of NASA's command center, this five-thousand-square-foot room served as the nation's early-warning hub against missile attacks. A minimum of ten people worked in here around the clock. Chief Shaw currently had Pave Three's thermal image feed on her computer's monitor.

"Explosions or fires?" Landon asked.

"Explosions," Shaw said. "They fit the profile perfectly."

"Let's see it on the main screen. When's our next bird overhead?"

"It clears the horizon in twenty-two minutes."

"Is it a LEO?"

"Yes, ma'am, Pave Fire Eight."

Damn. She wanted more time over the target and was willing to sacrifice some resolution for it. Currently, she didn't have that option.

"How long can we watch with Pave Three?"

"Another two minutes."

"Pull up the sats and plot the heat signatures."

"Yes, ma'am."

Landon addressed a different tech. "Sergeant Bailey, give me what we have on Jong Doo."

"Right away, ma'am."

Ten seconds later on a different TV screen, overlaid thermal dots could be seen on the satellite photos. A third screen showed GPS coordinates and basic information about the facility—size, personnel, commanding officer, commencing date of operations, and some other stats. She squinted at the top secret clearance required to view more than currently displayed.

Something heavy's going down. Did we do this?

"Opinion, Sergeant Bailey. What's going on?"

"There aren't any aircraft overhead, and there aren't any warm engine blocks. Based on the size, location, and near-simultaneous timing, I'd have to say . . . foul play." Bailey pointed to the main monitor. "Those bigger signatures correspond to the main and secondary entrances. I think it's fair to assume the smaller hot spots correspond to ventilation shafts."

"Agreed. Good call, Sergeant. We've got ninety seconds of real time left. Pan out and scan for departing vehicles. Five-mile radius."

"Aye, ma'am . . . We're too low to see the entire access road weaving through the canyon, but I'm not seeing . . . anything. Except for the explosions, it's cold."

"Zoom in and look for warm bodies. Search a thousand-yard radius from the complex's main entrance."

She worked her terminal. "Affirmative, ma'am. I've got three signatures on foot, moving due east. Looks like they're running at a medium pace."

"Anything out in front of them?"

"Negative, nothing but forest. Once they leave the open ground surrounding the pit mine, we'll lose them in the trees."

"Who are you?" she murmured. "Let me know as soon as our next bird clears the horizon." She addressed everyone seated at their monitors. "Stay sharp, people. This place is going to get really busy within the next few minutes."

She returned to her desk, picked up her handset, and punched a four-digit number. "Sir, we've got multiple explosions at Jong Doo."

There was a pause on the other end for a few seconds. "I'm on my way. Lock it down, Colonel Landon."

CHAPTER 8

Charlene Beaumont didn't like shopping for clothes, even with no upper limit on spending. It simply wasn't her thing. She preferred shooting handguns at indoor ranges over trying to pick the right colors for shoes, belts, and purses. And trying on a swimsuit? Forget it. She'd rather have a root canal without anesthetic.

Her two sons, Brian and Anthony, ages fourteen and twelve, looked understandably bored. Nordstrom wasn't their kind of store. She could've let them hang out at the house and stare at their phones, but she hadn't spent enough time with them lately, and their cell phone addictions had become an ever-increasing source of conflict. A saving grace? The devices offered her unlimited power over them. All she had to do was threaten confiscation, and they instantly transformed into model citizens. The few times she'd done it had been agonizing—for them. They'd acted as if their lives had no meaning or purpose. As if the universe were doomed to destruction.

A couple of days ago, her husband of twenty-seven years had made an offhand comment about their shoes looking a little "ratty." That's all it took.

Aye aye, sir. Message received. Loud and clear.

She supposed that's what she loved most about Vince. His practical approach to minor problem-solving. Delegation. Of course she could've blown off the *suggestion*, but he was right. "Ratty" had been an understatement. Their sneakers looked like they'd been dragged down a five-mile stretch of gravel road—in the rain. Vince had offered to take them shopping, but Charlene knew he hated it more than she did. Besides, it gave her a chance to embrace motherhood a little longer. The boys were getting less and less dependent with each passing year. In no time, they'd be off to college, married, and raising families of their own.

She didn't usually have to bribe them, but today's reward after enduring Nordstrom's footwear department would be a thirty-minute stop at San Diego's premier gaming superstore, where they could test-drive all the latest blood-and-guts video games. Apparently killing your enemy wasn't good enough—he had to be dismembered in medieval fashion. Nice. She knew the gaming material was a little too mature for them, but it kept them off the internet, where every depraved sex act imaginable waited only a few clicks away. What a world . . .

Leaving the store, she looked up to a crisp blue sky. Such a beautiful day. No wonder so many people moved here. If you could tolerate the high taxes, expensive cost of living, traffic nightmares, and noise, America's Finest City became an attractive destination.

Her phone rang. She'd been about to reach for it, when it occurred to her she ought to make a good example for her boys and ignore it. If it were urgent, they'd call back or leave a message. Just because the damned thing made a sound, it didn't mean she had to look at it right away.

It could wait.

She noticed a couple of young men wearing hoodies, immediately thought gangbangers, and regretted it. Besides, they looked Middle Eastern, not Hispanic. Plus, she didn't know them. They could be honor students. *Don't judge them on appearance only, Charlene. That's unfair and shallow.* Not surprisingly, their faces were glued to their phones. It wasn't cold, but she supposed the hoodie look was "in." Vincent drew the line there. His boys could wear their pants low and shuffle along, but hoodies were OOTQ—out of the question. She remembered seeing these two a few minutes ago; they'd been eying a couple of women at the cosmetics counter inside Nordstrom. She couldn't blame them. The two women could've passed for cover models. Long legs. Perfect hair. Full lips. *Oh, to be young again.*

Hanging back a few steps, her two sons trailed her across the second-level courtyard. She couldn't blame them for not walking next to Mom. They were at that geeky age where image was everything—except for their shoes. Perhaps well worn was a status symbol. Who knew? She glanced over her shoulder and wasn't as surprised to see her boys pecking away on their phones.

One of the hooded men must've said something funny because they broke out in laughter.

After going down several half flights of stairs, she reached the main concourse, her boys still trailing. She glanced in both directions, looking for a map kiosk, and didn't see one.

At the same instant she turned toward Brian, she caught a glimpse of the same two hooded men walking down the short flights of stairs, sports bags slung over their shoulders. Charlene absorbed five critical pieces of information from her brief glance at them.

One, they'd both been singularly focused on her and looked away quickly.

Two, none of their skin was exposed, only their shadowed faces.

Three, their cheap sports bags looked out of place with their expensive shoes and designer jeans.

Four, their earlier laughing had sounded forced.

And five, this wasn't the first time she'd caught them staring at her.

She could dismiss the first and fifth pieces of information. She was, after all, hot. She'd mostly maintained her high school physique, and her sheer, fitted blouse didn't leave much room for imagination.

Number three could be viewed as bad fashion, and number four didn't mean trouble per se. The kicker was number two: no exposed skin. That, in combination with the hoods, didn't pass the smell test.

Was it possible their bags held athletic shoes and workout clothes? Yes, but something seemed off.

At the same instant she eased her hand into her purse, her phone made a text message sound. She grabbed it and looked at the screen.

It was Vince.

Sending three numbers.

911

Her skin tightened with a sickening sense of danger.

Slowing her pace, she allowed her boys to catch up, then turned toward a store and pretended to look in its windows.

Anthony asked, "We're not going in there, are we?"

In a whisper, she told them to go inside.

Her boys seemed confused and just stood there.

"Go inside!" she hissed.

In the glass reflection, her pursuers reached into their bags.

Her eyes focused on the compact machine pistols being pulled free.

In the split second before their weapons leveled on her, she made the decision to knock both of her boys to the ground. She drove her shoulder into Brian, causing him to strike Anthony like a bowling pin. Both of them went sprawling on the concrete as the two machine guns roared.

"Run!" she yelled.

She didn't understand how the human brain worked at times like this, but her mind registered multiple impacts to her body. The sensation wasn't pain as much as vibration. Through it all, she managed to get her hand onto the butt of her handgun and yank it from her purse.

In the blink of an eye, the scene morphed into chaos. What had been a quiet and tranquil mall was now a hellish place of deafening gunfire, screaming, and death. She scrambled to her right, putting some distance between herself and her boys.

All down the mall, people clutched their wounds and fell to the ground. Others ran as the staccato roar of automatic gunfire slammed every hard surface.

Charlene saw two menacing arcs of expended brass flipping through the air, each casing representing a copper-jacketed slug arriving at twelve hundred feet per second.

She felt more impacts to her body. Over the chaos and thunder rocketing down the mall, she knew the bullets had to be small-caliber rounds because she hadn't been punched all that hard.

She stayed on her feet—one of the many things her husband had drilled into her over the years. Just because you get shot, doesn't mean you have to fall down.

She didn't yet feel pain but sensed massive tissue damage. Shock, she knew.

Riding the adrenaline, she aimed her Glock and squeezed off a shot—remembering not to jerk the trigger.

The shorter of the two gunmen shuddered, as though experiencing a chill. She'd drilled him for sure. Center mass. Like herself, the guy didn't go down but continued to fire his weapon.

To her horror, the other gunman aimed at her boys, who were still on the ground a few yards away.

No! Oh, please no!

At the same instant the gunman's weapon roared, she saw the most horrible thing imaginable. Her beautiful child took multiple impacts to his chest and stomach. His small face looked confused, then terrified.

Charlene felt rage burst up from the depths and fired her pistol as fast as she could pull the trigger until it stopped. Most of her shots missed, but one of them nailed the taller guy in the hip. Glass storefronts behind both gunmen shattered and fell. The taller gunman cursed when his magazine went empty and fumbled to pull a new one from his bag.

Now pain arrived. In force.

It started like multiple bee stings, then morphed into a flame-thrower-like burn.

She looked toward Brian and saw him bolting down the concourse, screaming as he ran.

Keep running! Don't look back! Please don't look back. She didn't want his last memory of his mom and brother to be this bloody mess.

A snarl formed on the taller man's face as he dropped the empty magazine and inserted a fresh one. In a quick and practiced move, he jerked the bolt back and let it spring forward. It slammed closed with a mechanical clack sound.

She limped to Anthony, dropped to her knees, and used her body to shield him.

This was it.

She'd never be able to reload her Glock in time.

With his lips curled back, the gunman shuffled forward. "Mr. A sends his regards."

Her voice sounded detached, as if coming from someone else. "Please . . . don't kill my son."

The man's expression didn't change.

As frightened as she was, she didn't close her eyes. Better to face death rather than cower from it. She'd met her husband in the Marines, and once a Marine, always a Marine.

She took a deep breath and winced in pain.

Oh, man, that really hurts.

So this is how I die? Huddled around Anthony like an exhausted mother bear protecting her cub from wolves?

Charlene flinched at the moment of truth when the report cracked down the mall.

What the hell? Had he missed? From there?

Impossible. Nobody missed from four feet.

So why didn't she feel anything? Was she already dead?

Could this be the beginning of her journey to heaven?

Then it dawned on her. The report had been a single shot, and its location had come from behind.

Something else too.

The gunman who'd been about to kill her jerked at the same instant a small hole appeared in his sweatshirt. The fabric instantly turned dark.

Another boom tore across the eerie silence.

Another hole. Two inches from the first.

The gunman looked down at his chest and back up just as a third bullet found the middle of his sweatshirt.

More automatic gunfire roared from her right, followed by more individual booms.

Still wanting to fight, she reached into her purse for another magazine but lost her balance and fell to her side.

A woman yelled, "Drop the gun!"

Two more booms thundered down the mall.

Directly above her, the gunman's chest exploded outward.

That's some damned fine shooting. She looked for the other gunman but saw no sign of him.

"Anthony . . . ?"

Nothing.

Firm hands held her in place when she tried to roll toward her son.

A woman's voice: "I've got you. Don't try to move, okay?" The voice was calm, soothing. Somehow she knew it was the same woman who'd returned fire on the shooters.

She turned her head but closed her eyes against the sun.

"Please hold still."

"Are the gunmen dead?"

"Yes."

"Please help my son." She tried to roll again.

"I will, but please hold still."

Looking the other direction, she saw ten or twelve people on the ground. Some of them writhed in pain. Others didn't move. She also saw both her boys' phones on the concrete. The irony felt absurd. Now that they really needed them . . .

The mall music, coupled with moans of agony, twisted into a surreal murmur. Could this be some kind of psychotic hallucination left over from her college years? Had this really happened? Was she really lying in a pool of her own blood next to her wounded child?

It defied understanding.

More quick footsteps. More hands touching her body. And something else. Pressure on her stomach and chest.

She heard hushed words about controlling bleeding and felt something press against her legs.

Thankfully, Brian got away. She'd seen him running down the mall.

"What's your name?" the woman's voice asked.

"Charlene."

"I'm a retired corpsman, Charlene, and I'm putting pressure on your wounds to control the bleeding. I'm sorry this hurts."

"It's okay." She listened to the woman give instructions to someone helping Anthony. "My son . . ."

"We're helping him too. You nailed both of the gunmen. All I did was finish them off. You were incredibly brave. I saw you knock your boys down and fight back. Are you retired law enforcement?"

"Marines."

"Well, Marine, you're in good hands. I did three tours in OEF. Lie still, okay?"

"Anthony . . ."

"We've got him."

"Is he okay?"

The woman lifted Charlene's head just high enough to put something underneath it. Her purse? She smelled leather and a familiar cologne.

The soft voice spoke again. "You need to hold still until the paramedics arrive. You might have a spinal injury."

"My son . . . please help him."

"We are, Charlene. We're helping him right now."

Like a teakettle starting to whistle, she felt her consciousness begin to fade. Sound became tunnel-like and distant. She sensed only a few people were around. Where was everyone else? Why weren't they helping the wounded?

There was something she needed to do before she lost consciousness. What was it? Something about her phone.

Pictures. She needed pictures of the dead gunmen's faces.

"My phone. I need my phone . . ."

"We've already called 911."

"Pictures . . ."

"Pictures?"

"Of the gunmen . . . their faces."

The woman helping her didn't respond.

"Please, it's important. Use my phone . . . in my purse. Please!"

"We'll take care of it. Don't move, okay?"

"Please don't . . . bullshit me . . . My husband needs the pictures. Promise me!"

"Okay, I promise. I'm going to lift your head a little. Let me do the work."

Charlene's pain seemed to be fading, and her eyes wouldn't focus.

"I need your pass code."

"Nine-six-six . . . seven-six-six."

Her hands felt wet, and she brought them up. *Oh, dear Lord, that's my blood.* "Please tell Vince I love him . . . will you do that?"

"You're going to tell him yourself."

Charlene heard the fake shutter sounds of her phone taking photos. Then the woman with the kind voice told someone to take pictures of the other gunman. Whoever she asked to do it started to argue, but the woman's voice became stern, insisting on it.

"Anthony . . . why aren't you . . . helping him?"

"He's right here. I'm going to lift your head again. Let me do the work."

"Thank you. You got . . . the photos, right?"

"We got the photos. Your phone's back in your purse. I'll make sure the paramedics take it with them. I'm going to stay with you until they arrive. Can you feel this?"

"Yes." She felt her left foot being wiggled.

"How about this?"

The other foot. She knew feeling her feet was good but wasn't sure why. "My lungs . . ."

"I think they're okay."

She thought that was good news too.

The inward spiral began. She'd only felt it once before in Iraq. Crazy thing was, it hadn't been a combat wound. She'd cracked her head on a Hesco bastion when she'd stumbled in the gravel on the way to the head. Of all the things . . .

"Thank you . . . for helping us."

A hand grasped hers. "Don't talk, okay? An ambulance will be here any minute. Relax your breathing and concentrate on lowering your heart rate. Can you do that for me?"

"I don't feel too bad right now."

"That's good. Don't talk. Take deep breaths."

The sun formed a yellow-white halo around the blonde woman's head. Charlene felt herself smile. "You're an angel."

The woman smiled. "I don't think I've been called an angel before. My husband might disagree with you. Charlene, listen to me, okay? It's really important that you keep breathing and relax as much as possible. Breathe in. Exhale slowly. I'm right here. I'm not going anywhere."

She felt her hand being held and couldn't think of anything else she should say except thank you.

A calmness washed through her, and she sensed more voices. People were doing things. Saying things. She closed her eyes.

Stay with me, Charlene. Stay with me. Charlene!

That was her name. Charlene. Retired US Marine staff sergeant. She had two children and a loving husband . . .

As her world compressed, she wondered if she'd ever see them again.

CHAPTER 9

Five Days Ago

The seventy-meter luxury yacht *Yoonsuh* pitched and rolled with a gentle six-foot swell. Its state-of-the-art GPS navigation, sonar, radar, and forward-looking infrared made collision with another ship or reef next to impossible, especially in the middle of the Philippine Sea. Captain Santino's presence on the bridge wasn't really necessary because his third in command had the watch for another hour, but he liked being up here just the same.

The last time he'd been in this region of the world, he'd rendezvoused with the massive container ship *Namkung Khang* for the transfer of several duffel bags. To this day, he still didn't know what the bags had contained and didn't care. Asking questions would lead to his employment termination, or worse. The man he worked for survived on stealth and secrecy. Creating news headlines meant losing business, simple as that.

He was pretty sure the *Yoonsuh*'s South Korean registry didn't reflect its true owner, a ridiculously wealthy Mexican crime lord with ties to cartels all over the world. Santino liked his new boss, as much as you can like a drug dealer, smuggler, racketeer, human trafficker, and cold-blooded killer.

Santino had no illusions about his role. It hadn't changed. When it came right down to it, he was little more than "staff," along with the private jet and helicopter pilots, limo drivers, bodyguards, cooks, hand-maidens, butlers, gardeners, and last but not least? Enforcers—killers who did the boss's wet work. The few times he'd been in the presence of such men, it felt like standing on the precipice of a cliff.

More times than Santino cared to admit, the cartel's enforcers had used this ship to dispose of bodies, which made him complicit in cover-ing up murders. There was no sense in worrying about it. Santino did what he was told, collected his twenty grand a month, and got to sail this elegant beauty across the open seas as much as he wanted. Not a bad life.

Under the close supervision of his two new passengers, two items had been placed into a special smuggling compartment. Looking like hard-shell camera cases, they were made of black plastic, not aluminum, and there were no markings on them at all. Each case was secured with two combination locks. The cases weren't heavy enough to contain bullion, but they could have held something priceless, an antiquity of some kind, like a sculpture or jewelry. Maybe even precious gems or prototype microchips. The possibilities were endless.

In their mid-thirties or so, his two guests were of Asian descent. That much was clear. An experienced world traveler, Captain Santino guessed they were from one of the Koreas or maybe eastern China. No way to know.

Late last night, without saying a word, they'd come aboard from a smaller yacht—plastic cases in hand—along with travel bags slung over their shoulders. Maritime courtesy wasn't lost on Captain Santino, so he'd exchanged a pleasantry with the captain of the other vessel. They knew each other from many previous rendezvouses.

After the uneventful transfer, he'd set sail for the Kaunakakai Ferry Terminal on Molokai, where he planned to top off his fuel tanks before continuing on to Cabo San Lucas.

His first officer entered the bridge fifteen minutes early with two cups of coffee. He thanked Javier for bringing the coffee, then told his third in command he could take the rest of his duty shift off.

"All quiet out there, Captain?" Javier asked. "Any contacts?"

"We passed a COSCO heavy about half an hour ago. Its captain said hello on the radio, but other than that, not a soul."

"Just the way we like it."

"Any sign of our passengers?"

"None," Javier said. "As far as I know, they haven't even left their staterooms."

"To each his own. Makes our job easier. They're placing mess orders for room service, then?"

"Yes. It seems they speak just enough Spanish to get by."

Santino had known from the start that this wasn't their usual smuggling run. It had the feel of something much bigger, much more lucrative and dangerous. The guests confirmed his hunch. The captain was accustomed to quiet and subdued passengers, but these guys were downright morbid. Mysterious, like their valuable but small packages—which he really needed to stop thinking about.

Time to change the subject.

"We came through some pretty rough seas last night. Anything to report?"

"There's some minor damage in the Acacia Suite," Javier said. "The TV partially dislodged and scarred the cabinet."

"Let's make sure we get that repaired right away. We don't want the boss to see it on his next walk-through."

"That's for sure."

Aside from their invisible passengers, there was something else odd about this voyage. The complete absence of women. The boss had made it abundantly clear there'd be no hookers on board for this particular mission. The most reasonable conclusion had to be that his boss didn't want anyone but the *Yoonsuh*'s crew to see the two strangers.

As far as the captain was concerned, this ship couldn't reach Cabo soon enough, but then again, he didn't look forward to his next assignment either.

After another stop at Molokai on the way back from Cabo, he'd be sailing into Seoul, and his next guests definitely wanted ladies of the evening on board.

He'd hosted them many times.

South Korean mafia.

Scary, scary men.

CHAPTER 10

When Charlene failed to answer her phone, Vincent had never felt so helpless and frustrated. Worse, he couldn't reach his boys either.

From Denise's, he'd raced home, praying she'd mistakenly left her phone, but all he found was an empty house and two very nervous Irish wolfhounds, their unease fueled by his frantic state. What was Charlene's schedule today? He wasn't sure. They'd had a little squabble this morning and left things a little chilly. Since it was Saturday, he knew his boys had volleyball practice. Was she taking them shopping afterward? Shit, he couldn't remember. In a near panic, he called Nathan and asked him to head over to the school gymnasium. Nathan said he'd do it right away.

He'd been about to start contacting hospitals when he got a call from an SDPD detective telling him Charlene and one of his sons had been shot. *Been shot? Which son?* The news slapped him so hard, he couldn't breathe.

His worst nightmare had come true. Someone had tortured Denise to extract his personal information, then used it to attack his family.

Now, racing toward the hospital, he called Nathan back, then contacted the emergency room's receptionist and said he needed to speak to his wife before they took her into surgery. The receptionist tried to explain hospital procedure with a bunch of boilerplate crap about regulations and policy. Since arguing proved useless, he played the legal card, saying in no uncertain terms if they didn't wait for him to arrive, they'd be facing a criminal lawsuit, or worse. Her indignant response was predictable and justified, but Vincent didn't care. He'd apologize later.

There was nothing more maddening than being in a hurry surrounded by clogged traffic. He'd avoided an accident so far but knew his luck wouldn't last much longer. Speeding toward a busy intersection, he laid on the horn at a Smart car driven by a kid with an oversized pompadour. Adding to his annoyance, the punk had purposely moved over to block the right lane, preventing him from running the red light at Kearny Villa. Vincent hit the horn again and waved for the kid to get out of the way.

When he got the middle-finger salute, that was it. He rammed the Smart car with enough force to give the punk's head a whiplash. When that failed to work, Vincent eased forward until his bumper made contact again. He shifted into low gear, then bulldozed the rolling coffin into the center of the intersection. Even with its brakes locked, it was no match for the Navigator. The roadblock cleared, he backed up but had to wait for several speeding cars to clear the intersection.

Cell phone in hand, the kid scrambled out and sprinted toward the sidewalk.

Since his window was down, Vincent thought, *Why not?* "Hey, snowflake, you ever had an emergency? Next time get the hell out of the way!"

What happened next was glorious. Trying to peck his phone while he ran, the millennial tripped over the curb and went sprawling onto the sidewalk. The guy protected his phone but sacrificed his elbows and chin in the process. *That's going to leave marks.* Feeling a slight twinge of guilt, Vincent gunned it across the intersection.

Because of all the storefronts, fast-food joints, and gas stations lining the street, Vincent thought there was a pretty good chance his little indiscretion had been captured on camera. Screw it. He'd deal with the fallout later. Right now, he needed to talk to his wife before they knocked her out for surgery.

After the most agonizing drive he'd ever made, he pulled in behind several ambulances waiting under the porte cochere. Maybe one of them was Charlene's. Inside the automatic doors of the ER, he rushed up to the counter. The waiting room held several other people, all with concerned and frightened looks.

"My wife's in here. Her name's Charlene Beaumont. I need to talk to her right now."

"You're the man who called."

He recognized the receptionist's voice. "Yes, I'm the man who called."

"As I tried to explain, she can't have any visitors right now. She's being prepped for surgery and—"

He pivoted away from the counter and ran toward the double doors.

"Sir, you can't go in there!"

"Watch me."

"Sir!"

It looked like controlled chaos in the ER, every stall occupied and buzzing with nurses and doctors. He knew these patients were also victims of the mass shooting at the UTC mall, a stark reminder that his wife and son weren't the only casualties. He spotted Charlene right away but didn't see either of his sons. Flanked by two nurses and a big orderly, his wife appeared to be covered in blood-soaked bandages.

One of the nurses tending to Charlene turned toward him just as the receptionist burst into the room. "Sir, I've called security."

"Ya think?" Vincent said. "Security should already be here."

The orderly stepped forward.

He pointed at the man's chest and said, "Don't even think about it, young man. I'll put you down hard. I'm allowed to be in here."

The orderly backed up a step as Vincent approached his wife.

A portable X-ray machine sat in the corner of the stall. Charlene looked deathly pale. He'd seen this before. Blood loss. Dripping at a fast pace, an IV delivered fluid into her forearm, and her head was wrapped with gauze. The worst looked to be her abdomen, where a large dressing soaked with blood wrapped her torso. Both her legs were also bandaged and bleeding. His wife looked like a war casualty. He glanced at the display on the vitals monitor and cringed. Her blood pressure was critically low.

Ignoring all the activity, he focused on his wife. "Charlene, can you hear me?"

Her haunted expression made his stomach tighten. He took her hand and gave it a gentle squeeze. "Charlene, where are the boys?"

"Don't . . . know."

She already looked and sounded sedated.

"Sir," the nurse said, "it would be really helpful to know your wife's blood type."

"A positive." Vincent turned toward the nurse. "Where are my sons?"

"I think it's best if you speak to the doctor."

Across the room, a man in scrubs who looked younger than Doogie Howser talked on a phone. Could that be the doctor? Why wasn't he tending to his wife? If one of his boys was also shot, where was he? Why wasn't his other son in the waiting area? Shit! He needed answers.

Charlene's eyes opened. "Brian . . ."

"What about him? Where's Brian?"

"Got away."

"Where's Anthony?"

Tears fell from her eyes. "I'm so sorry . . . I wasn't . . . fast enough."

"Charlene, tell me what happened."

"Sir, it would be best if you waited—"

He gave the nurse an expression that got through.

"Please keep it brief. The anesthesiologist will be here any second."

He said thank you without taking his eyes from his wife.

"Where's Anthony?" he asked again.

Her face contorted into the most hideous agony imaginable. "I don't know."

How could she not know? "Tell me what happened."

"Two gunmen. I shot . . . them."

"Did they say anything?"

She closed her eyes and pursed her lips.

"Think, Charlene. It's important. Did they say anything?"

She nodded, eyes still closed, fading.

"What? What did they say?"

"They said . . . Mr. Hey-sendsis . . ."

"I'm sorry, Mr. Beaumont, but we need to get her into the OR."

"Just a few more seconds." He touched her arm and leaned down. "Charlene, what does that mean? Who is Hay-sen-sizz?"

Her lips moved, but nothing came out.

"Charlene." He gave her a slight nudge.

"I . . . love you, Vince."

"I love you too."

She closed her eyes.

The ER doctor entered the stall. "I'm sorry, Mr. Beaumont, but we have to go right now." Without waiting for his approval, the doctor nodded to the orderly.

"Vince . . . ," said Charlene.

"I'm here."

"My phone . . ."

"What about it?"

"My purse . . . pictures . . ."

What was she saying? What pictures? "Charlene . . . Charlene!"

He watched in horror as her head lolled to the side. Had she just died? No, the heart monitor was still beeping. *Thank God.*

With the ER doctor and one of the nurses in tow, the orderly pushed the mother of his children out of the ER.

This can't be happening.

He wanted to scream until his throat bled. Who did this? Where were his sons? Someone had tortured his secretary to find his wife and children? Seriously? Why hadn't they targeted him? Why his family? Charlene had no enemies.

His mind felt ripped in half as feral rage boiled to the surface.

He intended to find whoever did this and make them suffer.

And he knew who'd help track them down.

Vincent pulled his phone and called Nathan McBride.

While it rang, he narrowed his eyes at the remaining nurse and put iron in his voice. "Where is my son?"

CHAPTER 11

Jin Marchand liked Washington, DC, especially the downtown area. Over the last three days, she and her sixteen-year-old daughter, Lauren, had worked their way around the National Mall, visiting the various museums and memorials. One thing impressed her more than anything else. The incredible number of capitol police. Washington certainly knew how to take care of its own. Nothing but the best security for the lawmakers.

They'd spent most of their vacation in public, something Jin didn't much like. If she didn't wear contacts, people stared at her unusual genetic trait: heterochromia. Her left eye was blue, like the color of deep arctic ice—the same as her father. The other? Dark brown, nearly black. When it came to her eyes, her genetic fusion had been evenly split. The rest of her, not as much. She had fairly dark skin and black hair with a smattering of gray strands here and there.

Being half-Irish and half-Korean, it was a small wonder she hadn't drunk herself to death. Not a fair thought, she knew. The Irish and Koreans didn't own the franchise on self-medicating destruction.

Lauren? Well, she looked stunningly beautiful. No other description fit. Three-quarters white, one-quarter Korean, she got an amazing mix from both genetic sources. Deep-blue eyes. Jet-black hair. Flawless pale skin. Jin's half brother, Nathan, had once likened Lauren to a mysterious science-fiction heroine, and Jin had a hard time disagreeing.

Her ex-husband, Lauren's father, was a tall, handsome, and blue-eyed Frenchman serving a ten-year sentence in a minimum-security prison for insider trading, money laundering, and tax evasion. The cartel criminals he'd aligned himself with had nearly cost Lauren's life. Had it not been for Nathan's heroic intervention, Lauren would've been captured, tortured, and eventually killed by a psychopath. Jin owed her half brother for that one, something he never mentioned.

People often mistook Lauren for her granddaughter, and while it used to bother her, it didn't so much anymore. She'd been in her mid-forties for Lauren's conception, a surprise pregnancy just before leaving Paris to begin a secret new life in America with her future jailbird husband. *You sure know how to pick them, Jin.*

Looking around, she couldn't help but notice how clean and litter free downtown DC was. She supposed tourism and trash didn't mix well.

"Can we move here?" Lauren asked. "I really like it. The Metro's cool."

Jin answered noncommittally. "It's a nice system."

"I really liked the natural history museum. There's so much left to see. Can we stay longer?"

"I wish we could, but we'd have to change our airline reservations."

"I'll bet Grandpa could do it. He's in a position of political power and influence."

Jin nearly laughed. To be young again, when life was simple—except she'd never had Lauren's life. She'd grown up in poverty. Hungry. Cold. And at times homeless. Existence for the unprivileged in DPRK was a mire of constant stress and suffering. Making things worse, she'd been arrested for stealing food when she was Lauren's age and sent to a prison labor camp for "reeducation." At age twenty, her life improved when a kind man—who'd held an office of power in the government— offered her a fresh start as a covert operations officer. He'd discovered her during a tour of the prison. He'd liked her eyes and looked past the bigotry that so many of his comrades couldn't.

She went on to become a highly skilled and deadly covert operations officer in North Korea's Ministry of State Security. In the MSS, she'd conducted all kinds of assassinations and spy missions. Over the years, she'd tried to convince herself she wasn't that person anymore, not altogether successfully. And there was still a price on her head—dead or alive.

"Lauren, I want you to put your cell phone on silent and keep it in your pocket during lunch. You can take it out for some photos, but nothing else."

"Okay."

Their lunch date was at Mabel's Diner—just down the street from the Willard, where she and Lauren shared a luxurious room, thanks to her brother's generosity. She'd heard a rumor about the term *lobbyists* being credited to the Willard, but when she researched it online, it turned out to be one of DC's many myths. The label of *lobbyist* had been around long before President Grant used it to describe the power-hungry vultures lurking in the lobby.

Walking in, she gave the dining room a quick scan before spotting her father seated at a table by himself. He waved and got up as she approached.

"Grandpa!" Lauren rushed forward and wrapped him in a bear hug.

"How's my angel doing? I hope you're not making your mother prematurely gray."

"I'm not."

"Jin, you look positively stunning."

"Thank you, Senator."

"Can't you call me Stone?" He smiled. "Since you won't call me Dad, at least use my first name."

"That just seems really awkward to me. How is your hip? I don't see a cane."

"I stopped using it three weeks ago." He lowered his voice. "It makes me look so old."

"How is Martha?" she asked.

"The woman's immortal. I swear she doesn't feel pain like the rest of us."

Have her try on a prison labor camp for size, thought Jin uncharitably. Four years on the verge of starvation had prematurely aged her. Not to mention, clearly twisted her psyche. The man sitting across from her had fought in her birth country long before it became the North Korea everyone knew today. She'd read Stone's bio on Wikipedia. Korean War hero. Small town mayor. State senator. Congressman. US senator. He'd spent his postwar life climbing the political ladder. No wonder Nathan rarely mentioned his childhood. She and Nathan had talked about it a few times, and from what she could gather, Nathan felt a certain amount of resentment toward his father's career choice.

She motioned with her eyes to the corner table near the window. "Who's the muscle with the subcompact?"

"You don't miss much. Secret Service. He's got the most boring job in town."

A server approached their table. Tall and lanky, she looked to be in her mid-sixties.

"Good morning, Senator McBride."

"Mabel, it's nice to see you again."

The people at the next table looked over at the sound of Stone's name.

"This is my daughter, Jin, and my granddaughter, Lauren."

Mabel couldn't hide her surprise. "I never knew you had a daughter."

"Until recently, neither did I. It's a long story. Her mother and I were going to be married. We lost track of each other during the Korean War and never saw each other again."

Jin watched her father's expression closely. The pain on his face couldn't be faked. For Lauren's sake, she hoped Mabel wouldn't pursue the subject further, a tragic chapter in her family's history. Her mother had loved this man, and he'd loved her. Because of her pregnancy by an American, Jin's mother had been subjected to the worst kind of ridicule and bigotry imaginable. Having an "impure" child was akin to birthing a monster from an alien planet. People accused America of racism? What a joke. North Korea's xenophobia made America's problems look paltry in comparison.

Mabel must've sensed the unease gripping their table and didn't inquire further. "Coffee, Jin?"

"Yes, please. With cream and sugar."

"Senator?"

"Earl Grey, please. With milk and sugar."

"You got it."

"You know something?" Stone asked. "I just realized I've never asked you how long you've owned this diner."

"Six presidents. And I'd always hoped you'd be one of them."

Stone offered a politician's smile, then winked at Lauren. "This town chews people up and spits them out."

"It broke a few teeth on you." Mabel looked at Lauren. "What would you like to drink, young lady?"

"A triple latte, please."

Mabel raised a brow and headed for the coffeepots behind the counter.

"That's quite a caffeine buzz you'll be working on," Stone said, taking a drink of water.

"Since I no longer get kid benefits, I might as well cash in on early adulthood."

Stone nearly choked.

"What exactly does *that* mean?" Jin asked.

"You know, the maturation thing. I'm getting in touch with my metropolitan side."

"Your metropolitan side?" Jin asked.

Lauren gave a sweet smile to her grandfather. "I feel very comfortable in DC. I could definitely live here."

"Well, aren't you full of surprises," Stone said.

Jin wouldn't spoil the lighthearted moment. Despite the offhand remark, it couldn't be denied. Her daughter was maturing into a beautiful . . . person. She had a hard time thinking of Lauren as a woman, perhaps because Jin had been forced to "grow up" at an early age, much younger than Lauren was now. Thanks to Nathan, the mother-daughter lines of communication were open. For a while, it had been touch and go. Nathan played a major role in Lauren's life, often filling in for her incarcerated father. He possessed an intuitive and empathic personality and knew how to connect with Lauren on an emotional level. They weren't afraid to share their lives, to be open and honest with one another. She cherished Lauren's respect and admiration of Nathan.

Jin owned too much baggage to be an ideal parent, but love went a long way. And she did love her daughter. Immensely. Despite having trouble showing affection, she did her best to make Lauren feel safe and appreciated.

Without a doubt, Lauren had already lived well beyond her years. At age twelve, what she'd done in that abandoned desert building to help Nathan defeat Hans Voda fell nothing short of miraculous. How many kids would've kept their cool in that situation? One in a thousand? A million? Adding to her arsenal, Lauren knew how to turn on the charm. She'd ensnared her grandfather the first time they'd met, forming an instant bond.

When Mabel returned, Jin found herself smiling at the owner's exchanges with Stone, and she couldn't help but notice the familiar tone of their conversation. It became clear Mabel had known Stone for a long time.

And from the look of things, her father wasn't alone in that regard. Every square meter of wall space was covered with autographed pictures of Mabel smiling arm in arm with what Jin guessed were politicians. She recognized three presidents and a few other retired legislators who'd found second careers in cable news.

Jin started scanning the photographs.

"Above your head to the left," Mabel said, answering Jin's unspoken question.

She and Lauren turned and spotted it right away.

"Seems like yesterday," Stone said. "Hard to believe that was taken thirty years ago."

Lauren asked Mabel if they were all politicians.

"Not all, but mostly. All three branches of government are represented."

"The judicial, legislative, and executive."

"I'm impressed, Lauren. Maybe you'll be on my wall someday."

Jin watched her daughter glow from the compliment. Fun to see. Lauren needed more experiences like this.

Jin waited for Mabel to leave, then lowered her voice. "Who's the other guy under the restroom sign? Private security?"

Stone's gaze brushed past her. "There's no one else."

Using the glass reflection from a large portrait, Jin watched a Middle-Eastern-looking man slide his right hand from his coffee cup to the inside of his coat.

He doesn't know I'm watching him.

"Lauren, don't turn your head," she said. "Just hold still."

It's been said things happen in the blink of an eye; in reality it happens much more slowly. Jin saw the unmistakable shape of a pistol-gripped AK-47 emerging.

She shoved her daughter in the chest, knocking her backward to the floor along with her chair.

"Mom!"

"Stay down!"

Stone's expression changed to disbelief just before his mouth opened to say something.

In a continuous motion, Jin grabbed her silverware and hurled it at the gunman. Flipping end over end, the chromium-iron alloys flew toward the threat.

The man's weapon came up at the same time the knife and fork reached their halfway point.

Jin's aim with the silverware was good, but not good enough. The utensils struck the man in the chest, not the face, but it saved lives.

The man flinched as he pulled the trigger, sending the salvo into the ceiling. The roar was beyond deafening, becoming its own weapon and drowning out Lauren's scream.

Jin upended their dining table, flipping it on its side to give Lauren and Stone some cover.

The gunman recovered and took aim again. More thunder slammed the room.

Jin saw the Secret Service agent start to rise from his corner table, then shudder from the impacts. He'd managed to pull his weapon free but not in time. In moving to save Stone, he'd made himself a target.

She caught motion in the hallway leading to the bathroom.

Two dark forms materialized, both holding the same kind of compact AKs. She thought she saw a third silhouette in the hall but wasn't sure.

Despite taking multiple wounds in the chest, the Secret Service agent returned fire before sliding from his chair to the ground. His three-round burst missed, but it made the killer flinch, buying Jin the precious seconds she needed.

She grabbed a captain's chair with both hands and hurled it toward the hallway behind the first gunman. With a little luck, the move should distract the new threats.

Less than a second later, the chair smacked the wall and broke apart. She'd thrown it with adrenaline-charged strength.

The gunman under the restroom sign crouched as shattered photograph frames and chunks of glass rained down around him.

Using his body as a shield, her father dived to the floor and wrapped Lauren up, but there wasn't time to admire his heroics. Jin needed a weapon. Fast.

If she could get the Secret Service agent's MP5 before the first gunman opened fire again, she'd have a fighting chance.

It didn't happen.

The underside of the table shielding Stone and Lauren exploded into splinters as multiple bullets sliced through its wooden surface.

And in that instant, she knew the shooter had purposely targeted Stone.

Lauren's screaming changed from fear to pain.

Her father yelled, "Get the MP5!"

More thunder pounded the diner, overpowering the collective screaming of people being slaughtered. The carnage intensified when the other two gunmen opened fire. Three fully automatic Kalashnikovs sounded like something out of hell.

Flesh tore.

Bones shattered.

Blood flew like wind-driven rain.

Fighting instinct, she ignored her daughter's shrieks of terror and leaped toward the dying federal agent.

CHAPTER 12

"Lauren, don't turn your head. Just hold still."

Stone McBride frowned. *What the hell's she talking about?*

The next thing he knew, his daughter shoved Lauren to the floor, grabbed her silverware, and threw it toward the rear wall of the diner. He couldn't believe how fast she'd moved.

Arms pinwheeling, Lauren went sprawling. Jin then overturned their table to hide Lauren from a man pulling a gun.

Pulling a gun? It was a compact AK-47, its distinctive shape unmistakable.

Jin yelled to stay down as an ear-splitting growl compressed the air, a sound he knew well from his time with the Marines.

He looked left and watched in horror as the Secret Service agent tasked with guarding him—a man he considered a friend—ignored two bullet wounds to the center of his chest and leveled his MP5 at the threats. Firing his weapon, the agent slumped, then slid out of his chair as more bullets tore through his midsection. Sadly, he'd seen this before—a severed spinal cord—all the man's motor function below the waist quit.

Stone might be pushing his mid-nineties, but that didn't make him useless. Ignoring the agony of slamming his knees on the hardwood floor, he thrust himself forward and wrapped Lauren up against his stomach, shielding her from the gunfire.

The table shuddered from impacts at the same instant he felt multiple punches to his lower back and legs. Not punches. *Bullets.*

Lauren screamed an ear-piercing, inhuman sound of pain and terror. She tried to fight her way out of his arms, but he kept a solid grip.

Someone was firing a fully automatic Kalashnikov into this room full of people.

He tried to deny it, but the truth slammed home.

Some of the bullets had passed through his flesh and found Lauren.

He hoped his body took most of the energy. If not, Lauren could be in a bad way. Until the shooting stopped, he wouldn't be able to help her. He'd been shot in Korea, but he remembered it had hurt a whole lot worse than this.

Another burst of fire blasted the room.

He told Lauren to stop struggling and play dead, then yelled, "Get the MP5!"

Stone wanted to claw his way over to get the weapon, but that meant leaving Lauren exposed, something he wouldn't do.

He didn't have to.

Jin launched herself toward the Secret Service agent like a base runner sliding headfirst into home plate.

The overturned table prevented Stone from seeing the source of all the gunfire, but he *could* see people being shot where they sat. Their faces, chests, and arms exploded as if charges had been placed under their skin. He knew there had to be at least two gunmen, possibly three.

Rage. It hit him like a Metro bus. He wanted to tear the gunmen apart with his bare hands, chew open their throats with his teeth. These savages were trying to kill him with no regard for Lauren or anyone else in the restaurant. Life meant nothing to them.

He saw a flash of Mabel's pink outfit as she bolted for the kitchen's opening. He hoped she'd make it to safety but knew she didn't have any guns back there.

Lauren cried out again and screamed for her mom.

"Don't move!" he yelled over the gunfire. "Play dead!"

"Grandpa, I think I'm bleeding!"

"Play dead, Lauren. Don't move."

After a brief moment of silence, more automatic fire erupted.

He watched in horror as people on the ground were systematically targeted and shot again. Drawing all the strength he had, he pulled her closer.

"Keep breathing, Lauren. Hold still and play dead. Your mom's fighting back."

Hurry, Jin. Hurry!

***

Both of Jin's elbows flared with pain when she landed.

Everything hinged on coming to a stop at the right place. If she fell short, she'd die. And likely, Lauren along with her.

Sliding headfirst across the floor, she extended her hands toward the MP5.

And ended up eye to eye with the Secret Service agent. His grimace of pain told all.

"I'm Stone's daughter."

"Kill the . . . bastards."

"Count on it."

A woman holding her abdomen with both hands ran directly toward her.

Where's she going? The door's the other direction.

The woman tripped over something, went sprawling, and cracked her chin on the floor. Her lips moved, but only blood emerged.

After a brief pause for the gunmen to reload, the nightmare began again, but the resulting bedlam actually worked in her favor.

Because of all the overturned tables and chairs, she couldn't see the rear wall of the diner, which meant the gunmen couldn't see her. She stole a quick look over the top of the slain woman and saw something from the lowest depths of hell. The gunmen were advancing, sending short bursts into the torsos of wounded people attempting to crawl away.

Her hands closed around the MP5 just as a man in a business suit tumbled toward her, his white shirt dyed with blood.

Scenes from her life didn't flash before her eyes.

She didn't reflect on regrets.

And she certainly didn't waver.

Jin Marchand flipped a mental switch and became an efficient killing machine.

A glance at the MP5's firing switch confirmed it was set to three-round-burst mode. Jin was no stranger to this weapon and knew how to maximize its deadly design. Knowing it wouldn't climb much, she came up on one knee, aimed center mass at the closest gunman, and pulled the trigger.

The discharge slammed her ears, but the trio of slugs found the man's chest.

She had the satisfaction of seeing him transformed from a deadly adversary into a rag doll.

She hammered the other gunman before he could react and line up on her.

For good measure, she sent another burst into each of them as they crumpled to the floor.

The last gunman—whom she'd first seen lurking under the restroom sign—kicked his table over and ducked behind its square form. She fired at its surface and watched three holes appear in a diagonal line.

Again, she detected motion in the hall and sent a burst in that direction. She felt confident anyone who wasn't part of this attack wouldn't be moving around back there. They'd be on the ground cowering, hiding in the restroom, out the back door, or dead.

Spooked from the shots blasting through the overturned table, the third gunman dived to his right and used his fallen comrades for cover. Jin kept pounding the downed murderers in an attempt to keep the shooter pinned. Problem was, she'd be out of ammo soon. She'd already blown through half the magazine.

Something brushed past her foot, and she looked down to see a fresh mag being pushed toward her. Because it might be the last thing he ever did, she wanted to thank the Secret Service agent, but there wasn't time. Pulling the trigger as fast as she could, she emptied the mag, purposely sending a few bursts high to make broken picture frame glass and wood splinters rain on the third gunman. With a little luck, he might get shards in his eyes.

She ejected the empty mag, slammed the new one home, and cycled the bolt.

What she saw next looked like something out of a horror movie. The floor of the diner writhed like a bed of worms, bloody people in the process of dying or trying to crawl away.

Keep fighting, Jin. This isn't over.

She didn't have a clear shot at the third gunman, who still hid behind his dead comrades.

"Mom!"

"Don't move, Lauren. Stay down!"

She rolled to the right for a clear line of sight to her daughter.

Huddled behind the overturned table, Stone still had her protectively clutched in his arms. Her father's wounds looked serious, but she didn't have time to help him right now.

"I've got her," he said. "Go!"

Go? He couldn't be saying she should leave. No, he meant, *Go*, as in, *Get going and kill these murderous animals.*

Suddenly, the last gunman raised his weapon over his fallen friends and sprayed the room again. Fortunately, all his rounds went high. More glass fell in sheets along the diner's storefront.

Time to end this insanity.

When the salvo ended, she jumped to her feet, sent two bursts into the human sandbags, and charged the gunman's position.

Jin knew another barrage was seconds away. From what she'd witnessed, these guys were fast at reloading their weapons.

To keep the gunman down, she fired twice more, drubbing the dead bodies.

In three more strides, she'd have a line of fire.

Either the gunman would be dead in the next two seconds, or she would.

She took in her opponent's shocked expression at seeing a woman charging forward with a machine pistol. She'd counted on the guy not believing anyone would do such a reckless thing. Terrorists never expected anyone to fight back. Most people either froze or fled.

Not Jin Marchand.

Welcome to my world.

In his awkward prone position, the killer must've realized he'd never bring his weapon to bear in time. He clenched his teeth and snarled in pure hatred.

The clunk sound of a door from the end of the hallway changed her strategy. Crap, she wanted this guy alive—how else could she learn who'd sent the assassins?—but someone new had just entered this fight . . . or left it. From her current position, she couldn't see straight down the hall.

No time to debate it.

She pointed the MP5 at the man's face and pulled the trigger.

Three slugs cleaved through the bridge of his nose and exploded out the back of his head. As if shocked by electricity, the guy's body went stiff, but his furious expression stayed. She hoped he'd carry it through eternity in the underworld.

After a final glance around the blood-spattered diner, she ran for the hallway.

***

Stone felt something smash the back of his head hard enough to shatter teeth. *Something? Don't you mean a bullet?* The fact that he could ask the questions meant his brain hadn't been scrambled. He located the broken pieces of teeth with his tongue and spit them out. Fighting the onslaught of unconsciousness, he kept a firm grip on Lauren as a white haze coated his mind.

No matter what, he had to keep her from getting up. If she tried to run, she'd be murdered.

More gunfire rang out, but it sounded different. Three-round bursts. The reports were so fast, they almost sounded like single shots.

Jin.

She'd grabbed Jason's MP5 and was shooting back.

All of a sudden, the diner fell eerily silent.

"Don't move, Lauren. Play dead."

"Grandpa, am I going to die?" she whispered.

"No, you're not going to die. You're going to have . . . beautiful children someday."

"My side and arm really hurt."

"Shh. Keep breathing and don't move. Help will be here soon."

"I'm really scared."

"I love you, Lauren. I wish . . . I could've been . . . a bigger part of your life. Tell your mom . . . I love her."

"Grandpa?"

"Nathan . . . tell him I've always been . . . proud of him." Awareness began to fade, and with it, his life. He hoped Lauren would never forget what he said next. "Your mom loves you . . . It's . . . it's just hard for her to—"

"Grandpa!"

He tried to fight the feeling of slipping away but knew he'd lost the battle.

Stone McBride had no complaints. He'd lived a full and rich life, seen and done wondrous things.

Not a bad way to go. Hugging my granddaughter . . .
Not a bad way at all.

***

Jin crouched at the opening of the hall leading to the rear exit and peered around the corner.

An empty corridor greeted her.

She rushed down the hall and was about to burst into the men's room to clear it when she saw two important things. Droplets of blood on the floor and duct tape covering the door's latch bolt. Someone— likely one of the gunmen—wanted to ensure the door remained unlocked. Right now, the door could be pulled open from the outside without any noise or resistance.

"Not good," she whispered. The killer—or killers—outside could reenter at any second.

The blood meant she might've winged one of them when she'd fired blindly into the hallway. Jin liked her odds better when facing a wounded man.

Decision time. Should she take a look? If anyone guarded the door, they'd see it move, and she might find herself on the business end of an AK again.

Right now, her daughter needed a tourniquet applied to her arm. The amount of blood she'd seen meant a clipped or severed artery. She also didn't like Stone's chances at surviving the next few minutes. His shirt had been completely soaked.

The heavy dead bolt above the door's emergency exit bar sealed her decision. She slid it to the locked position, being careful to avoid making noise. If anyone tried to muscle through this door, she'd hear it.

On her way back to the dining room, she quickly cleared both bathrooms, then raced back to the table sheltering Lauren and her father—who wasn't breathing. Gone, she knew.

Oh, dear Lord. Too much blood.

Using her good arm, Lauren clutched the left side of her rib cage. "Mom, I think I got shot."

She put on her best strong-mom face. "I see it, and you're going to be okay." She lifted Lauren's shirt and saw an entry and exit wound about fifteen centimeters apart. The bullet had grazed her rib cage but hadn't hit any vital organs. A serious wound for sure, but not life-threatening.

Of more concern, two angry-looking holes marred both sides of Lauren's bicep where blood flowed freely.

"Can you help Grandpa?"

"I'm sorry, baby. He's gone." She'd been tempted to lie, but Lauren deserved the respect of hearing the truth.

"Grandpa's dead?"

"Yes."

Lauren's face contorted.

"I'm going to tie your arm to stop the bleeding." Aware of passing time, Jin worked at maximum speed. She grabbed a cloth napkin and rolled it into a rope shape. After tying it as tightly as she could above the wound, she picked up a spoon from the floor, forced it under the napkin, and gave it a full turn to tighten the tourniquet.

"Hold this spoon in place and don't let go, okay?"

"Mom, that hurts . . ."

"Don't take it off no matter how much it hurts, okay? This is *important*. Don't let go until help arrives."

"I won't." Lauren's eyes swept past her to an approaching figure.

Jin grabbed the MP5 from the floor and whipped around. "Mabel! I nearly shot you!"

"I called 911."

"Hold this spoon," Jin said.

Mabel crouched down. "I couldn't believe how fast you were."

"You saw it?"

"Everything."

"I was motivated." She reached across Lauren and plucked a pen from a dead man's breast pocket. Next, she glanced at her watch, then wrote the current time on Lauren's skin above the tourniquet: 1:37.

There was so much blood in here . . . Making things worse, there were many wounded who needed immediate medical care. Jin wanted to feel more emotion but wouldn't allow it. She'd learned long ago to suppress her feelings, as it meant the difference between survival and death. Her stint in the prison labor camp hadn't been solely for manual labor. Multiple guards, often all at once, did whatever they wanted, whenever they wanted. She'd disconnected her soul during the worst of it, as she had to do right now.

The choice she faced felt agonizing: remain here with Lauren and the others and tend to their wounds, or try to catch the remaining shooter and find out who planned and ordered this murderous savagery.

Jin had learned one thing from her years in the DPRK: when threatened, you don't run; instead, you neutralize the threat. Given what had just happened, she saw little choice but to chase down the remaining shooter.

She looked to Mabel, then inclined her head toward her daughter. The diner's owner offered a single grim-faced nod of silent understanding. Mabel would watch over Lauren until the first responders arrived.

Jin hated her decision, what she had to do. Hated it more than anything in the world.

With a bloody hand, she touched Lauren's cheek. "An ambulance is only a minute or two away."

"Mom?"

She looked at Mabel again. "I need you to keep holding this spoon and put pressure on her rib cage." Jin folded a napkin into a square and pressed it over Lauren's wound.

"I will," said Mabel.

"Lauren, I have to find out who attacked us, or we'll never be safe again."

What her daughter said made her openly weep.

"It's okay, Mom. I understand why you have to go. Grandpa said you love me."

"I do love you, more than anything."

"I love you too, Mom."

"What's beyond the back door?"

"An alley," said Mabel.

Damn it. She had to go.

Now.

CHAPTER 13

Wiping away tears, Jin searched the Secret Service agent for additional ammo and found two more magazines. She stuffed them into her rear jeans pocket.

"You died a hero," she said softly.

She had one more thing to do before leaving.

Photos.

She wiped Lauren's blood—*Lauren's blood!*—on her pants. *Stop it. Stay focused.*

A quick frisk of the three gunmen revealed no wallets. No surprises there.

She pulled her phone, grabbed a handful of hair, and twisted the first killer's head so she could snap a photo of his face. The lighting wasn't ideal, but her iPhone worked well. She did the same thing with the other gunmen. They all looked Middle Eastern, with something else mixed in. Caucasian? Had the gunmen been Korean, they would've been tasked with killing her, not her father. For now, this looked like an assassination attempt against Stone, not a random terror attack. Her father had long been a leader in the battle against terrorism, both at home and abroad. No doubt he had countless enemies who wanted him dead.

She forced the image of her bloodstained hands into a mental locker. There was no margin for distraction right now, especially with not knowing what waited on the other side of the rear door. It could be an empty alley or full of men with Kalashnikovs ready to mow her down.

Only one way to find out.

She hurried down the corridor, left the dead bolt engaged, and pressed an ear against the door.

She heard nothing but the muffled wail of a police or fire siren—a reminder she was out of time.

The door appeared to be metal clad, but she doubted it would stop 7.62-millimeter rounds.

On the way to unlock the dead bolt, her hand froze.

Someone just tried to come through.

The dead bolt made a barely audible sound when the door shuddered.

She flattened herself against the wall and waited. Predictably, the person on the other side tried again and got the same result.

What happened next made her skin tighten.

Someone knocked. Three times.

Rap, rap, rap.

Who would knock on a door leading into a place where a mass slaughter had occurred? Add to that, there had to be fresh blood drops on the ground outside.

She considered shooting through the door, but her nine-millimeter rounds might not penetrate, and she didn't know with 100 percent certainty who was out there.

She backed away, leveled the MP5, and waited for the door to be forced open.

Nothing happened.

She felt like an idiot when she remembered the door opened toward the outside. It couldn't be kicked in without heavy breaching equipment.

Shit! She'd just wasted five seconds, close to ten now, and missed an opportunity to take whoever was out there by surprise.

Brilliant, Jin, just brilliant.

The opportunity gone, she slid the dead bolt back, crouched, and cracked the door a few centimeters. Because it swung to the right, she couldn't see more than a small sliver of the alley. What she wouldn't give for one of those little dentist's mirrors right now. From what she could determine, the alley wasn't wide. It might allow two small cars to pass side by side. Just left of the door, piles of bagged trash, big metal recycle bins, and flattened cardboard were stacked against the diner's wall. She had no idea what lay to her right.

There wasn't time to debate her next move. She needed to be unpredictable and aggressive.

Because the door had a self-closing piston, she reared back and kicked it with a prolonged force, like doing a quick leg press at a gym.

As predicted, the door flew outward, but it didn't swing completely freely.

It didn't matter.

The sound it made was glorious: the thud of kinetic energy being transferred to someone's head.

An AK skittered across the oil-stained concrete.

Its wielder fell to his knees, clutching a bleeding nose. She saw the source of the blood drops in the hallway. One of her bullets had passed through the man's hand.

Off to her right, an engine started.

She pivoted through the door and caught sight of a white minivan. No more than twenty meters away, it lurked on the opposite side of the alley. No other cars or trucks were in sight.

She thumbed the MP5's firing switch to its semiautomatic position and sent single rounds through both of the bludgeoned man's rotator cuffs, purposely missing the arteries. The blunt force trauma of being hammered by a metal door coupled with the fresh damage to his shoulders proved too much. He curled into a fetal position, moaning in agony.

Jin was sorely tempted to shoot out his knees as well, but she had to deal with the minivan first. She didn't think it a coincidence its engine had fired up the same instant she appeared in the alley.

Clasping the same kind of compact AK, the driver's left hand extended through the window. Fortunately, a Kalashnikov can't be easily controlled with one hand. Only the first few shots would be on target because an AK's recoil causes it to climb when fired.

Needing cover, she ducked back into the hallway as the Russian weapon roared. Multiple rounds blasted through the opening before the piston could close the door.

Whoever controlled that AK had to be strong. He'd managed to score four hits inside the hallway, all at chest level.

She stayed in a crouch, waiting for the next pause in gunfire to make her move.

Another burst rang out after the door had closed. Supersonic slugs sliced through the metal veneer, punching more holes in the drywall.

To anyone in the surrounding area, the rattle of fully automatic gunfire had to sound like an active war zone. And for Jin, that's exactly what this was.

She had little doubt it could be heard all the way to the steps of the Capitol. At this location, the law enforcement response would be fast and immense. Rifle fire in downtown Washington, DC, would draw every available police officer—and personnel from other agencies as well.

How long should she wait? If the driver pulled alongside the door and fired again, the bullets would come straight down the hallway. Without ducking into the men's room, she'd have no cover. Going out there now might be akin to suicide, but she couldn't allow the two surviving gunmen to escape. One way or the other, this needed to end.

She pushed the door open with her left hand and rolled out, coming up on one knee.

Moving faster than she thought possible, the minivan's driver shoved his AK out the window again. She'd never be able to line up on him in time.

This could be it.

She dived to her left and landed on a pile of bagged trash as the gunman opened fire. He obviously knew his stuff, firing in short controlled bursts. Shoot. Recover. Shoot. Recover.

If he'd been able to fire with both hands, she'd likely be dead.

Her luck ran out when something punched her leg just below the knee.

You just took one, Jin. And with your elevated heart rate, it's going to leak. A lot.

No time to dwell on it. She needed deeper cover.

She scrambled over the top of the trash bags and burrowed into a low spot next to a rolling trash container. Above her head, dozens more 7.62-millimeter bullets punched through the container's metal surface. She heard breaking glass and something else being destroyed inside the bin, but thankfully, the slugs didn't ricochet down to her position. She'd once heard her father refer to American cities as "garbage factories," and she was now glad they were. Saving her from certain death, the pile of bagged trash outside the container acted like the protective mound of a foxhole, but not all of the trash would be solid enough to stop high-powered rifle rounds. Only a matter of time before a bullet found its way through.

Pain.

It arrived in her calf like an electric shock. Crap, just what she needed. Another distraction. She was no stranger to bullet wounds. Her skin bore the scars from many over the years.

Forget it. Stay focused. Lauren's life is still at risk.

Right now, she was the only force keeping the murderers from returning to the diner to either retrieve their dead, finish off any survivors, or both. Someone had obviously wanted to enter the restaurant, or they wouldn't have knocked on the door.

In sporadic bursts, the gunman kept firing, and it was really starting to piss her off.

She covered her eyes as chunks of brick and mortar blew out from the wall above the mound of garbage. Some of the shrapnel stung her arms and torso. *More leaking to come.* Until the salvo ended, she'd have to endure the mind-numbing assault—which seemed to be lasting way too long.

Screw this.

Jin came up and aimed at the minivan.

The attacker's AK spit white fire again, but the salvo went high.

The shooter must've just run out of ammo because he pulled the AK back inside the window.

This would be so much easier if she didn't need this loser alive. She could easily drill him in the head from here, right through the windshield.

She saw the man freeze in indecision, probably wondering why she hadn't fired.

He must've realized he'd never get his weapon reloaded in time because she saw him toss it to his right and slump down, making himself a smaller target.

The man on the ground continued to writhe in agony.

For extra firepower, she thumbed her MP5's switch to the three-round-burst position.

The driver of the minivan didn't do anything for several seconds. For an instant, she thought he might actually surrender, then dismissed the thought as ridiculous.

His next move would be one of two things: race forward and try to plow her, or throw it in reverse and try to escape.

Why not make the decision for him?

Jin had done tens of thousands of push-ups in her life and was about to find out if all that upper-body strength training would pay off.

She tucked the gun into her waist, forced herself into the tight gap between the trash container and the wall, and shoved its two-meter-long form forward.

Not knowing how much the thing weighed, or if it would even move, she gave it everything she had.

Success!

It rumbled forward. Too easily.

The container impacted the building on the opposite side of the alley and bounced back a meter or so.

Good news and bad news. She had the result she'd wanted—the container now blocked the driver's path forward, but it left her completely exposed. She hadn't expected it to move so freely.

Time to be aggressive again.

She hobbled directly toward the minivan, purposely firing high as she advanced.

The driver looked over his right shoulder, threw it into reverse, and gunned it down the alley. When he swerved back and forth to make himself a more difficult target, the minivan began fishtailing.

Things got more complicated when a delivery truck entered the alley and blocked the gunman's escape.

Even though her right calf stung like all hell, she managed to maintain a pretty good pace. From the look of things, she wouldn't have to run much farther.

The minivan continued to fishtail in bigger and bigger arcs, until the driver lost all control.

Its right front fender smacked the brick wall of the building on her left.

Metal crunched, glass broke, and plastic shattered.

Simultaneously, she heard the loud bang of the minivan's airbag detonation. Perfect.

Temporarily stunned, the driver would need a few seconds to recover. Still in reverse, the minivan slowly crept across the alley at a sharp angle and stopped when its rear bumper found the wall.

The delivery truck froze about twenty meters inside the alley, its driver understandably shocked by what he saw: a wounded and bloody Asian woman armed with a machine pistol pursuing a reversing and out-of-control white minivan. Not something you see every day.

She formed a new plan, but it would have to be executed to perfection.

In six more strides, she'd be at the minivan.

Her idea went south when the truck began backing out of the alley in a big hurry; its reverse beep was nearly drowned out by its diesel engine noise. She hadn't expected the driver to react so decisively or quickly.

There was no way she'd have time to disable the minivan's driver and make it to the truck in time to kick the driver out and commandeer his ride.

With the truck out of the equation, she concentrated on the minivan.

Her leg felt weak, and the squishy wetness in her shoe confirmed it bled freely. She'd have to tie it off soon.

Her gun stayed up as she closed on the van, taking a wide berth to her right to create a better angle to shoot the guy if needed.

Stunned from the airbag deployment, the guy looked at her with an expression of uncertainty and fear, a good sign.

He looked Middle Eastern and fairly young—college age or a little older. He wore a pullover shirt with some kind of logo on the chest.

Screw him, Jin thought. He'd gone from predator to prey. He'd be fully realizing that soon enough.

Jin kept her machine pistol pointed at his face and yanked the door open. He held his hands up defensively, as if they could stop bullets. The empty AK sat on the passenger seat next to him.

She said nothing as she drilled him in the left knee.

Oops. She'd forgotten the MP5 was set to its three-round-burst mode.

What a shame.

His knee took three rounds rather than one.

She glanced back to the diner and saw the man she'd bludgeoned with the door. Looking like the victims inside the diner, he writhed in agony. She hoped he wouldn't pass out. Yet.

A quick look in both directions confirmed the alley remained empty. No one had entered, and no one stood at either end watching the action. She couldn't blame them. Automatic gunfire tended to scatter people.

Covering the wound with both hands, the man sitting behind the wheel of the minivan looked extremely unhappy.

Nine-millimeter slugs traveling faster than the speed of sound did a tremendous amount of damage to bone, cartilage, and ligaments. Not fatal unless an artery was severed. Agonizing, yes, but not fatal. This loser had a bona fide date with pain beyond anything he could possibly imagine. And part of her hoped he wouldn't spill his guts too quickly.

To make him manageable, she had to render him semiconscious. She'd never be able to stuff him into the back seat otherwise.

In a calculated blow she'd performed many times, she drove the butt of her MP5 into the guy's forehead. *Clunk.* The result immediate, the man went limp.

She glanced into the cargo area of the van. Its third-row seats were folded down, and five bags sat back there.

Five gunmen. Five bags. She felt confident there weren't any additional threats.

The wailing siren she'd heard earlier had grown in volume.

She yanked the gunman out of the driver's seat, dragged him to the rear sliding door, and pulled the handle. The automatic door moved in painfully slow motion, so she forced it open, not caring if the mechanism broke in the process.

Though small, this guy wasn't light. He probably weighed seventy-five kilograms. Again, Jin was going to find out if all her strength training would pay off.

Ignoring the pain in her calf, she hoisted him up by his collar and belt, got his torso onto the floor of the passenger area, and climbed in to finish the job. It was a whole lot easier pulling him than pushing.

More echoing sirens had joined the fray. The closest one sounded less than a minute away, but she still had another gunman to collect. Out of time, she torqued the sliding door closed and climbed into the driver's seat.

The delivery truck was long gone. Its driver would likely report what he'd seen to a 911 operator right away. With a little luck, the truck driver might get a busy signal. Hundreds of people had to be calling to report automatic gunfire, which meant every arriving cop would be high-strung and suspicious of anyone they encountered.

She couldn't do anything about the minivan's damaged front fender or scraped rear bumper except stay close to cars in front of her once she left the alley.

She drove forward, stopped next to the downed gunman, and climbed out. Grunting in pain, she limped over to the bullet-ridden door.

The loser with the destroyed shoulders hissed at her in Arabic.

She pointed the MP5 at the man's knee, was about to pull the trigger, and then remembered the weapon was still in its three-round-burst mode. *Why not?* she thought. *Screw him.*

The nine-millimeter screamed again, causing another groundswell of thunder to crackle across the city.

She didn't know what was louder—the triple report of the machine pistol or the man's cries of agony.

Not wanting him to bleed out before the cops arrived, she decided to spare his other knee.

After opening the door to Mabel's and ripping the tape from its latch so it would lock, she yelled, "Mabel, tell the police there's a wounded attacker out here. You got that?"

"Got it!"

Her hands. They were quite literally covered in blood. She stepped into the hallway and entered the men's restroom to wash her hands as best she could in three seconds. The blood swirling down the drain should've bothered her more than it did because much of it was her daughter's.

Was her heart that hard?

She avoided looking in the mirror before leaving.

What's the matter, Jin? Afraid of what you'll see?

Before leaving the hallway, she called out, "I love you, Lauren; I always have."

She entered the alley, made sure the door wouldn't open, and pulled away in the minivan. Her thoughts returned to the sobering image of Lauren clutched in the protective grasp of her dead father. She could hardly believe he was gone.

This whole thing felt like one of the many nightmares she regularly endured. But this one had a different ending—she'd been able to fight back. She wasn't bent over a steel table with her wrists and ankles manacled to its legs. There weren't multiple prison guards drooling, laughing, and sneering. The stink of their breath . . . their black, lifeless eyes . . .

Not this time. During this *real* nightmare, she'd been unchained and unafraid. If Lauren had ever doubted her mother's mettle, she wouldn't now. Jin had just proven you didn't have to cower and hide. You could fight back and win. If she didn't survive the next few hours, she hoped Lauren would remember her in a positive way—fearless and capable.

A sudden wave of rage took her. She smacked the steering wheel hard enough to hurt her wrist.

None of this was her fault!

All she'd wanted was a nice quiet lunch with her family.

The man behind her was going to pay for his crimes with open-ended pain.

Jin Marchand was no stranger to interrogation. If this man knew who was behind the attack, he was going to tell her. Common household items worked quite well. In the right hands, a pair of scissors became an awe-inspiring tool of encouragement.

Resisting the urge to speed as she exited the alley, Jin turned right, glad she'd washed most of the blood from her hands. Plenty of cars, taxis, and small trucks filled the road, but because of all the howling sirens, they eased along slowly.

Jin had no idea where the closest police cruiser was. She thought it was behind her. And it might not be the police. It could be a fire engine or an ambulance. Either of those would have to stage at a safe distance until the police arrived and secured the scene, which meant a slight delay tending to Lauren's arm.

The stinging throb in her calf reached a peak. She didn't think an artery had been cut, but she was leaking at a pretty good pace. Her wound made her think again about Lauren and her father.

Stone had given his life to save Lauren.

She now wished she'd called him Dad.

Too late now . . .

Setting the unwelcome feeling aside, she concentrated on driving. She needed to put several miles between herself and Mabel's Diner within the next few minutes or risk ending up trapped inside a roadblock. A glance over her shoulder confirmed her prisoner remained unconscious. Had she clocked him too hard? If so, she might not be able to conduct a proper interrogation. She'd need him fully awake.

Still battling the urge to speed, she turned left at the next intersection and scanned her surroundings with her eyes only. So far, no one walking or driving had focused on her.

Unfortunately, there were literally hundreds of traffic signals all through downtown DC, and she seemed to arrive at every one of them while it was red. Jin wasn't super familiar with DC but made the decision to head west on Constitution. She thought crossing the Potomac and going north on the George Washington Memorial Parkway would be the best way to put the most distance between herself and Mabel's in the shortest amount of time. To avoid the streets immediately adjacent to the White House, she went straight through a couple more intersections before turning south.

At another red light, she reached across and opened the glove compartment.

"Oh yes," she whispered. A beautiful Garmin handheld navigation device stared back at her. The gunman had likely used it to navigate the city, which meant it might contain recallable locations, and probably did.

She heard the gunman moan but didn't detect any movement. To be certain, she took a quick glance over her shoulder. Nothing. He was likely drifting in and out of consciousness.

Echoes of multiple sirens now surrounded her. The forlorn wailing sounded eerie and sad at the same time. As painful as it was to crawl along at fifteen miles an hour, she kept going south, blending with the flow of traffic.

That's when she saw it.

Red and blue flashing lights, heading straight toward her. Pulling over to the curb wasn't possible, so everyone did the next best thing. They stopped. She had to stop too.

She tightened her grip on the wheel as the police cruiser barreled toward her.

She edged forward, pulling in tight behind the taxi to keep the damaged fender screened from the approaching cop's view.

The moment of truth arrived as the cruiser screamed up to her position. Keeping her head slightly dipped, she felt tremendous relief as the vehicle raced harmlessly past.

Traffic started again but crawled at a painfully slow pace. It seemed to take forever, but she finally reached Constitution, turned right, and sandwiched herself between a couple of taxis.

The man in the back seat moaned again, this time louder. When she looked over her shoulder to check on him, he was attempting to crawl up from the floor. She pumped the brake pedal hard enough to jar him and felt a thump against her seat.

His response was a hissed curse of some kind.

When he tried again, Jin obliged him again.

"I can do that hundreds of times if necessary. Your choice." She didn't know if he spoke English, but the tone of her message couldn't be mistaken. He stopped attempting to get up from the floor.

Sooner or later, she'd have to pull over and deal with her bleeding calf, but she was still dangerously close to the action at Mabel's.

"Do you speak English?" When he didn't respond, she tapped the brakes again. "Okay, have it your way." Then she did it again for good measure. The man's knee had to be blindingly sensitive, even to the smallest movement.

"Yes," he grunted. "I speak English."

"Save your strength. You're going to need it."

CHAPTER 14

Seven Days Ago

The striped bark scorpion cringed at being exposed. El Lobo smiled and set the twelve-inch rock down to admire the creature. He couldn't blame it for being startled; he'd feel the same way if the roof of his home suddenly disappeared. What a magnificent creature. He didn't even consider killing it. How many of them lived in the Chihuahuan Desert? Hundreds of thousands? Millions?

As a young boy, he'd kept one as a pet until his father smashed it during one of his countless drunken rampages. A valuable lesson. Don't get close to anything; it might not be around tomorrow. When he turned eleven, he fought back against the verbal abuse, neglect, and beatings that his nine-year-old sister and he had endured since before he could remember. Love and warmth? It never existed in his household. He'd struggled through childhood and learned to disconnect from pain and anguish through hatred. The more he hated, the easier his life became.

Then, early one morning while recovering from a drunken stupor, his papa took a tragic "fall" and sustained a fatal head injury. His family found some measure of peace after that. Dirt-poor but no longer black and blue: a worthwhile trade. With no income and no support, his mom turned to prostitution to make money. At the time, his sister and he didn't know it was a bad thing. Years later, by the time they did, they no longer cared. Was their mom a loving caregiver and provider? No, but she never beat the crap out of them for no reason.

A distracted driver killed his sister on her sixteenth birthday. El Lobo saw the hit-and-run happen. All of it. The idiot was looking at his phone, jumped the sidewalk, and sent his sister cartwheeling through a plate-glass window. She bled out in front of him, pleading for help. He'd never seen so much blood.

Fortunately, he knew who the driver was, knew where he worked, and knew where he lived. The idiot had been one of his mom's best customers over the years. He didn't tell the police he recognized the driver because he had other plans. Later that night, the man took an unfortunate "fall" and sustained a fatal head injury. That's when it had dawned on El Lobo like a revelation: killing wasn't that hard to do.

Over the next twenty years, he worked his way up from a street-gang punk to a cartel gopher and, eventually, a made man. His street smarts combined with desert awareness and knowledge were valuable assets to Mr. A. He took pride in being a coyote and didn't care for the derogatory label. Smuggling drugs, guns, and people became a perfect fit for his personality and skill set, and he'd been doing it successfully for most of his adult life.

El Lobo found himself staring at the scorpion, having lost track of time again. He didn't fear the creature, but its sting produced a nasty and protracted burning sensation. He stepped a few meters away, placed some smaller rocks in a triangular formation, then searched for a suitable flat rock, and set it aside. Using his knife, he nudged the scorpion into his ball cap. It didn't look real happy about being evicted, but it beat the alternative. After setting it free inside the triangle of rocks, he set the flat piece on top.

El Lobo returned to the spot he had been setting up as his sniper's nest, placed the twelve-inch stone and several others at his two o'clock position, and repeated the process at ten o'clock. He now had a clear view to the exact location he wanted along the border fence. The rocks he'd strategically placed created a wedge, also giving him lateral visual cover.

After removing his backpack, he took a swig of water. The last vestiges of morning twilight were nearly over. This small bluff would be scorching in a few hours. Better to stay ahead of the dehydration curve.

His wait shouldn't be long. Through a series of planned incidents, El Lobo had ensured that this fifteen-mile stretch of the fence was under closer surveillance by the US Border Patrol. Not a difficult task: light a few bonfires, throw some carpet over the wire, paint the monuments and markers with threatening anti–Border Patrol slurs. What had been an isolated basin of empty desert was now being patrolled much more frequently. This meant that other areas were now less patrolled. A simple strategy: divert them away from the area where you want to smuggle people and drugs across.

Because he needed to execute a flawless crossing in eight days, he intended to up the stakes this morning, further diffusing the Border Patrol's assets. El Lobo bragged about being the best human smuggler in all of Mexico, and he'd proven it many times. In reality, it wasn't all that demanding, just a pain in the ass. At times he felt like nothing more than a babysitter.

The job had its benefits, though.

He and Quattro jokingly referred to the high-tech smuggling center's warehouse as the whorehouse. After arriving, his "customers" received a hot shower, new clothes, state-of-the-art fake green cards made on the spot, and $200 in authentic American cash. Many of the girls and women were willing to trade sex for an extra $100, one of the many fringe benefits of his business. There was even a picnic area that included a playground for children—although he didn't see that many kids. His air-conditioned fleet of shuttle vans, like the airports used, worked well for transporting his customers from the southern border of Mexico all the way to Mr. A's ranch, which occupied an eleven-kilometer stretch of the international border along the Rio Bravo, the same river the arrogant Americans called the Rio Grande.

Situated in the middle of the property, the ranch house, smuggling center, and training compound were only several kilometers from the border, making it an ideal staging location for Mr. A's smuggling operations.

Rancho Del Seco might be isolated, but a forty-thousand-liter fuel truck served as a mobile gas station. He also had a diesel tanker at his disposal. When it came to the business of smuggling drugs and people, El Lobo's services were highly sought after. Opioids were in such high demand, Mr. A's suppliers couldn't produce them quickly enough. Pain pills had now become his boss's number one commodity, surpassing marijuana, cocaine, meth, and heroin combined. Who could've known? He'd heard reports of high numbers of opioid overdose deaths in America, something like thirty-five thousand last year. How many a day was that? Almost a hundred? Incredible. He didn't feel guilty about it. Why should he? No one made the drooling junkies take the pills; they did it of their own accord. The loss of customers wasn't ideal, but there seemed to be an endless supply of new addicts ready to step up and pay. The street value seemed hard to believe. Again, depending on whom you talked to, the average price of an illegally sold pain pill had surpassed thirty-five US dollars. Mr. A usually bought five hundred thousand of them for seventy-five cents apiece and sold them to his criminal gang and cartel connections for five bucks each.

Most of the illegals El Lobo escorted across the border were from Central America. The price for the stroll across the desert into the land of freedom and opportunity? Fifteen thousand dollars. Each. All in advance. All cash. Mr. A preferred American money but accepted Mexican pesos. He knew it could take years for people to save that much money—not his concern. On an average night, Mr. A made over half a million dollars from a column of illegals. And that didn't even include the drugs. Most of the people he escorted into America, men and women alike, were willing to carry a backpack for a $200 discount. Adding opioids, heroin, or meth to the mix produced anywhere from $400,000 to $600,000 more income. Demand created supply, and for now, the illegal pain pill market showed no signs of tapering off.

Today's diversion promised to be exciting. He loved harassing the jackbooted bullies of the mighty US Border Patrol. He thought it ironic that the very thing he hated the most about America's immigration policy had made him a very wealthy man.

El Lobo enjoyed a sweet deal with Mr. A—20 percent, a generous chunk compared to his competitors. His share for tonight's haul should be close to $200,000. Trust ran both directions. El Lobo could easily skim, but that entailed certain death if ever discovered. Besides, El Lobo was doing just fine. Last year, he'd averaged $16,000 a day, 365 days a year. Had he been willing to work harder and take less vacation time, it would've been even more. It boggled the mind imagining how much money Mr. A made, but El Lobo felt quite comfortable with his salary. He drove the nicest cars, paid for the best hookers, and owned lots of real estate all over Mexico. He had use of Mr. A's private jet and helicopters, and he'd be taking his first cruise on Mr. A's luxury yacht soon.

Through trial and error over the years, El Lobo had found the optimum number for a column of illegals was thirty-five to forty. Fewer wasn't profitable enough, and more became too many to manage with a four-man escort. Most people had no clue how dangerous his line of work could be. There were bandits all throughout the Chihuahuan Desert. Lazy bottom-feeders who weren't willing to do the difficult work. At gunpoint, they'd rob a migrant column of all its cash, green cards, and drugs. And they'd often assault the women and girls. Without El Lobo's protection, his columns had a good chance of being intercepted. Once stripped of their cash and IDs, they had little chance of making it deep into US territory, but worse than that, El Lobo's reputation would take a hit.

Across the two decades he'd been doing this, he'd refined his smuggling skills to a fine art. As an example, he always had one of his own men accompany the convoy disguised as a migrant. You couldn't be "too careful." Truer words had never been spoken.

Years ago, Mr. A had built an incredible ranch house at Rancho Del Seco. El Lobo stayed there for free, as long as he maintained it. The place had eight bedrooms with full baths, a library, game room, sitting room, living room, full gym, and a kitchen bigger than most people's houses. The one drawback was a total lack of cellular service, but a high-speed satellite subscription allowed him to access online phone services. Making calls via the internet was easy but not secure.

He found it mildly amusing that Quattro, his right-hand man, had adopted the Italian spelling of the number four, but to each his own. Quattro was more than capable of running the day-to-day smuggling operations, but El Lobo liked being out here, liked hiking across the desert, and liked the thrill and danger.

Like right now.

In every sense of the definition, El Lobo was a hands-on man. His enemies feared him and didn't want to be on the wrong end of his infamous scorpion cattle brand. Many people had been marked by his red-hot iron over the years. Fear, he'd learned at an early age, went a long way toward keeping order in Mexico.

He watched through field glasses as Quattro, eight hundred meters away, tossed the last of the old tires out of the truck onto the second smaller pile of tires. The bigger pile, perhaps a hundred tires strong, sat ten meters away.

Quattro rounded up the strays that had rolled away and heaved them onto the smaller pile. Next, his first lieutenant dowsed the larger pile with a mixture of half motor oil, half diesel and threw the empty can into the truck. The motor oil assured the syrupy combination would stay wet for an hour or so, which ought to be more than enough time.

They weren't concerned about evaporation on the smaller pile, so they'd use pure diesel to get it going.

The image in his field glasses wavered with the beginnings of what would be a nice mirage today—not extremely hot, but comfortably warm. The conditions couldn't have been more perfect. A near absence of wind worked in their favor, for more than one reason. The column of dark smoke would be visible for miles.

Quattro placed a heavy L-shaped plate of steel about halfway up the larger pile of tires. He had to move a few tires to make it sit fairly level. He then set a twenty-liter red gasoline can on the base of the L shape so that the upright part of the steel was behind the can.

"How's that look?"

El Lobo answered the radio call. "Perfect. I've got a solid bead."

The last thing Quattro did was place a cardboard box on the near side of the bigger pile, away from the border fence.

He keyed his radio. "Good job, Q. Light it up and come on back."

"Copy."

Quattro sloshed an entire can of diesel on the smaller pile, threw the empty container into the truck, and rolled the door closed.

His lieutenant made a motion—like throwing a Frisbee—and within a few seconds, the smaller mound of rubber became fully engulfed in flames.

Quattro waved, climbed into the truck, and sped away from the pile.

It didn't take long for the dark smoke to reach a thousand meters above the desert. El Lobo glanced at his watch. Response time to this area ought to be about twenty minutes. Because of his strategically planned incidents, the US Border Patrol now had more assets assigned to this stretch of fence.

The dust from Quattro's truck slowly dispersed. Out of boredom, El Lobo grabbed his laser rangefinder and began taking readings from various objects. A rusted hulk without wheels or doors sat 763 meters away. A road sign on the American side registered at an astonishing 2,700 meters. He got a reading from an abandoned building at 921 meters and a passing car at 1,436 meters.

He told Quattro to park the truck and come on up for the show. Because his shooting position atop the twenty-meter knoll offered a shallow downward angle, the beeps would never see them.

His guests arrived ten minutes sooner than expected. A Border Patrol SUV appeared at the limit of his binoculars. He saw its dust cloud first. In the round image of his field glasses, the SUV slowly got bigger and bigger. When it looked to be about two minutes out, El Lobo set his binoculars down and shouldered his rifle. Today, he favored his Remington 700, chambered in 30–06.

Quattro grabbed the binoculars and looked at the vehicle. "Too bad it's only two of them responding."

"Two is enough." He acquired the red gas can in his rifle's scope and asked Quattro to check the mirage, a great way to determine the windage correction. "Right now, wind looks negligible in our immediate area, but there could be some downrange."

"The mirage is lying down a little more . . . Give it two additional clicks left."

El Lobo repeated the correction. "Two clicks left." His elevation correction was already set for 570 yards. Now all he had to do was pull the trigger. And score two hits, of course.

No problem, he owned this.

"Are you sure this is going to work?" Quattro asked.

"Yes, it's old and unstable," he said slowly, concentrating on the crosshairs. "It's been weeping nitroglycerin for years. I'm surprised it didn't go off when you lit the small pile of tires."

"Tell me you're joking."

"I'm joking."

"Come on, boss. You're being funny. Right?"

He half laughed and said, "Seriously . . . I was just"—the rifle kicked his shoulder—"kidding."

Downrange, the incendiary bullet punched through the gas-filled plastic container and smashed into the steel plate, setting off its miniature explosive warhead.

"Awesome shot, boss!"

"All in a day's work."

The gas didn't explode like in the movies, but it did create a nice fireball.

"Redneck entertainment at its best," Quattro said.

Smoke from the two fires merged into a single roiling mass. He focused on the approaching SUV, which seemed to have sped up. No doubt seeing the smoke column triple in size had motivated the beeps to hurry along. The SUV stopped about fifty meters away, and two agents climbed out. They walked a few steps and stood there with their hands on their hips. No doubt they were wondering why anyone would create a burning pile of tires in the middle of nowhere, forty kilometers west of Ciudad Juárez.

He'd give the pyre another minute to get really hot.

"How's our mirage look? The smoke column seems about the same. Any change mid-range?"

"Everything looks . . . good," Quattro said. "No change."

El Lobo moved the crosshairs onto the cardboard box and began a gradual increase of pull on the trigger. Anticipating the outcome, he nearly jerked the trigger.

The second report hammered his hearing again.

This time the result was spectacular.

"Oh, hell yeah!" Quattro yelled.

Even at this distance, they felt the blast's compression thump.

Looking like a fireworks accident, smoke trails arced through the air at a low angle to the ground. The TNT explosion essentially created an oversized claymore mine of burning tires. Covering their heads, the beeps crouched as smoking chunks pelted the area all around them. Sadly, none of the molten rubber found them. El Lobo smiled as they scrambled back to their SUV. Killing the responding beeps wasn't in his master plan, but that would change soon enough.

Tomorrow's action would prove far more enjoyable, albeit more challenging.

CHAPTER 15

Rebecca Cantrell's direct line came to life. A true direct line, it rang through without being vetted. The tiny screen on her telephone console showed a person she spoke with daily: Director of National Intelligence Scott Benson.

"Start another pot of coffee, Rebecca. Ethan's on the line with us. My staff is calling the other IC directors, but I wanted to talk to both of you in person."

Her longtime friend Ethan Lansing sat in the FBI director's chair. Lansing was a good man, and she felt comfortable sharing the call with him. She turned toward her bank of TVs. Since all the cable news networks were still covering the UTC mall shooting in San Diego, she wondered what else had happened. Whatever it was, it had to be big. Benson's office wouldn't call all the intelligence community directors otherwise.

Benson continued. "There's been another mass shooting, and this one's in our backyard. Multiple gunmen just shot up Mabel's Diner."

Just as Benson finished his sentence, the Fox News broadcast of the UTC shooting was interrupted to announce more breaking news. One by one, the other networks followed suit.

With the sound muted, she watched coverage of the shooting in San Diego switch over to the shooting in Washington, DC. The scrolling ticker tape on CNN rolled with: BREAKING NEWS: WASHINGTON, DC, DINER TARGETED BY MULTIPLE GUNMEN.

"You seeing it?" Benson asked.

"Yes," she said, focusing on the subtitles scrolling across the TVs. She had an uncanny ability to follow multiple TVs at the same time without missing anything.

Rebecca knew of Mabel's Diner, but she hadn't been in there in over a year. Mabel's was famous for being frequented by senators, members of Congress, cabinet personnel, and yes, IC directors.

"Was anyone there?" Realizing how that sounded, she asked, "I mean, lawmakers?"

"Yes," Benson answered. "Stone McBride was shot and killed."

Stone McBride? Dead? She ought to be prepared for any kind of news imaginable, but she suddenly felt flushed. Her voice cracked. "Is that one hundred percent confirmed?"

"Yes," Benson said. "The owner witnessed everything and gave a detailed report to MPD. The chief then called my direct line. I just got off the phone with him. There's more: Stone's daughter and granddaughter were with him."

"Please don't tell me they were killed," she said.

"They weren't, but his granddaughter was shot twice. She's being transported for surgery as we speak. She's expected to live. Stone's daughter is MIA after single-handedly taking down three gunmen before leaving through the rear door. Mabel reported hearing more gunfire in the alley. MPD found a seriously wounded man near the rear door to Mabel's, presumably one of the assailants, but he's unconscious and may not live. There was no sign of Stone's daughter. Her trail goes cold from there. Except for essential meetings, I want both of you to clear your calendars. Job one is to ID the DC and San Diego gunmen and find out if the two shootings are connected."

"What are the odds that two mass shooting attacks take place within the same hour?" Rebecca asked, somewhat rhetorically.

"Exactly. We should assume they're related until we learn otherwise and make sure every other metropolitan police department is on full alert. We've already updated the National Terrorism Advisory System to include the new attack in DC."

"I'm not seeing anything about Senator McBride on the networks," Lansing said.

"That hasn't leaked yet, but we can expect it to within the next fifteen minutes or so. When it does, things are going to heat up, especially for a certain San Diego resident. I want you to call him directly, Rebecca. He needs to hear this from us, not see it on TV."

"Actually," said Lansing, "my chief of staff, Holly Simpson, is dating Nathan McBride. I think the call should come from her. I'm walking over to her office as we speak. Here, she's coming my way."

"Did Stone have a Secret Service agent with him?" Rebecca asked.

"Yes," said Benson. "He took several rounds to the chest. Fatal. It seems he tried to return fire on the gunmen, making himself a target. According to Mabel, Stone's daughter fought back with the slain agent's weapon. It could've been much worse otherwise."

"Rebecca, Scott, please hang on a sec while I talk to Holly . . ."

She and Benson waited a moment until Ethan returned to the call. "Sorry, I'm back. Holly's going to call Nathan right away."

"Rebecca, could Stone's daughter have been the target?"

"It's definitely possible," she said, "but I'm giving that extremely low odds."

"Why?"

"She and her daughter are in WITSEC."

"That makes it unlikely, all right, but for now, nothing's off the table. We're going to work the two investigations and get answers."

"Rebecca, I'm going to need everything you've got on Stone's daughter," Lansing said. "I'm assuming you've got a file?"

"Yes," she said. "I'll make sure you get a copy ASAP."

Benson jumped back in. "Rebecca, what have you got on her? The short version, please."

Anticipating the question, she already had Jin's file on her computer screen.

"Her name's Jin Marchand and she has a colorful history as a DPRK spook. Remember the Exocet missile scandal? Well, that was her doing. To make a long story short, the French finally caught up with her and forced her into becoming a double agent. Once DPRK found out she'd been working for the French, they put a price on her head, and a mercenary assassination squad nearly killed her in a Paris hotel. Eight people were killed."

"How did she end up here?" Scott asked.

"I'm scanning for that right now . . . As I recall, it was around fifteen years ago."

"It can wait," Benson said. "We don't need to know right this second. Only take absolutely essential meetings. I want both of you immediately available. The president's going to want answers and want them quickly. If these two shootings are linked, we need to know how and why."

"If it's an assassination of Stone, there will be a long list of suspects," Ethan said. "As the former chair of the Committee on Domestic Terrorism, Stone made many enemies from many different groups."

"Ethan, make sure Nathan McBride knows we're going to keep him in the loop, but he's to do nothing and take no action until he hears back from us."

"Holly's calling him right now; I'll let her know."

"Will he be on board?" Benson asked.

Rebecca said, "He's a Marine; he'll follow orders."

"He just became your responsibility. We'll talk again in half an hour, sooner if anything comes up."

***

Scott Benson ended the call and shook his head. The news networks were going to have a field day. He just hoped the mass shootings stopped with these two incidents. The longer his IC agencies went without answers, the more ineffective they'd look.

He called Rebecca back, not conferencing in Lansing this time.

"That was quick," she said. "Do you have something new?"

"No. It's just the two of us now. I didn't mean to put you on the spot with Stone's daughter."

"Not at all. I'm still looking at her file."

"I thought you might be."

"It's a long story, but she's from a relationship Stone had in Korea near the end of the war. He'd planned to marry Marchand's mother, but they were separated and never saw each other again. Rather than dive into her entire background, I'll send you the file. In a nutshell, she was a covert operations officer for DPRK's Ministry of State Security. Several years after the Exocet missile leak, which was Marchand's op, the Chinese rolled out an upgraded antiship missile system. It doesn't take a lot of math skill to put two and two together. DPRK either sold or gave the specs to their neighbor."

"I remember it," Benson said. "I was at the Pentagon at the time. As I recall, we worked closely with the French to help track Marchand down."

"Yes, that's right," Rebecca said. "After the French caught up with her a few years later, they gave her two options. Spend the rest of her life in a French prison or go to work for their DGSE."

"So what's she doing in the United States?"

"The simplest answer is we wanted her."

"Because of her working knowledge of North Korea?"

"Yes, specifically because she had familiarity about a prison where several high-profile South Koreans were being held. The information she provided helped with the planning of a raid by ROK special forces to break them out. We supported the op with a force recon unit. DPRK denied it ever happened, but ROK had the hostages back as proof. A month later, the prison was shut down, and all the prisoners were transferred farther inland. We were able to pull it off because the prison was less than a mile from the Sea of Japan. FORECON got in and out quickly."

"Why didn't the French keep her?"

"She'd outlived her usefulness. The final straw was her surprise pregnancy. Rather than continue shelling out money to either protect or imprison her, the French released her from her obligation. She'd cooperated fully and given up extremely useful information. The French authorities have never admitted it, but we suspect she told them she was Stone McBride's daughter, which could've easily been proven through a DNA test."

"And being the biological daughter of a high-profile politician, her US citizenship was put on the fast track," Benson said.

"Only after we discovered who she was. She didn't tell anyone for a long time. Stone McBride didn't know she existed until fairly recently."

"Why would she keep that a secret?"

"She never said."

"Speculate."

"She could've been planning to use it as leverage at some future point."

"To what end?"

"To remain in the United States with her daughter."

"I see your point. It wouldn't look good on Stone's résumé having a long-lost, illegitimate daughter who'd been a North Korean spook. That's pretty solid leverage."

"To put it mildly."

"So how can we get her to make contact, assuming she's still alive?"

"We can't," said Cantrell.

"Shit, it's already breaking about Stone being killed in the diner. Look at CNN."

"I see it."

"Let's hope Holly's on the phone with his son by now."

CHAPTER 16

Six Days Ago

There's nothing out here but rattlesnakes and two-legged vermin. US Border Patrol Agent Hank Grangeland knew his dark mood was moored in frustration. This desert teemed with life; you just had to know where to look. He'd spent twenty of his fifty years on Earth guarding the border.

Driving toward the column of black smoke, he marveled at how beautiful it looked out here. Most people didn't have a clue. The Chihuahuan Desert encompassed Big Bend National Park and hosted some of the most pristine landscape in North America—in the world, for that matter. He admired all its diverse areas but favored the sinuous path of the Rio Grande the best. In many places, the contrast of its greenbelt set against the beige and brown looked like a tree viper on sand. Ever since childhood, he'd loved the desert, the summer heat, the winter frosts, the smell of spring rain, and the vibrant colors of blooming cactus and flowers. Everything.

Watching the murky water snaking its way toward the Caribbean, Grangeland wondered whether his new partner could handle the job.

Two decades ago, he supposed *his* first partner might've wondered the same thing. Rookies were notoriously hard to read. Some had what it took, and some didn't, but only time would tell. He gave the man sitting next to him fifty-fifty odds.

"You ever get tired of this, G-Man?" asked his partner.

Grangeland's full name was Horatio Cecil Grangeland. Horatio Cecil? Seriously? His parents were kidding, right? Apparently not. During his formative years, he'd become quite the brawler. Kids could be so cruel to each other. He'd adopted the nickname Hank long ago, although most of his fellow agents called him G-Man. The only person who still called him Horatio was his sister, Mary. She had always thought Horatio was a cool name, but she hadn't borne the brunt of relentless teasing all through childhood, high school, the Navy, and then the Border Patrol academy. If he hadn't shared the name with the famous English sailor, he would've been spared all manners of jokes and pranks. During his Border Patrol academy days, his locker had become the sole focal point of mischievous activity. But despite all the teasing, everyone at the academy liked him.

"Tired of what?" asked Grangeland. "You mean being out here?"

"I guess. It just seems so pointless at times."

"It's a lot easier if you don't second-guess the decision-makers. We don't make policy. We just enforce it."

Tucker nodded and stayed silent for a moment. "You ever meet Agent Jackson?"

"I think I met her a few years back. Can't remember."

"What those assholes did to her . . . it's hard to imagine."

Three months ago, Agent Jackson and her partner had been bushwhacked just north of the Rio Grande near the eastern border of Big Bend by two notorious and violent coyotes named El Lobo and Quattro. They'd killed her partner outright, but they'd had different plans for Jackson. Her torment lasted two days before they shot her in the gut and left her for dead. It was a miracle she'd survived.

If he ever crossed paths with those two, he'd make an exception to the "nobody's watching" rule and have no regrets.

He didn't like thinking about it. El Lobo hadn't simply wanted to kill Jackson; he'd wanted his men to humiliate and demean her. Violating her hadn't been enough. She'd been beaten, branded, shot in the stomach, then left for dead. An off-road motorcyclist, who'd been illegally riding on private ranchland, found her. Amazingly, Agent Jackson had been conscious. Sunburned. Dehydrated. Lacerated. Bug bitten. You name it, she'd endured it. Fortunately, the off-roader had a backpack and offered her water and food. She might not have lasted another hour.

Grangeland found himself gritting his teeth.

"You thinking about her?"

"Huh? Yeah . . . I hate the idea of those animals getting away with it."

"I heard about the scorpion brand he uses. What a sick asshole."

"Yeah, we think he heats it up with a cigar torch when he doesn't have a campfire going. I'd love to get my hands on El Lobo and personally teach him the error of his ways."

"What about your 'nobody's watching' rule?"

"Let's just say there are some rules I'll bend, others not."

"So if we come across El Lobo, he'll definitely *resist arrest*?"

"Absolutely." Grangeland's partner was a rookie Border Patrol agent, but not inexperienced. Before joining the Border Patrol, Tucker served ten years with the Plano Police Department.

"I heard your sister's in law enforcement too," said Tucker.

He nodded. "She's an ATF special agent. Before that, she was FBI."

"No kidding?"

"Yep. She's tougher than I am, but I hate the thought of her being brutalized like Jackson. It could've been her . . . She almost joined the Border Patrol."

"Why didn't she?"

"She had her heart set on the FBI."

"Then why'd she move to the ATF?"

He couldn't reveal the real reason, so he said, "I think she just wanted a change. She loved the FBI, but the ATF turned out to be a better fit."

If Tucker pursued this line of questioning further, he'd have to change the subject. Fortunately, they ended up talking about Tucker's brother, who currently served in the Coast Guard. Most people had no clue how big a role the Coast Guard played in preventing illegal immigration.

When they crested a small hill and started down toward the river, the source of the smoke became visible right away—definitely coming from the Mexican side of the river. The question became, why? Lately, he'd seen this kind of thing a lot, chalked it up to vandalism. But not all bonfires were harmless pranks. Over the years, he'd come across charred bodies, some of them belonging to children. He hadn't been kidding when—on their first day together—he'd told Tucker that monsters lurked in this desert.

"Go ahead and call in another bonfire, Tuck." All incidents along the border were categorized, plotted with GPS coordinates, and logged. They wouldn't have the exact lat and long numbers until they reached the spot.

Dispatch said a park ranger was on scene. Moments later, they spotted the SUV on the shoulder a quarter mile ahead. When they got close, the ranger climbed out and approached his window.

"Hey, G-Man, sorry you guys got dragged down here."

"Hey, TR. We've got the best assignment in the agency. Big Bend National Park and beautiful rangers." He could say that without worrying about being labeled a sexist or accused of harassment. They'd known each other for many years.

She offered him a genuine smile. The ranger's full name was Theresa Ragan, a super nice woman and a class act. Like Border Patrol agents, she wore a sidearm—all federal park rangers did. Compact and blonde, she looked a lot like his sister, probably the reason he felt so comfortable around her.

"Tuck, how you making out with this crusty old codger? You must be tired of hearing the same old fish stories over and over and over."

"It's unbearable," Tucker said.

"Hey, what's wrong with my stories?"

"How much time do you have?" she asked.

He smiled. "So can we get all the way down there?"

"Most of the way. We'll have to hoof the last three hundred yards or so."

"We aren't going to get too close. You heard about the tire fire west of Ciudad Juárez the other day?"

"Yeah, it exploded," she said.

"Like I said, we'll keep a safe distance."

"That's a foul-looking smoke column," Tucker said.

"It's tires again," she said. "I went down there for a closer look before you guys got here. It's a crappy thing to do. That stuff's toxic."

Even though the dark roiling smoke rose high above them, a slight stench of burned rubber hung in the air. Grangeland used his field glasses but couldn't see the fire's source through the trees. "Were you down this way yesterday?"

"Yeah, but I didn't see anything. I mean I didn't see a pile of tires."

"Then somebody dumped them there last night and waited until this morning to torch them. Why wait? Why not torch them last night?"

"Hard to say."

"Could it be a trash burn?"

"It's possible, but the locals are pretty respectful of the park. I've never seen this before. One thing's for certain: there aren't enough vehicles in Santa Elena to produce that many old tires. Somebody brought them into town."

"Do you know any of the locals? Anybody we could talk to?"

"Not really. It's a tiny community and they keep to themselves. If we see someone across the river, we can ask. Your Spanish is better than mine, though. I checked at Cottonwood Campground. No one saw or heard anything. It's pretty far away."

They didn't say anything for a few seconds.

"How's Jackson doing?" TR asked.

Grangeland shrugged. "I honestly can't say. I don't really know her. From what I've heard, she's still on paid leave and planning to return to patrol someday. In my opinion, she should get as much time as she needs."

"I totally agree. Well, let's go down there and see what we see," TR said. "Our access road is just past the Castolon turn."

Grangeland already knew that. He'd been down to the old Santa Elena crossing many times, just not lately. Out of respect for TR, he didn't say anything. He'd been patrolling this area of the river long before the park ranger had been assigned to Big Bend.

***

El Lobo's irritation grew with each passing minute. Where the hell were they? Didn't anyone work at the Castolon ranger station? Perhaps it was too early in the morning. If the response came from Boquillas, it could take a while.

He supposed another pile of burning tires didn't warrant a "drop everything and respond" type of call, but the last time he'd torched tires, there'd been a nice explosion to go with it. If the cavalry didn't show up in the next half hour or so, there might not be any response at all. This section of the river was, after all, extremely remote. Even so, the fire's proximity to the two-bit town of Santa Elena should merit some level of investigation, if only a drive-by.

So far, the USBP was batting a thousand. They'd arrived to investigate and log every bonfire he'd created along the border over the last week, and he expected they'd do the same thing here.

Patience. They'll come. They've got nothing else to do.

It didn't feel bitterly cold, but he was far from comfortable. It triggered a childhood memory of being cold. He and his sister used to stay away from the house until well after dark, waiting for their father to fall asleep, or more accurately, pass out drunk. He remembered being cold, huddling with his sister in the bushes of a neighbor's yard. A skinny dog used to keep them company. It smelled bad, but they still liked it. It never hit them or yelled at them. They'd save some of their food from dinner and feed it. Then one day, the dog didn't come inside the bushes to visit them. They looked for it the next day but never found it. He remembered feeling sad.

Never get close to anything; it might not be there tomorrow.

El Lobo shivered. Even with a heavy camouflaged jacket, he began to feel the onset of a chill. What he felt next was a huge pang of relief when a vehicle with a light bar came into view, too distant to know if it belonged to a park ranger or the Border Patrol . . . He'd have to wait until it got closer.

A minute later, he had his answer—a park ranger. He'd seen enough of their white SUVs to distinguish the difference. It kept coming and rolled past the Castolon junction. He had the impression a woman was behind the wheel.

A few minutes later, it emerged from the line of cottonwoods lining the sandy wash along the river. The ranger, definitely a woman, didn't get out. Maybe he'd have his way with her someday. Maybe someday soon. He liked law enforcement women . . . liked dominating them, in particular.

The park ranger used field glasses to study the fire for a few seconds, then backed away and disappeared back into the trees. A few minutes later, her vehicle returned to a position above the Castolon junction and parked on the shoulder. A good sign. She was obviously waiting to meet someone, presumably the mighty US Border Patrol.

He took a swig of water and focused on the fire with his scope. Some of the locals had crawled out of their holes to watch.

If no one showed up soon, he'd be forced to scrap this mission and try again. Problem was, the big move across the desert was about a week away, and he needed to make sure the Border Patrol assets were deployed where he wanted them. He had a backup plan to stage an incident at the Boquillas port-of-entry crossing, but he'd rather have the Border Patrol's efforts focused farther west, here at Santa Elena.

Boquillas. What a joke. He couldn't believe how idiotic the Americans were. Rafts full of people were legally allowed to cross the Rio Bravo and dump their occupants onto American soil. If the migrants didn't mind getting wet, they could just wade or swim across—legally. Once on the American side, the "visitors" walked up a short trail to the ranger's station where they were required to check in at a kiosk run by the US National Park Service. A kiosk . . . really? Didn't that assume they could read and write? During their stroll up the path, "visitors" could accidentally stray away from the tree-lined trail, hide out until dark, then catch a ride north. In reality, they didn't even need to wait until nightfall. He'd used the Boquillas crossing many times, and no, he and his charges didn't bother to check in. He always got a big kick out of the Department of Homeland Security emblem plastered on the kiosk. America, home of the great naive class. His profession as a coyote would be so much harder if America ever got serious about its border security. Until then, he'd just have to keep making obscene amounts of money.

His one fear was going to prison. He'd never survive it, being cooped up all day long, spending hour after hour, day after day, and year after year in a tiny cell. Ever since childhood, he'd hated being told what to do, and prison embodied that. No way. He'd rather die than rot in prison.

El Lobo scanned the highway's horizon with his optic and saw something. A speck on the road. He watched the speck turn into a vehicle. After several minutes, the vehicle became white. The white vehicle slowly transformed into an SUV with a light bar and a diagonal green stripe on its sides. *Stop the presses.* The US Border Patrol had finally arrived.

He smiled when it pulled alongside the park ranger. *Oh, that's so quaint. Say hello. Make small talk. Exchange some doughnuts.*

The Border Patrol vehicle followed the park ranger's SUV when it pulled away. He'd scouted this area with binoculars thoroughly and knew the exact route they'd take down to the old crossing, but he lost sight of their vehicles after they passed the turn to the old Castolon station. The cottonwood canopy along this stretch of the river made tracking them all the way to the water impossible. He wouldn't see them again until they emerged on foot. If they didn't dillydally, that ought to happen in just under four minutes. The two vehicles had to navigate the crappy road through the trees.

Right on schedule, he saw them emerge from the cottonwoods and park at the edge of the dry wash. They stopped at the same place where the park ranger had used her field glasses to look at the fire.

The two beeps got out and began walking with the ranger toward the river.

He'd chosen this spot because it had an ideal exit. All he had to do was make a downhill run to where Quattro waited with the Range Rover, then casually drive away, staying well south of the main part of town, if you could even call this dump a town.

He wondered what they were saying as they walked toward his trap. He didn't have any hard feelings for the park rangers, but business was business, and those other assholes in green were on his shit list. The mighty US Border Patrol was nothing but a bunch of overpaid bullies.

Maybe that's why he hated them so much . . . They were too similar to himself.

El Lobo gauged the wind and added another left click.

"Come to Papa," he whispered.

***

Grangeland drove behind TR through the trees and shrubs lining the dirt track, branches scraping their vehicles' doors. TR hadn't been kidding. Bumpy didn't begin to describe this. The Santa Elena crossing wasn't really a crossing unless you had one of those silly boats on wheels tourists liked to ride.

The low vegetation began to thin as they got closer to the wash. Just ahead, where a huge stand of cottonwoods towered over their heads, the road ended at a wide dry wash.

"We've got some lookie-loos," Grangeland said.

"I see them," said Tuck. On the Mexican side, several men, women, and children stood at a safe distance, watching the fire. "I guess we have our answer about talking to the locals. They're leaving in a big hurry."

"Yep, they see us for sure."

TR climbed out and walked a few steps toward the river. "You guys always scare away the wildlife."

"We're truly loved," Tucker said.

"Well, let's get over there and see what we see," Grangeland said.

"We'll see murky water, sand, driftwood, and rocks."

"Come on, Tuck," she said. "Where's your sense of adventure? We might discover some fresh footprints."

"You can't know how much that excites me."

"We have to walk over there anyway to get the coordinates," said Grangeland.

"If you say so. Can we avoid getting too close? I'd rather not take a molten-rubber shower."

"I second that," TR said.

The three of them emerged out of the trees. To reach the river's edge, which ought to keep them a safe distance from the burning pile, they had to hike about a thousand feet across open sand intermixed with river rock and driftwood.

TR took point. "At least the smoke column's leaning away from us. I wouldn't want to breathe that crap in."

"It looks nasty, all right," Grangeland agreed.

Separated by several yards each, they walked in silence for a few minutes. Too bad some idiot ruined a beautiful morning by torching a bunch of tires. What a dumb-ass thing to do. Monkey see, monkey do. Bonfires had become a disturbing trend recently. Agreeing with Tuck's sentiment, Grangeland didn't plan to get too close. The last thing he wanted was a burning chunk of rubber to ruin his magnificent hat. He liked wearing his formal cover rather than a ball cap. It kept the sun off his face and neck.

The fire's source was plainly visible now . . . and something else. Like a fuse, a line of burned tires extended away from the pile. They hadn't been able to see it from Santa Elena Canyon Road. "TR, hang on a sec. I wanna check something with my binoculars. Tuck, you see that burned line coming out of the pile?"

His partner brought his binoculars up. "Yeah, what do you make of it?"

"I think it acted like a fuse. Whoever set this fire wanted to delay the main burn."

"Why would they do that?"

He stopped walking. "I don't know. TR, did someone call this in to you guys? A camper or anyone? The park service called us, right?"

"Yeah. We got a report of a fire near the old Santa Elena crossing."

"I don't like the feel of this anymore. I think we should—"

A loud crack tore the air.

Shit! Grangeland knew the sound well. *A supersonic bullet.*

He yelled, "Sniper!"

More than a full second later, the distant thud of the report from the Mexican side of the river reached their position.

Her face contorting with pain, TR spun and collapsed.

"Theresa!" Grangeland crouched to make himself a smaller target. "Go, Tuck! Weave as you run! I've got TR. Call it in and get the M4! Go. Go!"

More supersonic cracks rang out, and thankfully, all the bullets missed.

As he scooped TR up from the sand, he heard Tuck shouting into his lapel mic for backup.

A fourth bullet screamed off a melon-size river rock next to his face. Chunks of shrapnel cleaved into his cheek and nose. *Shit, that could've been my eyes.* The sniper's attempted head shot hadn't missed by more than a foot.

"I've got you, TR."

She wrapped her arms around his neck. "I'm okay."

She didn't sound okay.

In retrospect, the wash had been an ideal ambush location. Nothing but open ground in every direction. No gullies or deep depressions to provide cover.

Making matters worse, they had no way to return fire on the shooter, so he didn't have to relocate. Based on the gap between the arriving bullets and the delayed report of the rifle, Grangeland put the sniper at one thousand yards, probably atop the low ridge to their southwest. It might even be El Lobo himself. Grangeland knew the coyote had taken Special Forces training in the Mexican Army, which would've included sniper school.

Whoever lay behind that rifle was a damned good shot.

The sand continued to explode at his feet as he ran.

"Keep going," TR said. "Go, go!"

"Yeah, that's the general idea."

The intensity of the supersonic cracks lessened as the shooter switched over to Tuck. Fortunately, his partner was on the move, and all the bullets missed. He hoped the sniper was really fast at operating a bolt-action rifle because the alternative meant they were on the wrong end of a semiauto and could be facing upward of twenty rounds without a break.

Not a pleasant thought.

This whole thing? A setup. The location. The delayed burn. The smoke column to gauge the wind. All of it reeked of El Lobo.

No time to lament.

With TR securely in his arms, he ran as fast as he could toward the tree line to the northwest. It was farther to go, but if he ran due north, he'd be an easier target to acquire. While running, he slowed down and sped up in an unpredictable pattern. Three strides, two strides, four strides. Every so often, he'd nearly stop then start again.

The feeling of being in a sniper's crosshairs had to be the worst dread he'd ever experienced. He sensed the shooter trying to get a solid bead on him.

Ignoring the early signs of muscle burn, Agent Grangeland kept pumping his legs.

He might die today, but he could live with himself if he survived.

***

Things progressed exactly as planned. It couldn't have been scripted better. El Lobo watched the three of them walk along the exact route he'd predicted. Looking through his $10,000 scope, his excitement built with every step they took.

Then they stopped.

What the hell are you idiots doing? Keep going!

They hadn't reached the spot he'd chosen at nine hundred meters. They were still a good one hundred meters too far away. If they didn't come any closer, his elevation adjustment would be way short. He ran a quick estimate in his head, calculating the additional bullet drop out to their current position. He'd need four additional minutes of angle, maybe a little more. Since adjustments were made in quarter-minute increments, he'd have to click his elevation knob sixteen times. Rather than do that, he made the decision to hold at about a meter above the target, which ought to be fairly close.

Even with the unplanned hitch, he loved the exhilaration and excitement of having their lives in his hands.

Then his mood changed, like a balloon popping.

Excitement turned into rage.

One second he felt power and authority; the next he felt teeth-grinding ire and resentment. His stupid mother had allowed the abuse to continue for years. She should've done something about it or reported it to the police. Something. Anything. But she did nothing. Nothing! Living in an orphanage would've been infinitely better. What hurt the most? The brutal truth. If the monster was beating him, he wasn't beating his mother. She'd traded her pain for his.

Simple as that.

At the last second, El Lobo moved the crosshairs from above the bigger Border Patrol agent to a spot above the park ranger.

Screw her.

After a full breath, he blew half of it out and began to apply increasing pressure on the trigger. He never knew precisely when the rifle would buck. It always surprised him, as it should, right about—

Boom!

The circular image in his scope jolted. The concussion from the Lapua Magnum raised a wispy dust cloud in front of his position, but he reacquired the woman in time to see her spin and fall. Beautiful! He'd drilled her for sure.

Reacting quickly, the smaller male agent bolted toward their vehicles.

The other agent rushed over to the woman's side. El Lobo fired three more shots and saw the sand explode with each arrival. Crap. Clean misses.

You're brave, I'll grant you that, but I'll bet you need a change of underwear.

The agent hauled the woman up from the ground and began an all-out sprint for the trees.

He sent more bullets at the two of them, then eased the rifle left, aiming at the smaller agent, who was already weaving back and forth as he ran. His shots missed, and he couldn't tell if they were left or right of the target. The distance was also increasing, so he had to hold a little higher to make the correction.

El Lobo was an excellent shooter, but he didn't have world-class skill, and the wind had begun to gust unpredictably. It would be a whole lot easier if the man carrying the park ranger had run due north, rather than laterally toward the west. He wondered if that had been intentional or just dumb luck.

At this distance, shooting at a laterally moving object meant you had to shoot out in front of it—at a spot it hadn't yet reached. He knew it took the bullet about 1.3 seconds to travel nine hundred meters. El Lobo thought his target was moving about three meters per second. That meant he had to lead the running man by four meters or so. The bullet and flesh would then converge on the same location. In the purest sense of the physics, the Border Patrol agent would quite literally run into the bullet's path.

He moved the crosshairs to a spot in front of the agent and gently squeezed the trigger. After the kick, he was able to reacquire the target in time to see the sand explode. He'd missed again. Good thing Quattro couldn't see this, but he didn't beat himself up for missing. The primary mission had already been accomplished.

Screw it, he thought, and began pulling the trigger as fast as he could.

***

Hank Grangeland found himself in a shooting gallery. The cadence of the arriving slugs increased by a factor of four. The sand began detonating all around him as miniature sonic booms pounded his ears in a relentless barrage. He knew the shooter was unloading his magazine in an attempt to score a lucky hit, and right now, Hank didn't like his odds. The effect wasn't merely distracting; every time the sand burst upward in front of him, he had to narrow his eyes, making it harder to see the ground. This stuff wasn't Hawaiian beach sand. Every arriving bullet blasted fine powder, pebbles, rocks, and grit into the air. He was at serious risk of falling. If that happened, he might never get back up. He tried to find a positive side to this madness. Because it was so damned dry out here, the resulting dust surrounding him worked in his favor, partially obscuring him from the sniper.

"How you doing, TR?" he said between heaving breaths.

"I'm okay. Keep . . . going."

"Almost there."

With no choice, he kept running. The trees were still fifty yards away, but each stride put him a yard and a half closer. Thirty-three. Thirty-two. Thirty-one. The countdown to cover. He hoped to run out of steps before the shooter ran out of bullets. The distant booms of the discharges mixed with the arriving cracks created an unnerving drum beat. *Crack. Boom. Crack. Boom.* Over and over, bullets pulverized the earth around him. Sooner or later, one of those miniature artillery shells was going to find him.

He heard it then—the roar of an engine. Looking left, he caught a glimpse of a white flash in the trees just before Tucker came barreling toward him in their patrol vehicle. He'd never seen a prettier sight. *Way to go, Tuck!*

"Stand by, G-Man, I'm coming to you! Divert right toward the trees! Divert to the right!"

He could hear his partner on the radio clipped to his waist, but he couldn't press the transmit button to respond. He saw what Tuck had in mind but knew they'd never have enough time to load TR into the

SUV without making themselves stationary targets. Add to that, if Tuck stopped, the Tahoe would likely get stuck in the loose sand.

The burning in Grangeland's legs from hauling TR across uneven and soft ground began to take its toll. Together, they had to weigh over three hundred pounds.

He got a break when the explosions of sand switched over to the SUV, which was now angling toward a spot about twenty yards out in front of him.

In an incredibly brave move, Tuck had drawn the sniper's fire.

He watched in horror as the Tahoe's windshield took an impact, but it kept pitching and bouncing along.

"I'm okay!" Tuck yelled. "Be ready to hand her to me!"

I'm ready, he thought. *More than ready.*

Just ahead, the Tahoe flew over the slope of a shallow gully, then rammed the opposite side of the bank, a perfect spot to offer them a visual screen for the rest of their retreat into the trees.

The passenger side ended up toward the shooter, but Grangeland knew the supersonic bullets would cleave through the Tahoe's sheet metal doors and panels easily. He saw Tuck scramble out with the M4 slung across his chest.

"Stay down!" Grangeland yelled. There was no sense in Tuck making himself a target. The crack-boom cadence of the sniper's fire slowed. The shooter was walking his shots onto the SUV now that he had a stationary target.

In ten more steps, Grangeland would reach Tuck's position.

Tucker came up, bench-rested his M4 on the hood, and began pounding away at the sniper's position. The odds were next to nothing he'd score a hit, but it might make the shooter hesitate.

It didn't.

Two more supersonic cracks made Grangeland flinch, but he'd made it to the Tahoe.

No explanation was needed. They both knew what to do.

Tuck slung the rifle back over his shoulder, took TR into his arms, and began running in a straight line for the trees. A brief pause in the shooting meant the sniper was probably changing magazines.

Grangeland couldn't leave yet. He opened the passenger door, climbed into the back seat, and reached for the medical bag in the rear luggage area.

Shit! A bullet smashed through the closed passenger door, flew through the interior, and impacted the sand where Grangeland had been only seconds ago. He sensed the slug miss his extended leg by mere inches.

With the medical bag in hand, he wasted no time and took off in Tuck's wake. His partner had already made the tree line and disappeared.

The man can flat-out run, Grangeland thought.

Shit!

Something smacked the side of his butt at the same instant he heard a whiplike crack. His mind registered it as a bullet wound and something else. He could keep going! Which was what he did—with renewed urgency. He'd never live this down and could already hear the teasing—shot in the ass.

Screw the teasing. Keep your damned legs moving.

The sand detonated several more times, but finally he made the tree line.

And saw no sign of Tuck.

"Tuck!" he yelled.

"Over here."

Grangeland thrashed his way through the head-high shrubs and bushes, but still didn't see his partner.

"Tuck."

"Over here."

He hobbled to the left, in the direction of Tuck's voice. A few additional cracks tore through the trees, but none of the impacts came close.

In a small clearing, he found Tuck kneeling over TR's supine form.

She managed a smile. "You Border Patrol guys are downright nuts."

"I don't know about you, Tuck, but I think she just paid us a compliment."

"It wasn't," she said, then pointed at his wet pant leg. "Did you get shot?"

Tuck looked up with a shocked expression. "G-Man?"

"It's nothing."

"Fuck nothing. Let me see it."

Grangeland turned, unbuckled his holster belt, and pulled his trousers down.

Tuck grinned. "Looks like the bullet went in and out. Something you're used to."

"Ha ha ha."

"Well, Forrest Gump, you're going to live."

"Life is like a box of chocolates," TR said in her best imitation.

"Cute, you guys. But need I remind you we're not out of danger yet? It's a good thing you park rangers are wearing vests these days."

"No kidding," she said, wincing. "I hated the change in policy, but I'm strongly reconsidering that sentiment."

Grangeland grimaced at a sudden wave of stinging pain. "I gotta say, Tuck, that took balls driving out there like that."

"You'd have done the same thing for me."

"I absolutely would've. Now if you're done admiring TR's attributes, I could use a field dressing on my backside."

Tuck had TR's vest off and her shirt open. "What's the hurry?" he asked.

TR gave him a look and buttoned her shirt. "I feel like I got hit by a baseball bat."

He winked. "The bullet nailed your vest at an angle. Good thing. You're all busted up, but you'll live."

"You sure know how to make a girl feel good."

"Tell that to my wife."

The distant booms started anew, but the supersonic cracks weren't close.

"Stay with TR," said Grangeland.

"Tell me you aren't going back out there," Tuck said.

"Don't worry. I'm not planning on getting shot again." He took the M4 and began limping through the trees. He didn't want eyes on the shooter, but he did want a visual of their Tahoe.

The thuds and cracks continued and other sounds too, the clatter of bullets passing through glass and sheet metal.

The son of a bitch was peppering their vehicle. He found a bush and watched the destruction unfold. Shot after shot hammered the Tahoe. It pissed him off. What an asshole, drilling their vehicle purely for sport. He was tempted to find a spot to return fire but knew it would be a waste of perfectly good ammo—which they might still need.

Enjoy it while you can, El Lobo. Your luck won't last forever.

CHAPTER 17

The call Nathan took a few minutes ago seemed surreal. Someone had tried to murder Vince's wife and children at the UTC mall? One of his kids was shot, the other MIA? Charlene in emergency surgery?

What the hell's going on?

He was about to leave his house for Sharp Hospital—where they'd taken Charlene—when his cell rang again. Now wasn't the time to ignore it, especially after seeing Holly's name.

"Are you okay?" she asked.

"Better than the Beaumonts," he said, unsure what she meant. Before leaving Denise Tabor's house, he'd texted Holly a complete update on what had happened. "Vincent's wife is close to death. She was shot six times. He still doesn't know—"

"Nathan . . . I'm sorry for interrupting, but I don't know how to say this . . . There's been another shooting. It's all over the news networks. I wanted to talk to you before you saw it on TV."

"Saw what?"

"It's about your dad."

He felt a sudden rush of blood in his temples. "Did something happen to him?"

Holly hesitated, and he knew the news wasn't good. He decided to spare her from saying it.

"Is he dead?"

"I'm so sorry, Nathan, but it's worse than that."

What's worse than that? he wondered. *Oh, please, no . . .* Jin and Lauren were in DC visiting his father.

"He was having lunch at Mabel's Diner with Jin and Lauren when multiple gunmen shot the place up—"

"Are they dead?" He couldn't believe how that question sounded. He felt his skin tighten.

"Lauren was shot twice, but she's going to be okay. The owner of the diner told Metro PD your sister pursued someone into the alley, presumably one of the gunmen."

"Unarmed?" Nathan asked.

"No, she managed to get the Secret Service agent's weapon and fight back after he was killed. She killed three attackers inside the diner, wounded a fourth in the rear alley, and now she's MIA."

"MIA?" He knew what MIA meant—missing in action—but he had a hard time believing Jin would've left Lauren behind. There had to be more to this, a lot more.

"By the time MPD arrived, there was no sign of Jin."

He consciously realized his mind couldn't yet process the death of his father. "What do the gunmen look like? White, Asian, Middle Eastern?"

Holly didn't hesitate with her answer. "Middle Eastern."

"Then it's possible—hang on, Holly. Harv's calling. I'm going to conference him in . . ."

Feeling detached from his body, Nathan merged the call. His father dead? Shot by gunmen in public? Lauren wounded? His sister MIA? Vince's family attacked? It was too much. Nothing seemed real right now. He felt like he'd awoken in a strange place where nothing looked familiar. He needed answers and fully intended to get them.

"Nathan, it's about your dad—"

"I heard, Harv. Holly's on the line."

"Hi, Harvey," she said.

"Hey, Holly. It's already on every news network. I just wanted to make sure Nathan didn't see it on TV first. How're you doing, partner?"

"I've had better mornings. Holly, can you tell Harv what you just told me?" He listened while she summarized what they knew.

"We've asked the ATF to help with the ballistics and shell-casing analysis. We might get a hit from a different crime scene and have a lead to follow. None of the gunmen had IDs, so we're using our facial recognition program to scour the databases. We're also looking at AFIS and INTERPOL to see if we come up with any fingerprint or DNA matches."

Harv said, "Knowing the ID of the shooters will go a long way in determining if Stone was the primary target and why."

"We're pretty sure Jin wasn't the target of the attack, but until we can confirm that one hundred percent, it's all speculation. Right now, we're trying to find a link between San Diego and DC. No matter who the targets were or the motivation behind the attacks, they're definitely acts of terrorism. I'm sorry, Nathan, but that's all we have at this point. We've got DC locked down."

"How long ago did this happen?" he asked.

"About twenty minutes."

Pacing the kitchen, he turned on the TV and muted the sound. From the image on the screen, it looked like every police cruiser, fire engine, and ambulance in DC had shown up. The aerial camera zoomed in on a sidewalk and showed a glimpse of a victim on a gurney being loaded into an ambulance.

"So there's nothing on my sister at all?"

"No. I figured you and Harvey would want to come out here right away, so I chartered a jet. I'll text you the flight information and pick you up at Reagan's jet center when you arrive. Count on around eleven p.m."

No one spoke for a few seconds.

"Does Nathan's mom know?" asked Harv.

"Yes. As soon as I found out, I sent a pair of agents to her house just to be safe. She's being escorted to the hospital."

"Thanks for doing that, Holly. I'll call her right after we hang up."

"Is Lauren really all right?" Harv asked.

"I'm waiting on a call back from the ER for more details, but yes, she's expected to make a full recovery. We don't have an exact number, but the diner was full of people when the gunmen opened fire. They used AKs. It's bad. Lots of people are dead, and many more are wounded."

He closed his eyes.

"I don't need to say this, but I will. Every federal, state, and local law enforcement agency is all over this, from the DOJ to the IC right down to the volunteer police patrols. Everyone's going to chip in."

"Please tell us anything else you know at this point." His voice sounded distant, almost as if someone else were speaking.

"The eyewitness reports are confusing, but it appears your father wrapped himself around Lauren and saved her life by taking the brunt of the gunfire. According to Mabel and other accounts, your sister saved a bunch of lives. Metro PD is doing its best to interview anyone who isn't going into emergency surgery. There's a massive amount of investigative work to do. We're looking into acquiring video from the surrounding businesses that might've captured the gunmen. People may also have video on their phones. Everyone's taking this attack personally. We're all highly motivated."

"Best guess—was Nathan's family purposely targeted or were they simply at the wrong place at the wrong time during a terrorist attack?" Harv asked.

"We think the odds are extremely low it was a random terror attack and not an assassination. Because of Jin's background, we can't rule her out as the primary target. But we have no reason to believe the gunmen knew who Jin Marchand is, including that she's Stone's daughter."

Harv asked, "Do you think the attack out here is somehow connected?"

"It's definitely possible. We just can't say yes with certainty yet. You should see it around here. It's literally a mad scramble right now."

Harv and Holly faded into background noise.

Nathan felt disconnected, as if floating above his body.

The first wave of fury hit him so hard, it summoned something dark within his soul. *Something? You know damned well what's down there.* The Other. Craving vengeance, it emerged from its slumber and oozed forward like a cat, its eyes singularly focused on the latch of its cage, hoping to find it unlocked. The Other grabbed the bars with both hands and yanked. Hard. The clank of steel on steel was a horrid reminder of what stood between sanity and madness.

Not now. Not without my permission.

He'd spent years learning to keep the vile thing in its cage.

Not an easy task. If he didn't stop this malignant surge of rage . . .

Shit. Shit!

The hatred driving such a cowardly attack on his family paled in comparison to the wrath he planned to unleash on his father's murderers. He desperately wanted to get off the phone and destroy something with a baseball bat. He now wished he'd broken every bone in Fred Flintstone's miserable body. Swing a meat cleaver at *me*? It would've—

Holly's voice broke in. "Nathan . . . ? Are you there?"

"Sorry, Holly. I missed what you said."

"Hey, you have nothing to apologize for."

"I'm okay. I just zoned for a second."

Harv said, "I'm starting in your direction. Are you at your La Jolla house?"

"Yes."

"I'll pack a bag and head over there right away."

"Thanks, Harv. My dad was in his mid-nineties. I hate to say it, but this probably spared him from a slow, convalescent death."

It wasn't public knowledge, but his dad had been suffering the late stages of prostate cancer. He might've lived another year at most. Harv and Holly knew, but few others.

"Will you call me as soon as you know more about Lauren's condition?" he asked.

"Yes, absolutely. We need to find your sister. Can you try calling her?"

Harv cut in. "I think it's better to let her initiate contact."

What Harv just said made sense, but he didn't know why . . .

His mind seemed to be experiencing a cascade failure, too many images flooding into his thoughts to process.

Trying to anchor himself, he grabbed a childhood memory.

A fishing trip. His father smiling as he reels the bass in. The lake's so beautiful. He knows why. It's the color of his father's eyes. It's the happiest moment of his life. Ever.

He pulled the memory closer, grasping it with both arms like the stuffed lion he'd adored. The lion had protected him, made him feel safe.

Memories. They were all he had now.

His poor mom. This was going to kill her.

Harv's voice emerged out of the void again. ". . . doesn't have me or Nate in her contacts. I don't want either of our numbers popping up on her phone until we know what her status is."

"On second thought, I agree," Holly said.

"Nate, did you catch that? Don't call Jin, okay?"

Harv knows I zoned again. "I won't."

"My house is being fumigated," said Holly, "so I've got Harvey in the Abraham Lincoln Suite at the Willard, and, Nathan, you're in the Jenny Lind Suite. I'm in a tiny hotel room with a single queen for the next few days. Nathan, I'd love to come over and stay with you."

"Count on it."

Harv said, "That private jet you chartered for us is a five-digit deal, especially on such short notice."

"Trust me, we all think you're worth it."

Nathan eased his grip on the phone.

"Listen, Ethan just came in. I have to run. I promise I'll keep you guys in the loop every step of the way. I'm so sorry this happened."

"Thanks, Holly. We'll talk again soon. Stay on the line, Harv."

"I love you," she said.

"I love you too. Thank you for calling." *Damn it, that sounded so cold and impersonal.* "Holly, I'm sorry. I didn't mean to sound like that. I'm just . . ."

"It's okay. I can't begin to imagine what you're feeling. Don't worry about Lauren. Metro PD has half a dozen officers guarding her and the other survivors—"

It hit him hard; his father wasn't the only one killed. Many families were hurt by this senseless butchery.

"We're sending some of our SAs as well. I've personally agreed to oversee the investigation. I think of Lauren as my niece. I've got to go. We'll talk again soon."

There was no sound, but Nathan sensed Holly leave the call.

"You still there, Nate?"

"I'm here."

"Don't worry about Lauren. Holly would never lie about her condition. She just wouldn't do it."

"Yeah, you're right. I'm just really angry right now. I'll never see my dad again. And Lauren had to watch him die."

"You'll see him again."

"I meant here, on Earth."

Harv said nothing for a long moment, then asked, "What do you make of Jin being MIA?"

"We shouldn't second-guess her motive. We weren't there." He thought for a few seconds and came up empty. "I told her if this sort of thing ever happened, she should contact me using the code words *Sierra Charlie.*"

He didn't state the obvious: *I hope the attackers didn't take her prisoner.*

"Let's hope you see those two words on your phone really soon."

"I probably shouldn't say this, but please don't feel like you have to come with me."

"You're right; you shouldn't say it."

He closed his eyes and rubbed his forehead. "Sorry, Harv."

"Already forgotten. Don't worry about it. Candace isn't home right now. She's visiting Lucas at Hillsdale College. I'm bacheloring it."

"Bring your dogs. They can hang with Grant and Sherman. Angelica can take care of them."

"What about the woman and her niece you rescued?"

He'd told Harv about his grocery store incident earlier. "They don't need twenty-four-hour care. They'll be okay."

"In the meantime, it would be wise for us to be on a higher level of alert even though no one should be able to find us."

"No one's totally unfindable, given a good enough tracker."

Nathan wouldn't say what they were both thinking. His sister could be strapped to a table, being rendered, holding out as long as possible. He hated the visual.

"Whoever it is, they found my dad. But he's easier to locate than you or me."

"And unless someone's hacked the state department or DOD, no one's going to get our personal information. The biggest variable is Jin. If they've got her, whoever *they* are, she could give us up."

Well, there it was. He didn't have to say it; Harv had. "That's assuming they want us, not her."

"Either way, it's an unhappy ending for her."

"If she's okay, she'll go after them and might get herself killed in the process."

Harv didn't say anything.

"Lauren needs her mom. I'm not parental material."

"Tell that to your dogs."

"Dogs don't drive and go on dates."

"Point taken, but I happen to know for a fact that Lauren would love to have you as her adopted dad."

"Do you have any idea how terrifying that sounds?"

"We're getting ahead of ourselves here. All we know is that Jin hasn't made contact. There are only two possibilities. She's unable to call, or she's unwilling to call. Let's stay positive and believe the latter. It fits her personality."

Again, he didn't say anything, and Harv waited through the silence. He really liked that about his friend.

"I need to call my mom."

"She's gotta be torn up over this. Promise me one thing, Nate. Don't watch the news coverage, okay? I'm serious. Don't watch it."

"I won't—" His phone made a telegraph sound. "Holly's text just came through. We're leaving in two hours."

"Since it's a private charter and we don't have to wait through long security lines, we've got enough time. I'll be there in thirty minutes, depending on traffic. Put Grant and Sherman on alert status."

"I will."

"Hang in there, partner. I'm on my way."

CHAPTER 18

During their drive to the airport, Vincent called with tragic news. One of his sons was dead. Anthony had died on scene from multiple gunshots to his chest. Charlene was still alive, but her condition remained critical. She'd be in emergency surgery for several more hours. The only good news in this whole sordid chain of events was that Vince's oldest son, Brian, had survived, and Denise Tabor was expected to be released from the hospital later this afternoon without major complications from the head trauma she'd sustained.

Hearing about Vince's murdered son hammered them. As did the growing realization that both the McBride and Beaumont families had been targeted almost simultaneously. The questions now became, who did it, and why? Nathan wasn't in the mood for much conversation, something Harv instinctively knew and respected. They spoke a little more about Nathan's concern for Lauren, Jin's MIA status, and his mom, but the death of his father remained at the forefront of his thoughts. He wanted to talk about it at some point but didn't yet feel in the right frame of mind.

They arrived at San Diego's jet center a little early, and their aircraft hadn't yet been cleared to leave. Jet pilots couldn't simply take off and land at will like they could at smaller airports.

So here they sat, waiting in luxury but feeling uncomfortable.

Nathan couldn't take his eyes off an annoying sight. Sitting across the room, a well-dressed man in his mid-twenties was either waiting to leave or waiting for someone to arrive. It didn't matter which.

Nathan shook his head. How could any human being become so deeply held hostage by a small electronic device? It defied understanding.

Five minutes into his surveillance, he'd discovered a predictable pattern in the young man's behavior. He'd pull his phone out of his pocket, peck away on it for about a minute, then put it back. That's when Nathan started his countdown. The kid wasn't able to go more than thirty seconds without looking at it again.

Cell phone out.

Peck, peck, peck, peck, peck . . .

Back in pocket.

Thirty seconds.

Cell phone out.

Peck, peck, peck, peck, peck . . .

Back in pocket.

On and on and on . . .

Nathan knew about the crippling effects of addiction all too well. He'd suffered from chronic alcoholism after returning from Nicaragua. Harv helped him beat it. Was cell phone addiction equally destructive? Maybe, maybe not. But he was willing to bet the mortgage this kid used his phone while driving. He'd seen a recent news story about a church van being plowed by a distracted driver who'd been texting. Twelve people killed. It pissed him off. A lot.

Harv's voice startled him. "Don't watch."

"Huh?"

"That kid. Don't let him bug you."

"It's friggin' unbelievable. He's a drooling addict with no situational awareness. None."

"In his defense, he doesn't need to be alert right now."

"Just like the people at the Brussels airport bombing didn't need to be alert?"

"He's not like you and me. Don't condemn him."

"Shit, Harv, you're right. I'm being a jerk. I don't know that kid's story. He could be an abuse victim or have some kind of mental condition. Maybe his phone is the only source of contentment he has. Why should I care?"

"Because someone with that degree of addiction also uses his phone while driving."

"Do me a favor."

"What's that?"

"If a cell phone addict ever kills me because he was texting while driving, deal with it." He knew Harv understood what he meant.

"Count on it. In a purely legal way, of course."

"Of course."

Harv nudged him. "Remember that conversation with Lauren you told me about? When she asked if it was hard to be a Christian? I totally agree with you. Right now, it's really hard. It's easy when things are going well. Your father's murder is tough to stomach. I'm sure Vince is dealing with the same emotional turmoil—worse."

"I'm so damned angry. I could scream until my throat bleeds. I've been having these dark fantasies of torturing the assholes to death with medieval devices."

"A certain amount of that is normal. I'm guilty of the same thing. Stone was more than a friend; he was like a father to me."

"He loved you, as much as me."

Harv didn't say anything.

"Don't let me stray, Harv."

"Don't worry. I won't. Forget about that kid. He's not why you're angry anyway. Given different circumstances, he wouldn't bother you at all."

"You're probably right."

"Thanks for putting your phone on speaker when you called your mom earlier."

"She also thinks of you like family."

"Same here. I was glad to hear Lauren's going to be okay."

"Yeah, me too."

They sat in silence for a spell.

"Don't worry about Jin," Harv said. "She's a survivor."

"I've got these horrible thoughts of what she might be going through right now."

"Let's not assume they took her captive. The reverse might've happened: she might've nabbed one of the shooters. I wouldn't put it past her."

"Me either. I just wish we knew which it was."

"Are you angry that she hasn't made contact, assuming she can?"

"Yeah, Harv, I am. It's so . . ."

"Cold-blooded?" Harv asked.

"I didn't want to use those words, but yeah."

"Maybe by the time we land in DC we'll know if she's okay."

"Let's hope so, for Lauren's sake."

***

Their Challenger touched down at Reagan National within one minute of the pilot's prediction of 11:23 p.m. eastern time. Not too shabby. He sent a text to Holly even though it wouldn't be a long taxi over to the jet center.

Neither of them had dozed off during the flight. Too much on their minds—like hunting down the people responsible for attacking his and Vince's families and *dealing* with them.

They'd reminisced about some good times he'd had with his father on camping trips, family vacations, and church mission trips. But neither had felt especially talkative. Understandable, given the events of the day.

Truth was, Nathan hated small talk. How's the weather? How's the family? How's the dog? It was so pointless. Oh, he made small talk when the situation called for it, but he didn't like the pretense. He and Harv were quite comfortable sitting in silence. At least the chartered flight had been stress free. He'd send a personal thank-you note along with a case of wine to Director Lansing.

Ever since college, he'd had a hard time with air travel because of his size. Coach? Forget it. His knees always pushed against the seat in front of him. Several years ago, he and Harv had considered buying a small jet. They'd run some numbers and determined they'd still lose money even if they rented it. Pilot salary. Maintenance. Fuel. Hangar rent. Management fee. Airport taxes. A loser all the way around.

Still, flying by private jet remained a guilty pleasure, but not without unforeseen risks. At one point, Harv had caught him staring at the liquor cabinet. His friend cleared his throat and issued a *don't-even-think-about-it* shake of the head.

Truth was, for the first time in many years, Nathan *had* been thinking about it, *strongly* thinking about it.

Holly sent a return text saying she was waiting on the tarmac.

Even as dark as his mood was, he looked forward to seeing her. Because of Holly's job, they only saw each other four or five times a year, mostly when Nathan traveled to DC. Being the chief of staff for the FBI's thirty-five thousand people, she didn't get a lot of free time. Much to Harv's chagrin, Nathan often flew his helicopter across the country. It took about seventeen to eighteen hours of actual flying time—including departures and approaches. The biggest challenge was the radio work, and in reality, it wasn't all that difficult. He always preprogrammed the frequencies for the next leg prior to taking off. There was something about sitting in the cockpit of a helicopter that appealed to him, something he couldn't explain to nonpilots.

At any rate, he'd be visiting DC a lot more in the future.

His mom was alone now.

The pilot taxied over to Signature Flight Support's jet center, the same place where he parked his Bell.

He crossed the aisle, looked out the window, and saw Holly standing near the building. She must've used her FBI badge to get through.

Seeing her made him feel light-headed, almost euphoric.

How does she do this to me? I must be under some kind of spell.

A minute later, the first officer emerged from the cockpit and opened the fuselage door.

Signature's staff offered to carry their bags, but neither of them needed help. Nathan had a lot of faults, but being stingy wasn't one of them. Everybody within eyesight got a twenty-dollar tip, except the pilots, who gratefully accepted $300 each.

With that taken care of, he and Holly practically ran toward each other.

No words were spoken. They simply merged.

It felt so good to hug this woman. One of life's unexplained miracles. The coldness and cruelty of the world disappeared into white noise. Nothing else mattered.

Life became Holly.

"You two are made for each other," Harv said.

They were.

"I'm sorry I live so far away," Nathan said. "I should move out here or buy a condo or something. My mom is going to need me."

"It wouldn't break my heart. I'd love to spend more time with you."

"Why don't you do it?" Harv offered. "I can handle First Security."

Nathan figured it was Harv's turn for a hug, so he let go of Holly and watched two irreplaceable people embrace each other. If anything ever happened to them . . .

Don't think about that. Enjoy the moment.

The pilots were in the process of doing a walk around, but they stopped and waved when the automatic door leading to Signature's plush interior whooshed open. He waved back.

"You don't have security?" Harv asked, looking around.

"I'm afraid I don't warrant it." She smiled. "I'm just not that important."

"You are to me," Nathan said. "Thank you for picking us up."

"Of course. Besides, I don't get to drive all that often. I need to keep in practice."

"Nate told me your house in Rockville is only a five-minute walk from the Metro station."

"I take the Red Line to Federal Triangle. The Hoover Building's only a couple of blocks away. I use a bureau car once I'm there. Seems like I'm doing a lot of traveling lately. More than I'd like."

Nathan said, "It's really great being here, Holly, even under the circumstances."

"I wish I could take tomorrow off to spend time with you guys. Actually, Ethan said I could, but I'm not comfortable being away from my desk right now."

"Hey, don't worry about it," Nathan said. "It would be really bad form. I'd never let you do it. The FBI's chief of staff doesn't take the day off after a US senator is assassinated. It's—" He cut himself off, feeling another wave of emotion.

They stopped walking, and Holly hugged him again. As before, the world lost focus, and the ache in his soul didn't feel as deep.

"I'm so sorry about all of this. How's your mom doing?"

"Not well, but it's a good thing she has Lauren to look after. I need to call her again. She's camped out in Lauren's room. If it's okay, we'd like to head over there right away, but I want to make sure Lauren's feeling up to it first."

"No problem. She's at George Washington University Hospital. It's been quiet the rest of the day. There haven't been any more attacks. Speculation is rampant on the news networks. Truth is, we don't have much right now. We haven't been able to ID the gunmen in either shooting. Unfortunately, the wounded gunman from the back alley bled out before the paramedics arrived."

"Jin?"

"We think she shot him in both shoulders and took out a knee so he couldn't get away or cause any harm. No other explanation seems to fit. The ballistics and shell-casing analysis will confirm our theory."

He nodded but didn't say anything. He'd reached mental burnout. All he wanted to do was hold her a little longer.

"Sorry, Nathan."

"It's okay. Just don't let go."

"Hey, listen, you guys, I can easily get a cab over to the Willard."

"Harv . . ." His tone said it all.

"Okay, sorry I mentioned it."

"We don't usually hug each other like this, but maybe we ought to."

Holly nodded into his shoulder; she must have needed it as much as he did.

They let go and walked across a small parking lot to a Lincoln sedan.

This wasn't her car. She drove a white Ford Explorer. "Don't tell me you came straight from the office."

"Okay, I won't tell you."

"That's what, a fourteen-hour day?"

"We're going full speed on the investigation. We need to ID the shooters. Everything hinges on it."

"Remember when we talked about burnout the first time we met?"

"It's hard to forget. You said I'd break down into tears without any good reason, but this isn't one of those times."

Harv let Nathan take the front passenger seat by getting into the back without asking. He was four inches taller than his friend.

"Any leads you can share?"

"Based only on their physical appearance, we're certain all six of them are of Middle Eastern descent."

"There were six gunmen?" Harv asked.

"That we know of. Two in San Diego and four in Mabel's."

Her phone bleeped to life.

"You should take a look," Nathan said. "I think under the circumstances, it's okay."

"Thanks . . . It's Ethan. I need to take it."

Director Lansing was a major figure in Washington, having kept his job through the change in administrations, a rare achievement.

"Hi, Ethan . . . Yes, they're with me right now . . . Okay . . . When? . . . We'll be there as fast as we can . . . Okay . . . I won't . . ." She ended the call and said, "Your sister just made contact."

CHAPTER 19

"That's good news," Nathan said. "As opposed to not knowing if she's alive or dead."

"I don't have anything more than that. DNI Benson called Ethan with the news. He knows I'm picking you up."

"Benson knows you're picking us up or Ethan?"

"Probably both. We'll need to delay your visit with Lauren."

She hadn't posed it as a question.

"Where are we going?" Nathan asked.

"The White House."

"The White House . . ."

She looked over her shoulder and accelerated into traffic. "We aren't going inside. The DNI's wrapping up a meeting with the president on the two shootings. We're meeting him outside the West Wing's entrance."

"You mean Benson?"

"Sorry, yes. We'll have to go through security. You guys don't have any of those, you know, *Crocodile Dundee* knives on you, do you?"

Harv said, "We left them in the car in San Diego—just in case we got summoned to the White House."

"If I'd known about this, I would've told you. Is there anything in your luggage?"

"Nope," said Nathan. "Just the normal stuff."

"Why do we need to meet with Benson?" Harv asked.

"Apparently your sister's refusing to cooperate until she talks to you first."

"Sounds like Jin, all right." He hadn't said it kindly.

"You okay?"

"Truthfully, I'm a little ticked off she didn't make contact sooner. I'm not going to tell Lauren about this until I have a green light from Jin. It's her decision when to tell Lauren, not mine or anyone else's."

"Hopefully, you'll be able to tell Lauren her mom's alive tonight or first thing in the morning."

Harv said, "Depending on how the rest of our evening goes, it might be first thing in the morning. It's already pretty late for a visit."

"Hang on back there," said Holly. "I'm going to be speeding a little."

"A little," Harv said flatly.

"We need to be there when Jin calls Benson back," she explained. "We should make it, barely."

"I guess Benson must've told Jin we were here," Harv said.

"Yes, the pilots called me just after you touched down, and I passed that on to Ethan, who then told Director Benson. Information travels fast around here."

He shook his head.

"It's not a bad thing, Nathan. It's supposed to work that way. Unauthorized leaking is bad, not the sharing of intel between agencies. The intelligence community directors have an unofficial hotline of sorts. It's a little different with the FBI. We report to both the Office of the Director of National Intelligence and the attorney general."

"Who has the last say?" Harv asked.

Holly smiled. "Depends on who you talk to."

"Do you guys mind if I call my mom and let her know we made it out here okay and that we may not be stopping by tonight?"

"Please do," Holly said.

"You call your mom," Harv said, "and I'll call 911 ahead of time to report our crash. And I thought I drove fast."

"Is he always like this?" she asked.

"Pretty much," he said.

His mom said Lauren was asleep, but otherwise okay. Although she'd love to see him, she thought it best if he came by in the morning. She'd be spending the night in Lauren's room in any case. She also assured him that there were police officers all over the place.

Overall, pretty good news. One less thing to worry about. He spent another five minutes on the phone, mostly listening. His mom needed to . . . vent? No, that wasn't the right word. She just needed to talk to her son.

"For not getting a lot of practice, you're a damned fine driver," Harv told Holly when Nathan ended the call.

"Thank you," she said, turning right on Seventeenth Street.

Nathan knew this area well. He'd been in his teens the first time he'd toured the hub of the executive branch with his dad.

After being carefully identified, they had to pass through two additional manned gates before rolling up to the West Wing's curb where three black limos sat waiting. Their Lincoln was approached again by men with bulges under their coats. Nathan had no idea who was who. Was he looking at the DNI's security people or the Secret Service? He suddenly felt underdressed; his 5.11 Tactical garb didn't seem formal enough.

"You feeling it, Harv?" he asked.

"Yeah, this is friggin' intense. These guys are some serious hombres. Let's just say I'm not planning to make any sudden moves."

"You guys are overreacting. Everything's fine."

"If you say so," Harv said.

Holly asked them to sit tight while she got out and exchanged some words with one of the men. She turned and nodded. They got out and walked toward the parked limousines.

Introductions were made. Then one of the Secret Service agents opened the door to the last black limo and gestured for the three of them to get in. Nathan had a sudden visual of entering a viper's nest but knew it wasn't a fair comparison. The life these public servants lived was mired in secrecy but lacking in privacy. He wondered how they coped with the near-constant pressure from day to day.

The big car's interior felt cramped and comfortable at the same time. Two opposing sets of couches faced each other. A man and a woman sat inside. He recognized Benson from TV but didn't know the woman.

"Thank you for coming on such short notice," Benson said, shaking hands with the three of them.

"We're glad to do it, Director Benson."

"First let me say I'm very sorry about your father. He was a true patriot in every sense of the word. How is your mom holding up?"

"Not very well. They were married for sixty-two years."

"Please offer her my condolences."

"Thank you, I will."

"I'm comfortable using first names." He introduced the woman as Ms. Kelley Ford, the ODNI's principal deputy director, second in line to the throne. She smiled at the reference and shook hands with everyone.

Ford started to look vaguely familiar, but he couldn't place her.

"I stole Kelley from Langley. She was the third in command over there."

"I met you a long time ago," she told Nathan.

He had it. "The wall . . ."

Ford nodded.

She'd been standing in front of the CIA's memorial wall, and they'd struck up a conversation about the absence of names under the stars. He remembered her amber-green eyes.

"I was a data analyst back then for Latin American ops." She glanced at Benson, then said, "I reviewed your files."

He didn't say anything. Neither did Harv.

"I was impressed with the content," she added.

"Thank you." He didn't know how else to respond. Fortunately he didn't have to. Benson's cell rang.

"Yes . . . They're here . . . Put her through." Benson put the call on speaker.

"Nathan, are you there?"

The voice on the phone end was definitely his sister; her voice still carried that strange combination of three accents.

"Yeah, Jin, it's me."

"Am I on speaker?"

"Yes."

"Tell me the exact time."

Benson held his phone out, and Nathan leaned forward for a closer look. "Nine fifty-one."

"What are the two code words we use in an emergency?"

"Sierra Charlie."

"Please tell me who's with you right now."

"I'm sitting in a limousine across from Director of National Intelligence Scott Benson and Principal Deputy Director Kelley Ford. Harvey and Holly are also with me. These people are the real deal, Jin."

"Where are you?"

"At the curb outside the West Wing of the White House."

"Are we being recorded?"

Benson nodded.

"Yes."

"Is Lauren one hundred percent safe?" she asked.

Another nod from Benson.

"Yes."

Jin paused for a long moment. "Is she okay?"

"Lauren's currently sleeping, and my mother's with her. She's expected to make a full recovery."

The pause on the other end was a good thing. He pictured Jin closing her eyes in relief.

"Would you trust DNI Benson with your life?"

"Yes. I've done it before."

"I know who's responsible for both attacks today, but I don't know why."

"They're connected, then?" Benson asked.

"Yes, they're connected."

Nathan let Benson continue even though he had lots of questions.

"Was Stone the primary target?"

"Yes."

"Are you willing to come in and be debriefed?" the DNI asked, glancing at Nathan as he spoke.

"Yes, but not yet."

"Have you told anyone else what you just told us?"

"No."

"What do you want?"

"I want your word my life with Lauren will continue as it was."

"If that's what you want, then you'll have it. By all accounts, you saved countless lives. Your presence in DC is . . . unexpected, but we're glad you were here."

Well played, Nathan thought. Wisely, Benson hadn't chided her about being in Washington. When he'd talked with Jin before the trip, he'd advised her—in the strongest possible terms—to let her WITSEC handler know she planned to visit DC. Obviously, she hadn't done that.

"Will you tell us where you are?"

"I'll call back in twenty minutes with an address. The scene is secure but bring an ambulance. I had to work on the fifth gunman for a long time before he caved. He's not in good shape. I'll be gone by the time you arrive."

"Ms. Marchand, the gunman from the alley didn't survive. He bled to death. We need the last man alive. Are you confident he's not in immediate danger of dying?"

"Yes."

"Will you give us a general area where we'll be going?"

"Friendship Heights."

"Are you okay communicating directly with me from now on? Do you want your brother present?"

"No, that won't be necessary."

"Jin," Nathan said, "you don't need to—"

The call ended.

"Re-lo-cate," he said slowly.

"Played like a veteran," Benson said.

"Can't say I blame her."

"Nor I. We've reviewed her file, at least everything we have. It's what we don't have that concerns us."

"Scott, may I speak freely?" Nathan asked.

"Yes, but hang on for just a sec. Holly, please get a special-response team moving toward Friendship Heights and arrange an ambulance for Jin's prisoner. Whoever gets there first is to stage until your people arrive. No one enters the house until the FBI's SRT is on scene. I'm not sure whose jurisdiction that is . . . might be Metro PD."

"I'll find out and get things rolling." Pulling her cell, Holly stepped out of the limo.

"Sorry, Nathan, please continue."

"I totally understand where you're coming from, but my sister has no agenda. She just wants to live out the rest of her life being the best mom she can to her daughter. She's not a sleeper agent, waiting to be activated. In fact, North Korea would love to get her back, put her on public trial for treason, and then execute her slowly. Now, I just told my sister she can trust you. Am I mistaken about that?"

"Absolutely not."

"Good, because she's not holding out for any other reason than to protect her daughter. My niece, by the way."

"Understood. We'll proceed on her terms. It seems we have little choice. I don't need to say this, but I will: the trust you mentioned has become a triangle. Her, us, and now you."

"You're loud and clear. I just put myself on the line for her."

Benson smiled. "I wouldn't put it quite that strongly. Let's just say we'll be . . . unhappy if she plays any games with us."

"Not her style."

"Let's hope not."

"May I ask a question?" Nathan asked.

"By all means."

"How did she get through to you?"

Benson's broad smile returned. "She used your name of course."

"And that's all it took?"

"Well, you do share the name with your father, and you're not exactly an unknown commodity in my circles."

He didn't say anything.

"Don't worry. It's a compliment. Rebecca Cantrell is one of your biggest advocates. Don't ever repeat this, but I consider her my best IC director. We go back quite a few years."

"We'd like to be included in . . . things to come."

"I hear you, but it's not my call. My office has no direct law enforcement powers. You'll need Ethan's approval. Given your history, I don't see it as a major issue. You'll have my endorsement as well."

"Thank you."

"Harvey, you've been awfully quiet," said Benson.

"Jin said the two shootings are related. I'm wondering what that relationship is."

"Rest assured, we're going to find out. Since there's a direct connection between your father and the Beaumont family, we'll be digging hard. I'm certain we'll know a lot more once the FBI's SRT reaches our mystery address in Friendship Heights. I'll keep you two in the loop. Kelley's going to give you her direct number. I can't tell you everything that's going on, but I will tell you that President Trump's personally monitoring the investigation into your father's assassination." Benson motioned with his head toward the West Wing's entrance. "I've got to head back inside. Give me Vincent's wife's name again?"

"Charlene. Retired Marine staff sergeant."

"Listen, we're going to find and prosecute the people responsible. Until then, you and Harv are in standby mode. Please be patient."

"We'll be ready."

"Over the next few hours, we're going to selectively leak information to the press. Primarily, that all seven gunmen were killed during the attacks, and we don't have IDs on any of them. Let's hope your sister doesn't contact the press."

"She won't."

With that, everyone climbed out of the limo. Nathan thanked Benson for being inclusive and open, then assured him that he and Harv were team players.

"You've already proven that," Benson said. "We'll be in touch soon."

Holly was still on the phone and gave them a one-minute gesture with a forefinger.

After Benson and Ford went inside, Nathan took a moment to look around and soak all of this in. It wasn't every day you got to be inside the White House grounds. With neutral expressions, the Secret Service agents stood guard on the curb, watching their every move. Never mind they'd already been cleared through security and thoroughly searched—including a meticulous pat down that made the TSA body searches pale in comparison. These guys didn't use the backs of their hands.

She finished her call and joined them near the Lincoln.

"That was quite a meeting," she said.

"I'm just really glad Jin's okay. Did you hear it, Harv? The tone of her voice?"

"Yeah, she sounded a little . . . distracted."

"Distracted?" Holly asked incredulously.

It would be best to drop it because he couldn't easily explain what he'd heard in Jin's voice.

"I'm sorry. I didn't mean to sound like that."

"Forget it, Holly. We're all feeling it. I keep seeing my dad's face."

"Me too," she said.

"It's definitely too late to visit Lauren, so let's head over to the Willard and check into our suites."

She leaned her head back and unclipped her hair bun. "Sounds good. I'd love to put my feet up."

When Nathan looked at Harv, she punched his arm.

"What?" he asked.

CHAPTER 20

Two Days Ago

El Lobo loved the open sea, especially in a high-performance boat like this one. Sleek and streamlined, this amazing Mercedes-Benz Arrow 460-GT was fourteen meters of comfort and power. Rumor had it Mr. A paid $1.5 million for it. Whatever the price tag, it made the two-hour round trip out to the *Yoonsuh* and back not only tolerable, but fun.

After returning to Puerto Los Cabos Marina, the next leg of their journey back to Rancho Del Seco would be much less enjoyable. Long helicopter rides had never appealed to him. And this one was colossal. Two legs. Cabo San Lucas to Chihuahua, then Chihuahua to Rancho Del Seco. Six hundred miles total.

With most fixed-wing aircraft, if you took your hands off the controls, the things flew themselves for a while. No so with helicopters. They became unstable almost immediately. He'd actually flown one a few times—straight and level—but he had neither the time nor the desire to become a helicopter pilot. He supposed there was a certain exhilaration associated with vertical takeoff and landings, but he preferred cruising at forty thousand feet in Mr. A's private jet, sipping a glass of fine wine.

Quattro was an excellent navigator and had them on an exact course to rendezvous with the *Yoonsuh*'s coordinates, some thirty miles offshore. The swell was moderate, around two meters, so the Arrow had no trouble maintaining a fast cruising speed.

El Lobo began to feel a little uneasy when they hadn't yet spotted Mr. A's luxury yacht. According to the nav screen, they were still a good fifteen nautical miles away, so there was no need to panic. Yet.

***

Captain Santino watched the navigation screen closely. The readout now showed 22°56'43" N 110°25'57" W. He cut his engines to make minimal headway into the swell and keep the *Yoonsuh* close to the rendezvous point.

His first officer reported an intermittent radar contact due east. Santino hoped it was Mr. A's Arrow. He couldn't get his creepy passengers and their cargo off his ship soon enough.

They'd come out of their staterooms last night to sit on the upper sundeck, but they'd summarily ignored the *Yoonsuh*'s cabin attendant when he asked if they wanted something to eat or drink, an incredibly rude and arrogant thing to do.

Rude and arrogant? Those two men were assholes.

Even if they didn't speak Spanish, they could've acknowledged the attendant's presence. They'd pretended like he didn't exist. Santino had watched from the diving platform, where he'd been enjoying an evening cigar, something he did when feeling troubled.

Five minutes after spotting the radar contact, it became clear the blip was heading straight for his ship. No words needed, he exchanged a glance with his first officer.

A few minutes later, as the Arrow approached the stern, the stark contrast wasn't lost on him: such a beautiful vessel carrying such ugly people.

Santino never judged people by their color, religion, or nationality—only by their actions. El Lobo and Quattro were as ugly as men came. Without conscience, they did whatever they wanted and never faced consequences. He hoped that would change someday. For now, he just wanted to get this transfer over with.

His first officer threw two lines across to Quattro, who secured them to the bow and stern of the Arrow with simple layman's knots.

"Welcome aboard," Santino said.

El Lobo hopped across, but Quattro stayed put.

"How was your journey?"

El Lobo looked back at the luxury speedboat. "She handles like a champ. I understand you chose this boat for Mr. A."

"Indeed I did."

"Where are our couriers?" El Lobo asked.

"They're still in their staterooms."

"Well, go get them."

"Certainly. Would you like something to—"

"We're a little pressed for time. We have a long helicopter flight back to Rancho Del Seco."

"Of course. I'll be right back."

Below, he knocked on the stateroom doors of his guests and told them in Spanish they'd arrived.

The two men appeared, didn't say a word, and brushed past him on their way topside. Rude as ever. Santino noticed the backpack right away; they'd obviously transferred the goods from the hard cases into the pack.

He followed his passengers to the sundeck and stayed behind while they stepped down to the diving platform. Without saying a word, the lead courier handed the backpack across to Quattro. El Lobo thanked them for making the voyage, then joined them on the diving platform—

In a quick move, El Lobo pulled a tiny automatic pistol from his front pocket.

What the hell? The move stunned Santino and he held perfectly still. Anything else might spell death.

The two Asian men reacted quickly but not in time.

They tried to lunge forward and grab the coyote, but El Lobo shot both of them four times in quick succession. Their brains and chest cavities destroyed, the two men collapsed to the platform and lay still.

It seemed surreal, like something out of a movie. Had he really just witnessed a double murder? Was he complicit? The answer sickened him. Of course he was complicit.

He realized he was squinting and relaxed his eyes.

El Lobo looked up and waved a hand. "Don't worry, Captain. I have full authority to do that. I trust you'll dispose of the bodies and clean up the mess?"

He put on his best "everything's normal" face, but his voice nearly cracked. "We'll take care of it." Captain Santino suddenly realized he'd never seen men murdered, and it surprised him how vile it was. Vomit rose in his throat, but he fought it off. Losing control in front of these men wasn't an option.

"Captain?"

"Yes, I, ah, was just wondering if you and Mr. Quattro would like to take some fresh yellowtail with you. I caught it a few hours ago. We can easily pack it in ice." He cringed inwardly, hoping his offer hadn't been as lame as it sounded.

El Lobo smiled. "Thank you, but no. We're looking forward to our cruise next month. I hear your crew's hospitality is second to none."

"Thank you," Santino said. "We're happy to host you."

El Lobo stepped onto the Arrow's stern, then slowly turned.

"The only people in the world who know about this . . . transfer . . . are you, your crew, us, and Mr. A."

"We don't know about any transfer," Santino said. "We're here to refuel at Puerto Los Cabos and be on our way."

The madman's smile returned. "Smooth sailing, Captain."

With that, Quattro untied the mooring lines, tossed them onto the *Yoonsuh*'s diving platform, and offered a friendly wave goodbye.

Santino waved back, then had to steady himself as a swell rocked the ship. He couldn't remember ever feeling such raw fear.

When the Arrow was several hundred meters away, he hustled up to the bridge and found his first officer—looking pale. Seasickness didn't begin to describe his friend's expression.

"Let's get the hell out of here," Santino said. "We'll deal with the mess later."

CHAPTER 21

Nathan turned off the TV at just after 3:00 a.m. Half an hour ago, Holly had returned to her office. Despite the concern he'd voiced, she intended to pull an all-nighter. So much for her spending the night with him . . .

Sitting alone in a constricting darkness, he felt emotionally torn in half. He and Holly had made love, an unbelievably warm and restorative experience, but the death of his father felt equally cold and crippling. Was this the human condition? A constant dichotomy of contentment versus wanting? How do people ever find true happiness? He knew there was no metaphorical pot of gold, but good grief . . .

It seemed like an alternate reality; he couldn't believe his dad was dead, especially the way it had gone down. Publicly murdered in cold blood. The last time he felt this level of emptiness, he'd been close to death. Part of him wanted to destroy the hotel suite around him, while another part wanted to weep in silence. So which was it? Uncontrollable rage or hopeless despair? Maybe it didn't matter. The result was the same.

Detachment.

He didn't feel human, and that scared him. The dark fantasies he'd been visualizing were beyond what a normal human being should think about, let alone ever do, but if he got his hands on the person or persons who'd ordered his father's murder, they would experience new heights of anguish and pain.

He should've heeded Harv's advice and not watched the news, but he'd turned it on anyway.

Including his father and Vincent Beaumont's youngest son, eighteen people had been slaughtered. Eleven in Mabel's and seven at the UTC mall. Twenty-one people were wounded, with five still critical, Charlene included. She'd fallen into a coma. Vincent's oldest son, Brian, had escaped death by running away, but it seemed like little consolation.

At least the coverage wasn't wall to wall anymore. The networks were cramming commercials into their broadcasts. One second he was watching gurneys being loaded into ambulances; the next he was being coaxed by a cheesy advertisement into buying a pillow. What a wonderful combo: murder and pillows.

The massacre at Mabel's remained the lead story, with the UTC shooting and Charlene Beaumont coming in a close second. The networks made it abundantly clear that the family of the nation's largest private military contractor had been targeted. Speculation and innuendo among the endless parade of talking heads ran rampant. The Beaumont family had been attacked because of BSI's alleged war crimes in the Gulf region. The Beaumont family had been attacked because BSI's personnel made three times what their US military counterparts made. The Beaumont family had been attacked because the moon was made of green cheese. Blah, blah, blah. On and on it went, hour after hour after hour . . . The coverage was unwatchable.

He'd never realized the true nature of the cable news networks until now. He'd watched coverage of high-profile terrorist events, but never in this state of mind. His father was being used as a tool to drive higher ratings. The harsh truth? People were making money from his family's tragedy.

Murder and pillows.

It came on suddenly, an overwhelming desire to belt down a few drinks. And why the hell not?

He walked over to the minibar and stared. Maybe he should've asked for the booze to be removed. Useless, he knew. Temptation wasn't distance sensitive. Five steps or five miles. What difference did it make? He found himself wondering why he'd quit drinking in the first place.

You know why.

Next came the lies, excuses, and justifications. All of them painfully familiar. What would it hurt to have just one drink? He didn't have to drive anywhere tonight, and he didn't have to be 100 percent alert. It's not like he and Harv were targets of whoever had killed his father. Having one drink didn't mean he'd automatically become an alcoholic again, did it? Just one drink to take the edge off . . . Who could it hurt?

You know who it will hurt.

He reached out.

Pulled the cabinet door open.

Well, there they were.

Right in front of him.

Shiny and clean. Small and colorful. They looked like secret elixirs. Like magic bullets.

Was he really going to dismiss twenty-five years of sobriety because a bunch of pathetic losers had murdered his father? Wouldn't that make him a casualty as well?

He pulled his phone and hit the calculator icon.

Twenty-five years multiplied by 365 equaled 9,125 days—not including leap year adjustments. He multiplied the days by twenty-four.

Incredible. He'd been sober for 219,000 hours. So where was the harm in one drink, just one, and no more than one?

You know the harm.

That's always how it started—with just one. One today, maybe one next week. Once a week turns into twice a week. Before long, it's three a week. Three a week quickly morphs into once a day. Then once a day turns into twice a day. Twice a day turns into three. Four. Five. Six. Ten. Bottom line? Hitting the bottle just once leads to becoming a full-blown drunk again.

So what?

Who gave a damn?

And more importantly, who would know?

The answer slammed him.

You'll know.

There's no escaping the truth. It can't be hidden, denied, or delayed. It is what it is. The truth.

Shit. This really sucked. The urge seemed to be intensifying with each passing second. The longer he stood here, the more inviting those enchanted little bottles of amber liquid looked.

When he realized his hands were balled in fists, he tilted his head back, closed his eyes, and prayed for strength and courage.

And the face that descended upon his soul was Holly's. He felt her touch, warmth, and kindness. Her unconditional acceptance of who he was and always would be.

You need to call her right now.

As if controlled by an unknown force, his hand reached down and tapped her number.

The voice on the other end held beauty and grace. "Can't sleep?"

"I'm standing in front of the minibar."

"Don't you dare!"

"What's wrong with me, Holly? I feel like I'm losing it. Nothing seems real right now."

"I'm real, and I love you."

He closed his eyes and steadied himself against the wall.

"I know why you called me."

He didn't say anything.

"You called because you knew how deeply it would hurt me if you destroyed yourself."

"I saw your face when I closed my eyes and prayed."

"I'll always be here for you, Nathan. Do you want me to come over?"

"I'll be okay. I just have to work through this."

"*We* have to work through it."

His phone vibrated. "Harv's calling. This isn't a coincidence."

"I just sent him a text. I don't want you to be alone right now."

"Hang on." He brought Harv on to the call. "Holly's on the line with us."

They said hello to each other.

"How're you doing, old friend?"

"I'm okay. I had a weak moment in front of the minibar."

"So why didn't you do it?" Harv asked.

"Holly said it was selflessness on my part."

"What do you think?"

"I'm not sure. I guess I didn't want to hurt the people I love."

"You knew that becoming a drunk again would do that."

"I'm not very good at sharing my feelings, but you and Harv are more than family. You're part of me. Without you guys, I'd feel . . . I don't know . . . empty."

"That's very sweet of you to say," Holly said. "I feel the same way about you."

"The three of us are a team, Nate. We'll never betray each other."

"I'd die first." And he would, no questions asked.

"You asked me something," Holly said, "during our drive up to the cabin, when we were pursuing the Bridgestone brothers. I'll never forget it. You asked, 'Am I really that transparent?' I also remember my answer like it was yesterday. I said, 'Not at all. Just truthful.'"

He gripped the phone tighter and didn't say anything.

Harv took command of the call. "You are not going to drink alcohol under any circumstances. Are we clear on that, Marine?"

"Aye aye, sir."

"I'm coming over. You aren't the only one who can't sleep. I'll be there in two minutes. There will be no booze on your breath."

"Thanks, Harv. I don't know what I'd do without you guys."

"Get a pot of coffee going. I'm on my way."

"Okay. Holly, would you stay on the line?"

"I will."

There was no sound when Harv hung up, but he felt it. "Thanks for asking Harv to call."

"I didn't think you'd mind."

"I'm an alcoholic, and I always will be. It doesn't hurt admitting it anymore."

"You've accepted it about yourself."

He nodded, then realized she couldn't see him. "Yes. It'll never go away. Tonight's urge just felt really intense."

"I'm glad you called."

"Honestly, I saw your face. You looked like a descending angel. Holly, we're not married by law, but in the eyes of God, I feel we have a covenant with one another."

"I feel the same way."

"I love you, Holly." There'd been a time in his life when he never said those words to anyone.

"I love you too."

He ended the call, walked away from the minibar, and used the security latch to block the room's door from closing. He felt short of breath and couldn't believe what he'd been about to do. Was he really that vulnerable, after all these decades? Did other alcoholics go through this? Were they all just a *bad moment* away from becoming drunks again?

A sobering question, no pun intended.

He thought about Grant and Sherman, just then, about how giving and accepting they were. He loved interacting with his dogs, admired their uncomplicated lives. No envy. No greed. No wrath. They were never tempted by the seven deadly sins. Well . . . maybe gluttony.

A funny comic came to mind; he couldn't remember where he'd seen it. The comic showed a bunch of dogs in a lifeboat with a sinking ship in the background. The caption of the comic read, WHY DOGS DON'T SURVIVE DISASTERS AT SEA. The lead dog was asking the question, "How many vote we eat all the food now?" Every dog in the lifeboat had its paw in the air.

Nathan smiled at the memory. Whoever had written the comic knew dogs well.

A soft knock announced Harv's arrival, and he gave his friend a tight embrace. They had, after all, been through life and death together.

"I don't know how you do it, Harv. Seeing you feels like descending out of the clouds." A sentiment all pilots understood.

"Let's go have that coffee," Harv said. "I want you to tell me all about your dad. Things you've never shared, things you've been afraid to tell. I want it all. Don't hold anything back."

"I'm sure there's a method to your madness, Harv."

"There is, and it will be clear to you soon enough."

CHAPTER 22

Carlos Alisio's private jet flight from Mexico City to A.G. International Airport in Ciudad Juárez had taken forever. He couldn't stop thinking about the payback for the death of his father.

He wanted news.

Immediately after entering the jet center's lounge, he asked the staff to turn on one of the American cable news networks. He didn't care which. Since English was a second language, he had no problem following the lead stories.

Stone McBride was killed, but the Beaumont bitch was still alive, and one of her offspring too. His attempt to emotionally destroy the great Vincent Beaumont by killing the murderer's entire family had failed. He wanted *all* of them dead, not some of them.

El Lobo had some explaining to do.

He didn't plan to fire or kill the crafty coyote; El Lobo remained too valuable to his smuggling empire. More importantly, the man could be trusted—his most valuable asset. Relatively speaking, Alisio wasn't all that disappointed by the result, but he'd never signal that to El Lobo. Better to keep him guessing a little.

He wanted to head straight for the Rancho Del Seco, but later this morning, he had an important breakfast meeting with the mayor that couldn't be canceled or postponed. Not all his sources of income came from illegal activity; he'd developed quite the portfolio of hotels, restaurants, and retail shopping centers, many of them here, in beleaguered Ciudad Juárez.

He could've used the helicopter to fly out to the ranch, but his breakfast location was well east of the city. It made sense to use the limos, then continue on to the ranch rather than return to the airport. Besides, one of his three helicopters was already at the ranch. El Lobo and Quattro had used it to transport the goods from Cabo. He'd use the helicopter on the return trip and have his people drive the limos back to Ciudad Juárez.

He felt like he owned this town. He could have anyone in local government fired with nothing more than a phone call. The same was true about hiring. For now, he was happy with the status quo. Well, almost. A city planner had been waffling about the environmental impact of his two-hundred-acre luxury resort project. Yes, it encroached into the Chihuahuan Desert, but that's what people wanted. They wanted a desert experience coupled with every imaginable amenity. The planner didn't need to go away yet. There was still a chance he could retain his job—as long as he didn't interfere with the permit process.

After a successful powwow with the mayor and city manager, his motorcade of three limousines worked its way east, leaving the vast metropolitan area behind in favor of a dry and inhospitable landscape. Why anyone wanted to live out here defied understanding. There was nothing. No restaurants. No spas. No nightclubs. No hotels. And no women—except for imports.

His surprise visit to Rancho Del Seco was designed to keep his right-hand man on his toes. There were limits, though. Alisio wouldn't drive through the entry gate completely unannounced. That would've been disrespectful and in bad form. But he hadn't given El Lobo more than two hours of advance notice.

When his three limos arrived at the entry gate to Rancho Del Seco, two heavily armed men in tactical clothes stepped out of the shack and approached. Today, Alisio sat in the second limo. Yesterday in Mexico City, he'd been in the third. It made sense to be random and unpredictable. Surprise visits ensured everyone did their jobs properly. Most importantly, El Lobo wasn't allowed to warn the guards the boss was coming. Such information could be leaked to his enemies, enabling an assassination or a kidnapping. Alisio relaxed when he recognized the two guards.

The lead driver exchanged a few words, and they were waved through.

A few miles farther in, a narrow dirt road forked to the right. Manned by a Middle Easterner who didn't smile or wave, a smaller guard shack sat next to the road. The man stared with the emotionless eyes of a viper as they drove past.

Stupid punk, Alisio thought. He was willing to overlook the smug superiority because the ISIS leadership paid a small fortune to lease his land. Because of Rancho Del Seco's location—directly on the US border—they forked over a premium to be here.

Yesterday, El Lobo had said their jihadists had been a little friendlier lately, and their Spanish was coming along to the point where they could have two- or three-sentence conversations. Their Syrian-born interpreter kept trying to convince El Lobo they had a common enemy: the evil empire of America and its countless millions of infidels. Yeah, sure. Whatever.

Alisio didn't give a rat's ass about their caliphate, their radical jihadist views, or their misguided desire to impose Sharia law on the world. None of that mattered. As long as the cash kept flowing, they could believe anything they wanted.

And flow it did.

The most recent windfall? Twenty-eight million dollars.

That's what these fanatics had agreed to pay for the North Korean WMD grenades—in Bitcoins, the preferred currency of the underworld.

As part of the deal, his militant guests were required to carry out the attacks on Stone McBride in Washington, DC, and the Beaumont family in San Diego. For their services, Alisio agreed to a $4 million discount on the purchase price of the grenades, dropping it down to $24 million—an astounding $2 million apiece. The discount was an equitable trade, in Alisio's opinion.

Of course he hadn't relied on the jihadists to plan the attacks—El Lobo and Quattro handled that. Tragically, the attacks had been only partially successful. Two of the four targets were still alive.

Alisio kicked himself for not stipulating total success in his deal with the ISIS hierarchy. As far as they were concerned, their end of the agreement had been met—the attacks took place. He couldn't welsh, or he'd lose credibility with both ISIS and his fellow cartel bosses. How would it look if he reneged? It wasn't an option. He'd make another attempt on Beaumont's family at a future date and insist that El Lobo and Quattro personally handle it. Revenge was only delayed, not derailed.

Cash-wise, he'd already collected $12 million as a good-faith deposit from his ISIS connection. Once he received the second half of his payment later tonight, he'd turn the grenades over—and make sure he had plenty of muscle surrounding him for the handoff.

Concerning the use of the grenades? Alisio didn't care where the terrorists deployed them as long as they excluded Mexican soil. The line had to be drawn there. The ISIS leadership agreed and seemed more than eager to move forward under those terms. He had no illusions about what the jihadists intended to do—not his business. Alisio got what he wanted: millions in cash and revenge for his slain father. They got what they wanted: dead American infidels. If the chemical agent killed a few hundred, or even a few thousand, innocent people, so be it. Innocent people were killed every day. He remembered reading somewhere that drunk drivers killed twenty-eight people every day in America. So why didn't that little statistic ever make it into the news? He supposed it was dull and uninteresting. But a deadly gas attack? Now *that* will get some coverage.

He wasn't worried about blowback. All the grenade attacks would be suicide missions. What could be more perfect? No link to him, and even if the authorities found out, he had safeguards in place to lay the blame squarely on El Lobo and Quattro. He'd miss the income they produced, but little else. When it came right down to it, the two coyotes were expendable assets.

Fifteen minutes later, his motorcade pulled up to the ranch house and El Lobo came out to greet him. A few pleasantries were exchanged, but Alisio wasn't in the mood for small talk. El Lobo took the hint and gave him plenty of space. Three of his six bodyguards removed all the suitcases from the trunks of the limos and entered the huge Spanish-style house ahead of him.

Following his men inside, he admired the sculptures and the artwork adorning the walls. This collection of oil paintings and marble statues far exceeded the value of the entire hacienda, by a large margin.

After reaching his bedroom suite, he picked up the nightstand phone, called his personal butler, and said he was ready for company. *Company* meant high-end hookers, the best money could buy.

His thoughts returning to the attacks in DC and San Diego, he plopped down on the bed and stared at the ceiling. It had been bad luck, nothing more. Eyewitness accounts in the DC attack seemed to be mixed, but a common thread involved a woman in the diner shooting back. Much like Charlene Beaumont had fought off her attackers in California. Remarkable, really . . . and not what the jihadists expected. They didn't care who they killed, but they hadn't planned on dying themselves. The attacks weren't designed as suicide missions. All seven jihadists had fully expected to return to the training compound at Rancho Del Seco. Their demise didn't break Alisio's heart. What was the expression? Dead men tell no tales. In hindsight, it was good fortune he'd told El Lobo and Quattro to stay clear of the San Diego mall attack, or his best coyotes might've ended up dead as well. More importantly, his men hadn't been picked up on the mall's security cameras.

A soft knock announced the woman's arrival and he told her to come in. She was stunningly beautiful, no doubt about it. Over the next hour, he indulged himself in every carnal pleasure imaginable, and then some.

So here he was, laid out on a bed with a hooker, less than a day away from being another $12 million richer. Life was grand.

He rolled out of bed and strolled over to the humidor atop the dresser. He grabbed an Opus X Double Corona cigar and fired it up with a torch lighter. There were more expensive cigars, but he liked Arturo Fuente's flagship line the best. He dismissed the woman with a wave. She'd been pretty good, but he'd had better—and younger. He knew a forced smile when he saw one but didn't care.

He stepped out to the patio and looked across to the mountains. They looked so barren, so different from the southern part of Mexico, where everything was green and lush. He didn't love the desert like El Lobo did, but that didn't mean he couldn't appreciate it. Many of the sunrises and sunsets were spectacular—the most colorful he'd ever seen.

In hindsight, El Lobo should've killed Vincent Beaumont's secretary. So why hadn't he? His man hadn't offered any good reason. Fortunately, the disguise El Lobo had worn worked. The sketch shown on American TV looked nothing like him. El Lobo had always enjoyed using disguises; they'd served him well over the years.

He took a puff, tilted his head back, and let the smoke pour out of his mouth.

El Lobo's efforts had produced a good week of revenue. The last two columns of El Salvadorans had been successfully delivered across the border, along with half a million opioid pills. Chalk up another $4 million in profit.

Alisio's life revolved around the pursuit of money. Deep down, he knew it wasn't spiritually rewarding, but he honestly didn't care.

What else really mattered?

Goodwill? Friendship? Charity?

Hardly.

Power's reins were held by the wealthy. He knew he'd never reach Carlos Slim's stature, but he was determined to get his eleventh digit of net worth. Unfortunately, the wealthier he became, the more enemies he seemed to make. One thing he never did was swindle the other cartels. He had a good working relationship with his fellow crime bosses. Mutually profitable.

Alisio stepped back into the suite and turned on the TV. Watching the cable news babes and ugly old men spewing the same old talking points was amusing at best, annoying at worst. The blowhards had been wrong so many times, it was a wonder anyone believed anything they said. Maybe the news was like product advertising: if people heard it enough times, they'd start to believe it.

He turned the TV off when that annoying pillow ad came on . . . *again.*

Sleep well, Americans, you naive fools.

CHAPTER 23

Deep within the Liberty Crossing Intelligence Campus, just west of Washington, DC, DNI Scott Benson walked into the conference room and made eye contact with everyone present while an assistant worked his way around the room, placing a file in front of each person seated at the massive oval table. Four people had arrived early for a pre-meeting brief: CIA Director Rebecca Cantrell; her deputy director; Commissioner Tim Haley of the US Customs and Border Protection; and the top man in the US Border Patrol, Chief Ryan Switzer.

Everyone present used first names for meetings like this.

Benson took a seat at the far end of the table. "Thank you for coming in at oh-four-thirty, but I'm afraid the situation warrants it. We have a lot of ground to cover in a short amount of time. You'll have a chance to review your briefing packets later, so please wait to do that. In a couple of minutes, Kelley Ford's going to walk us through more detailed information on what we have to date. We now know that the shootings at Mabel's Diner and the UTC mall are related. Thanks to

Stone McBride's daughter, Jin Marchand, who captured and interrogated a gunman from Mabel's, we also know who's behind the attacks: a Mexican coyote called El Lobo. A San Diego Police Department detective provided us a physical description of El Lobo he'd obtained from Vincent Beaumont's personal secretary, who'd been interrogated just prior to the murders. Clearly the man tried to disguise himself, but based on what Ryan has told us about El Lobo, we're certain he carried out the interrogation and planned both terrorist attacks. Obviously, El Lobo's not his real name. We're scrambling to find out what it is. Ryan believes he moves back and forth across the border at will, using multiple fake IDs and passports. At this point, we don't yet know the motivation behind the attacks. Once we question our prisoner further, we're hoping to get that information.

"Here's what we *do* know. El Lobo has set up a terrorist-training compound and staging area on a ninety-thousand-acre property about a hundred miles southeast of Ciudad Juárez. How does a Mexican coyote come to own ninety thousand acres? We have no idea, and we're not sure he even owns it. Getting the property ownership records at this hour is next to impossible. We think it's in the municipality of Guadalupe in the state of Chihuahua. What makes this ninety thousand acres especially alarming is its location. Its northern boundary is the Rio Grande—approximately seven miles' worth. We know this because Jin Marchand's prisoner disclosed it. We're officially calling this compound and its occupants 'the Rio Grande cell.' Let's be clear. We're talking about a terrorist-training site and staging area within a ninety-minute walk of US soil. To put it bluntly, that sucks."

Benson received nods from around the table.

"We've all wondered why there hasn't been a major Islamic terrorist attack in Mexico. Well, we might've just discovered a possible answer. The jihadists don't want to bite the hand that feeds them. By our best estimates, there are over ten active radical Islamic terrorist cells operating within Mexico's borders, waiting for marching orders from their ISIS and Al-Qaeda hierarchy. Most of these cells are hosted by narco cartels."

The room had gone silent. Everyone in here knew that Mexico had a terrorist problem, but they hadn't known a cell sat literally on the international border.

"For a lot of reasons," Benson continued, "it's easier for terrorists to blend in down there, and it's certainly easier for them to get in and out. We have direct evidence from captured intelligence in San Diego, El Paso, and Tecate that terrorists are crossing the border at will in remote areas along the Rio Grande and other regions. They're constantly scouting for potential terror attack sites in the United States. Between the terrorist cells and their narco cartel hosts, the worst possible crimes against humanity are going unanswered and unchallenged. Making matters worse, the money generated from the jihadists' illegal activities is huge. Hundreds of millions every year, and a significant percentage of it ends up in the terrorist watch list countries. The ISIS hierarchy is learning the tricks of the narcotics trade from the cartels and implementing them to make money to support their jihad.

"As everyone at this table knows, these radical fanatics view all non-Muslims as lower life-forms. The vast majority of Muslims don't believe that crap, but they aren't the ones trying to kill us. Memories are short. September eleventh has been all but forgotten."

Benson made eye contact with everyone present again. "Well, not at this *fucking* table. Pardon my language, but I wanted my point . . . emphasized. We believe the compounds in Mexico are not only training and recruiting grounds; they're also staging grounds. The man Ms. Marchand interrogated said the numbers vary, but at any given moment, there are fifteen to twenty radical Islamic fanatics in the Rio Grande cell.

"Because the Mexican narco cartels own many of the local law enforcement officers and politicians, it's extremely hard to penetrate their organizations. Despite the threat these terrorists pose to our Western way of life, some of the crime lords—not all of them—look the other way because the money's so huge. Ryan's going to give us a report about some activity along our southern border that we think is related to the Rio Grande cell. After that, we'll get up to speed on what we learned from Stone McBride's daughter." He nodded to the Border Patrol chief.

Ryan Switzer clicked the remote that controlled the projector, and a map of Mexico's northern border filled the screen. "Thank you, Scott. I promise to be brief. Everything I'm about to report is in your packets. We've plotted the last six months' worth of incidents. The last thirty days are noteworthy." He used the laser pointer to illuminate a series of plotted locations on the map. "As you can see, there's a pattern." He zoomed in to the Texas border and made a circular motion with the pointer. "There's a hole right here. Anyone care to guess where the Rio Grande cell is located? Yep. Right in the middle of the hole. It's clear that whoever's behind these incidents wants us to divert asserts and patrols away from this area of the border. We've also considered it's a ruse, designed to make us think something's going to happen in the hole when it's not. Now we know otherwise.

"As you all know, less than a week ago, a national park ranger and one of my senior agents were ambushed after they responded to an arson fire at the old Santa Elena crossing site right here. We believe El Lobo was the shooter, and he managed to hit the park ranger from eleven hundred yards. Her vest saved her life. While my agent carried the wounded ranger away from the ambush site, the shooter scored a hit on him. He's going to be okay." Ryan put some levity in his tone. "He took a Forrest Gump shot."

That got some smiles, but no one laughed.

"We sent a small team across the border, found the sniper's shooting position atop a ridge, and recovered close to fifty spent casings, all of them from a Lapua Magnum. It's also worth noting that the effective range of a Lapua is over a mile. I'm having my staff work up a topographic map and redline all areas where my agents will be the most susceptible to sniper fire. As you can imagine, it's a massive project. Despite the risk, we aren't going to let El Lobo interfere with our job of guarding the fence. We also found something else at the shooter's nest." The screen changed to a photograph of a small piece of paper with a hole punched through it and the image of a black scorpion burned into its surface.

"This was stabbed into the sand with a mesquite branch. El Lobo obviously knew we'd find it." The screen showed a close-up of a blackened scorpion brand, about an inch in length. "It's El Lobo's signature. The scorpion image is identical to the one branded into the lower back of one of my agents several months ago after she'd been assaulted. Her partner was murdered outright, but she endured two days of pure hell. The details aren't necessary right now. They're in the file."

The screen went dark.

During Switzer's brief pause, Benson said, "We want El Lobo's head on a platter, but we'd prefer to take him alive, as we'd like to know how exactly the Rio Grande cell came to be. Contacts, money transfers, and any connections to other cells . . . lone wolves or otherwise."

Benson nodded, and Ryan continued. "At this point, we think El Lobo's basically a gun for hire, although many of the cartels want him permanently on their payrolls. As far as we know, he's resisted all the offers and remains a freelancer. Before my agent was shot, the worst we'd faced over the last ten days was an explosion that sent a burning pile of tires across the border. My agents weren't injured, but they could've been."

Ryan took a seat, and Benson took over again. "Now, about Jin Marchand. Her file is included in your packets. She used her phone to dictate a very detailed report of the massacre inside Mabel's. She also used it to video a confession by the surviving gunman. The details of how she forced him to talk aren't included. Needless to say, he didn't give up the information without being physically tortured.

"Now, before we continue, Kelley's going to bring you up to speed on a recent event that we think is directly related to the attacks yesterday. President Trump has already authorized immediate military action, and you'll soon know why. We're going to act quickly, within the next eighteen hours." Benson held up a hand at the groans and body language offered around the table. "I know that's an impossibly short amount of time, but that's all we've got. Everything will be clear to you within the next few minutes. Kelley?"

His principal deputy director thumbed the remote, and the image of a mining operation, like that of a giant circular borrow pit, filled the screen.

"Here's what's not in your packets," she said. "Ten days ago, the Jong Doo military research facility came under attack by unknown forces. North Korea's denying it happened, but we have photographic evidence to prove otherwise." She triggered the next slide, a side-by-side comparison of the before and after imagery. "Here is actual footage of the explosions, picked up by our Pave Fire Three satellite just before it slipped below the horizon. As you can see, the heat flares correspond to Jong Doo's primary and secondary entrances. The North Koreans did an excellent job disguising the entry points inside old-looking warehouse buildings, but the explosions were so powerful, they blew the roofs open. Fortunately, the duty officer at NORAD had the presence of mind to pan out and look for warm engine blocks or people on foot leaving the facility. Three human heat signatures were detected, running toward the eastern tree line. Unfortunately, Pave Fire Eight didn't clear the horizon in time, and we didn't reacquire the people on foot.

"Jong Doo isn't your run-of-the-mill underground military facility. It's a state-of-the-art bio- and chemical weapons development laboratory complex. We learned of its existence several years ago, just before one of Rebecca's operations officers turned up missing. She's now one of the unnamed stars on the CIA's memorial wall."

Benson watched Rebecca shift her weight slightly. It didn't take much imagination to know her officer died badly over a long period of time.

"Thank you, Kelley," Benson said. "The man Ms. Marchand captured and interrogated provided some valuable information. Had the attack in Mabel's gone as planned, we wouldn't know of the catastrophic threat we now face. And I mean catastrophic. The attacks in San Diego and DC were not intended to be suicide missions. All seven gunmen intended to return to Mexico and rejoin their comrades in the Rio Grande cell." Benson stood and leaned on the table. "The captive told Ms. Marchand that there were going to be thousands of dead Americans within the next few days. Not dozens. Not hundreds. Thousands." He let that soak in. And based on the expressions around the table, it had.

He looked at Kelley and pursed his lips. "What we're about to show you will turn your stomachs, and I wouldn't blame any of you for closing your eyes, but you need to understand the gravity of the crisis we're facing. Make no mistake about it. We *are* in crisis mode. Four days ago, a thumb drive was found on an intercepted ISIS courier near the Syria-Iraq border. The courier was killed, so we haven't been able to determine how he got the thumb drive or what he planned to do with it. All we know is that he was heading deeper into ISIS-held territory at the time he was intercepted. Yes, the president has seen this video."

There was absolute silence in the room.

The video began with four emaciated people in gray jumpsuits manacled to a steel table inside a small white room. Three men and one woman.

"Those are North Korean labor camp prisoners," said one of the directors under his breath.

"Yes," Benson said. "That's our assessment as well."

Armed guards then entered the room through a thick door with a round small hatch. The prisoners held perfectly still while the guards removed their handcuffs from metal rings bolted to the table. It was clear the prisoners were accustomed to being restrained.

Everyone knew what was coming when the guards left and a flashing, strobelike beacon came to life. Even though he'd seen this footage numerous times, Benson found himself holding his breath.

A gas grenade was dropped through the round hatch. Its spring-loaded safety handle flew free, and three seconds later, the can began spinning wildly on the floor. On the wall above their heads, a large digital timer began counting seconds—presumably in Korean—its red symbols menacing. The prisoners reacted defensively, shying away from the grenade, but they had no place to hide.

The grenade made a loud hissing sound as the compound spewed in every direction.

"Kelley, please mute the sound. We don't need to hear it."

The IC directors watched in stunned horror as the chemical agent took effect. At the thirty-second mark, they looked itchy and irritable, as though being pestered by a swarm of flies. Things went downhill from there. A minute into the video, they'd become nothing more than savage animals hell-bent on tearing each other to pieces with their teeth. At two minutes, they were all on the floor, convulsing in death spasms.

"Dear Lord," Ryan said. "Please tell me this is an enactment."

"It's not. We've had it analyzed by our video experts, and it's real."

"So what the hell are we going to do about this?" Ryan asked.

Sounding like chaos, everyone started talking.

Benson didn't take Ryan's emotionally charged question personally. It was, after all, a fair thing to ask.

Benson held up both hands. "That's why we're all here, Ryan. If we play out the scenario and connect the dots, we're looking at direct evidence of a North Korean WMD connection to ISIS. Based on the explosions at Jong Doo, the intercepted thumb drive, and the intel from Ms. Marchand's captured gunman, we can almost certainly conclude the WMD grenades are in the hands of the Rio Grande cell, *just five miles from our border*. Now to answer Ryan's question, we're going to eradicate these murderous fanatics from the face of the earth. I'm already working on a plan. In the meantime, Rebecca's specialists will be interrogating Jin Marchand's captive extensively. And by interrogating, I do not mean that we'll be torturing this man with physical abuse. We'll use drugs, subterfuge, sleep deprivation, and visual and audio disorientation. There will be no more physical abuse. We don't do that on my watch. Everyone clear on that?"

Everyone nodded.

"Here's where things rise to the level of direct military action. Each chemical grenade—and we don't know how many they have— has the potential to kill hundreds. If what our captive said is true about the Rio Grande cell's goal to kill thousands, it's reasonable to believe they have more than just one or two grenades. As early as tonight, El Lobo could be escorting ten to fifteen radical Islamic terrorists across the border, each carrying one of those grenades. We're in a bin Laden type of situation, but this time, we aren't waiting weeks and months to act, nor do we have weeks and months to plan the strike. We've got *hours*.

"In the meantime, we're tending to our captive's wounds, showing him compassion, and dispelling all the garbage he's been brainwashed with over the years. These people are fueled by hatred, and reflecting it back onto them only hardens their resolve. Don't think for a minute the stolen chemical weapons were simply given to the Rio Grande cell. Whoever's funding this attack probably paid millions to get the WMDs smuggled into Mexico. That's where El Lobo comes in. We need him alive to determine who the ringmaster and financiers are, assuming they could be different people. Clearly whoever's in charge has a strong connection to ISIS. Our objective is simple, but its execution is complex. As the intelligence community directors, you're going to make sure every agency inside the IC is working with every other agency. Can we keep this out of the news indefinitely? No. We have no idea if other copies of the WMD video are on the loose. Time will tell, and it's clearly only a matter of time before it gets posted on YouTube. Once that happens, we're either going to be seen as heroes or goats. I'd prefer heroes.

"I've ordered breakfast sandwiches and lots of coffee from the mess. Our chow should be here any minute. Text your wives and husbands and let them know you'll be sequestered until further notice. We're locking ourselves in this conference room until we have a working plan to attempt ahead of my fail-safe backup plan. No, we aren't nuking the Rio Grande cell. If we can covertly get in, seize the WMDs, and get back out, great. If that fails, I want all the logistics of a massive conventional airstrike in my pocket. Basically, I want the ability to carpet bomb the entire Rio Grande cell and reduce every building—and person inside of them—to quarter-inch pieces. Clear?"

Everyone nodded, but no one said anything. Now wasn't the time for dumb questions.

"I know what you're thinking. It's Mexican soil. I'll remind everyone that the compound where bin Laden was holed up was Pakistani soil. I don't need to tell you how the president feels about any of this. Despite how things are portrayed in the mainstream media, the president has a very solid relationship with President Menendez, and I've been in regular contact with my counterpart down there over the last sixteen months.

"President Menendez is no fan of El Lobo. Mexico's justice department has been trying to link El Lobo to several murders of local and state lawmakers who've openly voiced their desire to see El Lobo arrested and brought to trial. It's a reign of terror down there. Menendez ran on the promise to do something about the corruption plaguing his country. He knows we're going to take action, but he doesn't yet know what we're going to do, or when. He's agreed to keep this under wraps with the exceptions of several key cabinet positions that have to know—his defense secretary and several others. If we pull this off covertly, Menendez saves face, but one way or the other, the Rio Grande cell is going to be destroyed. Metaphorically speaking, there's a turd in our neighbor's pool, and we're going to sanitize it with prejudice."

CHAPTER 24

Two and a half hours after Nathan's close call with alcohol, he and Harv were still talking. Neither of them could've slept, even if they'd wanted to.

Had this been his normal routine back in La Jolla, he would've climbed out of bed or risen from the floor—depending on how his dreams went—by 0530. After that, he'd take a twilight jog around the neighborhood, followed by giant schnauzer training and playtime, the three S's, foreign language study, and then morning chow.

Harv's pattern was nearly identical.

Harv got up from the living room couch and looked out the window. "I'm not sure I've ever been this angry."

"I have."

"You're used to it."

Nathan joined him at the window. "You *are* bent this morning."

"I feel terrible for your mom. They really loved each other. How long were they married?"

"Sixty-two years," Nathan said, hardly believing it.

"Yeah, that's a bad deal. She was ten years younger, right?"

"Eleven. He was her summer camp counselor. They first met when she was fifteen, but they didn't date until she was in college. Their second meeting was a one-in-a-million-chance encounter."

"Tell me."

"He knocked her onto her ass running toward the men's room in a department store. He had a bladder infection. She'd just come out of the women's room and, *bam*, down she went. They recognized each other right away, and the rest, as they say, is history."

"You owe your existence to a bladder infection?"

Nathan laughed. "I'm afraid so."

"What are your thoughts on Jin? You know, about her wringing information out of the captured gunman?"

"I'm okay with it, but let's hope Lauren never finds out."

"Somehow I don't think Jin will disclose that."

"My sister had a hellish life, Harv. Growing up underprivileged in North Korea is as bad as it gets. She spent four years in a prison labor camp and told me she literally ate whatever she could catch to stay alive. Rodents, insects, whatever she could find. It's a miracle she was able to conceive after the brutal assaults she endured. I hate thinking about it. The guards at those prisons are the most depraved and sadistic tyrants on the planet. They're embodied evil in its purest form."

"Yeah, they're not accountable to anyone. I hate to say this, but it's crappy to keep Lauren in the dark. She should tell her daughter she's okay."

"We both know this kind of thing isn't new to Lauren. My sister's disappeared before, often for days at a time without calling. Look, it's easy to judge her, think of her as a bad mom, but she's doing the best she can. Considering the abuse she endured, I think she's done a damned fine job as a mother. I totally understand her reasons for . . . withdrawing at times."

He knew Harv wouldn't respond, but sensed his friend wanted to say, *You mean like you used to do to me?* Like Jin, there'd been times when he hadn't wanted any human contact at all.

Harv had been a godsend and still was. If Harv hadn't rejected his attempts to shut him out, he might've killed himself and become another statistic in a veteran suicide file.

"Thanks for not saying it, Harv."

"Ancient history."

They watched a police cruiser with its light bar on race down the street. No siren, though.

"We have to remember that Jin never got any counseling for her PTSD. She didn't have anyone to fall back on, like I did with you. She dealt with her demons alone. Truthfully, it's a wonder she's as balanced as she is."

Harv nodded agreement. "Lauren's finally old enough to under-stand her mom's history, what she went through."

"She doesn't resent her mom anymore, at least not like she used to. Their level of trust isn't where it should be, but they've made a lot of progress. We've talked about this a lot, Harv. Lauren doesn't want to be bitter. She wants to appreciate the good times they've had and not dwell on the bad times."

"You've helped her have that attitude."

Nathan said, "We've talked a few times."

"A few times? You've been really generous with your time."

He didn't say anything.

"Is she still struggling with school?"

"Not as much. She's super smart but doesn't like the structured environment of a classroom. I told her not to stress about it. I told her to play the role, pass the tests, and get her diploma. It's a rite of passage, nothing more."

"You told her that?"

"Well, not in those exact words, but yeah."

"Good for you," Harv said. "Please don't tell me your sister expects her to get straight As?"

"No, but she doesn't think Lauren's trying hard enough."

"Is she right?"

"Probably. She's bored to tears in class."

"Like uncle, like niece?"

"I'm afraid so. I hated school, especially college. Regurgitating meaningless crap isn't an accurate gauge of intelligence."

"Adaptation and improvisation," Harv said.

"Problem-solving—it's the true measure. I couldn't wait to graduate UNM and join the Marines."

"Go Lobos!"

He hadn't heard that game cry in a long time. "Back then, the happiest day of my life was the day I found out I'd made it into OCS at Quantico. My grades were borderline, but my dad used his political clout. I plan to do the same thing for Lauren if she's serious about officer-candidate school. She wants to fly Ospreys."

"Why not? She's already flying our 407s."

"I'm not sure how much Jin likes the idea of Lauren becoming a Marine pilot."

"If I know Lauren, the more her mom objects, the more she'll want to do it. She's lucky to have you in her life."

"Thanks for saying that. I feel the same way about her."

Neither of them spoke for several seconds.

"My dad saved her life by sacrificing himself."

"Doesn't surprise me at all."

"Me either." Nathan closed down the visual of what it must've been like in the diner. He'd thought about it enough. "My mom's sleeping in her hospital room, and I told her to let me know when Jin calls. I think we should both spend some time with Lauren today. She's gotta be feeling pretty bad. Mentally and physically. I want her to know we'll be there for her."

"She thinks of you like her adopted dad."

"Yeah, I know, and it really worries me."

"Nonsense. You're a huge part of her life. If I can be a dad, anyone can. You just have to put in the time—which you've been doing with Lauren. How many times have you taken her shooting, gone to her softball games, to the movies?"

"I don't know, a bunch."

"You've also been teaching her fighting and survival skills. Not one in a thousand kids can make a fire from scratch or create a snow cave or break down a 1911 in the dark and put it back together."

"Not too many adults can do those things either."

"Well, if the zombie apocalypse ever happens, she'll survive it."

"I don't know about you, Harv, but I don't want to live in a world where people are killing each other over a can of tuna. I mean, what's the point? It has nothing to do with being a survivalist. It's about human dignity. I'd hate living in that world."

"Like you said, what's the point? It's too bad Holly needs to be at the office."

"She's amazing. A perfect fit. I can't explain it. It just feels like she was custom-built for me."

"Maybe she was."

"Amen, Harv. Want to take a jog around the National Mall and blow off some steam? I've never done it at sunrise. I hear it's beautiful, and I could use some beautiful right now."

"I'll go change. Lobby in ten?"

"See you there."

CHAPTER 25

During their run, they pushed themselves hard, going much faster than they normally did. When running or doing anything else, for that matter, they never competed with one another. They were always together, always a unit.

In many ways, DC felt like a second home to Nathan. He'd spent a lot of time here and knew the city fairly well. He'd always loved viewing the monuments. Seeing Abraham Lincoln sitting in that chair was quite literally breathtaking. Being an amateur Civil War historian, he'd often tried to put himself in Lincoln's shoes, unsuccessfully. He'd never fully understand the tremendous personal cost Lincoln had paid by sending hundreds of thousands of men to their deaths to end slavery and preserve the union. The only reason people claimed the Trump-Clinton presidential election was the most vicious of all time was because they didn't know their history. The 1860 election of Lincoln made 2016 look like a kid-glove fight. The country had been quite literally tearing itself apart, the draft riots of New York City remaining a sobering testament.

After their run, they cooled off with a slow walk along Fourteenth back to the hotel and decided to meet in the lobby in half an hour. From there, they'd walk over to the hospital to see Lauren and his mom.

Along the way, they stopped at a coffeehouse and got a couple of breakfast sandwiches to go. Nathan had been tempted to walk by Mabel's Diner but decided against it. He preferred to remember it the way it had been when he'd been there with his father, years and years ago.

In the hospital, they rode the elevator in silence. They weren't alone; an elderly couple accompanied them. They smiled when Nathan and Harv got in. Given who their co-occupants were, Nathan did his best to return a smile. This slow elevator ride made him flash back to yesterday's elevator ride in the grocery store. Had his fight with Flintstone been only twenty-four hours ago?

Whatever good mood he'd felt earlier this morning suddenly vanished.

He was ready to chew glass at this point.

Harv must've sensed his tension because his friend softly cleared his throat.

Nathan mouthed the words *thank you*, relaxed his jaw, and tilted his head back. After pulling in a deep breath, he let it out slowly. He noticed the elderly pair staring at him and said, "Sorry, rough night."

The man asked, "You two retired military?"

"What gave us away?" Harv asked.

"Your silent way of communicating and your high and tight haircuts."

"Marines, one-eight," Nathan said.

"Outstanding."

"You?" Harv asked.

"Squids. My guys kept the Connie's Phantoms in the air during Vietnam."

Nathan hadn't heard that name in a long time. Connie was the nickname for the USS *Constellation*, a Kitty Hawk–class supercarrier, decommissioned in 2003.

The man grinned. "You Marines did a good job on board as ballast."

That put a genuine smile on his face. Nothing like a friendly rivalry with the swabbies.

"Wait a minute. You're Stone McBride's son. And you must be Harvey Fontana. Your father bragged about you two a lot."

"Thank you, Senator Kemper. I appreciate you saying that."

"You recognize me?"

"Absolutely. You're the chair of the Senate Arms Services Committee. We've met before, but it had to be twenty-five years ago."

"I remember it. Mabel's Diner." He looked down for a few seconds. "I'm damned sorry about what happened. Stone was a fine man. We're here to pay our respects to your mother. Your parents were our closest friends. Still are . . . I mean your mom still is . . ."

Nathan sensed the awkwardness and smiled. "I know what you meant."

"So how are you holding up, Marine?" Kemper asked.

"Right now, I need an ax and several hundred rounds of oak." Splitting firewood allowed him to be destructive and constructive at the same time.

"Copy that. I'd join you, but my shoulders are toast. We'll make our visit brief. We know you'd like some time with your mom and niece." He held up a hand. "Don't worry; it's not common knowledge. Your father and I go way back."

"Thank you, Senator."

"Please, call me Bill."

"Your mom and I have lunch every month," Mrs. Kemper said. "I'm so sorry about your father. Our thoughts and prayers are with you and your family."

"Thank you." He didn't know what else to say.

She looked at Harv. "They both thought of you like a son."

Harv said thank you as the elevator doors opened.

"Why don't Deb and I wait in the visitor's lounge while you and Harv sit with your family?"

"Bill, you and Deb are more than welcome to come in the room with us, but let's gauge how Lauren's doing. If she's awake, she'll get a kick out of meeting the chair of the SASC, especially when she finds out how much money you're in charge of."

"Are you sure? We don't want to intrude."

"I'm positive."

"They're in room four twenty-five," Deb said.

They walked past the nurses' station and saw Lauren's room right away. It was hard to miss. A Metro police officer sat in a folding chair to one side of the door. Nathan admired the lack of a cell phone in his hand. Keeping their voices low, everyone introduced themselves and shook hands. Nathan thanked the officer for his service to the city.

Lauren's door was partially closed. He pushed it open.

"Uncle Nate!"

Lauren practically jumped out of the bed, but then she remembered the IV hooked up to her wrist and slowed down.

"Easy, Lauren. You got shot twice, remember?"

"They're just flesh wounds."

"Just flesh wounds?" *Oh, to be young again,* he thought.

He looked at his mom, who made the happiest face possible, but she couldn't conceal the pain and loneliness. An inch short of six feet tall, she had blue eyes and short gray hair. She once said she'd never dye it, and so far, she hadn't. She wore a light apricot pantsuit and a scarf to cover up a recent scar from cervical surgery.

He hugged Lauren gingerly, then embraced his mother.

No words were spoken. This was a silent mother-and-son hug for the ages, one he'd never forget.

Lauren grabbed Harv next. "Uncle Harv!" She closed her eyes and winced when she tried to hug him.

"Easy, Lauren," Harv said. "You'll tear your sutures."

Again Nathan studied her body language. She didn't seem all that upset. Maybe she hadn't fully processed what had happened. *Join the club.*

Harv continued. "Metro PD said you gave them a very detailed report while you were on the way to the hospital."

She shrugged. "I told the policeman it was okay to ride with me. It didn't hurt all that bad. I liked him; he was really nice. He said it was important to get as much information as soon as possible."

"Well, that was very brave of you," Harv added.

"Hey, you," his mom said, "back in bed."

Lauren made her exaggerated pouty face and eased onto the bed, being careful to keep her hospital gown from climbing. Even though she was several years older now, Nathan saw the same beautiful and fiercely intelligent girl who'd won his heart the first time they'd met. She'd been twelve at the time. Her questions had dissected him, especially when she'd said, *"You don't have any children, do you?"* It hadn't been a question. Clearly, she'd already known the answer. He remembered her blue eyes penetrating his protective veneer like an ice pick. Then she'd asked about his service in the Marines.

"Did you ever kill anyone?"

"Yes."

"Was it hard, you know, like . . . did you feel bad about it?"

Thank goodness a passerby came along at the right moment, ending that line of inquiry.

A smart kid for sure *and* stunning. Knowing those losers in Mabel's Diner had tried to murder this beautiful child caused another swell of anger. He suppressed it. Now wasn't the time. That would come later.

His mom embraced Senator Kemper and Deb. Yep, these three knew each other well.

Nathan said, "Lauren, I want you to meet someone very special. This is Senator and Mrs. Kemper."

Lauren's face shone with excitement. Nathan knew she admired politicians from their many discussions over the years.

Well, nobody's perfect, he mused.

"Senator Kemper is the chairman of the Senate Armed Services Committee."

"You mean like the boss?"

Kemper half laughed. "Try telling that to my Democratic colleagues."

"Would you sign my cast?"

Kemper stepped forward. "I'd be honored, young lady."

By phone, his mom had briefed them on Lauren's condition. In addition to opening her brachial artery, the AK round had splintered part of the bone. She'd be in the cast for eight weeks while the bone graft took hold.

He watched Kemper write:

To the bravest girl in the whole world! Senator William A. Kemper.

"This is way cool!" Lauren said. "I can't wait for my mom to see it."

Nathan watched her smile fade quickly before she looked away.

His mom said, "I'm sure you'll hear from her soon."

She didn't say anything.

Nathan asked, "What are you watching, kiddo?"

"It's a *Magnum, P.I.* marathon," she said. "It's so eighties. His shorts are *really* short, and he's a total babe."

Harv looked away and smiled.

"I'm going to pretend I didn't hear that," Nathan said. "I keep forgetting you're sixteen. Someone needs to invent an antihormone pill."

Lauren rolled her eyes in a kind way.

"Listen, we just stopped in to offer our condolences. Please call on us if you need anything."

Nathan said thank you again and shook Bill Kemper's hand. Harv did the same.

His mom left the room with the Kempers, probably to walk them over to the elevator.

Looking at Lauren's sweet and innocent face, he wondered what kind of a parent he might've been and how much worse this would've felt had Lauren been his child. Vince had to be a basket case. His son hadn't been wounded; he'd been murdered. A very shitty deal.

"Harv, I'd like a few minutes alone with Lauren, please."

Harv winked at Lauren and filed out.

Alone with his niece, he pulled up a chair, looked her in the eyes, and didn't say anything.

"What?"

"I'm just wondering when you were planning to tell me."

"Tell you what?"

"Lauren, you're not very good at subterfuge." He held up a hand. "It means pretense. Faking . . . you get the picture."

"She told me not to tell anyone!"

"Hey, it's me, Uncle Nate. When did your mom contact you?"

"Last night."

Nathan waited again.

Lauren looked at the closed door with a guilty expression. "I waited until Grandma went out for dinner to send her a text. She texted me back right away and asked what hospital and room I was in."

He nodded toward the nightstand. "So a few seconds later, she called you on the hospital phone?"

"Uh-huh."

"What did she say?"

"She told me she was okay even though she got shot."

Nathan couldn't hide his shock. "Your mom said she was shot?"

"In the leg."

"Have you talked to her since?"

She shook her head. "She told me not to call or text."

"Did she say when she'd call again?"

"No."

"Anything else?"

"She told me not to worry and that no one's going to attack us ever again."

That's a given, Nathan silently added. Maybe this wasn't the right time to ask, but there wouldn't be a good time anytime soon.

"Did Grandpa say anything, you know . . . before he died?"

Lauren's face contorted. "He said he wished he could've spent more time with me. He told me my mom loves me, but she has a hard time showing it. He also said he was proud of you."

Nathan felt short of breath. His thoughts spiraled into a black hole of emotion. He couldn't remember the last time he'd openly wept, but he was damned close right now. So much for putting on a strong veneer. He didn't know how or why, but Lauren connected with him on an emotional plane that couldn't be understood or explained.

Like himself, his niece was on the verge of tears. "She told me not to tell anyone, even you! Please don't be mad at me."

And in that instant, Lauren *was* the same little girl he'd first met, saying the exact same words: *Please don't be mad at me.*

"I'm not mad at you."

She didn't respond.

"Listen carefully, Lauren. You and me? We don't lie to each other. If I tell you I'm not mad, it's the truth. We share a combat bond built from trust that few people will ever own." He reached out and held her hand. "You were in a horrible position. If you didn't tell me, it felt like you were betraying me. If you did tell me, you'd be betraying your mom. Now it's my turn. I knew your mom was okay last night, and I didn't tell you."

"You knew? Last night?"

He nodded. "I could've called you, but I didn't." It wasn't entirely true, but he wanted Lauren to feel better.

"So we're even?"

"Yeah, kiddo, we're even."

"Mom said you were going to know everything last night anyway."

"But that's not the reason you told me."

"We're supposed to tell each other everything because of our combat bond. Like you and Uncle Harvey have."

"That's right. He loves you. You know that, right?"

"I love him too," she said.

"Tell him that sometime."

"I will."

He put a finger to his lips, turned up the TV's volume, and leaned in close. "Big Brother could be listening," he whispered.

She looked around. "People are listening to us? Seriously?"

"Shh . . . Keep your voice in a whisper. Probably not, but it doesn't hurt to be cautious."

"Okay. It's kinda exciting, huh?"

He smiled. "The reason I know your mom's okay is because she has issues with trusting people."

"What do you mean?"

"She wouldn't talk to the authorities until she talked to me first." He lowered his voice even more for effect. "Last night Harv, Holly, and I were at the White House."

"No way!"

He cringed and motioned for her to tone it down.

"Sorry . . . No way."

"We didn't go inside, but we met with someone really important. Your mom wanted to know if she could trust the person I was with."

"Was it the president? I remember when you told me you could talk to him about secret stuff."

This girl had an amazing memory. What he'd said was he still had a security clearance high enough to allow him to sit in on presidential briefings. So yeah, she was right.

"No, we didn't meet with the president. Your mom needed to know she could trust the person I was with."

"Was it Senator Kemper?"

"No."

"I guess I don't need to know."

"What's odd is your mom didn't say anything about getting shot last night. I'm worried about her." He now knew why Jin had sounded stressed.

"You mean like getting an infection?"

"Yes. I'll be back in a few minutes." He looked at the IV hooked into her arm and winked. "Don't go anywhere."

She rolled her eyes again. "That's *so* not funny."

"Then why are you smiling?"

He found Harv and his mom holding hands in the waiting area.

"Mom, may I have a moment with Harv? I'm pretty sure Lauren misses you already." It was one of those little white lies he could live with.

After his mom left, he lowered his voice a little. "Lauren told me Jin made contact with her late last night."

"I'm really glad to hear that," Harv said. "For a lot of reasons."

He conveyed what Lauren told him.

Nathan's phone rang and now wasn't one of those times to ignore it. "It's Rebecca . . . Good morning, Director Cantrell."

"I only have a minute."

"Okay . . ."

"Be down at the corner of Twenty-Third and First in six minutes."

She knows where I am. Dumb thought. Of course she knows. "What's going on?"

"This time the motorcade's coming to you."

"Rebecca . . ."

"Five minutes, fifty-five seconds."

"Okay, okay. We're on our way."

"We need you standing at the curb when we arrive. We'll be coming from Washington Circle. When you see the limos approach, walk out to the curb. We'll be stopping right next to the Foggy Bottom Metro station sign. Get into the third vehicle when its door opens. We'll only be stationary for a few seconds."

"We'll be ready."

"Say your goodbyes quickly."

"Where are we going?"

"Reagan."

"We haven't even checked out of the Willard. What about our clothes?"

"We're taking care of it."

"Okay. Can you tell me what's going on?"

"Not over the phone. Five minutes, twenty seconds."

CHAPTER 26

Their rendezvous went as planned. Rebecca's motorcade pulled in behind a waiting taxi. Less than five seconds later, the convoy was rolling again.

Seated inside, Rebecca Cantrell had her legs crossed with two files on her lap. The man seated next to her spoke four words into his phone: "We're on the way."

Rebecca introduced him as her personal aide. He looked familiar, and Nathan was pretty sure they'd met before.

"You certainly know how to make an entrance," Nathan said. "Why all the cloak-and-dagger? We could've come up to Langley."

She didn't smile, and it became clear something heavy was happening when she said, "We go back a ways, the three of us."

Neither of them said anything.

"That's what I like about you guys: you're good listeners. You'll need to be because what I'm about to tell you is complex and detailed. Before we start, DNI Benson wants you to see something. It's a three-minute video. We're ninety-nine percent sure it's from the Jong Doo underground research facility northeast of Pyongyang."

Her aide pulled a laptop from a soft case, opened it, and handed it across to them.

Four gaunt Asian prisoners were shackled to a metal table. The white room looked clean, too clean. It didn't take long to realize something bad was about to happen.

"Rebecca, I don't want to see North Koreans being—"

"It's not that," she interrupted.

"We're not watching this until you tell us what it is," said Harv.

"It's a chemical weapon demo."

"Shit, Rebecca."

"It's important. Benson wants you to know what's at stake. We all do."

Using the touch pad, Nathan tapped the Play arrow.

Rebecca said, "The sound is muted. There's no need to hear it."

One minute into the video, it became clear why the guards had removed the prisoners' handcuffs. At the two-minute mark, Nathan felt sick to his stomach and hoped it would end soon.

A few seconds later, it finally did.

Neither of them spoke.

There were times in Nathan's life when he found his faith in humanity tested—when the human race seemed doomed to extinction. This was one of those times.

"So now you know," she said.

"I'm sure there's a good reason for showing this to us," Nathan said, not softening the edge in his voice. He could've lived ten lifetimes without seeing this crap.

"There's a very good reason," she said.

It took most of the drive to the airport for Rebecca to explain what her people had learned from his sister's interrogation and their own follow-up questioning. "Our guest caved at the two-hour mark. Jin had already worked him over pretty hard. We didn't have to do much. We traded him pain relief coupled with quiet sleep time for some additional details. We now have a pretty good picture of what's going on. Speaking of, how much sleep did you guys get last night?"

"Not much, a couple of hours."

"Take a look at the inside flap of your files."

They did. Light blue in color, a small oval pill was scotch-taped to the flap.

"Triazolam, twenty-five milligrams," she said. "I want you guys to take them right away. You'll be sleepy within thirty to forty-five minutes. It should keep you asleep for the entire flight out to Santa Fe."

Harv looked skeptical, but Nathan knew all about this drug. It worked well and had no groggy aftereffects.

"I've used it before, Harv. All it does is help you fall asleep; it doesn't keep you asleep like surgical anesthetics. It's totally safe in this dosage." As proof, Nathan popped it into his mouth and swallowed it.

Harv did the same.

"You'll be on a company plane. One of our G280s."

Normally Harv would've said something like *nice*, but the mood in their armored limo had turned dark.

"Your pilots are operations officers, just like you guys used to be. They'll be accompanying you all the way to the BSI's academy and training ground. Needless to say, those files will not leave your possession or be duplicated. A BSI helicopter will be waiting for you at the aviation center at Santa Fe. You'll be flying directly to BSI's academy, where you'll receive a comprehensive mission-op briefing. You'll be reviewing topo maps, aerial photos, and a 1:500 scale mock-up of the ranch compound and the ranch house. We don't have anything on the interiors of the buildings, but BSI's people have made cardboard representations of the buildings and their relationships to one another.

"Once El Lobo's name surfaced during your sister's interrogation of her captive, a special agent from our San Diego field division spoke to Denise Tabor and showed her one of the few photographs we have of the man. The same photo's in your file. She couldn't identify him as either of her two assailants, but she did see something that's not in your file. Several months ago, a female US Border Patrol agent was brutally assaulted over a two-day period. She described El Lobo in great detail, including a scorpion tattoo on the back of his right hand. Ms. Tabor described the exact same tattoo on the back of her attacker's hand. From Ms. Tabor's description, it's clear El Lobo was wearing a disguise. He wore dark glasses and had a mustache and goatee.

"From the physical description she gave of the other man, we think he's El Lobo's lieutenant, Quattro. We have very little information on him, but a facial sketch of him is also in your file."

"How is Denise Tabor doing?"

"She's going to need plastic surgery on her face, but she's expected to make a full recovery."

"Physically," Nathan said.

"That's what I meant."

"I'm sorry, Rebecca. I didn't mean to sound cold." He shook his head. "I seem to be apologizing a lot lately."

"He's not the only one," Harv said.

"Look, you don't need to apologize. We're all on edge. If one of those grenades gets released into a crowded space, there could be hundreds of casualties. Maybe more. The insidious aspect is the pretoxin effect of making people go berserk. We can only speculate on how it works. Many secondary injuries and deaths will likely occur to people who weren't even exposed to the compound."

"So how do Nathan and I fit in?" asked Harv.

"You're on one of the fire teams, assuming you want to go."

Harv exchanged a glance with him, then said, "Absolutely. Are we going in with SEALs or recons?"

"Neither."

Nathan started to say something, but she held up a hand.

"President Trump has already authorized direct military intervention, but he doesn't want the US military used."

They both understood at the same time.

"He wants to use BSI private military contractors," Harv said.

"Because . . . ?" she asked.

"Because the op's on the Mexican side of the fence."

"And . . . ?"

"It gives the United States credible deniability. If the op fails miserably and it's leaked to the public, it could be seen as a purely retaliatory strike by a man furious about the murder of his son and attempted murder of his wife."

"Isn't it a little harsh to let BSI take the fall?" Harv asked.

"Vincent Beaumont volunteered knowing his company could take a PR hit. We assured him his contracts with the US government aren't in jeopardy."

"Aren't the stakes a little high to entrust this entirely to BSI?" asked Nathan.

"Actually no. BSI's operatives are some of the most highly trained combat and special-op veterans in the world. Few people know how big a role BSI played in the Iraq and Afghan wars. You guys do, but it's not common knowledge. When the CIA needed prisoners to interrogate, BSI teams often went out and got them. You both need to be clear on something. The operation against the Rio Grande cell is going to be under BSI's command. Vince will be leading the teams. Understood?"

"Fully," Nathan said.

"To answer one thing you might be wondering—yes, Vince approved your inclusion. It was part of the . . . negotiation. He said he wouldn't agree to the op without you guys. We could've approached a different military contractor, but based on the advice from his cabinet, the president decided to go with BSI."

Nathan raised his eyebrows.

"Yes, this situation rises to the presidential decision level. Think about what we're doing. We're conducting a military operation on the south side of the fence without support from the Mexican government.

Although President Menendez knows about the raid, and he's on board with it, it's purely a BSI mission."

When Nathan started to speak, she held up a hand.

"Contrary to the way the mainstream media portray things, President Trump's relationship with Menendez is strong. They personally spoke on the phone a few hours ago."

"Then the need-to-know circle on this op is small?"

"Extremely small. A few of Menendez's cabinet secretaries only. Look, we'd never do this without his permission. Trust me, he doesn't want it leaked that terrorist cells are operating inside his country with impunity."

Nathan didn't say anything.

"One more thing. As a fail-safe backup plan in the event BSI's raid isn't successful, three B-2 Spirits will be in a holding pattern just north of the border. On the president's command, they will accidentally stray a few miles south and drop sixty tons of general purpose bombs. We're going to obliterate every building on the property and anyone who's inside of them."

"Including us," Harv said.

Nathan locked eyes with her. "I should've given my mom a longer hug."

CHAPTER 27

After being dropped off at Reagan's jet center, Nathan yawned and realized the pill had begun to work its magic. "You feeling the effect yet?"
he asked Harv.

"Yeah, it's like I've only had two hours of sleep in the last two days."

His friend's sarcasm wasn't lost on him. "We've gone longer."

They didn't say anything for a spell.

"Harv?"

"Yeah, Nate?"

"If we get exposed to that toxic crap, will you . . . you know, do
whatever it takes?"

"Only if you'll do the same for me. Chances are we'll be together
anyway."

"I hate the thought of hurting you, Harv."

Harv smiled. "What makes you think you'll get the upper hand? I
might be the one whooping ass on *you*."

"That video . . . It has to be the most disturbing thing we've ever
seen. And we've seen a lot."

"Maybe the B-2s will spare us," Harv said.

"Yeah, that would be quick, all right. Those people looked out of their minds. I wonder if they knew what they were doing but just couldn't help themselves."

Harv nodded. "I think I know why it's bothering you so much in particular. You're worried about unleashing what's inside you."

"Yeah, I am. It's already crazy enough. It doesn't need any help."

"Try not to think about it."

"Are you going to call Candace?"

"You mean like a goodbye kinda call?" Harv asked.

He shrugged.

"Absolutely not. She once told me if I ever made that kind of call and I survived, she'd kill me when I got home."

"She really said that?"

"Yep."

"Yeah, that sounds like Candace, all right. Can't say I blame her, though. 'Good night, honey, and oh, I forgot to mention that we may never see each other again. Sleep well.' Yeah, that's a crappy call to get."

"Besides, we've already said our goodbyes. Did I ever tell you we did that a long time ago? Said our goodbyes?"

"No."

"We were having a discussion, kinda like this one, and we both agreed we'd say goodbye right then and there and never, ever do it again. And we've honored that agreement ever since."

"I guess I need to do that with Holly."

"You absolutely should."

"Hey, aren't we supposed to be retired?"

"You remember what Rebecca said."

Nathan nodded. It was hard to forget: *You're never retired.*

Harv offered a closed fist, and they touched knuckles. "For king and country."

"For king and country."

***

Rebecca had called it. Nathan awoke when the Gulfstream's wheels touched down.

He looked across the aisle at Harv, who stretched his arms. "How're you feeling? Hungover from the pill?"

"Not at all."

Their G280 taxied over to Santa Fe's small aviation center where several private jets, a couple of twin-engine turbo props, and one beautiful BSI helicopter were parked.

Local time was just after 10:30 a.m.

They both made head calls before being escorted off the jet by its first officer. Soft cases in hand, they waited while a man wearing sunglasses came out of the aviation center and walked toward them. He introduced himself as one of BSI's pilots. The jet's first officer said they'd need a few more minutes to shut down and secure the craft.

BSI's pilot asked if they wanted to wait inside the jet center, but Nathan preferred to remain on his feet. Harv agreed.

Fifteen minutes later, the five of them were flying north along the base of the Sangre de Cristo Mountains. He didn't know how the mountain range had gotten its name, but he understood the translation: Blood of Christ.

The next twelve hours seemed to blur into a single event without shape or definition. After landing at BSI's academy, several miles from the town of Nambé, they were escorted to their quarters across what looked like an oversized summer camp. All told, BSI's academy and training facility encompassed just over four square miles. Nathan thought it must've cost a small fortune getting this place set up. Someday when they weren't pressed for time, he'd like to take a tour with Harv. A security fence—topped with dozens of cameras—surrounded the entire twenty-seven-hundred-acre facility. Clearly, Vincent Beaumont took the safety of his cadets and PMCs seriously.

Vince arrived about an hour later and met up with them at the cafeteria. The two CIA operations officers introduced themselves, and the five of them settled down at a quiet table in the corner of the room. The boss's arrival turned heads, but everyone respected Vince's privacy and didn't approach. A few waved in a subdued way, and Vince waved back. Everyone here knew his family had been attacked. The news was hard to miss.

After eating a light lunch, they took a long walk across the campus to the academy's headquarters, a fairly large building. Nathan liked the architecture—low-pitched roofs, extended eaves, and a hint of pueblo mixed in. It fit perfectly with the area.

Inside, they were escorted into a large conference room. The center table held the cardboard scale model Rebecca had mentioned.

After a few minutes, they were joined by their fellow BSI operatives who'd be making the raid with them—athletic-looking people with high and tight haircuts like Nathan's. They all appeared to be in their late twenties to mid-thirties. Nathan recognized their 5.11 Tactical clothing right away. Harv and he currently wore pretty much the same thing, only different colors.

Introductions were made all around.

BSI's ranking system didn't have all the intermediate titles of its US military counterparts. There were corporals, sergeants, lieutenants, and colonels, in that order of ranking. There were no officers or enlisted in the sense of the military definition. The way Vince described the hierarchy, it closely mirrored that of a police force.

Even before reading the background info, he knew many of these BSI contractors were seasoned Iraq and Afghanistan combat vets, Vince included. Every private military contractor present had the same training as every other.

For tonight's op, the men and women seated around this table were divided into three four-person fire teams with code names of hotel, sierra, and tango.

Hotel team would consist of himself, Harv, Vince, and BSI's communications specialist. Nathan would be designated as Hotel one; Harv, Hotel two; Vince, Hotel three; and their radio specialist, Hotel four. Once the operation began, everyone would be using their code names only. Even though their radios were encrypted, they weren't taking any chances.

The only difference between a tango fire team member and a sierra fire team member was specialization. Each tango member had additional training in explosives and demolition. When Nathan read what sierra fire team's specialty was, he was surprised to hear it was cyber skills. Those guys weren't only warriors; they were IT experts.

Deadly hackers.

It was no secret that BSI's personnel were paid three times what their US service member counterparts made—often a source of contention.

But Nathan knew blood was blood. It didn't drain any slower from a higher paid warrior.

And tonight, that truth might just be proven.

The two women at the table were part of tango fire team, both munitions specialists. During the introductions, the two women had watched Harv and Nathan closely. In this male-dominated world, they'd probably expected to receive ambivalent greetings from the two "outsiders." Not so. Nathan and Harv had worked with female operatives and federal agents for decades. There wasn't a misogynistic cell in either of their bodies.

"All right, everyone, have a seat," Vince said. "I know this is a little awkward, so in order to ease some of the apprehension you may be feeling, I've prepared a small outline for you to review." Vince handed sheets of paper to the man closest to him, who took one and passed the rest along. "What you're looking at is considered top secret and may not be shared outside this room."

Both his and Harv's résumés topped the form, followed by the individual résumés of the BSI personnel seated around the table.

These guys are some heavy hitters, Nathan thought. The PMCs' prior missions were worthy of SEALs and FORECONs—everything from hostage rescue to surveillance to infiltration. Their work also ranged well beyond military-type service. As he and Harv had already known, BSI now trained undercover personnel for local, state, and federal law enforcement agencies, the first program of its kind ever.

By the time everyone finished reading, there were raised eyebrows all around the table.

Vince continued. "The purpose of what you just read is self-evident. There are ops that Nathan and Harvey successfully conducted that can't be revealed here. Same with my people. Everyone in this room was handpicked for this specific assignment. It's important to mention that this is a BSI mission, under BSI command. Now if anyone here can show due cause why we shouldn't all be joined in holy matrimony, speak now or forever hold your peace."

Vince's colorful reference perfectly stated what needed to be said. Now was the time to voice concerns, not once the shooting started.

No one said a word except Harv. "Just don't declare us husbands and wives."

That got a few low-key laughs.

"Leave it to Harvey to find some levity. All right, we've got a lot of material to review, so let's get started."

***

Ten hours later, they were rolling south through a pitch-black desert in a column of four BSI Humvees. Their "trucks," as the military liked to call them, and all their equipment had been driven down to El Paso's international airport earlier in the day. Nathan and Harv, along with the other fire teams, were flown down to the airport in Black Hawks, courtesy of the US Air National Guard. The two CIA operations officers who'd accompanied them from Washington, DC, flew back to Santa Fe in the BSI helicopter they'd used on the way to the academy. As Rebecca had requested, the two CIA officers retained possession of the top-secret files.

The lead truck held a BSI driver—who wasn't going on the raid—and a Border Patrol agent they'd picked up on the east side of El Paso.

His hotel fire team occupied the second Humvee. The other two fire teams rode in the third and fourth Humvees.

After leaving Interstate 10, they followed a paved road for a few miles, then turned south on a dirt track. Talk about the middle of nowhere . . . Nathan was no stranger to remote areas, especially deserts, but this region of southern Texas redefined remote. For the last thirty minutes or so, he hadn't seen any signs of civilization. Not even a single light bulb hanging outside a shack.

Their uniforms were desert MARPAT with ballistic vests, kneepads, elbowpads—the works. Just before crossing the border, they'd put all their gear on. For the time being, their M4s and duffels—containing all the ammo and equipment they'd need—were strapped to the corrugated shelf between their seats. Nathan's seat was a tight fit; he didn't have a lot of legroom.

During the drive, Harv hadn't been especially talkative. What could be said at this point? Like himself, Harv dealt with pre-mission stress by internalizing it. The last thing any of their team members wanted to see was a fellow member acting nervous and jittery.

In the near-black interior of the Humvee, Nathan turned off his radio, leaned across the duffels, and nudged Harv. He gave his friend a hand signal to turn his radio off—a twisting of his thumb and forefinger to simulate changing the volume, then a semiclosed fist indicating zero. He watched Harv reach down to his waist, then signal okay.

Still leaning, he spoke just loud enough for Harv to hear him over the rumbling of the engine. Vince and the driver had no chance to hear them because of the headsets they wore.

"You okay?" he asked.

"Yeah, you?"

"I'm good." He nodded toward Vince.

"Hard to say."

"Best guess?"

"He's focused and alert. I'd say he's good to go."

"That's my assessment as well. He's also in command."

Harv said, "I'm okay with it."

"Me too."

Vince's head turned slightly, but it didn't come all the way around. If Vince knew or suspected they'd just spoken off the comm, it didn't seem to bother him.

They turned their radios back on, returning them to manual mode. In this mode, they'd need to press the transmit button for their team-mates to hear them. Once the op started, they'd switch into autovoice mode so all they had to do was talk to transmit, no button needed. They'd have to override the autovoice mode when they whispered because their lapel mics didn't always pick up hushed conversations.

They rode in silence for several miles until Vince's voice came through their earpieces: *"Three minutes. Turn on NV and observe blackout protocol. Sierra one, Tango one, verify all team members copied."*

Vince turned his head to make sure Harv and he copied. They both issued thumbs-ups.

In the glow of a quarter moon, their Humvees crested a low ridge, and an expanse of flat desert interspersed with small hills and low ridges stretched for miles out in front of them. There was no sign of the Rio Grande or the fence. He kept expecting to see something, a dark line or stand of trees.

Everyone saw the quick flash from their one o'clock vector.

"Don't worry; that's an infrared signal," Vince said. *"Our Border Patrol contact is right where he's supposed to be, and we're right on time— something they appreciate."*

"I don't see the border fence," Harv said, using the radio.

"It's on the other side of that low bluff," Vince answered. *"About half a mile farther. We didn't want to risk being seen from the Mexican side. By the way, Nathan, there's someone up ahead who's looking forward to meeting you. Well, several people, actually."*

"Who are they?" he asked.

"No way," Vince said. *"I'm not going to spoil it. Let's just say you'll recognize one of the names when you hear it."*

"Harv?"

"No comment."

"Come on, you guys, out with it."

"Sorry," Vince said. *"You'll have to wait until we get there."*

"You guys suck."

"Some things are worth the price of admission," Harv said.

It was just like Harv to pull a stunt like this. He'd find a way to get some payback on his friend later.

They dropped down through a dry wash and came up the opposite side with plenty of speed. The lead Humvee launched over the far rim, getting five feet of air before landing.

Their driver whooped like a kid and yelled, *"Get* some! Hang on back there."

As in the Star Wars ride at Disneyland, they were pressed back in their seats as the vehicle climbed the far slope. Everything went smooth as they became weightless. Two seconds later, their vehicle found earth again and bounced along the track.

They went through a shallower wash and leveled out on a straight section of road. A few seconds later, they received a sixty-second warning from the driver.

Six Border Patrol vehicles materialized as they got closer and something bigger—a thirty-foot motor home with no markings at all. Indicating the motor home's purpose, several satellite dishes and large antennae sprouted from its roof.

"This is it. Everyone look sharp," Vince said.

Nathan felt his stomach tighten with anticipation. Somebody in this group knew who he was, and that unsettled him. He wasn't overly concerned because Harv would never reveal his identity to anyone who shouldn't have it.

Their convoy fanned out and parked facing the Border Patrol vehicles. After the dust drifted past, they climbed out and formed up with Vince and their radio specialist.

"Hang on a sec." Vince pressed his transmit button. "Sierra and tango, stretch your legs and make a head call. Do a complete equipment and weapons check. We're moving out in ten minutes."

Nathan's NV monocular allowed him to see six agents standing in front of their parked vehicles. One of them supported his weight on crutches and appeared to be in his fifties. Three of them were a generation younger than Nathan and decked out in tactical garb with grenade-launcher-equipped M4s slung over their shoulders. One of the tactically outfitted agents was a woman. The last two were dressed in khaki pants and dark sweaters and looked to be in their sixties with high and tight haircuts. The two older men didn't appear to be carrying weapons.

They're probably in charge, Nathan thought. He lowered his voice. "Those three are carrying some serious firepower. They're not what I expected."

"BORTACs," Vince said. "Border Patrol Tactical Unit."

Nathan wanted to ask why they were needed this far from the river but didn't. He supposed they'd find out soon enough. Keeping his voice low, Nathan said, "Vince, I've been meaning to ask you something. How did you assign the fire team members?"

"That was easy," Vince said, lowering his voice. "My people didn't want any unknowns with them. No offense . . ."

"None taken," Nathan said.

Vince touched his chest. "Don't worry; they feel the same way about the old man."

The female BORTAC agent walked over and asked them to follow her. Nathan was familiar with their "all business" body language, but these BORTACs embodied a new plane of seriousness. It didn't bother him. All Border Patrol agents, including the BORTACs, were the uniformed law enforcement arm of the CBP—Customs and Border Protection—and they took their jobs seriously. Back when he'd been a Force Recon, if a bunch of unknowns had walked into his camp, he would've acted the same way.

He wondered how many of them knew what tonight's mission was. Probably none, except for the two men in sweaters.

Nathan and Harvey fell back a step, letting Vincent take the lead.

The BSI commander walked up to the shorter of the two men wearing sweaters and shook his hand. "Chief Switzer, good to see you again."

"Likewise, Mr. Beaumont."

Nathan and Harv exchanged a surprised glance.

The chief of the US Border Patrol? In person? It wasn't every day you got to meet the top man of the third largest federal law enforcement agency in the country.

Vince shook hands with the other sweater. "Deputy Chief Lopez, thank you for coming."

"I wouldn't miss it," Lopez said.

Nathan knew Vince's formality was protocol. It wouldn't be appropriate to use first names in front of Switzer's agents.

Vince stepped aside and said, "Chief, Deputy Chief, this is Nathan McBride and Harvey Fontana." Vince also introduced their radio specialist.

Firm handshakes were exchanged. Then Chief Switzer said, "I knew your father well. A true patriot in every sense of the word. I'm very sorry for your loss."

"Thank you, Chief."

"I'd sing your praises to my men, but we're keeping this op under the radar." Switzer must've sensed his question. "Deputy Chief Lopez and I would've come even if the DNI hadn't asked us to. It seems you two have quite a reputation in DC."

"I hope that's a compliment," Nathan said.

"It is. I want to introduce you to someone who's been quite eager to meet you."

This is it, Nathan thought. *The other mystery person.*

The man on crutches came forward and offered his hand.

"This is Special Operations Supervisor Hank Grangeland," Switzer said. "He's on medical leave after pulling a Forrest Gump on us."

Nathan found himself grinning. This had to be Mary Grangeland's brother. The family resemblance was hard to miss, even in the dim moonlight. He'd first met Mary—who'd insisted on being called "Grangeland"—on a mission several years ago. Their introduction had been less than cordial, but they'd become close friends over the last few years. More than friends. Both he and Harv thought of Grangeland as a sister. The three of them had, after all, shared life and combat together on more than one occasion.

Switzer continued. "I've tried to keep SOS Grangeland out of harm's way, but he insists on being out in the field. He's currently breaking in a rookie and claims it's the most important job in the BP. Can't honestly say I disagree."

Hank said, "My sister considers you family, so you can count me in that category as well."

"A pleasure," Nathan said, pumping hands. He introduced Harv.

"How's she doing?" Harv asked. "We haven't spoken in over a year. I guess I owe her a call."

"She's with the ATF now."

"You're kidding," Harv said. "I thought she had her dream job with the bureau."

"Let's just say her work is a little more challenging than it used to be."

"She's got the mettle for anything the ATF can throw at her," Harv said.

Hank looked at Nathan. "Mary told me about your legendary first encounter in that Sacramento hotel room. She used to do the same thing to me on a regular basis when we fought."

Nathan shook his head.

"What's wrong?" Hank asked.

"It's hard to think of her as Mary. She's always been Grangeland to us."

Hank leaned toward Chief Switzer and lowered his voice. "Nathan employed an interesting technique to break the half nelson my sister had him in."

Looking up and down at Nathan, Chief Switzer said, "Your sister had *this* man in a half nelson?"

Nathan cleared his throat. "Aren't we a little pressed for time?"

Chief Switzer nodded at Agent Grangeland, then back at Nathan. "You, Vince, and Harv, you're with me. You too, Agent Grangeland. Let's take a walk."

Deputy Chief Lopez tagged along as well. The six of them strolled over to the drone launcher and formed a huddle.

Keeping his voice low, Switzer said, "There's something we discovered in our mission planning that you need to know. Well, there's . . . ah . . . no easy way to say this, so here goes. The ranch where the Rio Grande cell is operating belongs to Carlos Alisio."

"Alisio . . . ," Nathan said slowly.

"Yes, the oldest son of Alfonso Alisio."

He looked at Harv. Clearly Chief Switzer knew about the McBride-Alisio showdown a few years back north of Yuma. Vince's father had also been involved, along with Mary Grangeland. To put it mildly, things hadn't turned out so well for Alfonso.

Vince's voice betrayed his shock. "So the attacks against my family and Nathan's father were about revenge?"

"Yes," Switzer said. "Two things happened that Carlos Alisio couldn't have predicted. Nathan, your sister's presence in Mabel's Diner, and, Vince, Charlene's training and quick reaction when she returned fire on the shooters. Charlene bought a few extra seconds, which allowed a retired Navy corpsman to kill the gunmen. The same goes for your sister, Nathan. She saved many lives by fighting back. There's no doubt things would've been much worse otherwise."

Nathan was glad it was dark out here. He couldn't imagine what his expression looked like right now. Anger came on suddenly, like a dropped plate shattering on the floor.

Carlos Alisio, the bitter and depraved spawn of a heartless monster, had murdered his father, shot his niece, and tried to kill Vince's entire family.

Like father, like son. What a piece of shit. Your ass better not be in the ranch house when we bust in or you'll be joining your father in the underworld . . .

He felt Harv nudge his hip, which broke the dark thought pattern before it fully took hold. He touched Harv back—a silent thank-you.

Switzer continued. "We looked into the background of El Lobo and found a connection to the Alisio family that goes back over ten years." Switzer looked at Hank Grangeland. "You didn't hear any of this."

"No, sir. None of it."

"You three have a right to know who you're up against. That's why I was authorized to tell you. DNI Benson wants El Lobo and Alisio alive for interrogations. We don't know if Alisio's at the ranch house, but the presence of limousines seems to indicate it's likely."

"Limos?" Nathan asked.

"You'll see what I'm talking about inside the command post. It's also possible that more than one crime family's involved in the WMD smuggling operation. Obviously Benson wants any cartel brass you find in there alive."

"That won't be a problem," Harv said.

Vince spoke up, saying something Nathan didn't trust himself to say. "Look, this is shocking news, but it doesn't change anything. We're going to execute this op as planned. We'll bring you live prisoners—assuming it's physically possible."

"Apparently Scott Benson knows you three well. That's what he said you'd say . . . Well, now that we've got that behind us, let's go inside and review some last-minute intel." Chief Switzer gestured, and they walked toward the CP.

"I think my entire team should see the intel," Vince said. "Can we all fit inside?"

Switzer said it would be a tight squeeze but yes. "Deputy Chief Lopez and I don't need to see it again. We'll wait out here."

Vince turned to the fire team members who stood a dozen yards away and motioned them over.

Grangeland spoke into his lapel mic. "Go dark; we're coming in."

Fifteen seconds later, the mobile unit's door swung outward, exposing a completely black interior. When Nathan stepped up the entry stairs, all he saw were lots of micro-LED lights: red, white, green, and yellow, some blinking, most not. He felt the presence of another person in the room before he saw the figure's black silhouette against the multicolored LEDs.

"Okay," Grangeland said. "We're all inside."

Nathan heard the door clunk as it closed.

"Everybody hold still for a second," a deep voice announced. "The lights come on gradually."

Nathan became more and more aware of his surroundings as the illumination increased. His mind kept returning to the rock quarry where Alisio Sr. had met his end, but he couldn't afford the mental distraction. Right now, he needed to concentrate on the mission at hand. Each team member would be counting on every other team member to make it through the next two hours alive.

The right side of the interior was covered with large flat-screen TVs, all of which were currently dark. Nathan had never been inside a sportscasting trailer at a sporting event, but he imagined it looked a whole lot like this. Must've cost a fortune to set this up.

The man seated at the table stood and offered his hand. "Jack Harkin, Department of Homeland Security. I'm going to go over a last-minute update." Harkin laid an aerial photo on the table. Everyone present had seen it. It was the same image they'd used at BSI's academy to formulate their plan. "There are two things. Well, three, really. We're not one hundred percent sure, but we think this is a sniper's nest." Harkin pointed to a peak about five hundred yards north of the ranch's barracks building, which housed the ISIS fighters that El Lobo and Alisio were hosting. "There's a foot trail going up there we hadn't noticed before. It's barely visible. Also, it's a perfect strategic location with a three-hundred-and-sixty-degree view of the entire area. There's a patch cleared of rocks and bushes about the size of a king bed." Harkin put an eight-by-ten photo on the table. "When we enlarged the area, we saw this. We think this boxlike object is an ice chest. Notice how it's surrounded by a circle of rocks to screen it from below? Whoever set it up didn't think about the ice chest being seen from above. Had those rocks been irregularly shaped, we might not have noticed it."

"Good eye," Vince said. "Nathan? Harv?"

"We concur," Harv said. "It looks like the best way to get up there without being detected is from the north side, but we didn't bring any climbing gear."

"It's not a smooth vertical wall. The limestone formations are cracked and collapsed in places. I think you'll be able to get up there without too much trouble. The contour map indicates it's about fifty feet high, plus or minus. As you can see, the south side of the mesa fac-ing the compound doesn't have nearly the vertical element.

"The next thing we changed is your extraction point. You'll have to go a little farther on your exit hike, but it's a better place for the Black Hawks to get in and out." He pointed to the large-scale aerial. "By changing to this location, the Black Hawks can hug the dry wash of this canyon and stay below the horizon."

Harkin placed another photo on the table. "This was taken earlier today. It's a low-angle shot because it was taken from nine miles up on our side of the river. Three new vehicles are parked at the ranch house, and they're clearly limos. So far, we've seen no evidence of K-9 patrols anywhere on the property, but as you can see in this same photo, there are two sentries with some kind of assault rifles guarding the ranch house. There's no need to go over anything else in these photos—those are the only changes."

"Thank you, Mr. Harkin," Vince said.

"Hang on while I cut the lights."

Like the beginning of a Broadway show, the illumination slowly dimmed, then winked out.

Once outside the command post, everyone formed a circle. Switzer and Lopez joined them.

"All right, everyone, listen up," Vince said. "Sandra, can your demo team handle the limos, if needed?"

"Yes, no problem."

"Obviously, we'll have to clear the sniper's nest. We'll talk about it on the way. We've got a ninety-minute trek ahead of us. Everyone gear up and power down some water." Vince turned toward the Border Patrol brass. "Chief Switzer, Deputy Chief Lopez, no goodbyes. We'll see you in a few hours."

"We'll be waiting. Supervisory Agent Mark Ristow will escort you over to the frontage road along the river and then part company. You'll follow that to the east and look for the infrared beacon we planted. It marks the exact spot where you'll cross. There's a small raft with a rope that's anchored to both sides of the river. You guys know the drill. It's set up over a deeper spot, so the water won't be moving quickly. Good hunting, everyone."

Nathan felt the familiar sensation of butterflies as he walked with Harv and Vince back to their Humvee. The news of Carlos Alisio being behind the assassination of his father and the deadly attack against Vince's family still buzzed in his head. Purely revenge driven, the shootings had been cleverly disguised as terrorist attacks. Perhaps if the shooters had been Hispanic, he might've seen the connection. What pissed him off the most? The senseless slaughter of so many innocents who had no connection to Alisio's twisted quest for vengeance. It showed how vile the second-generation cartel boss was. Life meant nothing to him. In a way, Nathan was glad this news hadn't been discovered sooner. Vince, Harv, and he might have been excluded from tonight's action, or at a minimum, he would've had to cash in some IOUs to participate.

Three minutes later, they were walking downhill through the desert. He heard SA Ristow check with their sentry atop the ridge off to their right and receive an all clear. No one was present at the river-crossing site. Nathan wondered if the bomb-bearing B-2s were already circling overhead; if not, they were on their way.

They walked about three hundred yards through some good-size ravines. In some places, they had to scramble on all fours to make it back up the opposite sides.

Once they arrived at the dirt road, Ristow wished them luck and turned back. Since they now followed a maintained road, they didn't need to use their night vision, but Harv kept turning his on and taking a look every few minutes. His friend seemed on edge, more than their current situation called for.

The point man reported having the beacon in sight. Since their radios were currently in manual mode, Vince pressed his transmit button and acknowledged.

"Harv?" Nathan asked.

"What?"

"What's on your mind?"

"I think we need an advanced scout along our route once we're across the river," Harv said. "We won't have eyes overhead until we're a lot closer to the compound."

Nathan found himself agreeing but let Vince respond.

"He's got a point," Vince said. "We could launch our drone early, but that'd mean losing orbit time on the back end."

Harv continued. "I hate to say this, Nate, but we can accomplish two things at once if you're willing to be the scout."

"All right, you have my undivided attention," he said.

"I want everyone in on this," Vince said. He ordered all three fire teams to form up. "Okay, Harv, you're on."

"Once we cross the river, I think Nathan should scout ahead with a ten-minute lead. I'm sure everyone here has rock-climbing skills, but Nathan's an excellent free climber. He should be able to scale the north side of the rock face, come in from behind, and take out the sniper quietly. If no one's up there, he'll come down the easier southeast slope and rendezvous with us."

"I concur," Vince said. "It's likely we'll have our drone overhead by the time Nathan makes it to the base of the sniper's bluff. Since our drone's got a high-res thermal imager, we'll know if a shooter's up there. If the drone doesn't see anyone, Nathan will stop in his tracks and turn east. If a shooter *is* up there, Nathan will proceed as planned."

Harv put a hand on Vince's shoulder. "I'd feel better if we sent one of sierra's men with Nathan, one minute behind."

"Good idea," Vince said.

A member of the sierra fire team volunteered right away and stepped forward. "I'll go," he said.

"All right, Nick, the job's yours. I didn't mention it during our mission-op briefing, but Nick's worked with you guys before." Vince added some lighthearted tone. "Could be why he volunteered so quickly."

And then Nathan had it. "Were you part of Delta Lead in Santa Monica?"

Delta Lead had been the call sign for BSI's surveillance team assigned to help him and Harv during an impromptu mission last year. The BSI team had probably saved their lives.

"Yes, sir, I left you the note."

"You guys did a great job. Thank you."

"I was in Tanner Mason's unit in Afghanistan," Nick said. "It broke my heart to hear how he'd betrayed everything we stand for. He seemed like a good man."

"He *was* a good man," Vince said. "He took a wrong turn and kept going."

They resumed their hike down the road.

Nathan knew Vince wanted to change the subject. "It's hard to believe a terrorist camp is only a few miles from our border. How can a place like that exist without local law enforcement knowing about it?"

"It can't," Vince said. "Sadly, a local cop can make more money from a single bribe than his entire annual salary."

"Dirty cops are the worst," he said.

Five minutes later, they were taking turns pulling the small inflatable raft back and forth across the river. They formed a group in a small clearing of sand about fifty yards south of the water. There was lots of cover in this spot because bushes and trees flourished along the river.

Waiting for the last two members of tango fire team to cross, Harv said, "I don't know what I'd been expecting to see, but except for the river, there's nothing. No fence, no monuments, no barbed wire on either side. Hell, our freeways are better protected."

"I've got news for you," said Vincent. "Our border with Canada? Security wise, it's worse. There's not even a river. There's nothing but trees."

Harv shook his head. "I guess I'm beginning to understand what the definition of *porous border* means."

"The Rio Grande swells and shrinks every season," Vince said. "You can't really put a fence or wall right next to it. It has to be above the hundred-year flood plain. There are many areas where a wall or fence simply won't work, especially farther east in Big Bend National Park. It takes boots on the ground to guard areas like this. Lots of them."

The last two members of tango joined them.

"Okay. We're going to get Nathan and Nick going. Everyone leave their radios in manual and do a final check. If anyone needs to switch out a radio, now's the time. Verify long guns are on safety."

One by one, all twelve members did a radio check. Everyone heard everyone else's transmission. They were good to go. Since they'd gone over the logistics and planning many times during their six-hour briefing, Vince wouldn't repeat too many things.

"Our scatter point is anywhere on American soil. If the shit hits the fan, everyone works their way north, takes a swim, then gets their wetback asses back to the CP ASAP."

That got a few chuckles. Vince was a lot of things, but politically correct wasn't one of them. There were several Hispanic team members, and they wouldn't be the least bit offended. Everyone here would be fighting side by side and possibly intermixing each other's blood. If you couldn't take a little teasing, you had no business working for Vincent Beaumont.

"All right, Nathan, get going. Nick will be sixty seconds behind. The rest of us are moving out in ten minutes. Tell us once you have the sniper's bluff in sight. Nick will cover your six on the ascent."

"Good hunting, old man," Harv said.

"Hey, I'm six months younger than you." With that, Nathan began marching south through the canyon.

***

The hike, which paralleled a dry stream bed, wasn't difficult from a physical standpoint, but because of the near absence of moonlight, he had to keep his NV monocular deployed and spend a lot of time looking down, watching his step. This wasn't a vast expanse of sand—far from it. Some areas were worse than others, but this landscape was riddled with things to trip over. Face-planting into an agave lechuguilla would definitely ruin his evening and might cost him an eye. A fall could be more than painful and inconvenient; it could jeopardize the mission.

He settled on a pace mixing efficiency and stealth, not purely one or the other. Just ahead, where the dry wash turned left, he'd leave the visual cover of the arroyo and begin a fairly steep climb up the side of a small hill to maintain a due south route.

Whenever he turned to look back, he could usually see Nick, trailing by five hundred feet or so. He pulled the handheld moving map from his waist pack and checked his location. Right on target.

Except for the sporadic rasp of crickets, it was quiet. The insect and frog sounds from the river had slowly faded away.

At the crest of the small hill, he scanned the route ahead and saw no movement at all. So far, so good. Knowing Nick would temporarily lose sight of him, he started down the slope.

The next forty-five minutes went by without incident. When he came around the western edge of a low rise, he spotted the sniper's bluff right away. He couldn't miss it—a solitary crown of limestone sitting atop an asymmetrical cone. It didn't look too foreboding. On a smaller scale, it looked like a tilted ham tin sitting atop a three-foot pile of sand. From his current position, he couldn't yet see the compound. He'd need to gain elevation.

Gain elevation? Don't you mean scale that rock formation in near darkness? Way to cheer yourself up, Nate.

He froze in place when he heard it.

The unmistakable clatter of fully automatic gunfire.

***

Harv felt his skin crawl at the crackling sound reverberating through the canyon.

"Form up," Vince said. "Hotel one, Sierra two, you copy?"

"Affirm," Nate's voice came through every team member's earpiece. Nick copied as well.

Harv felt his heart relax. Shit, he hated that anxious feeling. He should've been trailing Nate, not Nick.

"Hotel one, report."

"It's coming from the compound, but it's not directed at us. We're still over a mile out."

"Do you have eyes on the sniper's location?"

"I can see the bluff, but that's all."

"How fast can you get up there?"

"If the vertical climb isn't too bad, maybe ten minutes. Hang on; I'm taking a look with my thermal."

Vince ordered Nate and Sierra two to hold position for sixty seconds, then said, "Harv, what do you make of it?"

"Hard to say. It could be—"

Interrupting him, a muted boom echoed through the canyon, followed by another and then the sound of more automatic clatter.

In the green image of Harv's night vision, the southern horizon flashed, as if illuminated by distant lightning. "Those are smaller detonations, probably from grenade launchers. Unless someone else is engaging the Rio Grande cell and no one told us about it, the most reasonable conclusion is that they're out there practicing."

"I concur."

"Do we scrub?" Harv asked.

"Not yet. Let's get our eyes overhead a little early. It can be here in seven minutes." Vince addressed Hotel four, their radio specialist. "Greg, get on the horn to command. Tell them to launch right away. It will cost us some orbit time, but we need to see what we're dealing with."

"You got it."

Greg stepped away from the group and made the call. Harv then watched him pull out a large tablet and tap open an app.

"Well, there's one saving grace to this development," Harv said.

"I'm hard-pressed to think of one."

"They don't know we're coming. There's no way they'd be out there firing away like this if they were expecting anyone. They'd be lying low, waiting to bushwhack us."

"True enough, Harv. For now, we keep going. The compound's on the far side of that next ridge. We're still twenty minutes from getting eyes on it."

Automatic gunfire continued, and from the sound of it, those guys were blowing through some ammo. Thousands of rounds. Every so often, a break in the clatter lasted for several seconds, then began anew.

Harv said, "Let's turn Nathan loose."

"Right." Vince pressed the transmit button. "Hotel one."

"Copy," Nate answered.

"Proceed as planned, best possible speed. We're launching the drone a little early."

"On my way."

"Sierra two, double-time over to Hotel one's position; then circle the vertical wall to the east. See if you can get eyes on the compound before our drone arrives. Avoid visual contact with the shooter at all costs. Do not proceed if you have any chance of being spotted. Hotel one, check in when you've scaled the vertical wall."

Both Nate and Nick acknowledged.

They all heard their radioman say, "Say again, say again . . . Copy . . . Stand by . . ." Greg walked back to the group. "We lost our drone. It crashed on launch. Some kind of steering malfunction. HQ asked if we want to scrub."

Vince didn't say anything right away, but Harv felt his anger radiating like an oven. A good leader wouldn't swear or kick the ground, Harv knew. A good leader would say something like, *All right, listen—*

"All right, listen up," Vince said. "We're not scrubbing. If the B-2s have to level that compound, we've failed, and we aren't going to fail. This complicates things, but we can handle it. We're doing this the old-fashioned way. Sierra one, if you can avoid being seen from the sniper's bluff, scout ahead to the ridgeline and get eyes on the camp. Give me your best speed. Let me know when you see Hotel one's and Sierra two's footprints where they turned to the west. Our route into the compound isn't scouted beyond that point, so slow down from there on."

"Yes, sir."

Sierra one began a cautious jog through the mesquite, creosote, and other bushes, then disappeared.

"Maybe we can turn this into an advantage," Harv said. "If we can hit them while they're practicing, we might be able to take five or six of them down simultaneously."

"That's a possibility," Vince said. "Once Sierra one gets eyes on the compound, we'll know what we're dealing with. Everyone take a few seconds and pound some water. We're moving out. Ten-yard separation."

They moved at a quick pace. At the point where Nate and Nick had turned to the west, they kept going straight, following Sierra one's solo footprints.

After crossing another sandy wash strewn with river rock, they began their final ascent up a gradual slope to a ridgeline that overlooked the compound.

Gunfire continued, but they didn't hear any additional detonations.

The hike they needed to make wasn't steep, but it was long. They had to go over half a mile at around a fifteen-degree slope. Vince slowed their pace a little. There was no sense in being gassed when they reached the summit, some four hundred feet above.

Harv felt a strong desire to race forward but kept pace with the rest of the squad.

***

Nathan took a few seconds to check the area in front of him, mainly the steep slope leading up to the base of the vertical wall. He didn't expect to see anyone, and didn't. The closer he got to the rock face, the more ominous it looked. At this point, he had his NV on a high gain setting in order to find the best place to make the climb. He saw something promising, but he wouldn't know until he got closer.

"Hotel one, copy?" It was Vince.

"Copy," he said.

"We lost our drone on launch—some sort of steering-control malfunction. You're going up there for sure. I've sent a scout ahead of our column to the compound's northern ridge, but you'll be our best eyes from up there. What's your ETA?"

"Five minutes or a little more, depending on the climb."

"Check in from the top."

"Copy."

The machine-gun fire continued but seemed to be decreasing a little. If he could get up there before the shooting stopped, he wouldn't have to worry about every little sound and could make a much quicker approach.

Off to his right, he saw what he needed: a dark vertical line that extended most of the way to the top. He diverted around a large rockfall and nearly lost his footing as a large rock gave way and tumbled down the slope, making a boatload of noise. He cringed when the shooting paused just as the rock came to rest. Sloppy. He should've tested its purchase first.

The fissure looked pretty good. About thirty inches wide, it would allow him to make a chimney climb straight up. The problem occurred at the halfway point, where the chimney appeared to be blocked. He'd have to leave the chimney and climb the vertical face, using much smaller foot- and handholds to get above the blockage before he could return to the chimney. There'd be zero margin for error on the limestone wall. Had time not been a huge factor, he would've looked for a better spot.

He removed his kneepads and elbowpads in order to get a better feel for climbing, then turned his pack around so his back would lie flat in the chimney. He put the pads into his pack and began using leverage to hoist himself up the shaft. Anyone with claustrophobia wouldn't be able to do this. Fortunately, it wasn't one of his phobias. He wondered what the fear of one's self was called.

Now there's a nice cheerful thought, Nate. Anything else? How about ending up as a crumpled mass of broken bones and dislocated joints at the bottom of this shaft? He nearly laughed when an old adage popped into his mind: *I don't get paid enough for this.*

Time to concentrate. He'd reached the spot where he needed to leave the fissure and move vertically up the cliff's face to continue the climb. As he'd seen from below, there weren't any handholds or foot-holds that he'd trust his life to without a belaying partner. Then he noticed something. Rather than leave the fissure and risk a fall from the cliff's face, he could go deeper into the chimney and maneuver himself around the backside of the blockage.

But, damn, it looked tight.

Up above, he could clearly see stars in the void created by the fallen hunk of limestone. If he got himself stuck, the mission would suffer a serious time setback rescuing his ass. It might even ruin the op. What if his radio didn't even work in here? He reached down and pressed the transmit button.

"Hotel three, radio check. How do you read?"

"Loud and clear."

"I'm in a chimney climb and wanted to make sure my radio worked."

"You're good to go."

"If all goes well, I'll be on the top in three or four minutes."

"Copy."

His NV monocular made coping with the stress a whole lot easier. This would be unnerving enough in daylight. Going deeper into the limestone fissure presented a new problem—his backpack. He couldn't wear it, even with it turned around on his chest. This vertical crawl space was way too tight.

Using just his knees, he wedged himself in place, slid the backpack off, tied its carry handle to his bootlace, and let it dangle. Satisfied it wouldn't come loose, he moved deeper into the narrowing crevice to a point where his knees could barely bend. So here he was, thirty feet inside the fissure, surrounded by cold limestone that seemed to be getting tighter with each breath he took. No problem—he owned this.

On second thought, maybe this hadn't been such a good idea after all. He still had to go four or five feet deeper into the fissure before clearing the backside of the fallen mass.

Shit! What was that?

The walls just shook.

He froze, waiting.

A crippling sensation of being trapped inside a giant trash compactor slammed home, and he hoped his death would be quick. Partially crushed and slowly suffocating to death wasn't on his bucket list.

The sound of his breathing made things worse. He closed his eyes and rested his head against the rock.

Whatever he'd felt didn't return. *Come on, Nate. The walls didn't move. You're imagining things.* The crack wasn't collapsing. His brain had played a trick on him. There was nothing but stable limestone all around him.

He kept inching deeper until his chest began making intermittent contact with the limestone, creating the illusion of not being able to breathe. *You can still breathe. Relax.* He inhaled deeply and felt even more pressure. *Well, duh.* A glance above his head confirmed he could now start ascending past the blockage. The narrow belt of stars lightened his mood. All he had to do was go ten feet higher, and he'd be able to rest his weight on top of the fallen mass.

He felt the onset of fatigue take hold in his forearms, quads, and calves. Because it was so tight in here, he couldn't get the right kind of leverage to make the climb less strenuous. He wedged his palms and elbows and took the weight off his legs for a few seconds.

Almost there. Just a little farther.

All I have to do is keep going.

CHAPTER 28

Like a spider crawling out of a hole, Nathan emerged from the crack, grateful he didn't have to battle any clumps of cactus or agave. He took a few deep breaths to calm his nerves. As tempting as it was to take a breather, he didn't have time. Harv and his fellow team members were counting on him to clear the top of this bluff. Lives could be lost if he failed—not only lives, but the entire mission. Unacceptable. There might not be a sniper or sentry up here, but he needed to find out. He'd rest his legs and arms while he advanced toward the opposite rim.

He looked at the fissure he'd ascended and felt good about making it up here. The sense of accomplishment made up for the suffocating feeling of being entombed inside countless tons of limestone.

After turning the radio back to auto mode, he untied the backpack from his boot; put on his elbowpads, kneepads, and gloves; then checked the wiring of his radio to make sure nothing had pulled loose during the climb. Next, he donned his ammo vest, followed by the backpack. This wasn't his preferred setup for carrying spare ammo, but he now had eight additional thirty-round M4 magazines and five pistol magazines within easy reach. He also carried twelve high-explosive grenades—six on his pistol belt and six more in the waist pack. Every team member also had four tear-gas grenades, two white-star parachute flare rounds, and four gray smoke rounds. His pants pockets held all kinds of other tactical tools and items. Harv had the identical setup. Not exactly the look of FORECON Marines, but they had everything they needed.

Satisfied he was ready to continue, he made radio contact. "Hotel three, I'm on top of the bluff, proceeding to the south end."

"Copy."

From the satellite photos, he knew the sniper's nest lay at least a hundred yards distant. He focused his night-vision scope to infinity and held perfectly still, listening for sound.

The plant life surprised him. He'd expected to find barren rock with a cactus here and there. The vegetation wasn't as abundant as in the desert below, but everything still grew up here—mesquite, creosote, ocotillo, grasses, agave, and of course, all other kinds of cactus. It seemed like every plant in the Chihuahuan Desert poked, pricked, punctured, or scraped.

The terrain sloped gradually downward in the direction he needed to go. Once again, he had to focus his NV on the ground to advance. He stopped when a sudden glow came to life. Directly ahead. Some sort of light source illuminated an area of bushes and medium-size rocks. The glow varied in intensity, almost as if . . . Oh, no way . . . Could the fool really be using his cell phone while on sentry duty? If so, he had to be playing a game or using an app that didn't require a cell signal. He could be reading a book or scrolling through photos. Anything really.

"Hotel three," he whispered, "I've got something at my one o'clock. Stand by."

"Copy, Hotel one. Sierra one, status?"

"I can't go any farther without being seen from the bluff. It's at my three o'clock right now. If the sniper has a thermal imager, he'll see me."

Vince said, *"Sierra one, hold position. We're closing in on you."*

"Copy."

"Hotel one, we can't proceed until that sniper's eliminated. Best possible speed."

Nathan clicked his radio and kept weaving his way forward through the shrubs and cactus.

He got his first direct look at the sniper after moving past a small group of mesquite trees.

Wearing a dark coat with an AK slung over his shoulder, the man sat in a low-profile folding chair, like sunbathers used at the beach. Incredibly, he held his phone up without any concern for the light it emitted in every direction. Nathan shook his head, planning to take full advantage of the situation.

He pressed his transmit button and whispered, "I've got eyes on the target. He appears to be a sentry, not a sniper. He's got an AK without a scope."

"Proceed, Hotel one."

Nathan heard that loud and clear.

He was grateful for all the gunfire noise still grinding across the plateau up here. It wouldn't be easy to walk silently through this dry and brittle foliage. A snagged piece of clothing would likely be heard.

Everything changed when the automatic clatter suddenly ended, and didn't resume.

He waited a few seconds, but no more gunfire emanated from the compound. It seemed they'd finished practicing. *Great timing.* He couldn't believe his luck. *Quit lamenting and deal with it.*

Knowing the slightest sound would make the sentry turn and look, he froze in place.

Still a good fifty yards from the sentry, Nathan evaluated the situation.

He had two advantages. The first, and perhaps the biggest, was that the man remained engrossed with his cell phone. At this distance, Nathan didn't even need his NV to see it. The second advantage? The terrorists of the Rio Grande cell obviously weren't expecting trouble tonight. If they were, they'd have put a bona fide sniper up here who wouldn't be staring at his phone, and they certainly wouldn't be outside firing their weapons.

The disadvantage—a big one—was that he'd have to go much more slowly to avoid being heard. Every shrub, kicked rock, or snapped twig would make noise. In the silent landscape of this bluff's plateau, any noise might as well be a loud sneeze. How could it be so damned quiet? Looking ahead, there wasn't a bush thick enough to hide behind, and the biggest rock looked about eighteen inches high.

He changed the NV's focus back to the ground, which made distant objects blurry. Conversely, focusing at distant objects made the ground blurry. He couldn't have it both ways. If only he had dual scopes . . .

It is what it is. Deal with it.

He decided to split the difference and focus at about fifteen feet. It still gave him a fairly clear picture of the desert floor and made objects in the distance less blurry.

The Sig's laser sight combined with the night vision made an ideal point-and-shoot setup. The bullet went where the bright dot illuminated the target. In this case, it would be the back of the sentry's head. If he could just get fifteen yards closer, he'd feel a whole lot better about making a single-shot kill. He wasn't overly worried about the suppressed shot being heard down below. His biggest concern was dropping the sentry with a single shot, because if his target somehow managed to return fire with the AK, the element of surprise would be lost.

Nathan looked down, memorized all the objects that could make noise if stepped on, then looked back up to watch the sentry. Trusting in himself, he took three steps without looking at his feet. He then stopped, looked down, found two more safe steps, and focused on the sentry again. Two steps later, he was ready to repeat the process.

He'd need to do this five or six more times before he would reach a comfortable head-shot range.

Nathan marveled at his good fortune when, thirteen steps closer, he detected a trip wire.

A foot off the ground, each end of the fishing line connected to a cowbell hanging over a small branch. Beyond the cowbells, the string continued as far as Nathan's NV could see. It looked like it extended all the way across the bluff. Had he not been using this glance-and-advance technique, he might not have seen it.

He took a few seconds to focus his NV directly on the line to see its exact height and path before stepping over it.

Safely on the other side, he scanned the area for a secondary line. Seeing none, he continued forward using the same method.

He was about to take another step when the unmistakable sound of a radio transmission broke the silence, definitely in Arabic. Even though the radio was much louder than it needed to be, he caught only pieces of what was said. He shouldn't have been able to hear anything from this distance—a sloppy mistake on the sentry's part. The man on the other end of the transmission said relief was on the way in twenty minutes, then something about staying alert.

The sentry cursed and stretched his arms.

Nathan was in the process of crouching when the man stood, turned directly toward him, and—

Froze.

Had he been seen? He wasn't sure. It was damned dark up here, but the human eye can detect motion against a still background.

Motionless, the man seemed to be considering whether his eyes had played a trick on him. Nathan had definitely been moving when the guy looked his way.

A five-second staring match stretched into ten.

Then fifteen.

Nathan willed the man to turn back around.

It didn't work.

In the vivid image of his NV scope, Nathan watched the guy slowly unsling his AK.

There were times in life when you had to double down.

Like right now.

If you win, you win big. If you lose, it costs you your life.

Nathan came up from his crouch.

Speaking perfect Arabic with a Syrian accent, he put command tone in his voice. "What the hell are you doing on your phone? Are you some kind of idiot? I was able to climb the rock face and easily sneak up on you! The trip wire was sloppy and easy to spot."

The man froze. He had to be thinking this was some sort of a joke or prank. "W-who are you?"

Nathan began marching forward. "If I don't hear the right words out of your mouth, I'll kill you where you stand."

"I'm sorry! I've been up here for a long time. I was supposed to be relieved three hours ago. I just spoke to Mahdi. He's sending Tariq."

"Tariq had better do a better job than you. I should report your inexcusable carelessness."

"I'm sorry. I was supposed to be relieved."

"Relieved from what? Staring at your phone?"

"I—I was checking for a signal."

"Don't make excuses." Nathan continued his march forward, remembering how dark it was up here. At best, the man could make out only the dark silhouette of someone approaching. He'd also been looking at a bright cell phone screen. It would take his eyes a little longer to fully adjust. Nathan wanted to yell louder to disguise his voice, but he didn't want to risk being heard in the compound.

He maintained a quick pace. In ten or fifteen more steps, this charade would be over.

Sooner, it seemed.

He watched the lookout take a hand off the AK, reach into the cargo pocket of his pants, and pull an object out.

Shit! A night-vision scope. And it was turned on.

"You fool. I can see your night-vision scope lighting you up like a spotlight."

The man stiffened and took a defensive stance, but he hadn't brought his weapon to bear quite yet. Nathan continued the bluff. "You should've turned it off to preserve its batteries."

Five steps. Four.

"I'm very tired."

Two.

The sentry brought the scope up to his eye. "Who are you?"

"Retribution."

"What?"

In one fluid movement, Nathan took a Weaver stance, brought his suppressed pistol up, and activated its laser. Starting low, he swung the bright dot onto the man's chest. He didn't have the two extra seconds needed to walk the beam onto the man's face and send a precisely aimed bullet. He'd have to make two center-mass shots and hope for the best.

At the instant he double pulled the trigger, the area in front of him flashed like camera shots.

In less than a tenth of a second, the copper-jacketed slugs flew into their target.

The man went stiff, as if zapped by a Taser.

Hoping to sever all motor function, Nathan sent a third bullet through the man's throat.

It didn't work.

Sounding like a thunderclap, the man's AK erupted with a short burst, exploding the earth next to the ice chest.

Shit!

He sprinted forward and found the man writhing on the ground. Realizing he could be seen from the compound, he crouched and sent a fourth bullet through the man's forehead. That did the trick.

A few feet away, the sentry's radio squawked to life in Arabic. "What the hell's going on up there?"

Nathan knew this Motorola model well, and unfortunately, it had pretty good sound quality. Its user's voice would definitely be recognizable.

The question spat from the radio again.

He turned the volume to a medium setting, then pressed and released the transmit button repeatedly when he spoke so the man on the other end would hear a broken and intermittent transmission. "I shot at some kind of dog. Everything is okay. Repeat your transmission."

Nathan squinted at the harsh tone of the reply. Apparently they were having a bad night. He continued to press and release the button as he talked. "I dropped the radio. Your transmission is broken. I can't hear you clearly. It was just a dog. I chased it away."

Nathan heard the response clearly. *"It was a coyote, you dumb shit. Don't waste ammo on them. They're harmless. Stay there. I'm sending up a new radio. You just earned two more hours up there. Don't fire again unless you want to be there all night."*

Nathan thought it would be best not to respond because no question had been asked. And based on the harsh tone coming from the compound, anything he said would be wrong anyway.

"Hotel three, did you copy all of that?" Nathan hoped Vince had heard everything.

"Affirm. Smart thinking."

"Be advised the sentry up here was using NV, but I don't see a TI."

"Copy that. Status in the compound?"

"Stand by." Nathan took a few seconds to use his thermal imager and detected no warm signatures. The compound looked exactly like the scaled-down cardboard mock-up, allowing him to easily identify the barracks building. His TI registered a slight variation in the color of its windows compared to the background. About the size of a basketball court, the barracks were surrounded by smaller structures in a semicircular pattern. He could see some picnic tables and portable awnings, the kind that folded and unfolded. Just like the aerials showed, the practice range lay to the east. All kinds of derelict cars were intermixed with framed targets. Some sort of primitive obstacle course bordered the shooting range to the north. The geographic center of the compound appeared to be about six hundred to seven hundred yards away, and several hundred feet lower in elevation. The barracks were about one hundred yards closer. Heading to the west, toward the ranch's main house, a dirt road weaved its way up a shallow canyon and disappeared over the top of a ridgeline. He couldn't see the ranch house from here; it sat on the other side of the ridge. Several cars and trucks were parked near the barracks, and several others sat in a small group on the west end of the compound. Nathan spotted an overhead power line, its terminus pole clearly fitted with a transformer for reducing voltage.

He gave Vince a quick summary.

"Affirm, Hotel one. Sierra one, double-time up to the ridge and get eyes on the compound. ETA?"

"Three minutes."

Vince continued. *"Sierra two, form up with Sierra one. Everyone be advised I just sent tango fire team to the west. Tango one's going to divert over to the road coming down the canyon to sever power and phone lines while the rest of the tango team hustles up to the west ridgeline to get eyes on the ranch house."*

"Sierra two copies; I'm on my way to the compound's north ridge. I have eyes on Sierra one."

"Copy," Vince answered.

Nathan saw a warm body emerge out of the barracks building and begin walking toward the trailhead, likely a courier with the replacement radio.

"Hotel three, I've got company coming. One man on foot, heading for the trail leading up here."

"Prosecute, then stand by."

He offered a squelch click in reply, then grabbed the sentry's radio. He turned its volume down to zero and secured it in his waist pack. Thankfully, the vertical cliff face on this side was only ten feet high, and the trail coming up from the compound worked its way up a collapsed section, sparing him a vertical descent. At the cliff's base, he began searching the footpath for a good location to set up his ambush. Figuring the man coming up here would use the trail they'd seen on the aerial photos, he headed for a five-foot-high piece of the bluff's limestone that had tumbled down the slope.

The courier didn't appear to be using night vision. Confirmation came when the guy turned on a small flashlight. It wasn't bright to the naked eye, but his NV made it look like a phosphorous signal flare.

Nathan made it to the rock and ducked behind its square form. Several feet away, the trail made a gradual arc around a large gathering of agave and a nasty looking patch of cactus.

The man moved at a good clip, but Nathan didn't want to wait the two minutes it would take for him to arrive. He stole a look around the boulder and saw another hiding place fifty yards farther down the trail: a four-foot-high patch of thick brush. He focused his NV on the ground and crept toward it in a crouch.

He preferred using his Sig to take out the courier, but he was a good two hundred yards closer to the barracks building now and didn't want to risk the clap-like sound of a suppressed shot being heard.

He made it to the bushes with about a minute to spare. Bleed light from the approaching flashlight created jumpy shadows all around him. He reached down and pulled the Predator knife from its sheath strapped to the side of his calf.

He heard the man's footsteps as the jittery light reached a peak.

Walking at a fast pace, the man moved past the clump of bushes.

Using a technique he'd learned long ago, Nathan jumped the courier from behind and used his left hand to cover the man's mouth while his right hand drove the knife upward under the man's rib cage, perforating his right lung and heart.

Within ten seconds, it was over.

After his prey went limp, he let go, then turned off the man's flashlight. He picked up the spare radio and made sure it was off before securing it and the other radio in his backpack. Having two of the enemy's radios might come in handy.

Time to move on.

He wiped the Predator clean on the man's shirt, returned it to its sheath, and took a few seconds to make sure all his equipment remained secure. The man's initial thrashing had been severe.

"Hotel three, the courier's down. Request permission to approach the compound for a closer look. I can safely get within a hundred yards."

Vince's response wasn't immediate. He knew his friend was considering all the options, but given the lack of activity in the compound, a closer reconnaissance wasn't a bad idea.

"Proceed, Hotel one, but maintain cover. Do not enter open ground."

"Copy."

"Sierra one, we have you in sight," Vince said. *"We're double-timing up to your position."*

Nathan started a countdown of sorts, figuring they had a little less than five minutes to maintain the element of surprise. After that, things could get dicey. The terrorists would definitely become suspicious when two of their comrades failed to answer their radios.

All the more reason to get as close as possible.

Just ahead, he saw a way to get closer to the buildings without being seen from the barracks, but he wouldn't make the attempt without clearing it with Vince first. There were two parked pickups and a small sedan about fifty yards southwest of the barracks. If he went a little farther, he'd be able to keep the trucks between himself and the barracks, allowing him to advance with a better chance of not being seen.

Sierra one's transmission broke the silence. *"Hotel one, confirm you're moving due east about one hundred yards southwest of the compound."*

"Affirm, Sierra one, that's me. I don't have eyes on you."

"I'm with Sierra two at your ten o'clock, atop the ridge."

"Give me a fisted flashlight."

"Stand by . . ."

Nathan's NV saw it easily. "I've got you, thanks."

Sierra one's radio clicked in reply.

The barracks building was nothing more than a big rectangular box with an extended gable roof supported by wood posts. The overhanging roof allowed people to sit in the shade. A few chairs were present, but no one occupied them. The other buildings surrounding the barracks looked like storage sheds and small barns.

Nathan didn't see any motion with his night vision, but he did detect—

Cigarette smoke.

He halted, not knowing where the smoker was, then slowly lowered himself to one knee.

Since the air was so still, the smoker could be anywhere, even inside one of the buildings.

"Hotel three, someone's smoking out here. Attempting to locate the source."

"Copy."

Something didn't add up. If the smoker had been outside when the radio courier started up the trail, why hadn't the sudden disappearance of the courier's flashlight beam caused any alarm? The most reasonable explanation? The smoker hadn't been tracking the courier, which meant they still had the element of surprise.

He flipped his NV up and took a look with the TI. No warm bodies registered. He brought the NV back down and turned its gain to maximum. He slowly scanned the compound from one end to the other.

There! A super dim glow, emanating from between the trucks. He didn't see anyone, but a cigarette's glow definitely registered with the NV. The area between the trucks brightened for a few seconds, then went faint again. He'd seen this before: the smoker takes a drag, and the ultrasensitive device detects the increase in illumination.

Sierra one's line-of-sight vector wasn't much better than his, but he had a much higher elevation. "Sierra one, do you have eyes between the pickup trucks with your TI?"

"Stand by . . . Affirm. I've got a warm signature. I can see his head. He appears to be sitting in a truck with the door open. I can't see any weapons from here."

"Is he in the truck with the oversized tires and off-road light bar on the cab?"

"Affirm."

"Sierra one, can the smoker see the sloped area below you?"

"Affirm. If he's got NV or a TI, he might see us when we come down. For now, he's just sitting there. He doesn't seem to be on sentry duty."

"Hotel three, I think I can take him out if I approach from my current position. I can keep the smaller of the parked pickups between myself and the smoker." Nathan wanted to say he'd spare the guy from a slow death by lung cancer but figured it wouldn't sound professional.

Vince didn't delay in responding. *"Stand by, Hotel one. Sierras one and two, advance to the edge of the compound. Keep checking that smoker. Make sure he doesn't see you."*

"Copy. We'll be most visible near the top where it's steeper, but once the slope levels out a little, we can use vegetation as cover until we reach the level ground of the compound."

"Proceed to the closest cover you can find to support Hotel one while he approaches the smoker. We'll make contact once we reach the ridgeline."

"Copy."

"Hotel one, you're cleared to take the smoker down. Verbal copy please."

"Copy."

"Good hunting."

He clicked the radio in response. Staying low, Nathan moved downhill through the thinning shrubs, careful to avoid kicking any rocks or stepping on dry brush.

He paused at the bottom and took a moment to study the open span between the vehicles and him. It was mostly dirt and sand with smaller rocks here and there. Some curved tire tracks marred the surface, but he didn't see any footprints.

"Sierra one, do you still have eyes on the smoker? I'm about to traverse open ground over to the smaller truck."

"Affirm. No changes. He appears to be staring toward the barracks."

In a crouch, he moved across a dry creek bed at the bottom of the slope and began easing toward the vehicles. *This is going to be a long hundred yards,* he thought. How long before the man who was sent out with the replacement radio became MIA to the others? Another two or three minutes at most?

Nathan wondered why the smoker chose to sit in a truck as opposed to sitting on the patio surrounding the barracks. Perhaps he wanted some solitude. Being a good fifty yards away from the barracks, the pickups offered the man some privacy. Nathan knew about barracks life: he had, after all, spent years in the Marines.

Halfway across the open ground, he began to slow his pace, being extra careful with his steps. The dry earth didn't crunch, but it wasn't completely silent.

At the three-quarters mark, he slowed to a step every few seconds. The last twenty-five yards were going to take about a minute. *Perhaps a minute too late,* he thought.

Suddenly, the area between the trucks flared to life with a bright glow.

"You're good to go, Hotel one. The guy just lit another."

Nathan clicked his radio in response.

The smell of smoke permeating the air made Nathan's tension spike when he reached the tailgate of the smaller truck.

Looking like a small rug, more than a thousand cigarette butts littered the area between the trucks. His jab about lung cancer hadn't been far off the mark.

Sig up, he eased along the tailgate like a cat stalking an unaware bird.

No matter how many times he did this, he always thought his prey would turn at the last second.

Stay focused . . .

Slowly, he reached down with his left hand and unsheathed his Predator knife. He tucked the Sig into his waist pack and switched the knife to his right hand.

After adjusting his night-vision scope's focus to three feet, he ducked below the rearview mirror's reflection and slid down the left side of the pickup.

For the third time tonight, Nathan severed all doubt about killing. Now wasn't the time to second-guess the decision makers. He was an instrument of his country, saving lives by taking lives. It wasn't more complicated than that.

Here goes.

In a lightning-quick movement, he pivoted to face the open door and thrust the knife like a piston, sinking into the left side of the man's neck. He pulled the blade out, grabbed a handful of the man's shirt, and yanked him from the driver's seat. Although his victim couldn't utter a sound, he could honk the horn if he had the presence of mind to do it. Better to remove the variable.

Sierra one's voice sounded off in his earpiece, *"Hot shit, Hotel one! That was friggin' textbook!"*

Nathan clicked his radio in response.

"Let's keep chatter to a minimum," Vince said.

With a grunt, the man hit the ground hard but still managed to cover the gushing wound.

Nathan put a boot on the man's chest and applied most of his weight. In a different circumstance where noise didn't matter, he would've sent a bullet through the man's forehead, even knowing this jihadist wouldn't have shown him the same mercy—just the opposite. These barbarians burned captives alive in steel cages, beheaded live prisoners, and buried defenseless people up to their waists before hurling stones at them until their heads became red mush. And those were the *nice* things they did.

Should he feel badly about killing? Maybe, but he didn't. The world was better off without these people. Did they believe in their cause? Yes. Did they think their murderous actions were justified? Yes. Did they think the entire world would someday be governed by Sharia law? Again, yes.

None of that mattered.

What mattered was taking out the trash, and the sanitation engineers had arrived.

Nathan didn't hate Muslims. Not at all. He judged people by their actions, not the color of their skin or who they worshipped.

So no, he didn't feel badly about killing these men. In his opinion, they'd died too easily.

The man stopped squirming and lay still. His final breath sounded like a sigh of relief—and maybe it was.

Vince said, *"We're at the north ridge. Thanks to Hotel one, we've got three less hostiles to deal with."*

Nathan looked at the barracks, specifically the glowing windows facing this direction. Some of the windows had drawn curtains. Others didn't. If anyone had witnessed the action over here, they should've engaged him by now.

He looked south, to the top of the ridge, and saw the barely perceptible snakelike movement of six team members—three from sierra, three from hotel—hustling down the steep part of the slope.

Vince said, *"Hotel one, we're double-timing the rest of the way. ETA two minutes to level ground."*

"I've got eyes on you. I'm between the parked trucks at your two o'clock. No movement from the barracks. All quiet."

He heard a click in response.

Nathan wanted to conceal the body, but he needed to watch the barracks during his teammates' advance down the steep portion of the ridge.

Reconsidering, it wouldn't take him more than five seconds to scoop the dead man up from the ground and deposit him in the bed of the smaller truck.

The decision made, he picked the dead guy up, hauled him to the tailgate, and gently placed the body into the smaller truck's bed.

What happened next startled him so fiercely, he nearly dived to the ground for cover.

CHAPTER 29

The damned truck lit up like a Christmas tree, and an obnoxious car alarm began blaring. The deafening howl sounded like a nuclear-missile launch warning.

Shit! SHIT!

This shouldn't be happening! The truck was unlocked. He'd seen its door locks in their upper positions.

Nathan wanted to empty his magazine into its dashboard. "So much for the element of surprise," he said under his breath.

The door to the barracks opened, and a man wearing loose, dark clothes stepped out. Holding a compact AK, he asked, "Muhammed, what's going on out here? Turn that damned thing off."

Nathan stayed low and reached for the passenger door handle. He yanked it open and saw the keys and a remote dangling from the ignition. Light flooded the interior, but Nathan stayed below the dashboard. Guessing which button to press, he picked the largest one and pressed it once. The vehicle chirped, flashed, and went silent. He slid back out but left the passenger door open.

"Sorry," he said in Arabic, half under his breath, hoping it would disguise his voice.

The glow from the truck's interior didn't offer that much light, and the approaching man was still a good forty yards distant. Hopefully, his opponent would see only a dark form.

Nathan unslung his carbine and thumbed its safety 180 degrees to auto.

"Muhammed? Where's Sahib?"

He stayed in the shadows.

A second man emerged from the barracks, also holding an AK. "What's going on?"

"Muhammed, what are you doing? Where's Sahib?"

Nathan figured it would be worse to say nothing, so again, he said, "Sorry."

The man slowed and leveled his AK. He obviously didn't like the unfamiliar voice he'd heard.

That was enough for Nathan.

He brought the M4 up, triggered its laser, and painted the man's chest.

With a quick pull, Nathan sent four or five rounds.

The staccato roar hammered his ears, but it was much worse on the other end.

His heart and lungs perforated, the man dropped the AK and collapsed.

Vince's voice boomed through his ear speaker, *"Tango one, blow the power and phone lines!"*

"I'm still three hundred yards from the transmission line." Her voice sounded amazingly calm.

"All-out sprint, Tango one. Attempt a hit with your launcher when you reach fifty yards. Do whatever it takes. I want those lines cut!"

"Copy."

Before the other guy on the porch could react, Nathan painted him and let loose with an extended burst, then walked the bullets along the wall and inside the door. If any of the chemical grenades were in there, he wondered if he'd be exposed at this distance. Probably not, he hoped. A little late to worry about it.

To his left, he saw flashes coming from the slope where the hotel and sierra teams descended, then heard the corresponding thumps of their grenade launchers about a second later.

"Incoming on the barracks," Vince announced.

Multiple explosions rocked the area surrounding the barracks building. Two of the M406 high-explosive grenades landed just shy of its north-facing porch, and the others fell short by ten yards or so.

"Impacts are short by ten yards!" Nathan yelled over the explosions. Like ants emerging out of a disturbed hole, running men poured out of the barracks in single file, each carrying an AK assault rifle. "Aim for the area between my position and barracks!"

"Copy. Hotel four, contact the CP and report we've engaged."

Nathan emptied the rest of the magazine at the men pouring out of the door, pressed the ejection button, and rolled the M4 slightly away from his shoulder. Keeping the weapon level and pointed in the right direction, he slammed a full magazine home, used his palm to work the action, and rolled the carbine back into his shoulder. The entire process took about three seconds to complete.

Before he could shoot again, he heard one of the terrorists yell, "The trucks! He's by the trucks!"

Multiple AKs began hammering his position. The truck vibrated as rounds penetrated its sheet metal.

He hugged the front left fender, keeping the engine block and the oversized tires between himself and the shooters. His NV offered much more information than he wanted. The stroboscopic flashes merged into a continuous blinding light as hundreds of 7.62-millimeter bullets whizzed and zinged past. His ballistic vest didn't feel like a whole lot of protection right now.

He thought he heard Vince say *incoming* but wasn't sure.

He became sure when a second volley of grenades peppered the enemy's line. The sound of fully automatic AKs was replaced by half a dozen concussive blasts and something biotic—men screaming.

A glance over the lifted truck's hood revealed more casualties squirming on the ground. Other fighters took knees, reaching for magazines secured in ammo vests not unlike his. He had to give these guys credit: they were fearless and tough. Not many men would hold position in the middle of a maelstrom of detonating grenades and machine-gun fire.

Taking advantage of the shock and carnage created by the grenade rounds, he pivoted away from the fender, shouldered his M4, and let loose with an entire thirty-round magazine, walking it back and forth across the group of men.

It took less than two and a half seconds.

The result was devastating.

Anyone who'd been out in the open got torn to shreds by copper-jacketed bullets traveling at three times the speed of sound. Flesh was no match for physics. The slugs cleaved through organic material and slammed into the wall of the barracks. Some of his rounds broke windows that the salvo of grenades hadn't shattered.

He reloaded his carbine and fired controlled bursts at chest level through the open door and broken windows until his weapon stopped shooting. He then moved his finger down to the grenade launcher, flipped its safety forward, and lined up on the door. At this distance, aiming at the top of the opening ought to do the trick.

Only one way to find out.

The weapon popped loudly. A split second later, the door's opening and all the broken windows flashed from the interior detonation. Nathan worked the action of the M203 much as he would an oversized pump shotgun, loaded another round, and closed it. He sent the next grenade through the window on the left side of the door. Again, the interior flashed, but this time, a string of foul language followed. He repeated the process a third time through a different window.

Nathan reloaded the launcher, then his M4, and sprayed the ground in front of the downed men with half the magazine. The bullets skipped off the dirt surface, raising a huge cloud of dust and providing him visual cover while also demoralizing the enemy.

He saw a satellite dish mounted on the south-facing eave, painted it with his laser, and destroyed it with a burst of fire. Even though tango fire team was about to kill the power, it was better to be safe and take the dish out.

Time to relocate.

He hustled to the tailgate of the smaller truck and took off toward the off-white sedan about twenty feet distant. It wouldn't offer nearly as much cover as the trucks, but it would have to do. His other alternative was to retreat all the way back to the dry wash and lie prone. *Not in this Marine's world.*

Good thing he moved.

Several windows of the barracks ignited with star-shaped blossoms of light. The remaining terrorists were firing on the trucks. He heard a pop; then half a second later, the front end of the truck he'd used for cover ignited in a concussive blast. Its hood blew skyward, flipping through the air like a tossed playing card.

If he'd still been there . . .

Coming from his four o'clock position, a single thump reverberated across the basin.

"Hotel three, the power and phones are severed."

"Good work, Tango one. Rendezvous with the rest of your fire team and get eyes on the ranch house. We need to know if anyone's coming over here in a big hurry."

"Copy."

Vince continued. *"Sierras two and three, we've got three rabbits leaving the east side of the barracks armed with AKs. Get after 'em!"*

Crap, Nathan thought. *There's a door on the other side of the barracks. Of course there's a rear door; there's always a rear door.*

"Hotel three, they're heading for an outbuilding on the south side of the compound. They might have motorcycles or ATVs stashed in there. We're on 'em."

Nathan assumed that was Sierra two's or Sierra three's voice.

"Hotel one, what's your position?" Vince asked.

"Off-white sedan just north of the pickup trucks."

"Stand by, Hotel one. We're going to flush everyone out of that building with CS rounds. I seriously doubt they have masks."

Sierra two said, *"Our rabbits just opened a garage door on building oscar three."*

Nathan pictured the cardboard mock-up in his head. Oscar three was the designation for the largest of the five outbuildings surrounding the barracks. It had to be about three hundred yards from the base of the slope where Vince and Harv would be arriving.

"Sierra two, light 'em up with your M4," Vince ordered. *"Sierra three, launch on oscar three."*

He watched individual white tracers tear across the desert as Sierra two opened fire in semiauto mode. Nathan didn't hear the launcher's discharge, but he saw and heard the projectile explode. It overflew the garage building and lit up the far side. Because he had a lateral view of the trajectory, he could gauge the distance.

"Sierra three, you're long by twenty yards."

"Copy that."

Nathan watched more of Sierra two's M4 tracer fire zip across the desert like luminous ribbons. He'd always liked the look of it.

Nathan heard Sierra three's launch this time, a barely audible pop. After a three-second delay, the interior of the garage flashed. "Good hit! Fire for effect."

A second grenade flashed in the garage.

The third high-explosive round must've found stored gasoline because the garage went up in a roiling mushroom cloud. Even from here, Nathan heard men screaming. Once again, his NV delivered more information than he wanted. All three of the men who'd fled into the garage were now burning. They dropped to the ground and rolled.

More tracer ribbons connected to the smoldering forms. At three hundred yards, the M4 was an accurate carbine, and Sierra two looked to be a skilled marksman. Tracer after tracer disappeared into the downed men.

He'd never been on fire or sustained a serious burn, but it didn't take a lot of imagination to guess what it felt like. Mercifully, Sierra two put them out of their misery.

The remaining terrorists inside the barracks fired from the windows again. They didn't seem to be focused on any one spot. They were simply firing blindly, fighting back as best they could.

Rather than give his new position away by firing on the barracks, he waited through several more enemy salvos, all aimed at the truck with the missing hood.

Someone inside the building was yelling in Arabic, and he heard only part of what was said because of the gunfire.

"Sahib! Tariq! *Tariq!* Where are . . . under attack! . . . phone's dead . . . under attack! . . . Muhammed!"

***

Harv felt so helpless up here while Nathan engaged in a full-blown firefight below. Seeing the action at the barracks reminded him of just how deadly his friend could be with an M4 carbine. In the right hands, an M4 equipped with an M203 grenade launcher could dispatch a lot of bad guys. And dispatch Nathan had. From the look of things, he'd killed a minimum of six jihadists in addition to the three he'd taken down silently.

He hasn't lost a thing, Harv thought.

Watching the action from above looked . . . what? Awesome? No other word seemed to fit. The rattle of small-arms fire and deep booms echoing across the desert sounded equally impressive. He needed to get down there and join the fight.

"I'm picking up a transmission on the scanner," said Hotel four. "It's in Arabic."

"Sierras one and four, keep going." Vince stopped running, turned to his radio operator, and motioned Harv over. "Let Har—Hotel two hear it."

Vince had nearly used his name—not the end of the world given their encrypted radios. He caught the frantic soldier's metallic voice mid-sentence. "... *Tariq! Where are you? We're under attack! Sahib! Can you hear me? The phone's dead. We're under attack!*" A nasty string of foul Arabic followed, then, "*Muhammed!*"

Harv translated it all for them.

"We need to get the gas grenades into the barracks ASAP," Vince said. "Let me know if anyone answers that radio call."

Nathan's voice came up on the net. "*That transmission originated inside the barracks. Tariq, Sahib, and Muhammed won't be answering.*"

"Copy that, Hotel one. Sierra two, check the downed rabbits for survivors and prosecute. Sierra three, send HE rounds into the other outbuildings. We need to make sure no one's home. Hotels one and two, load CS rounds and prepare to fire into the barracks on my command." Vince looked at him. "Haul ass down to the white sedan and support Hotel one. Here. Take the scanner in case there's more radio traffic in Arabic. We're gassing the shit out of that building in thirty seconds."

Harvey needed no further prompting. He took off in a full sprint along the dry creek bed toward Nate's position at the sedan.

"*I've got eyes on you, Hotel two,*" Nate said. "*They might have NV inside the barracks. Divert upslope a little and use the thin vegetation for cover. Hotel three, I'm good to go with a CS round.*"

"*Stand by. Sierra two, status?*"

"*The rabbits are dead.*"

"*Load CS and hustle back to Sierra three's position. Tango fire team, ETA to the west ridge for eyes on the ranch house?*"

"*Three minutes.*"

"*Make it ninety seconds and give me a report of what you see. Sierra and hotel fire teams, stand by to launch gas. Sierra's covering the east and south walls of the barracks. Hotel's got the north and west. We're hitting them in a ninety-degree formation just like we planned. Avoid M4 crossfire. I say again, avoid M4 crossfire.*"

Harv had to hand it to Vince. The man sounded confident. There was no waver or hesitation in their commander's voice.

The men inside the barracks were firing less frequently, probably conserving ammo. Either that or they were bleeding to death. HE rounds send shrapnel in every direction.

Another burst of M4 came from Sierra two's location. A Colt M4 sounded quite different from a Kalashnikov.

"*Hotel three, several men just attempted to flee the building. They're down. We're relocating to the—*"

A salvo of AK clattered across the basin.

"*Sierra two's hit! He's down! He's down!*"

Vince's voice cut in. "*Launch gas! All units, launch gas now!*"

Harv gritted his teeth and stopped running. He pushed the launcher's safety forward, rotated the M203's side-mounted laser to one hundred yards, and painted the barracks window.

His weapon bucked with a *thunk* sound.

Crap. The grenade smacked the wall under the window, bounced off, and began discharging tear gas.

He quickly reloaded. Just before he fired, his NV registered two dim flashes inside the structure: gas detonations from his fellow team members. He aimed a little higher and pulled the trigger. Perfect. The CS round sailed into the dark interior. He sent another into a different window.

Several more flashes lit the interior with an eerie flickering as more grenades detonated.

Harv reloaded the launcher with a high-explosive round, ran to the edge of the dry wash, and waited for the enemy to come out.

***

Nathan gritted his teeth at the radio call announcing Nick was down.

Vince's voice came next. *"Launch gas! All units, launch gas now!"*

Half a second later, Nathan sent a grenade through the open door, then sent another through a window. The result was immediate. All AK fire evaporated, replaced with loud coughing and choking. Anyone inside that building could no longer breathe without extreme distress. Their eyes watered and burned, and their noses became faucets. Nathan knew about tear gas—he and Harv had been exposed during their recon training. The terrorists had two choices: asphyxiate on the fumes until they passed out or come out fighting. Given those options, he fully expected them to burst out of the doors, shooting as they came. These men would never surrender. It simply wasn't in their nature.

So be it.

A figure emerged from the front door. Hunched over, coughing, and disoriented, the guy leveled his AK and fired blindly, sweeping it back and forth in a desperate attempt to kill his attackers. All his rounds sailed harmlessly high.

Nathan took in half a breath, flipped his safety to the semiauto position, and sent a single round. The man stiffened as the slug slashed through the center of his chest. He fell to his knees, then keeled over and lay still. Harv nailed the second man to emerge with another single shot. He and Harv shot the third man simultaneously. There was no glory in doing this, but there *was* necessity.

One by one, the terrorists poured out of the building, and one by one, they were mowed down.

Vince ordered everyone to load high-explosive rounds and launch.

Nathan complied, sending an HE through the open door. Almost simultaneously, more detonations flashed and boomed, making the place look and sound like a creepy haunted house. The fragmentation grenades, combined with the near blackness and suffocating gas, created pure terror and agony for the men trapped inside.

He could almost pity them.

Almost, but not quite.

The rout continued for a solid minute. Men were quite literally falling dead on top of each other on the porch. The rattle of M4 gunfire surrounding the building slowed to sporadic bursts. Nathan heard shots inside the barracks that stood out—single reports from a smaller weapon, a few seconds apart. It almost sounded like .22 long rifle rounds. They made a distinctive whiplike crack.

A creepy silence descended onto the compound.

"Sierra three, report," Vince said, his voice subdued.

No response.

Vince waited a few seconds, then repeated the order.

"Sierra two's gone." The voice sounded detached, unemotional.

Nathan squinted. Everyone knew it could happen to any of them, but the news hit him harder than he'd expected. Nick was a good man. He wondered if the fallen hero had a wife and kids. Probably did. Damn it . . .

The silence became unsettling.

Come on, Vince, say something, Nathan thought. *We need to get past this; our mission's not over.*

As if on cue, Vince said, *"Sierra three, put on your mask and clear the interior. Tango fire team, maintain auto mode on radios. Fire teams sierra and hotel, switch radios to manual and maintain ceasefire until the barracks is cleared."*

"Hotels one and two, copy the ceasefire," Nathan said, then added, "I think Sierra three should give it a minute or two before going into the barracks."

Vince didn't respond right away. *"What's on your mind, Hotel one?"*

"I think they just shot each other. I heard small-caliber reports just before our M4s went silent."

"Okay . . ."

"There could be an IED rig—"

In an ear-shattering explosion, the barracks detonated in a blinding white flash. Nathan felt the heat of the blast as smoking pieces of the walls and roof flew in every direction. The concussive shock wave seemed to compress his internal organs. For an instant, it felt as if the air had been forced down his lungs, then violently sucked back out. Along with the other vehicles, the sedan rocked from the force of the blast.

Nathan was amazed at what the human mind could register. Just before the explosion temporarily blinded him, he saw the bodies outside the door hurled like rag dolls. Some of them tumbled, but most became airborne in a macabre ballet of flailing corpses. He hoped the visual wouldn't be with him for the rest of his life.

Smoldering pieces of the building began raining down like meteorites. Nathan squeezed closer to the sedan as something thumped the ground a few yards away.

The building wasn't burning, because it simply didn't exist anymore. One second it was there; the next it wasn't. Nothing standing taller than a few feet remained.

"Sierra and hotel fire teams, any casualties from that blast?" Vince asked.

Including himself, everyone was rattled, but otherwise okay.

He visually reacquired Harv as his friend hustled along the bushes lining the dry creek.

"Hotel three, we're at the summit of the west ridge overlooking the ranch house. We're going to have company. A dark pickup's heading toward

the road leading to the compound. Whoever's driving will have eyes on the compound once they reach this ridge and start down the canyon."

Nathan knew that transmission originated from tango fire team.

"Tango one, has the vehicle sped up since the blast?"

Vince obviously recognized the female voice as Tango one's.

"Negative. It's maintaining a constant speed. It doesn't appear to be in a hurry."

"Can you intercept it on our side of the ridge where you won't be seen from the ranch house?"

"Affirm."

"Proceed. Take out the driver and try to preserve the vehicle if possible, but no unnecessary risks. Clear?"

"Clear."

Vince continued. *"Tango team, since we don't know if the Rio Grande cell uses heavy explosives during training, we can't know if the barracks blast raised any alarm. El Lobo has a Lapua, and we don't know what kind of an optic he's got. The ridge is seventeen hundred yards from the ranch house, so it's definitely within range. I want continuous eyes on the ranch house, but do not advance down the slope yet."*

Nathan listened to tango's transmissions as two members angled down to the road to intercept the pickup. He looked in that direction but didn't see anything. Since the road leading to the ranch house followed the canyon's snakelike path until it reached the ridge, he couldn't see all of its length. He could, however, already see the bleed glow from the truck's headlights on the surrounding higher peaks and bluffs. The sensitivity of these devices never ceased to amaze him.

Harv arrived, barely breathing hard.

"Shit, Nate, how did you know about the barracks?"

"I don't know. I just felt something weird about the small-caliber shots."

"Maybe it's that finely honed intuition of yours."

He didn't say anything.

"How you holding up?"

"I'm assuming you're asking about my mental state?"

"What else?"

"I've killed a lot of people tonight."

"You okay with it?" Harv asked.

"I keep thinking about Lauren and Dad . . . So, yeah, I'm okay with it."

"Me too."

"It's fair to assume someone from the ranch house tried to contact the compound and couldn't get through, so they're sending a messenger to find out what all the shooting's about."

Harv looked toward the west ridge. "I'm betting El Lobo tried to call and tell them to knock it off. At least it confirms they're not in radio contact with the ranch house. The biggest variable is the WMD grenades. If they were in the barracks, they're toast, but since we don't know for sure, sierra team will need to search the compound, and this is a huge area. They could be anywhere out here. Buried in a secret place, anywhere."

"It kinda makes you wonder why we have a blanket order to kill everyone in the compound except Alisio and El Lobo."

"And only if it's convenient," Harv added. "If either of them looks at us funny, we're lighting 'em up."

"Take a look at the dashboard of this sedan. What do you see?"

"The keys are dangling in the ignition."

"Yep, and since our work down here seems to be over, it's time to take out the rest of the trash."

"Nate, we can't do that. I mean just take off. Vince is in command."

"Just a harmless fantasy, Harv. I'm a team player."

"Here comes the truck Tango one reported seeing."

Nathan turned and saw its headlights bouncing along the ridge. "We'll lose sight of it any second."

And they did, but the eerie glow continued, changing in intensity as the pickup navigated the curvy canyon road, bouncing across ruts and potholes.

The light stopped shifting and seemed to freeze.

"Tango's engaged," Harv whispered.

"Yep."

No sound came from the canyon at all.

Nathan found himself holding his breath.

Then their earpieces cracked to life with three identical sounds— the quick pops of suppressed pistol fire.

"Hotel three, pickup driver neutralized, no passengers, vehicle intact. It's a Ford crew cab. Based on the descriptions we have, I don't believe this man is El Lobo or Quattro. He's in a suit, and there's a compact HK on the passenger seat. He appears to be a bodyguard or hired muscle. Do you want me to bring the body?"

"Affirm, Tango one," Vince said. *"Do you see a radio?"*

"Negative."

"Head down to Hotel one's position at the white sedan. Tangos two through four, maintain eyes on the ranch house. Everyone keep your heads down up there."

"Hang on, Harv. I'm gonna contact Vince . . . Hotel three, can we huddle up?"

"Affirm. We're coming to you. Sierra three, secure Sierra two's body, then form up with your fire team and stay together. I want a thorough search of the remaining oscar outbuildings to look for hiding holes or tunnels. Look for the WMD grenades while you're at it, but your primary objective is to verify there aren't more combatants. Assume this fight isn't over. Check in as you clear each structure."

"Copy."

The bleed light in the canyon began shifting again as Tango one drove the truck along the winding road leading down here.

Tango one said, *"Hotel three, we've got more vehicular activity at the ranch house. Some kind of sports car just left, and it's heading south on the main access road away from the house. Whoever's driving isn't in a big hurry. He's not speeding."*

Crap, Nathan thought, *that could be our WMD grenades leaving.* Nick had given his life on this mission; he hated the idea of it being in vain. Killing the radicals was secondary to their primary objective: recovering the WMDs—at all costs. If only he hadn't tried to conceal that stiff in the bed of the truck, setting off the car alarm, everything might've unfolded differently. *And maybe for the worse,* he conceded. *The barracks might've gone up with some of us in there.* It was entirely possible the accidental car alarm had saved lives.

Vince answered Tango one's radio call. *"Let me know if it keeps going south or makes a right turn toward the smuggling center. Affirm you'll be able to see that."*

"Affirm. We're on it."

The Ford came roaring out of the canyon and barreled straight toward their position.

Harv said, "Whoever sent that messenger will expect him to return to the ranch house pretty quickly."

"I agree," Nathan said. "We need to figure out our next move."

"During our mission briefing, we talked about using one or more of these vehicles to get to the ranch house. The pickup changes the dynamic a little and might even work to our advantage. We can still stay close to the original plan."

"I think so too. Let's hear what Vince has in mind first."

Intermittent radio calls from Sierra three announced their progress clearing the outbuildings.

Its diesel engine rumbling, the truck stopped a few yards away. The dust cloud kept coming and drifted past.

A dust cloud . . . , Nathan thought.

A few seconds later, Vince and their radioman arrived.

Vince squared up to Nathan, and for an instant, he wasn't sure if the mission commander intended to rip him a new asshole for setting off the car alarm.

In fact, Vince shook his hand and said, "Well done, Marine."

"Thank you, Vince. Let's just say I was . . . motivated. Still am."

"Roger that. Let's take a few seconds and check out the stiff."

Nathan waited while Vince dragged the dead man out of the passenger seat of the pickup and laid him out on the hardpan.

"I agree with Tango one," Vince said. "This looks like a bodyguard or one of the limo drivers. It's definitely not El Lobo or Quattro. I think we can assume this isn't Alisio either. He'd never come over here alone."

Nathan didn't say anything. Neither did Harv. They both wanted to get going.

"I've got an idea," Vince said. "Tango one's going to give us a ride in this truck all the way to the ranch house like we own the place. You two will be concealed in the back seat. I can't tell you what to expect, because quite frankly, there's no way to know."

"May I suggest something?" Nathan asked.

"Make it quick. Whoever sent this truck is expecting it to return."

"If we use this sedan, none of us will have to ride in the bed of the truck. The keys are in the ignition. It's a small vehicle. If we bust out its headlights and taillights, it can tuck in behind the pickup and hide in the pickup's dust cloud." He looked at Tango one. "Sandra, right?"

"Yes, sir."

"As I recall from the aerials, the last part of the road leading up to the ranch house is a straight shot before it diverts to the south around the place."

"Yes, that's right," she said. "The landscaped area with grass and hedges extends about a hundred feet from the house in every direction, and the road becomes paved about twice that far out. If we stop the sedan on the dirt, just before the road becomes asphalt, I doubt it will be seen. From there, my fire team can fan out and surround the house."

Vince nodded approval. "I like it. Let's bust out the pickup's taillights to minimize the chance of the sedan being seen."

"Hotel three, we've cleared the last outbuilding."

Vince pressed his transmit button. "Sierras three and four, position yourselves where you can observe the entire compound. Sierra one, double-time over here. You're going with us to the ranch house."

Nathan knew the other sierra members wanted to be included in the ranch house assault, but it would be reckless of Vince to assume the compound was clear just because they didn't see any remaining combatants. Like Vince said, there could be holdouts, and leaving only a single member of sierra fire team behind was tactically unsound.

Nathan thought about Nick. Even though their team member's death was on everyone's mind, no one would say anything. This remained a live combat mission, and everyone had to stay focused.

Sierra one arrived, and Vince told him to fire up the sedan. "If it doesn't start," Vince continued, "we're all cramming into the truck, so keep your fingers crossed."

Everyone breathed a collective sigh of relief when the sedan turned over. While Harv broke the F-250's taillights, Vince used the butt of his M4 to shatter all the sedan's lights, both inside and out, making it totally dark.

Vince ordered Tango one into the driver's seat of the truck, then climbed in next to her. Looking around the interior, he said, "Leave the doors open and take a few seconds to break all the interior lights back there. We'll do the same up here. Harv, check the rear of the cab on the outside. There's usually a brake and reverse light mounted above the rear window."

The truck swayed as Harv climbed into the bed and shattered plastic and glass. With all the lights destroyed, the interior of the crew cab became pitch-black. Adding to their stealth, the truck's windows were darkly tinted.

"Hotel three, the sports car just stopped along the main road leading away from the ranch house. It's probably fifteen hundred yards out."

"What's it doing? Is it turning right?" Vince asked.

"It's just sitting there. It stopped short of the intersection to the smuggling center. Okay, the driver just got out. He's running west into the underbrush with something in his hand. It's hard to say what. Looks like a linear object of some kind. Could be a shovel."

"Tango two, stay on the ridge and keep eyes on the driver. Tangos three and four, hustle over to the road and position yourselves on this side of the ridge where you won't be seen from the ranch house. You're coming with us. We'll be slowing for no more than five seconds, so be ready to pile into the rear seats of the sedan. Our radioman will be in the front of the sedan with Sierra one. Copy?"

"Tango fire team copies. Three and four will be in position at the road in ninety seconds."

"That ought to be just about right," Vince said. "Let's roll."

The sedan maintained a safe separation from the pickup while going up the canyon, but as soon as they crested the ridge, that sedan would be glued to their bumper like the slot jet in a Blue Angels diamond formation.

One of the tango fire team members came up on the net. *"Hotel three, you're thirty seconds out. We're just around the next curve in the road."*

Vince acknowledged.

Nathan leaned to his left to look through the windshield and nearly butted heads with Harv, who was also leaning to look.

Even in the headlights of the F-250, the tango members were hard to see. Their uniforms blended perfectly with the tans and beiges of this desert. Nathan turned to watch as they rolled past.

The sedan slowed, and the two tango members climbed in while the vehicle was still in motion—not an easy task, but they made it look effortless.

And just like that, they were on their way again.

"We're getting close to the top. Sierra one, close to within twenty feet back there, closer if possible."

"I'm on it."

Tango one asked about the truck's headlights—whether she should turn them off when they got close to the ranch house.

Vince said yes, if anyone was outside waiting. Then he asked, "Sandra, where exactly did this truck come from?"

"We didn't see it until it emerged from the far side of the house—which is where the garages are. One of them is attached to the main residence's south wing. The other is freestanding next to the helipad. It's probably a hangar."

"Okay, as best you can, I want you to drive the exact route this truck took coming out here."

"No problem," she said.

"Here we go. We'll be visible from the ranch house in a few seconds."

Nathan glanced over his shoulder and couldn't see the sedan. It was so close, the truck's tailgate screened it from view.

Sierra one said, *"Let me know if you need to slow down up there. Your brake lights are out, so give me as much advance warning as possible, or I'm going to be wearing your bumper."*

"Will do," Vince said. "We're going to speed up a little to raise a bigger dust cloud."

They trundled along, but it wasn't a terribly rough ride. No doubt the truck was handling the ruts and potholes better than the sedan.

Nathan watched the valley on the far side of the ridge materialize. He saw the dim lights of the ranch house right away. Several windows glowed. His NV registered all kinds of little solar landscaping lights weaving around the structure. They probably followed exterior walkways and paths.

The aerial photos they'd reviewed showed a classic Spanish-style residence. Underneath a large porte cochere, the entry opened into a porchlike hall that provided access to the entire house. Basically, the residence was a two-hundred-foot square with a one-hundred-foot square interior courtyard. The courtyard held a pool, hot tub, and plush landscaping. The attached garage where they suspected the truck and sports car had come from was kitty-corner to their current approach vector, so they couldn't see it.

Even from this distance, the place looked huge—all thirty thousand square feet of it.

Probably beautiful inside, Nathan thought. Cartel kingpins tended to spend their blood money extravagantly on themselves. Apparently Alisio didn't like stairs—the mansion lacked a second floor, but it probably had a basement.

"We're looking good," Vince said. "Okay, Sierra one, get ready to brake a little. We're coming up on a curve in the road to the right."

"Copy."

Over the next three hundred yards, Vince coached their tail through several more turns as they descended from the ridge until the road found level ground and led them straight toward the house.

"Okay, great job back there. Stay tight; it's a straight shot from here. I'll give you a ten-second warning as we approach the pavement."

Nathan felt his stomach churn again. They'd already been through a firefight and were about to do it again. He wasn't sure why, but it felt more menacing this time. Clearing structures meant facing potential danger around every blind corner, piece of furniture, and closed door. Plus, the WMD grenades had yet to be located. First things first . . . they needed to get inside the residence undetected.

Vince brought his TI up. "We're looking good so far. I'm not seeing any warm signatures. Sandra, I want you to cut the phone line and locate any satellite dishes. Cutting their coaxial cables is best, but short of that, you'll have to shoot their LNBs with your silenced pistol. After that, find the main breaker box to the house and stand by to cut power on my mark."

"Yes, sir."

"Tango two, what's that sports car doing?"

"It's still parked on the main access road. I don't have eyes on the driver. He's still out in the brush."

"Sierra one, stand by back there. We're coming up on the pavement and fence."

"We're ready."

"You all set, Harv?" Nathan asked.

"Good to go."

Nathan reached across the seat and clasped his friend's hand. "We can do this."

"Absolutely."

Just ahead, Nathan saw the faint outline of an ornamental fence and gate—currently open. Huge illuminated palms seemed to grow out of the house's roof, an illusion created by the courtyard within. The satellite imagery didn't do this place justice. Nathan wanted to admire it, but this massive oasis, built with dirty money, reeked of human suffering.

"Sierra one, begin braking," Vince said. "Hit it hard in five seconds. Pile out and surround the place. Verify all your radios are on manual."

"Verified."

Nathan looked back and saw the sedan fade into the dust cloud. He wished them a silent good luck.

Sandra made a slight right turn toward the house at the fork in the dirt road. Their ride jarred, then became smooth as the truck's wheels found pavement. At a slow speed, they drove through the ornamental gate and followed the asphalt around the south side of the property. Alisio must have had a good water well because a vast expanse of lawn extended out from the house. Everything appeared verdant and manicured. Nathan kept expecting to see one or more dogs come bounding around the corner, but none appeared. He'd hate having to kill dogs, but he wouldn't jeopardize his colleagues' lives or the mission over them.

Sandra said she spotted the transformer pole for the house. It sat just outside the ornamental fence on the access road coming in from the south. Power went underground from there.

The attached garage came into view as they moved past a tall hedge. Two of the five garage doors were open, revealing empty slots. Probably where the pickup and sports car were kept.

"The front of the house is around the next corner," Vince said. "Get ready to engage."

When she rounded the corner, Sandra said, "Nice."

Sitting under the porte cochere, three huge limos dominated the circular driveway.

"I seriously doubt those belong to El Lobo," Vince said.

"Let's hope they're Alisio's," Nathan said.

This place looked like a high-end Hawaiian resort, right down to the landscape lighting. It never ceased to amaze him—the bewildering amount of money these scumbags made. He wondered if they felt any guilt at all. Probably not.

"Keep going," Vince said. "We've got company. Looks like hired muscle or bodyguards."

Two nicely dressed men with compact machine pistols slung over their shoulders stepped down from the flagstone entry steps. They weren't acting suspicious or aggressive. As they discussed, Sandra killed the headlights.

This is it, Nathan thought. *The moment of truth.*

Apparently, all the gunfire and explosions from the compound weren't out of the ordinary. Yes, the training compound was more than a mile and a half away, and all the grenade detonations had sounded like distant thumps from here, but judging from these two gunmen, even the huge barracks explosion hadn't raised any undue suspicion—except maybe for its late hour. Their expressions reflecting boredom, the men fanned out, stopped walking, and stared like caged gorillas.

Working in their favor, the dark tinting of the truck's windows combined with the ambient landscaping light made the interior of the truck completely black.

"Harvey, Nathan, left and right respectively," Vince said. "Stand by to engage."

"We're ready," Nathan said.

"Sandra, go a little farther."

If the men made any kind of hostile move, he'd be out the door and shooting before Vince could give the order.

"Stand by . . . Now!"

Twenty feet from the men, Sandra braked hard.

Simultaneously, he and Harv jumped out.

The bodyguards' expressions changed at seeing the rear doors of the crew cab open. By the time they realized the threat, it was too late.

He and Harv painted their lasers on the bodyguards' faces before the men could unsling their compact machine pistols.

Two shots. Two kills. All in less than two seconds.

Vincent got out. "Nathan, cover us. Harv, you're with me. We're going to move those bodies."

Nathan took a knee at the fender of the truck where he had a clear view of the front door. With Harv on his tail, Vince hurried over to the downed men.

Sandra was out of the driver's seat and on the move, sprinting toward the transformer pole on the south end of the fenced area. Telephone companies tended to use the same poles as the power companies. Once she reached the terminus pole, she should be able to sever the phone line at a point before it dropped into its underground conduit.

Vince and Harv each grabbed a dead man by his coat collar and dragged him into the bushes lining the circular driveway.

Nathan saw the front door hanging wide open, so he hustled up the steps and flattened himself against the stucco. On either side of the entry, three huge ferns sat in terracotta pots. He could see the entire covered area of the porte cochere from here. At his two o'clock position, approximately two hundred feet distant, he spotted the detached garage and a beautiful Bell 427 sitting on a sled on its helipad. The lighted wind sock indicated a slight westerly breeze. He wondered why the helicopter hadn't been towed into its hangar.

The muffled sound of a television came from within the house. He took a peek and saw all the way through to the huge lighted pool.

This guy's pool is bigger than most people's houses.

Just inside the door, beyond a classic sitting room, a glass-lined hallway offered two choices: left or right. He knew the right side led to the attached garage and south wing of the house. The left probably led to the kitchen, living room, and bedroom suites.

"I'm at the terminus pole," Sandra said. *"I just cut the phone line."*

"Good work," Vince said. "Look for satellite dishes on the south-facing eave of the house and take them out. The main breaker's probably in the garage. Proceed."

"I'm on it."

Nathan considered his options. If he and Harv entered here and went left or right at the main hallway, they'd be vulnerable from the other direction. Their job would be a whole lot easier with Vince covering their six.

He pressed his transmit button. "Hotel three, can you—" Nathan heard footsteps inside the house. "Stand by," he said in a whisper. "Someone's coming toward the door." Whoever it was wore hard-soled shoes and didn't seem the least bit concerned about noise. The foot-falls stopped, and Nathan held perfectly still. He caught only pieces of what was said, but heard two voices—both male, and neither of them sounded young.

A second pair of footsteps approached, and this time he caught what was spoken in Spanish.

"Hang on, Hector. E. L. wants me to go with you."

The footsteps began anew. Two sets this time. "At least those ISIS idiots stopped shooting," one of the voices said. "Jose should be back by now."

"He really hates those clowns."

"He ain't the only one."

Nathan heard their footfalls get louder as they rounded the corner of the main hallway and entered the sitting room.

He hustled over to the potted ferns and ducked behind them.

If the approaching men intended to check the black pickup truck, they'd have to walk directly past this spot.

In slacks and white shirts, they stepped out the front door and looked toward the pickup. Like the others, they had compact machine pistols slung over their shoulders.

"Jose, you out here?"

The man got no answer.

"Martin! Carlos! Where are you guys?"

"They're probably snorting blow in one of the limos."

"Well, go find their dumb asses."

"*You* go find them."

"Shit."

The bigger of the two men walked toward the limos.

"Jose, you in there?"

"Hotel one, hold position," Vince said. *"Let's see what he does when he finds the limos empty."*

Nathan clicked his radio and watched the man standing near the front door light a cigarette.

The other bodyguard opened a limo door, cursed, and closed it. He circled the other two, rapping on the glass with his knuckles.

Heading toward the pickup, the smoker started across the flagstone, but stopped at the steps and frowned. He crouched and stuck his index finger into a drop of blood, then rubbed it between his fingers.

"We're blown," Nathan whispered. "My guy just found blood."

The smoker's body language instantly changed for the worse.

He spat out the cigarette, stood up straight, and unslung his machine pistol. Rather than call out to his comrade, the man made a beeline for the front door. Nathan had less than three seconds to acquire and shoot.

Vince's voice rang out in his earpiece, *"Engage, engage!"*

Nathan activated the laser and lit up the back of the man's head. This time his target's finger wasn't on the trigger. There would be no reflexive contraction, but if he didn't make a single-kill shot, the man would go crashing into the sitting room, making noise, and spreading more blood.

Nathan executed a perfect trigger pull.

The bullet slammed into the back of the guard's skull. With no real estate to spare, the bodyguard took a final step before doing a face-plant onto the welcome mat.

Coming from Vince's direction, three suppressed reports swept across the driveway. Then a fourth. He saw Vince dart out of the landscaping and sprint toward the limos.

"Hotel one, the other bodyguard's down," Vince said. *"I'm on him. Get ready to enter the house with Hotel two."*

Harv materialized at the edge of the driveway and called out softly, "Drag him over here."

Nathan came up from his crouch and rushed to the downed man. Like Harv and Vince had done, he grabbed the man by his collar and hauled him across the flagstone. Some blood smeared along the way.

He entered the ferns and laid the body next to the first two men they initially killed.

Nathan pressed his transmit button—he wanted Vince to hear it. "El Lobo's in there for sure. I heard these guys refer to him as E. L."

"Copy," Vince said. *"Stand by; I'm concealing this fourth body."*

"What do you think?" Nathan asked Harv off the comm net.

"I hope Alisio's in there."

"Yeah, me too."

Harv didn't say anything.

"Don't worry. I'm not planning to kill him on sight."

"Tempted?"

"Yes."

"Me too," Harv said. "But Benson needs him to trace the WMDs. Killing him could end up costing lots of lives."

"Agreed."

"I think we're facing at least one more bad guy, not including any personal security El Lobo might have beyond Quattro. In any case, we've got less than a minute before they start missing their friends."

"Then let's get in there before they figure it out." Nathan keyed his radio. "Hotel three, we're ready to enter the house."

"Stand by, ten seconds."

Tango two's voice cut in. *"The driver's returning to the sports car . . . He's carrying something . . . It looks like a small suitcase or backpack."*

"That might be our WMDs," Vince said. *"If that sports car doesn't turn around and head back to the ranch house, I'm going after him. What's he doing?"*

"Stand by . . . He's turning the car around . . . Okay, he's heading back to the ranch house."

Nathan wondered how Vince would respond to this development. There was no way to know what the guy had retrieved from the desert. It could be anything. Gold. Jewels. Cash. Bonds. Or their WMD grenades.

Tango two came back up on the net. *"A vehicle just turned toward the ranch house from the road leading to the smuggling center. It's going a little faster than the sports car. I can't determine the type of vehicle yet."*

Vince said, *"Confirm there are two vehicles heading toward the ranch house?"*

"Confirm. It looks like the second vehicle will catch the sports car in about thirty seconds."

"Copy. Tango one, where are you?"

"I'm about to enter the garage. I rigged a radio-controlled charge on the conduit running down the terminus pole in the event I can't locate the breaker box. I'll set it off on your command."

"Good thinking, Tango one. I'm on the two arriving vehicles. Proceed into the garage, try to locate the breaker box, and stand by. All other members, maintain your positions on the perimeter. Hotel four, update command on our situation. Let them know El Lobo's inside the ranch house, possibly Alisio as well. Tango two, I want to know every move those vehicles make. Verbal copies."

The team members copied.

"The arrival of the second vehicle seems suspect," Harv said. "Its timing doesn't seem like a coincidence."

"What do we know at this point, Harv? About five minutes ago, a sports car left the house and drove out the main access road. Its driver stops along the way and seemingly digs up something from a remote area of the ranch. He returns to the sports car with something other than a shovel, and at the same time, a second vehicle is approaching from the smuggling center. What do you make of it?"

"It's hard to say, but the two vehicles being in motion at the same time doesn't feel like a coincidence. Whoever's inside the house is definitely expecting to hear back from the pickup's driver by now, not to mention the extra men they sent outside. I'd say we have under a minute left before things turn to shit."

He was about to respond when Vince's voice broke in.

"Hotels one and two, begin sweeping the house. Maintain stealth as long as possible. You'll be giving Tango one the command to cut power at the breaker box or detonate the charge on the terminus pole. Obviously, the later you give the order, the better. We're still undetected, but depending on

who's in the approaching vehicles, it might get loud out here. Tango two, ETA on the vehicles?"

"Three or four minutes, max."

"Copy."

Nathan started a mental countdown. Both he and Harv had a good sense of passing time in situations like this.

They watched Vince sprint across the circular driveway toward the access road to confront the approaching vehicles.

"All right, Harv, we're on."

"Let's do this."

"I'll take point. We'll go left at the main hallway."

And with that, they slipped inside.

CHAPTER 30

With Harv covering his advance, Nathan hurried across the forty-foot-deep sitting room and peered around the corner to the left. The main hallway, which had to be ten feet wide, extended well beyond a couple of closed doors—probably a coat closet and guest bathroom. He glanced the other direction and saw nearly a mirror image. Straight ahead on the other side of the glass, a tropical landscaped area surrounded a huge meandering pool. It appeared as if this main hallway followed the courtyard all the way around the house and ended up back here. Most of the light in the hallway came from the courtyard landscaping. The effect looked beautiful and, most likely, planned this way. Small spots mounted above huge paintings provided additional ambient light.

He waved Harv over to his position.

"Marijuana," he said. The hallway reeked of pot smoke.

"Yeah, lots of it."

"I'm going to check those doors. If we hug the left side, we can use the reflection in the glass. The lighting in this hall is—"

Sandra's voice broke through. *"Hotel one, I've located the breaker box, but it's a subpanel. The main breaker isn't here. There must be fifty individual breakers, all labeled. Count on about three seconds for me to flip all of them. I can detonate the power conduit outside, but it won't be stealthy."*

"Copy, Tango one," Nathan whispered. "We're inside the main hallway. Stand by." His radio clicked in response.

Halfway down the hall, they encountered a rare sight: an original oil by Albert Bierstadt depicting a landscape that looked a whole lot like the Chihuahuan Desert.

"I've got dibs on that," Harv said.

"You'll have to fight me for it."

They both heard it—a burst of female laughter, then a barely audible male voice. They couldn't make out what was said. A different kind of sound filtered down the hall—a strange clicking, like someone tapping on a hard surface with a hard object.

What the hell would make a sound like that? He looked at Harv. "What's that noise?"

"Razor blade on glass. Someone's chopping cocaine."

"And you know that because . . . ?"

"I've seen it in the movies."

"Uh-huh. Cover me; I'm going to get eyes into the next room. If anyone appears in this hall, take 'em down."

"Women?"

"Shit, Harv, I don't like it, but there's too much at stake." Being ultraquiet with his footfalls, he moved deeper into the house.

The room on the left was a home theater. And from the look of things, a really nice one. The furniture in here probably cost as much as an average American home. On the opposite side of the home theater, a narrower corridor connected to the next room, probably the kitchen. The light was substantially brighter.

Nathan pressed the transmit button. "Does anyone have eyes inside the northwest corner of the house? It's pretty bright. Could be the kitchen."

All the members outside reported seeing the same thing: closed window shades. It made sense. Men like Alisio and El Lobo lived in constant paranoia.

He looked back along the hallway toward the sitting room and signaled for Harv to join him. "I've got your six while you advance," he whispered.

Suppressed Sig in hand, Harv arrived a few seconds later. With his tricolor face paint, desert MARPAT uniform, tactical garb, and an M4 equipped with a grenade launcher, Harv looked like a Special Forces badass.

"We'll enter the next room simultaneously. I'll use the opening on the other side. I think it leads to the kitchen or maybe an adjoining dining or living room. Use the glass when you've got the reflective angle to see in there."

Nathan crossed the room and stopped at the corner of the opening.

An irritated voice boomed, "Where the hell is everyone? Where the fuck's Quattro? Quattro! Get your ass in here! Shit. Go find him."

They'd run out of time. Harv would have company in mere seconds.

He pressed his transmit button and whispered, "Now, Hotel two. Engage, engage!"

Nathan whipped around the corner of the opening and found a vast open space. The main hall became part of the kitchen, dining room, and living room before continuing around a corner. Seated in boy-girl/boy-girl formation, three sharply dressed men and three bikini-clad women looked up with shocked expressions. All of them were seated on a huge semicircular sofa wrapped around a glass coffee table. Each woman wore a primary-colored bikini. Red. Yellow. And blue.

Piled on the glass, a mountain of cocaine rose like a dump truck's load.

Nathan saw the scorpion tattoo right away. A twisted trademark, it dominated the back of El Lobo's hand like a cattle brand.

"Nobody moves!" Nathan yelled in Spanish.

From the other side of the room, Harv shouted the same thing as he stepped in.

Not everyone obeyed.

The man at the end of the sofa reached for his belt.

His hand never made it.

Harv drilled him through the back with three quick shots. One of the bullets passed through the man's torso and found the mound of white powder. It went up like a volcano. Glass shattered and fell in huge pieces.

Red and Blue screamed and covered their chests. Yellow just froze in place.

"Who's next?" Harv yelled.

Nathan closed the distance, keeping his Sig's laser painted on El Lobo's face. "Everyone keep your hands where we can see them!" he yelled. "Anyone who makes a sudden move dies."

Blue bolted from the couch.

Shit.

He painted her butt, careful to avoid her sacrum, and squeezed off a shot.

Shrieking in pain and fear, Blue tumbled and began squirming on the floor. He hated shooting an unarmed woman, but she'd given him no choice.

His heart and lungs perforated, the man Harv had shot slumped sideways. His head plopped into Yellow's lap. She yelped and shrank away in revulsion.

"That's far enough," Nathan said to her, then glanced at Harv. "We're not secure."

Keeping his Sig pointed in El Lobo's direction, Harv crouched at the end of an unoccupied sofa.

Nathan keyed his radio. "Tango one, leave the power on, exit the garage, and enter through the front door. Turn left at the main hall and proceed to our position. Best possible speed. Copy."

"Copy, on my way."

El Lobo looked at the dead man's nickel-plated pistol, but must've realized he'd never be able to lunge across Yellow's lap in time to grab it.

"Don't move," Nathan told him. "The same goes for you, Alisio."

El Lobo and Alisio glanced at each other.

"Yes, we know who you are."

Nathan focused on Yellow. She was incredibly beautiful, even with her face a mask of terror—a shame she'd fallen in with these criminals. He had a better chance of getting information out of her than El Lobo or Alisio.

He put command tone in his voice. "Who else is in the house?"

"No one," she said, but her eyes glanced toward a closed door.

"Harv! Behind you!"

The door burst open.

His friend dived for the floor.

And a huge man filled the doorframe.

Nathan's mind registered multiple things. An aloha shirt. Slacks. A toilet and sink. Shiny black shoes. A snarl of rage. But most importantly, a machine pistol.

Leveled for business.

He noticed one more thing. A bright red laser dot on the man's chest—from his own weapon. Before he could consciously think about it, he popped off two rounds.

At the same time, the man's weapon discharged.

Cutting the room in half, the bullets walked across the floor, sliced into the couch where everyone sat, then climbed up the far wall into the carved wood ceiling. Amazingly, the slugs passed harmlessly between El Lobo and Yellow but struck the man Harv had nailed, making his body shudder.

Aloha Shirt looked down at the holes in his chest with disbelief. When he tried to bring the weapon up again, Nathan nailed him in the throat, just below his chin. All motor function severed, the man melted.

"Tango one, ETA?"

"I've got eyes on Hotel two. I'll be there in a few seconds."

He clicked his radio, pointed his Sig at Yellow, and narrowed his eyes.

"Please," she pleaded. "I was scared. I wanted to tell you!"

He moved his aim to Red. "Your turn. Who else is in the house?"

She pulled her legs to her chest and shook her head.

"I didn't ask a yes or no question." He fired a bullet into the seat cushion next to her, making her yelp in fear.

"No one!" Red said quickly. "The staff doesn't live in the house."

Sandra arrived and kept her expression neutral. He admired her emotional control. This wasn't something you saw every day. Without being told, she assumed a defensive position where she could watch the hallway she'd just traversed.

Tango two's voice sounded in his earpiece. *"Hotel three, the two vehicles stopped side by side on the access road. They're just sitting there. No one's getting out."*

"Copy," Vince said. *"Let me know when they're in motion again. I can't see straight down the road from my location."*

Tango two acknowledged.

"You're real tough against defenseless women," El Lobo spat.

Nathan ignored the jab. "What about more bodyguards?" he asked Red.

The woman shook her head no.

El Lobo's voice held pure venom. "They ain't telling you shit."

Alisio said nothing but kept his eyes on Nathan.

Nathan turned toward Harv and waved his gun at the woman he'd shot in the butt. "Grab a field dressing from your pack. Better yet, grab two. Here's why . . ."

Nathan carefully aimed his Sig and fired.

He purposely grazed El Lobo's right calf, creating a channel of torn flesh. Grunting in pain, the coyote clenched his teeth and covered the wound.

"Is there anything else you'd like to say, Mr. Lobo?"

The coyote's face showed pure rage, but he remained quiet.

Alisio didn't move; like El Lobo, he looked extremely pissed off. Clearly these two men were used to being in command and despised being told what to do.

With the bandage packs in hand, Harv said, "We'd better tape their wrists and ankles first."

"Good idea. They still look a bit defiant. Tango one, update Hotel three on our status in here."

After setting the field dressings on a sofa end table, Harv pointed his Sig at their prisoners.

Nathan ordered El Lobo to lean forward and put his hands behind his back.

"Hey, I'm sitting next to a fucking dead guy," El Lobo said. "Do you mind getting his ass off the sofa?"

Nathan nodded an okay to Harv, then said, "Keep your hands and feet still. Any sudden moves will result in more discomfort."

Harv yanked the body to the floor and dragged it several paces away.

While taping El Lobo's wrists, Nathan asked a third time if anyone else was in the house.

Yellow said there were six more men, not including the dead guy near the bathroom door.

He asked if the count included Alisio and El Lobo. She said it didn't.

Nathan ran the body count in his head. Including the pickup driver, they'd killed six bodyguards. So who was the seventh?

Quattro.

He'd heard El Lobo call out to him.

The man he'd just shot couldn't be Quattro—he was too big and didn't have fully tattooed arms. Assuming Yellow knew who El Lobo's right-hand man was, he asked, "Where's Quattro?"

"He left."

"Yes, we know that. Where did he go?"

She looked at El Lobo with an uncertain expression. Clearly, she didn't know how to respond.

"Here's the deal. These men? Their lives are over as they've known them. Their next residence will be a prison cell at Guantánamo Bay, Cuba. You don't have to pretend they're attractive or desirable in exchange for money anymore. Now, listen up. I don't want to hurt you. All we want is information, so please tell me where Quattro went."

El Lobo looked furious but remained silent.

She bit her lip, obviously considering her situation. "I don't know. He just grabbed the car keys and said he'd be right back."

"Did El Lobo ask him to go out?"

"I don't know. They left the room and talked in the kitchen. I didn't hear what they said."

"But Quattro went out right after that?"

She nodded.

"How long ago?"

"I don't know, maybe ten minutes."

He keyed his radio. "Hotel three, one of our guests said Quattro left the house around ten minutes ago. Pretty sure he's the one driving the sports car."

Vince copied the transmission as Nathan secured Yellow's hands behind her back, then focused on . . .

Alisio.

The man who'd ordered the assassination of his father and nearly killed his sister and niece in the process.

The man behind the torture of Vincent's secretary.

The man who'd orchestrated the death of Vince's youngest son and come within an eyelash of killing the rest of Vince's family.

And last but not least? This man was responsible for the cold-blooded murder of sixteen other people in San Diego and DC—the collateral damage price tag of his quest for revenge.

Nathan wanted to put a bullet through this jerk's face so badly, it physically hurt to restrain himself.

What a piece of crap.

He ordered Alisio to lean forward, then duct-taped his wrists tightly. Short and heavyset, Alisio looked like a younger clone of his father. Wispy mustache and goatee. Double chin. Heavy gold chains. Diamond studs on his lobes. He even wore the same white fedora with a gold band. The only real difference? His stubby fingers weren't adorned with rings.

Nathan taped everyone's ankles, stepped back, and crossed his arms while Harv applied field dressings to El Lobo's calf and Blue's butt. She groaned in agony when Harv helped her off the floor and sat her on the couch.

Finished with his first aid, Harv said, "If we was fishing, I'd throw 'em all back."

"Very funny, asshole," Alisio said. "Do you have any idea who you're fucking with?"

"Yeah, we do," Nathan said. "The trust-fund child of a dead cartel kingpin. You look just like him."

That stunned Alisio. His lips moved, but nothing came out.

Nathan raised his brows in a *figure-it-out* kind of expression. "Don't strain yourself."

"You were there?"

"Let's just say your good ol' dad didn't know when to shut up."

At that, Alisio began a verbal tirade—annoying at best, deserving a bullet at worst. Unfortunately, Alisio represented DNI Benson's best hope of tracing the WMD-grenade-smuggling sequence all the way back to North Korea—a vital step in preventing this kind of threat from emerging again. Instead of shooting him, Nathan stepped behind the couch and smacked the butt of his pistol onto the top of Alisio's skull. It sounded like a dropped watermelon on concrete.

The man groaned, turned his head as far as he could, and spat in Nathan's direction. The saliva missed its mark, but it seemed another demonstration was in order. He clocked Alisio again, on the exact same tender spot.

"Oh, man, that's gotta hurt," Harv said.

El Lobo squirmed and cursed, not at his captors, but just in general. Nathan let the outburst slide. It was, after all, understandable.

Alisio became much more docile after that. Perhaps the reality of his situation had become clear: no escape and no one to rescue him.

"Let's get the women out of here. We'll tape them all together and put them in a bedroom."

Sandra guarded their prisoners while Harv and he moved the three women through the kitchen and into a spare bedroom. The woman with the bullet wound cried out but managed to limp along on her own. To make sure they couldn't escape, Harv taped all of them to a heavy reading chair. Even if they managed to get up, which was unlikely, the chair would act like a ball and chain. These women weren't going anywhere.

Back in the sofa room, Nathan said, "Let's get these two situated in the middle of the living room. It's wide open in there. Grab two dining room chairs and set them face-to-face so our guests here can witness each other's interrogations."

It took Harv a moment to arrange the chairs. They secured Alisio first, wrapping multiple layers of tape around his torso and the back of the chair. They repeated the process with El Lobo.

"The tape keeps you from falling out of the chair when you pass out, assuming we have to get . . . What's the word I'm looking for?"

"Rough," Harv said.

Sandra maintained an even expression, but Nathan got the impression she'd never witnessed an interrogation of this type before.

"It's a little understated, but *rough* will do. See, we'd like nothing better than to go home and get some sleep, so the sooner you cooperate and tell us what we want to know, the sooner this will be over. How *rough* we get depends entirely on you two."

"Do you think I'm scared of you?" El Lobo asked.

"You misunderstand. This isn't about fear; it's about pain. I'm sure you've tortured many people over the years. Now it's your turn to be on the wrong side." Nathan put on his warmest smile. "Welcome to my world."

Alisio began squirming, testing the tape.

"Save your energy," he said. "From now on, you will speak only when spoken to, and the first and last words out of your filthy sewers will be *sir*. Do you maggots understand me?"

Harv sounded slightly amused. "I doubt they've seen R. Lee Ermey's performance."

Nathan shrugged. "Okay, we can drop the *sir* part, but the rest stands. Let's get right to it. Where are the gas grenades?"

When El Lobo refused to say anything, Nathan backhanded him hard enough to split his lip. "The grenades—where are they?"

El Lobo spat blood. "You still don't have any idea who you're screwing with here."

"You mean a two-bit coyote-for-hire?"

"Oh, I'm much more than that."

"I'm sure you believe that, but you'll soon discover you're nothing but a miserable little cuss screaming in agony."

He turned to Harv. "Since our friend here seems unwilling to cooperate, let's get a little rough. See if you can find an ice pick in one of the drawers. I'd settle for shish kebab skewers if they're made of bamboo. I'll need something to drive them in. Look for a meat tenderizer. Oh, and see if you can locate some ammonia to wake them up after they've passed out. While you're at it, round up a flyswatter. I'm curious to see how well our friends can handle several hundred smacks to their rosy red cheeks."

"You got it."

Nathan locked eyes and didn't say anything as Harv began tossing the contents of the kitchen drawers on the floor.

Tango two announced the sports car had a one-minute ETA, and Vince copied the transmission.

El Lobo looked left and right.

"You expecting someone?" asked Nathan. "Quattro? He's dead." It wasn't true, but he wanted his captives to have zero hope.

El Lobo didn't say anything.

"Sorry, there's no one left. Here's the deal. I'm going to duct-tape your mouth closed before we begin driving skewers into your flesh. You won't be allowed to speak for fifteen minutes. The bleeding is minimal, so we'll have plenty of time. After your first fifteen minutes have passed, I'll remove the tape and ask you where the grenades are again. You'll have five seconds to answer. If I think you're stalling or giving me bullshit, the tape goes back on, and another fifteen-minute period will begin. Time will pass very slowly for you—"

"I found the shish kebab sticks," Harv called out. "There's probably over a hundred of them."

"Are they bamboo?"

"Indeed they are."

"Perfect. Did you find a meat tenderizer?"

"No, but I found a cast-iron skillet. It should work well as a hammer. Do you want me to heat it up? It can cool back down in El Lobo's lap."

"We'll keep that option open. Bring the equipment in. Tango one, you don't have to watch this, but please keep an eye on our six while we discuss the location of the grenades with these gentlemen."

"I wouldn't miss it," she said.

Nathan nodded. "Now, where were we? We were talking about time passing slowly. You'll be amazed how long a single minute can last. If you'd like to know the record, it's thirteen. We once had a guy hold out for thirteen fifteen-minute periods. He was a drooling basket case by the time he caved, but we got what we wanted."

He looked at Harv. "Duct tape, please. We're going to get started. Mr. Lobo, tell you what . . . Before we do, I think you should know what you're in for. Maybe you'll change your mind and tell us where the grenades are. Hand me one skewer and the skillet."

Harv stepped forward and extended both items.

Nathan set the frying pan down and removed his bloodstained Predator knife. As if sharpening a pencil manually, he sculpted the tip of the bamboo to an ultra-fine point, then tested its sharpness with his forefinger. "Nice. Where should we start?" he asked Harv, indicating El Lobo.

"How about his eyes?" Harv suggested.

"That's a good idea, but I want him to see what we're doing."

"His ears?"

"Then he won't hear himself screaming. Let's begin with his quadriceps. Sometimes the skewers break on the first impact, but once they're an inch or so deep, they're less likely to snap. I gotta tell you, though, it's quite unpleasant." Nathan looked at Alisio. "You're next. You ready, Mr. Lobo?"

"You're crazy . . . ," said the cartel boss.

"Certifiable."

"Wait," Alisio said, "I'm sure we can make some kind of deal. I have cash. American cash. Lots of it."

"And that cash is here, in the house?"

"Yes, it's in the basement. Five million."

"That's a lot of money." He looked at Harv. "Do we need any cash, partner? Is there something you've always wanted to spend five million dollars on?"

"No, not really."

"Seriously? Nothing?"

Harv shrugged.

"Well, I guess we don't need cash." Nathan placed the tip of the skewer on top of El Lobo's leg, grabbed the frying pan, and raised his eyebrows. "Well, what's it going to be? Information or pain?"

"I think he needs a demo," Harv said. "I'll bet he caves within—"

Vince's voice interrupted them. *"The sports car's a Porsche. It's waiting for the electric gate to open. The second vehicle's an SUV. Shit! The passenger in the SUV's pointing at the power pole. They've spotted Tango one's C4 charge. We're blown. They're racing toward the house. Tangos three and four, maintain perimeter. Don't let anyone leave! Tango one, I need you out front!"*

"Go," Nathan said to Sandra. "We've got this. Be ready to blow the power. Turn on the hall lights."

Without hesitation, she bolted from the room. A few seconds later, the main hallway became bright.

Nathan continued. "Hotel three, Quattro might have the grenades." *"I'll keep my rounds low."*

Everyone heard the muffled roar of automatic M4 fire, followed by a smaller-caliber automatic weapon, likely a machine pistol.

Alisio's expression changed. "It seems things have taken a turn for the worse for you."

Nathan clocked him on the jaw and took a defensive position near the kitchen's island. From here, he could see down the hall toward the bedroom where they'd confined the women, but he couldn't see more than halfway down the hall in the other direction. He glanced at Harv. "Cover the hall leading to the front door."

Harv repositioned himself.

Vince cut in again. *"I nailed its tires, but the Porsche is still making a beeline for the garage. Tango one, ETA?"*

"Five seconds."

More deep-throated M4 gunfire came from out front, then the roar of an engine, followed by machine-pistol fire. Tires screeched briefly, then went quiet. A loud explosion boomed, and Nathan hoped it was Vince's grenade launcher taking out the SUV.

"I nailed the SUV with an HE round, but the Porsche made it into the garage. I couldn't verify the driver's Quattro."

The clatter of machine-pistol fire sounded again, followed by another burst from an M4.

They heard Vince groan in pain and curse under his breath.

"Hotel three . . . status?" Nathan asked, his voice low.

Nothing.

"Hotel three!"

"I'm okay. It's not too bad."

Not too bad? Nathan thought.

What they heard next sounded like deep throaty booms from a large-caliber handgun.

Three quick shots.

Then two more handgun reports rang out from a smaller-caliber weapon. And something else: the shots had been fired inside the house, from the direction of the garage.

"Hotel three, status?"

"I'm okay. Keep Alisio and El Lobo secure. Tango one, where are you?"

"I'm on the steps outside the front door. I don't have eyes on you."

"I'm in the landscaping about twenty yards south of the pickup."

"Hotel three," Harv asked, "who fired the large handgun shots?"

"Unknown; they came from inside the garage. Could've been Quattro."

Nathan looked at their bound guests, who couldn't hear the radio's transmissions.

Despite that, Alisio's smile widened.

Don't worry, Mr. A, Nathan thought. *You won't be smiling for long.*

Vince's voice sounded strained. *"Stay alert in there. I fired an ankle-height salvo under the Porsche, but I have . . . no idea if I nailed Quattro. I need to check the SUV for survivors. Shit, I need a field dressing first. I'm leaking at a pretty good clip."*

"Where are you hit?"

"Left hip."

"Tango one, we're good in here," Nathan said. "Take care of Hotel three."

Vince said, *"Tango one, divert to the right around the circular drive-way and stay in the landscaping. I don't want you going across open ground with Quattro loose in there."*

"Copy, on my way. Hang in there, Commander."

The lighting in the hallway suddenly went dark.

The effect was eerie. The only illumination now came from the pool area, which wasn't much.

Looking down the hallway, Nathan lowered his NV but didn't yet see anyone.

He sensed a presence.

Malevolent and ugly.

Time seemed to stretch as something chilling emanated from the hall, a repeating *clomp-slide* sound of someone limping with a useless leg.

"Nate, we've got company."

"I see him."

What they saw belonged in a horror movie.

Shuffling like the undead, a bloody mess materialized in the hall. Quattro.

The man's right hand held a pistol.

And his left hand held—

A gas grenade.

Nathan focused on the device. Both its safety pins were pulled and looped around Quattro's trigger finger.

"Hold your fire," Nathan whispered to Harv. "The pins are pulled."

"Yeah, I'm seeing that, and he's only got one grenade. We need the others."

Quattro kept coming, his right leg nearly useless.

With a look of pure insanity on his face, the man limped into the living room.

In full color, he looked even ghastlier.

The lower half of his body looked like it had been dipped in a vat of red paint. His muscular arms and shaved head were covered with expensive blood-smeared tattoos. Nathan felt it. Evil, in its purest form.

"Drop your weapons and untie them," he said in a raspy voice. "We're leaving."

"Or what?" Nathan asked.

Quattro switched his aim over to Harv, then back.

"If you shoot one of us," Harv said, taking a step forward, "the other's going to drop you where you stand. You'll be spared a chemical weapon death, but you'll still be dead."

"Don't come any closer. I'll drop it. I swear I will!"

El Lobo smiled and licked his lips. "Well, well, well, Mr. G.I. Joe, what's it going to be?"

"Nobody's leaving," Nathan said.

"Then we all die together," Alisio said. "One big happy family, no?"

Nathan kept his eyes on Quattro. "Do you honestly think we're going to let you three just walk out of here? Seriously?"

Alisio half laughed. "You don't seem to understand the situation. If you don't let us go, we all die. Right here, right now."

"And that scares you?" Nathan asked.

Alisio hesitated but recovered quickly. "We'd rather die than go to prison."

"Drop your guns and get on the ground!" Quattro yelled.

"Then what? You shoot us?" Nathan put some pressure on the trigger. "That's not happening."

He wondered if they'd have time to bolt out of the room before being affected by the grenade's toxin. From what Cantrell had described, there was virtually no chance of that. As soon as the safety handle flew free, the gas spewed immediately. They'd be exposed, no way around it. Even if they held their breaths and tried to run, the microdroplets would nail them.

"I'll do it," Quattro said, his wounded body swaying.

"If you let go of that grenade, your usefulness is over," Nathan said. "Guess what happens next: I drive a bullet through that corn mush you call a brain."

El Lobo leaned his head back, laughed, and looked at Harv. "And what do you have to say?"

"Me? I'm just wondering why your sewer rat hasn't already dropped it. Maybe he doesn't have the balls."

"Don't make me do it!"

"He's full of shit," Harv said. "Call his bluff."

Nathan took a step forward. "No one's leaving."

"Don't come any closer! I swear I'll do it!"

"I'd listen to Quattro if I were you," Alisio said. "It's very nasty. Death doesn't happen quickly."

"We've seen the demo."

"Then you know what it does."

"Tell you what—if your sewer rat hands us the grenade and you tell us where the rest of them are, we can all live happily ever after. You three will be in prison, but you'll be alive. The food's bad, but I hear you get good dental." Nathan made an inclusive gesture toward Harv. "At this point, we have nothing to lose. If we drop our weapons, we die. If we don't drop our weapons, we die. Since death seems to be inevitable, I think we'll take you two losers with us."

That seemed to cause some concern.

Alisio's expression changed. "Surely we can work out some kind of deal."

Nathan took another step, focusing on Quattro. "Hand me the grenade. I'm done talking."

"Easy, Quattro," El Lobo said. "Calm down, okay? We can find a way out of this. Everyone has their price. We have to find how much these guys want."

Nathan frowned and looked at Harv. "Sorry, El Lobo, we're not for sale."

"Last warning!" Quattro yelled. "Put your guns down or I'll drop it!"

"Easy, Quattro," El Lobo said.

Nathan tried to reason a way out of this and came up short.

If they tried to run, he had no doubt Quattro would shoot. Maybe only one of them would take a bullet, but Nathan needed to be sure it would be him, not Harv.

He looked at Harv, and in that instant, they both knew what the other was thinking. Neither of them wanted to survive this knowing the other hadn't.

No, they'd die together.

In English, Nathan said, "Harv, you ready?"

"I'm okay, Nate. I'm glad we're going together. I'd always hoped we would."

"Me too. It's been an honor."

"Wait!" Alisio shouted. "We can still make a—"

Too late.

Nathan pulled the trigger.

CHAPTER 31

The bullet slammed through Quattro's nose. The result spoke for itself. The back of his skull erupted.

Quattro's mouth formed an O shape at the instant he crumpled to the wood floor.

The grenade rolled out of his grasp.

Nathan's eyes focused on the safety handle as it cartwheeled through the air.

"You dumb shit!" Alisio yelled. "You stupid dumb shit!" The cartel boss began thrashing against the tape in a futile effort to free himself.

Hissing like a punctured can of soda, the grenade spun like a top, ejecting its deadly poison in every direction.

Nathan covered his eyes, but he felt the micro droplets nail the back of his hand, lips, chin, and neck. Grasping at the weakest straw imaginable, he hoped the face paint would protect him but knew it was wishful thinking.

Across the kitchen, Harv crouched, also covering his eyes.

The canister continued its spastic pirouette, then went silent. A thin layer of frost now coated the device. Its discharge hadn't lasted more than four or five seconds.

Like honey combined with jasmine, a sweet odor dominated the room. Before he realized he was doing it, Nathan inhaled through his nose, sampling the fragrance. He wondered if the chemical engineers added the odor for just that purpose. It didn't matter. There was no use in holding his breath at this point.

He and Harv were infected . . . No way around it.

El Lobo kept thrashing, but he couldn't get the leverage needed to tear the tape.

Nathan had the presence of mind to key his radio. "We're exposed in here. We're exposed. The toxin's been released!"

Vince's frantic voice came back, *"Shit, Nathan, confirm a grenade went off. Confirm. Confirm!"*

"Yes, the WMD's loose. Get as far away as possible. Go north or south; then turn west into the wind."

"All fire teams, you heard him! The ranch house is hot. I repeat, it's hot! I want a thousand yards between us and that place. We're taking the truck. Sandra, you're driving. Let's move, move, move!"

Nathan didn't blame Vince for bugging out. There was nothing anyone could do at this point. He felt his face become flushed and hot.

Incredible as it seemed, the creation of a twisted chemical engineer was going to kill Harv and him—badly. Their earthly journey ended here, but thousands of innocent lives would be saved, beautiful lives like Lauren's. He felt some gratification knowing that, but he'd wanted to see Lauren get married and have a family—continue the McBride line. Now, he'd never have the chance.

In anger, he swung his pistol at a wineglass and had the satisfaction of seeing it destroyed.

"Nathan, it's okay," Harv said. "We did the right thing."

Only if the rest of the grenades are contained, he thought.

Nathan pointed his Sig at Alisio's face and began to put pressure on the trigger. The man who killed his father was going to die anyway, so why not?

Why not indeed?

Harv said something, but the voice seemed far away, like a distant echo.

Two pounds.

That's all the pressure it would take to prompt the Sig's hammer onto its firing pin, sending a bullet through Alisio's brain. A fitting end to the murderous criminal secured in the chair.

Or was it?

And then everything became clear.

Suddenly. Plainly. Totally.

Maybe he'd never fully grasped the power of life and death, or worse, he'd misunderstood his role in it. This man's life *wasn't* in his hands. It was in God's. Nathan was an instrument of good, not evil. The killing he'd done tonight—and all through his life—had served a purpose, and it hadn't been to satiate his desire for revenge. Yes, he felt overwhelmed with feelings of hatred and retribution. Who wouldn't? But if he killed Alisio, would he bask in righteousness? Savor the moral high ground by avenging his father's murderer? Not likely. He'd regret it, even for the few seconds he had left. Had killing Alisio's father, at the time it happened, been justified? Maybe, maybe not, but Nathan wasn't going to repeat history.

He lowered the pistol. "I'm not like you."

"Do it, you coward," Alisio spat. "The idea of dying alongside a chickenshit like you sickens me." The murderer's thrashing reached a peak. Perhaps the toxin affected him more quickly. "You're going to be my slave in hell. You'll be licking my boots through all eternity."

Nathan looked at the man and felt pity. So much fear. He couldn't imagine living with constant fear. Of all the human emotions, fear brought out the worst in people.

Alisio started another vile tirade. The language coming from the man's mouth needed to end. Nathan might die, but he didn't have to do it listening to a lunatic's twisted ranting.

He stepped up to Alisio and said, "I forgive you," then swung his pistol. The Sig's suppressor caught Alisio on the jaw. Like a KO from a heavyweight, the effect was instantaneous. Alisio's head snapped back, then lolled forward.

Ironically, he'd just spared the man from the horrid and violent death he'd been wishing upon him. El Lobo came next. He pistol-whipped the coyote's jaw, rendering him unconscious. He didn't like the idea of El Lobo seeing him lose control.

He didn't know how much time he had before the toxin ripped his mind to shreds, but he'd die without compromising who he was—while he still had the choice.

The truth hit him hard.

In a few more seconds, he'd begin to feel the poison coursing through his nervous system, and the choice of killing or not killing would be stripped away. Did the people who jumped to their deaths rather than burn to death on September eleventh truly commit suicide? No, they hadn't. Facing that scenario, they'd shown themselves mercy. Simple as that. And God didn't condemn them for it.

He'd faced death before but never like this. Being turned into a stark raving nutjob without reason or control? The savage violence he might wreak on his friend made him physically ill. No, that wasn't going to happen. He'd turn his Sig on himself before hurting Harv. He'd lived a good life. Yes, he'd lashed out at everyone close to him at one time or another, even Harv, but he'd made amends for it.

"Nathan."

Holly. Would she understand or feel betrayed? No. She'd be okay with this. Some things were worth dying for, like saving the lives of several thousand innocent people. The brave souls on board Flight 93 did it. They died trying to regain control of the aircraft. This was no different. He and Harv would die so that others would live.

He moved the pistol toward his head.

It's better this way.

The alternative was too horrible to imagine. He'd never allow himself to hurt Harv.

God will understand.

"Nathan!"

He felt his body flush with sudden heat. It had begun. If he didn't shoot himself right now, he'd lose the free will to make the choice. The ultimate sacrifice. The Marine who dives onto a grenade to save his fellow Marines. A mother who runs from a bear to draw its attention away from her child. Was this any different?

As the pistol neared his temple, he felt controlled by someone else. Some*thing* else.

The Other.

He sensed its presence emerge from his soul with a sly smile of satisfaction.

It was only a matter of time, Nate old boy. I was going to win in the end. You've always known that, haven't you? It's nice to see you're finally admitting it. Denial is so self-serving... Go ahead and kill those lousy vermin. They have it coming.

No! It's *my* decision, not yours.

If you keep telling yourself that, you might actually believe it someday.

Go away!

Or what? You'll kill me? A little late for that, isn't it? Kill them. Kill them while you still can.

No! I won't give in to this!

He forced the Other back into its cage and took command.

The pistol reached his head.

Its warm steel found his temple.

This is it, then.

No regrets.

"Nathan, STOP!"

A blur caught his eye.

Before he could react, two hundred pounds slammed into his rib cage.

At the same instant, an ironlike hand seized his wrist and twisted the Sig away from his head.

He resigned himself to a different kind of death.

Not from himself, but from Harv.

Maybe it was better this way.

Yes, better.

Fully aware.

Facing death.

Like a Marine.

CHAPTER 32

Nathan landed hard and felt the back of his head smack the hardwood floor.

Fighting off the dizzying effect of the impact as he lay half-conscious, he wondered, *Why isn't Harv tearing my throat open?* He fully expected to be fighting for his life. They'd been poisoned for sure.

"Harv."

"Nathan, you okay?"

"I don't know."

"You were unresponsive, so I kinda . . . took you down before you . . . you know . . ."

"Blew my brains out?"

"Well, yeah. That."

"May I ask a question?"

"Sure, Nate, anything."

"Why are you still on top of me?"

"Well, I'm not enjoying myself, if that's what you're implying."

"Then get off, ya lug."

"I just wanted to be sure *you* were *you*."

"Yeah, I'm me."

Harv rolled off and lay next to him. They stayed that way for several seconds.

Nathan tilted his head toward Harv. "May I ask another question?"

"Fire away."

"Why aren't we dying?"

"Because I switched the grenades two minutes ago."

They both sat up and pointed their weapons at the voice that had spoken perfect English, albeit with an accent Nathan thought he recognized.

"The real ones are in the pack I'm wearing." A man in a black butler's uniform stood in the hallway with his hands held chest-high. His right pant leg was wet with blood, dripping onto the floor. A small patch of ruined fabric gaped above the knee.

"Who are you?" Nathan asked as he slowly reached down to his radio.

"Perhaps the better question is, who are *you*? Needless to say, your appearance here is a huge surprise, but also quite fortunate." The man took a step forward, then stopped, wincing.

"That's close enough," Harv said as they got up.

The newcomer took another tentative step, seemingly unafraid of the Sig pointed at his chest. "I don't think you want to risk a bullet passing through my body. I assure you the grenades in my pack are real."

The man looked to be in his mid-thirties with dark hair, dark eyes, and a touch of gray in his temples. Although in a household staff uniform, he possessed a commanding presence. Clearly this man was no butler.

Nathan exchanged a glance with Harv, checked his still-unconscious prisoners, then looked back to the butler. "So who goes first?"

"Since you seem to be the ones out of place, you do."

"May we assume you aren't who you appear to be? Part of Alisio's household staff?"

"Yes, that's a fair assumption."

"Undercover."

The man offered the thinnest smile, then shifted his weight to ease the pain of his injured leg.

Nathan lowered his Sig, but Harv kept his leveled. "For all we know," Harv said, "you could be a last line of defense, a sleeper of sorts."

"Yes, that's definitely true." He pointed at Alisio's unconscious form. "Just not for him. If I were, we wouldn't be talking." He slowly turned, revealing a large revolver tucked into his belt under the heavy backpack.

"Point taken," Harv said. "So the gunshots we heard coming from the garage . . . that was you?"

"Yes. As you can see, he got me." He inclined his head at Quattro's body. "I thought I'd killed him. I shot him three times with a .357 Magnum. Tough little man, and fast. When he collapsed, I switched the grenades and left the garage to hide the real ones. You can only imagine my surprise to find him gone when I returned."

"The women said Alisio's staff doesn't live in the house," Harv said. "How did you know where Quattro was going?"

The disguised butler reached up to his ear and removed something that looked like an earbud, then smiled. "I bugged the sofa room and kitchen, where they discuss all their business. Now, I'm pretty sure you're Americans, but you're a little old for SEALs, Rangers, or Recons."

He and Harv didn't say anything, although Nathan felt tempted to smile.

"Sorry, no offense intended."

"None taken," Harv said. "We *old guys* did pretty well tonight."

"I can't argue with the results. So you're Americans and . . ."

Nathan said, "We're not US service members. We're private military contractors."

"Ah, yes, I see. That makes sense."

"Don't move!" Vince's voice boomed from the hallway's opening where the butler had entered.

"It's okay, Vince. He's not a threat." Shit, he'd just used Vince's name. A stupid and inexcusable error.

His M4 leveled at the man, Vince limped forward, a blood-soaked field dressing covering his hip. "He's got a hog leg tucked into his back."

"We know," Nathan said, looking at Vince's trigger finger, which was properly lying flat on the receiver and not curled around the trigger. "He showed it to us. He's also got the real grenades in his pack."

Their commander lowered his weapon upon hearing that, then labored over and stood next to Harv and him while Sandra eased behind the butler.

"Who are you?" Vince asked.

The man looked at Nathan. "Perhaps you should disable the auto-transmit feature of your radio first."

Nathan asked, "You saw me switch it . . . ?"

The man smiled again.

Amazingly calm under pressure, Nathan thought. *Even with that leg wound . . .*

A small pool of blood had already formed on the floor under the man's pantleg.

"Vince . . . ," the stranger said slowly. "Private military contractors . . ." This time a wide smile split his face. "You're Vincent Beaumont? The president and CEO of BSI. And these men are working for you."

Vince didn't say anything.

"You may not remember me, but we've actually met before. During the Wolf armored vehicle trials at Hatzerim. I was the man who asked the question about the Ford F-550 chassis—if it was heavy enough to accommodate the MRAP variant."

"I remember you," Vince said. "My company ended up buying five of them. I'm sorry, but I don't recall your name. Hang on a sec." Vince pressed his transmit button. "All fire teams, we're secure inside the ranch house. Maintain positions and stay alert. Hotel four, contact the CP and tell them we're in possession of the items. Tell them to expect a personal report from me in a few minutes."

"Aye, sir."

The man limped forward and offered his hand to Vince. "Gavriel Masalha. I'm very sorry about your wife and the loss of your son."

"Thank you," Vince said, "but I'm not the only one who's suffered a loss. This is Nathan McBride."

"McBride . . . Senator Stone McBride's son?"

Nathan nodded.

"I'm sorry for your loss too. Your father was a good friend to Israel over the years."

Vince introduced Harv.

"Mossad?" Harv asked, shaking hands.

"Being who we all are, and being that my mission here is terminated, I'm comfortable answering with a yes."

Harv offered to apply a tighter field dressing to Gavriel's leg. The Israeli agent gratefully accepted.

"Why bother to plant the fakes?" Harv asked. "Why didn't you just take the real grenades and leave?"

"I had no way to know who or what I'd be facing outside. For all I knew, there was a small army out there. I also had no idea who'd win the fight in here. If Alisio and his men managed to ward off your attack, they'd have the fake grenades and likely bug out."

"And that's a good thing?" Nathan asked.

"Trackers," Harv answered for the Mossad agent. "Right? The fake grenades are bugged."

"Yes, that's exactly right. We wanted to know where the ISIS insurgents planned to take them. That's not in play anymore."

Nathan didn't say anything.

Gavriel continued. "The most important thing is having possession of the real WMDs. Anything more than that was merely a bonus. In any case, it made sense to track their movement."

"Doing our job for us?" Harv asked.

Gavriel shrugged. "There was no guarantee the grenades were going to be used in America. They might've ended up in my country or France, Germany, Spain. Anywhere really. Based on the location of this ISIS cell, we suspected they were bound for America, but we couldn't be one hundred percent certain. I was hoping to salvage twenty-two months of undercover work and planning. I've been waiting for an opportunity to make the switch, but I didn't know where the grenades were until Quattro went out and retrieved them. I can only assume it had something to do with all the gunfire and explosions that came from the compound. We've all heard munitions practice at night, but never with that much intensity. When El Lobo couldn't reach the compound by phone, Alisio decided to play it safe and send Quattro out for the grenades. I took advantage of the opportunity you guys created."

"You undercovers are a special breed. I don't know how you do it," Nathan said.

Gavriel gave a humble shrug. "I wish I could say one gets used to it."

Vincent nodded. "Well, I hate to say it, but *our orders* are to take possession of the grenades."

Gavriel smiled. "Now what?"

"Why don't we use the bigger gun rule?" Vince suggested.

"The bigger gun rule?"

Vincent patted his M4. "Yeah, the man with the bigger gun rules."

"I, ah, see your point."

"How about a compromise?" Vince said. "In order to keep American and Israeli relations healthy, you'll come with us, pretending to be part of Alisio's staff."

"I was hoping you'd offer. I seem to need some medical attention too. I'm assuming you have an exit strategy?"

"Black Hawks, two clicks north of here," Nathan said.

Gavriel looked at Vince's wound. "He'll never survive the hike," he told Nathan, "even on a stretcher. It looks like he's got a clipped artery. He needs emergency surgery."

"Why don't I just stand here and bleed to death while you three discuss my medical history."

"A bit testy, isn't he?" Gavriel asked.

"Bullet wounds tend to do that," Harv said. "He'll be okay once I shoot him up with morphine. Would you like some as well?"

"Absolutely," said Gavriel.

Nathan reached out in a hand-it-over gesture.

Somewhat reluctantly, Gavriel gave him the backpack.

"It's unsettling," Nathan said, "what's in here . . ."

Gavriel winced again and nodded. "What you guys did—without knowing the WMDs were fakes . . ." He shook his head.

It was Harv's turn to shrug. "Like you said, we wish it got easier."

Nathan suddenly smiled.

"What?" Harv asked.

"I know how to speed up our exit. Gavriel, do you happen to know where the keys to Alisio's Bell 427 are?"

"As a matter of fact, I do."

CHAPTER 33

DNI Benson quite literally paced the halls of the West Wing. He really hated waiting like this, especially with the stakes so high.

When his phone vibrated, he yanked it from his pocket.

The display indicated Border Patrol Chief Ryan Switzer.

The moment of truth had arrived.

"Ryan, what's our status?" He wished his voice hadn't sounded so . . . desperate.

"I just spoke to Beaumont thirty seconds ago. His fire teams were successful. They've got the WMDs."

Benson closed his eyes and nodded. "Casualties?"

"One member of sierra fire team was killed at the compound."

"I'm very sorry to hear that."

"Beaumont took a round to his hip, and McBride's likely got a concussion."

"Did we get El Lobo?"

"Yes, we have him in custody. Carlos Alisio too. Quattro was KIA."

"The Rio Grande cell?"

"I don't have exact numbers because the barracks building was completely destroyed by a suicide explosion. All the insurgents from the Rio Grande cell are dead, along with half a dozen more of Alisio's bodyguards. One of Alisio's household staff was wounded. A woman too. Harvey Fontana's going to commandeer Alisio's helicopter to shuttle all the wounded—from both sides—out to the Black Hawks, where a medic will get them stabilized. McBride insisted we treat the wounded from Alisio's staff."

"What's Beaumont's condition?"

"He sounded okay, but it's hard to say. He brushed off his wound, wouldn't talk about it."

"Let's get our dead PMC out of there right away."

"I'm on it. After Fontana drops off the wounded, he and McBride are flying over to the compound to retrieve the body."

"Is Rancho Del Seco secure at this point?"

"Yes, the remaining eight members of BSI's fire teams are staying behind to assist Cantrell's officers when they arrive."

"Let me know when Beaumont arrives at the command post. McBride and Fontana too. I want to personally thank them."

"I'm sure they'd appreciate that."

"You too, Ryan. You and your agents did a fine job setting up the op."

"I wish I could take the credit, but it's a team effort. Ah . . . Beaumont told me something you need to know."

"All right . . ." Benson listened while Ryan laid out the sacrifice McBride and Fontana thought they were making to ensure the grenades didn't get loose.

"Incredible," Benson said, "although I'm not surprised. Like father, like son."

"So it would seem."

"No goodbyes," Benson said as he hung up. When he spoke to the president in a few minutes, he planned to give the Border Patrol a nice plug for its role in the success of the mission.

He leaned back and looked at the ceiling. He felt terrible about losing a man, but he sat in the director's chair because he could make the tough decisions, fully knowing the cost in human life. Even so, a single loss was too many. He planned to personally contact the dead PMC's family with his condolences.

Walking toward the Oval Office, he called Rebecca. "It seems your faith in BSI isn't misplaced. We've got the WMDs."

"That's great news. Did we lose anyone?"

He told her what Chief Ryan had relayed about losing a BSI contractor.

"At the risk of sounding callous, it could've been much worse."

"It's not callous; it's the truth."

"Thank you for trusting me about using BSI."

"Of course. Listen, I need to call off the B-2s. Menendez was on board for the surgical strike, but he didn't know about our fail-safe backup plan. If we'd had to drop sixty tons of bombs on Mexican soil, it would've been a diplomatic crap sandwich."

"Good thing we don't have to take a bite."

"No kidding. McBride and Fontana did well. I'll be in touch with you later this morning. You get some sleep."

He made a call to the secretary of defense, who was more than pleased with the news.

The door to the personal secretary to the president lay open, but he still gently knocked on its jamb. Madeleine Westerhout looked up and smiled.

"You're working late, Maddy."

"It didn't feel right going home. Go on in; he's just finishing a call."

Benson walked in front of her desk and stopped at the open door. Still on the phone, President Trump waved him forward. He kept a respectful distance until the president finished the call.

"The First Lady says I need to call it a day. From your expression, sounds like she'll get her way. Is the news good?"

"Mr. President, the news is extremely good. We've recovered all of the WMD grenades."

"Did we lose anyone?"

"Yes . . . One BSI contractor . . . He was KIA on site."

"I'd like to personally offer my condolences to the family, if that's okay with them."

"That shouldn't be a problem. I'm sure Vincent Beaumont will be more than willing to make all the arrangements. You'd like to do that here, in your office?"

"Yes." The president must've sensed there was something else because he said, "You look like a man with something more to say."

Benson nodded. "You aren't going to believe what Nathan McBride and Harvey Fontana did to make sure we kept control of the grenades."

EPILOGUE

Being inside the green-and-white landscape of Arlington's hallowed grounds felt humbling and, honestly, a little unsettling. Even though Nathan fully understood the cost of freedom, he had a hard time wrapping his mind around so many fallen heroes—more than four hundred thousand were laid to rest here.

Holly slowed her SUV when a black squirrel scurried across the road.

Seated between Jin and his mom in the back seat, Lauren didn't comment at seeing her favorite animal. Normally, she would've, but the mood in the car had been subdued during the drive over from the Willard. He knew Lauren's arm and rib cage served as constant reminders of what she'd been through.

Physically, his niece was okay. Mentally, not so much.

It would take her a long time to get over seeing her grandfather murdered, especially the way he'd sacrificed himself to save her.

The lead vehicle, driven by Vince's brother, turned at a fork in the road. It made Nathan think of a choice he'd made early in life: to join the Marines rather than pursue a theatrical career. He couldn't help but wonder how starkly different his life would've been.

Off to the west, the sky looked sharp and menacing. A few booms of distant thunder had rumbled across the cemetery but, so far, no rain.

Twenty other vehicles were part of today's small motorcade, nothing compared to the two-mile-long procession at yesterday's public service, where his father had received a full military honors burial.

Nathan had appreciated every aspect of the age-old ritual: the horse-drawn carriage carrying the draped casket, the flag-folding, rifle volleys, bugling of "Taps," the chaplain's prayer. Everything. The service had been masterfully performed by a multiservice honor guard with every branch of the armed services represented. Stone McBride had served in the Marines, but the secretary of defense—a close friend of Stone's—had requested the mixed honor guard.

He'd wanted to sit next to his mom, but the high-profile nature of the service—live coverage on every cable news network because President Trump had attended—meant their faces would've been seen by millions of people. Not an option, especially for Jin. Besides, Cantrell had strongly suggested—ordered, really—that they blend in with the crowd during the public service. Knowing this smaller private service would take place today, his mom had been okay being seated next to Senator Kemper and his wife—her closest friends—instead of her immediate family.

Holly pulled to the shoulder along with the rest of the motorcade, and they climbed out. He felt a wave of dizziness and steadied himself against the fender.

"Are you okay, Uncle Nate? Here, I'll help you." Lauren took his hand as the five of them walked deeper into the grounds.

Limping from the calf wound she'd sustained in the alley, Jin stayed next to Holly. His sister wasn't the only one limping. Off to his left, Vince hobbled along on crutches while his brother pushed Charlene's wheelchair across the grass. Vince's hip had required replacement surgery because the bullet had smashed through his femur head, severed the ligament, ruined cartilage, and shattered his acetabulum.

Nathan watched Jin take in the vast latticework of headstones and wondered if North Korea had something similar. Probably not.

His sister looked nice in a formal black dress. And Holly? She looked stunning. No other word fit.

"You were a little quiet on the drive over," he said to Lauren. "You okay?"

"I guess. It's hard to believe Grandpa's gone. Everything happened so fast."

"Yeah, that's usually how it goes. How's the rib cage?"

"It only hurts when I breathe."

He liked the wry humor; it reminded him of his dad.

"Then don't breathe."

"Funny."

"Lauren."

"Yeah?"

"I'm really proud of you. I mean the way you've handled all of this."

"Thanks. I try not to think about it too much. It seemed like a bad dream . . . still kinda does."

Harv and his wife, Candace, converged with them from where they'd parked. After a two-minute walk, they were close to the grave site.

"Wow," Lauren said. "Is that Vice President Pence?"

"Yes. Try not to drool on his shoes, okay?"

"Ha ha ha. I get to meet him, don't I?"

"Absolutely."

"Hey, there's Senator Kemper. Who are all these other people?"

"Do you know what the intelligence community is?"

Lauren looked up at him and thought for a moment. "Not really."

"It's the term for all agencies under the Office of the Director of National Intelligence. I recognize some of the directors, but most of them I don't know on sight. Good thing Holly requested name tags for everyone."

"No kidding."

Quietly, he asked his niece, "Do you remember how to address people? Do you want to go over it again?"

"If it says 'Director' on their name tag, I say 'Director,' then their last name."

"That's right. Same with 'Senator' and 'Secretary.' If you're not sure, then just say 'sir' or 'ma'am.' Call the vice president 'Mr. Vice President.' The Speaker of the House is here, so use 'Speaker,' then his last name. The Department of Defense is also well represented. I don't recognize all of them, but the secretary of the Navy, the commandant of the Marine Corps, and the sergeant major of the Marines are here."

"Their uniforms look really cool."

"I'm also seeing several Supreme Court justices, so use 'Justice,' then their last name, except for Chief Justice Roberts, add 'Chief.'"

"Got it," she said. "I'm a little nervous."

"You aren't the only one," Holly said.

"You're nervous too?"

Holly nodded. "You know what keeps me out of trouble, Lauren?"

"No, what?"

"When I'm uncertain what to say, I don't say anything."

"That's the best advice you'll ever get," Nathan added.

"Don't worry," Holly added. "Everyone you're going to meet loves to talk, so let them."

"I will."

Two semicircular rows of seats were arranged surrounding a lectern with the Marine Corps emblem. Attired in dress blues and holding American flags, a squad of Marines stood behind the seats.

Nathan didn't know how such things were decided, but he was pleased to see his father's grave lying next to George Beaumont's—they'd served together in the Korean War.

"Holly, this is . . . beautiful. Thank you again for arranging it."

"Of course, it was my honor."

Hands down, the best part of this memorial service was seeing Charlene Beaumont. She seemed aware and alert. From what the doctors could determine, she hadn't suffered any permanent brain damage. She'd come out of the coma during their raid against the Rio Grande cell. Vince had found out about it when he'd called his son from El Paso's emergency room. *His only son now,* Nathan thought. Losing a child like that was the worst tragedy imaginable. He hoped Vince and Charlene would find a way to cope. Had Charlene not acted so quickly and fought back, Vince would've lost his entire family.

As Nathan approached, he felt the scrutiny from many pairs of eyes. It didn't bother him. No doubt everyone attending knew of BSI's successful mission, and they were understandably curious.

Nathan, Harv, and Vince shook hands with everyone present, including the Marines holding the flags. Lauren and Jin were right behind them, also shaking hands. Vice President Pence thanked Nathan and Harv for their service, both recently and as retired Marines and CIA operations officers. Most of the people present—men and women alike—had worked with his father at one time or another. It felt good seeing them pay their respects.

The groundskeepers had done an amazing job. Transplanted sod made it look as though nothing had been disturbed. Nathan couldn't help but notice the available plot next to his father's and hoped he'd be laid to rest there, though not too soon.

He took his seat, this time next to his mother. Not a single reporter or photographer could be seen, which suited him just fine.

The service opened with a prayer, beautifully delivered by a member of the US Navy Chaplain Corps. FBI Director Lansing read a eulogy that Holly had written. Anyone who wanted to say a few words or recap a brief story about his father took a turn at the lectern. No one spoke for more than two minutes.

When it was Vince's turn, he thanked everyone for coming, specifically mentioning the vice president. He then put both hands on the lectern and started. "Stone wasn't Senator McBride's birth name. It was Matthew, named after the apostle. We called him Stone because of the incredible bravery he displayed during the Korean War. His Marine Corps platoon had been assigned to shore up an Army battalion that had come under heavy fire. Hunkered down in their foxholes, his platoon had endured half an hour's worth of near-constant mortar bombardment. In an act of sheer defiance, what some might call recklessness, he climbed out of his foxhole, stood on its rim, and emptied his M1 at the enemy line, some two hundred yards distant. My father, George, who'd been in the foxhole with him, yelled, 'Get down from there, Stonewall Jackson, before you take one where it won't bounce off!'"

That drew a few laughs.

"Senator McBride's act of bravery inspired everyone along the line, and they charged the enemy's mortar position, overrunning it, and ultimately winning the battle. From that moment on, everyone called him Stone, a name that truly fit. He died protecting his granddaughter from certain death, the very definition of a hero. It was my honor to know him."

The moment had arrived.

Nathan's turn to speak.

Even knowing exactly what he planned to say, the words almost escaped him. He stepped up to the lectern and took a few seconds to compose himself. He'd been through a lot over his lifetime, but this solemn duty felt like the most difficult thing he'd ever attempted.

He took a deep breath. "I'm not very good at this, so I'm only going to offer two sentences . . ." He looked at Holly for strength, then said, "The measure of a man isn't determined by his life's accomplishments; it's determined by how badly he will be missed. My father's passing is an ache on all of our souls."

With emotion threatening to overwhelm him, he stepped away from the lectern and embraced Holly. He closed his eyes, trying to hold it together. He didn't want to break down in front of these people.

Holly wiped her cheeks. She'd known his father well; they'd been friends for several years. More than that. She'd once told Nathan she thought of Stone as her father-in-law.

Vice President Pence immediately got up and offered his hand. "Mr. McBride, those could be the two finest sentences ever spoken here."

"Thank you, Mr. Vice President."

After the chaplain's closing prayer, everyone converged on Nathan to pay their respects again and shake his hand. He motioned for Harv and Vince to join him. They deserved this gratitude as much as he did. The assault against the Rio Grande cell had been a team effort. He wished every member of BSI's fire teams could've been here.

Off in the distance, a three-round volley echoed across the grounds as another hero was laid to rest.

The service concluded, and people began walking across the lawn back to their cars.

He asked Lauren to stay with his mom and Jin when he saw Director Benson nod him over. Harv, Holly, Vince, and Charlene joined him.

Rebecca Cantrell stood next to Benson, along with Border Patrol Chief Ryan Switzer. "Hello, Holly. Still keeping good company, I see."

"It's good to see you again," Holly told Cantrell.

Benson offered Charlene his hand. "I'm very sorry for your loss."

"Thank you, Director."

"I can't begin to imagine what it was like at that mall, but from what I heard, you acted decisively. A Marine, through and through."

She said thank you again.

Benson continued. "I haven't had a chance to thank you three in person, so on behalf of myself and every American, who will never know what you guys did, thank you."

Nathan liked DNI Benson. There was nothing pretentious about the man—probably why Benson and Rebecca got along so well.

The vice president finished a conversation with the Marine Corps commandant, waved goodbye, and started back to his motorcade—Secret Service detail in tow.

"Ladies, if it's okay, I'd like a few moments with your men," Benson said.

Several yards back, two men in suits accompanied them as they parted ways with the women and walked down the row of white headstones. Security for the DNI, Nathan knew. Benson didn't say anything until they were well out of earshot.

"I thought you'd want to know that Alisio and El Lobo caved without much trouble. All we had to do was threaten to turn them over to the Mexican authorities. President Menendez wants them back for a high-profile public trial and sentencing. It's all part of the game. We offered to protect them from what would surely be a living hell in a Mexican penitentiary in exchange for everything they knew about their ISIS connections. Bank accounts, contact names, dates, locations . . . you get the picture. Right now, they believe they aren't being extradited, but once we're finished with them, they're heading back to Mexico to face multiple charges of murder, extortion, racketeering, money laundering, et cetera. They'll both get life without parole."

"That's good news," Nathan said. "Will you be able to trace the WMDs all the way back to their source in North Korea?"

"That's our goal. The captain of Alisio's private yacht is offering his testimony in exchange for full immunity and a new life inside the WITSEC program. There might be some politics in play if we can establish the WMDs were stolen or sold. Either way, it's equally damaging and embarrassing to DPRK's regime. The rest of the world won't be pleased to learn the North Koreans failed to control those WMDs, especially given their nuclear efforts. It might be enough to push things over the top and get the international community to go beyond sanctions and implement a complete boycott of all trade."

"Let's hope so," Harv said. "It might still be possible to avoid military action."

"Are you confident we recovered all of the grenades?" Nathan asked.

"Yes. The ISIS leadership paid two million apiece for them . . . in Bitcoins. We found the good-faith deposit on Alisio's computer."

Nathan shook his head.

"What?"

"It's discouraging to know that ISIS has that much disposable cash. Let me guess. It's a proverbial drop in the bucket for them?"

"More like a cup of water than a drop, but yes, they have state-sponsored sources of cash. We're working hard to shut them down."

"It's like a leaking dam," Vince said. "You stick your finger in one hole, and it begins leaking somewhere else."

"Sadly, there's a lot of truth to that. We're doing what we can. If there's a silver lining, it's that the president's going to recommend a substantial increase in funding to my intelligence community to combat terror. It doesn't take a lot of imagination to realize how close we came to an event bigger than September eleventh. I had the FBI run a couple of worst-case scenarios, and just one well-placed grenade at someplace like Penn Station during rush hour would've killed three or four hundred and wounded several hundred more. Multiply that by twenty-four . . . Well, you get the picture."

"Now what?" Nathan asked.

Benson smiled. "I thought you'd never ask."

"Uh-oh . . . ," said Harv.

"You're going to the White House. President Trump wants to thank you in person."

He exchanged a glance with Harv. "When? Right now?"

"Yes."

Benson answered his unasked question. "And, yes, Charlene and Candace are invited as well. Holly too."

"I'd like to bring my sister and niece."

"I'll have to clear it. Hang on . . ." Benson pulled out his cell phone. After a minute of being on hold, he said, "Mr. President . . . Yes, they're coming . . . Nathan wants to bring his sister . . . That's the one . . . Yes, I'll personally vouch for her. His niece also wants to meet you . . . She's Stone's granddaughter . . . Yes, she was in the diner during the attack . . . Thank you, Mr. President. We'll see you in about twenty minutes." Benson ended the call and smiled.

"Lauren's going to be unstoppable after this," Harv said. "Maybe she'll become a politician, not an Osprey pilot."

"I think my father would've liked that career choice."

"What about you?" Harv asked.

"I never thought I'd say this, but I'm okay with it."

Walking back to his father's grave, the sky seemed less threatening. Less ominous.

Rest in peace, Dad.

AUTHOR'S NOTE

When writing a manuscript, I often leave my comfort zone. The last thing I want to be is a cookie-cutter novelist who cranks out material without caring about its quality or content.

Having said that, there are certain elements of Nathan's stories that, for realism's sake, need to be present. For example, Nathan and Harv regularly use radios, night vision equipment, and thermal imagers. Their preferred pistols are Sig Sauer P226s chambered in nine millimeter, and they like Predator knives. I once received an email from a reader who claimed a nine-millimeter round was too small for adequate "stopping power." I didn't have the heart to ask him if he'd ever taken one to the chest. I could only assume he hadn't. It would be artificial to take those elements out of a Nathan McBride adventure just because I've used them in past novels. Having said that, each situation in which Nathan and Harv face danger is unique.

The climactic scene in *Hired to Kill* definitely propelled my writing ability to the edge. The challenge was to keep the action intense and quick but also convey the inner turmoil and emotions Nathan and Harv felt. It's possible to do both, but it's a fine line. I sincerely hope you weren't disappointed with how our two heroes dealt with a harrowing no-win situation. In *Star Trek* terms, they took the Kobayashi Maru test.

Thriller heroes by pure definition have to be bigger than life and be willing to make the ultimate sacrifice. They wouldn't be worthy of the title otherwise. Readers of the Nathan McBride series want to see Nathan and Harv take on the tough assignments. How our two characters deal with stress defines who they are at their cores. Heroes have to step up. Talk is cheap. Action isn't.

Writing a thriller series, or any series for that matter, is a double-edged sword. It's easier than writing a stand-alone because I don't have to invent new protagonists for each story. But conversely, it's difficult because I have to describe Nathan and Harv (and their extremely close relationship) in every book. People who are reading *Hired to Kill* might be seeing them for the first time.

I wish I could say writing novels is all roses, but it's not. Truth be told, it's just plain hard work. It takes me about a year to produce a novel that readers will—hopefully—consume in a few days—or even hours. Please accept my apology for the longer interval between *Right to Kill* and *Hired to Kill*. Life got in the way, and I had to resolve some personal issues. Jessica Tribble, my editor, and Gracie Doyle, Thomas & Mercer's editorial director, were kind and understanding about my delay in delivering the manuscript. For that, I owe them heartfelt gratitude.

I've received many email inquiries from people who are curious about my writing process. They're basically asking, "How do you do it? How do you write 100,000-word novels? Where on earth do you get your ideas?" For me, the answer's roots are found within a theoretical principle: Occam's razor. Without getting too deep (over my head), Occam's razor basically states that the simplest answer to explain a phenomenon tends to be correct one. It's not absolute, hence the word *tends*. Think about it. For each accepted explanation of a phenomenon, there's an endless number of other possible explanations that are more complex, *but they're also incorrect.*

So how does Occam's razor apply to novelists? We create *if/then* scenarios. If *this* happens, then *this* happens as a result. Let's examine a simple example: a car broadsides another car in a four-way-stop intersection.

So what are the possible explanations for why it happened? If you apply the theory of Occam's razor, there's a pretty good chance the offending driver was distracted and not paying attention at the moment of truth. How many other explanations are there? An infinite number, growing in complexity and unlikeliness the further from the truth they go. Make sense?

Here's a possible explanation: the offending driver may not be at fault at all. The other driver may be attempting an insurance scam. He might've purposely raced in front of the offending car in order to collect "pain and suffering" money. Not very likely, but possible. Another explanation: the offending driver might have dissociative identity disorder (DID) and a reckless alter took over and purposely rammed the victim's car. Again, it's possible, but highly unlikely. A third possible explanation—and even more unlikely—is that the offending car's brakes temporarily malfunctioned. The driver could claim he pressed the brake, but the car didn't slow down. The odds of that happening? Millions to one. But it's still possible. Maybe the offending driver had an overturned bag of groceries on the floor, and a large can of lima beans accidentally lodged itself behind the brake pedal. That's far more likely than a pure brake malfunction, but it still has pretty remote odds. At the extreme end of the scale, little green men from Mars may have taken control of the vehicle and forced it into the intersection. The explanations are quite literally endless.

What's the most likely cause? The offending driver was distracted at the instant of the collision. He wasn't paying attention and didn't see the other car. The simplest answer *tends* to be the correct one.

You can see how a simple phenomenon has generated all kinds of ideas as to why it happened. As a novelist, I'm constantly facing tangents and forks in my plotlines. One idea spawns many, but few of them will end up in the story. It's all too easy to get distracted and pursue irrelevant or frivolous subplots. If you're trying to climb a tree in an efficient and timely manner, then it's best to stay close to its trunk and not venture out onto all its branches.

To keep me on track and focused, there's a sticky note on my computer reminding me of my nine writing tips:

1. POV: Whose, and why?
2. VOICE: What is the tone? Lighthearted, serious, angry, contemplative . . .
3. SCENE: Can the reader see it? Sights, sounds, smells, textures . . .
4. STORY: Does the scene move the story forward?
5. Stay mostly in Nathan's POV.
6. Show, don't tell.
7. Less is more.
8. Keep it simple.
9. Is there tension in every scene?

I also have a sticky note reading: Try to minimize uses of the words *that*, *had*, and *was*. I firmly believe keeping these tips in mind when I write makes the product stronger. In a good movie, you don't notice the directing. The same concept is true in novels: in a good book, you don't notice the writing. If you suddenly look at the clock and several hours have passed, I've done my job.

Complex sentence structures or big, fancy words aren't necessary. Indeed, I'd argue they're inappropriate in the vast majority of novels. As far as sentence structure and prose are concerned, I write at a junior high level. Most novelists do.

Seriously? you might ask. *You really write at a junior high level?*

Absolutely, and here's why. It's not because I think my readers aren't sophisticated—just the opposite. I write at a basic level for a very simple reason: *it's easier to read.* We've all slogged through legal jargon at one point or another. How many of you read the purchase contract for your car or all the fine print at your doctor's office? Technical or legal documents are rife with run-on sentences, abstract words, and meanings we can't understand without re-reading the material several times. In novels, it's the kiss of death. People read novels to be entertained, and having to reread something over and over dulls the experience.

The Nathan McBride books aren't intricate mysteries, whodunit stories with lots of subterfuge and misdirection. Don't get me wrong, I love those kinds of stories, they're fun to read, but my novels are mainstream thrillers. Yes, they'll have an element of mystery in them, but it's not the driving force. The McBride series is fueled by action and fast-paced scenes.

You learn who Nathan is by the way he views and reacts to the world around him. (Tip #6 above.)

Look at any *James Bond* movie. Generally speaking, mystery and subterfuge aren't key elements. People watch *James Bond* movies for the action. They want to see Bond foil the bad guy's plot, kill all the vermin, and—let's be honest—have a romantic encounter at the end. Boiled down to basics, Bond kills the bad guys and rides into the sunset with the girl. It's what people want to see in a Bond movie, and they'd be disappointed with any other outcome.

There's one more tip to which I strictly adhere, and it might be the most important. All the Nathan McBride books are available in audiobook format from Audible.com with Dick Hill as the narrator. So whenever I'm writing, I'm thinking about how it will sound with Dick Hill reading it. He's my barometer. If I don't think it will sound right with Dick's narration, I edit it until it will. Dick Hill is not only an award-winning audiobook narrator, he's a trusted friend.

So there you have it—a behind-the-scenes look at my writing process. As you can imagine, it's a little more complicated than writing a grocery list!

In closing, I'd like to share a quick story with you I once heard from Gayle Lynds, *New York Times* bestselling author and friend. I don't remember the exact specifics of what she told me, but in a nutshell, she was seated at a dinner table at some kind of a fund-raiser with various professionals, and they were introducing themselves and saying what they did for a living. When it was Gayle's turn, she said she was a novelist. Well, at hearing that, a man sitting across from her said, "You know, that's something I've always wanted to do when I retire." As the introductions worked their way around the table, the man who'd expressed interest in being a novelist said his name was "Dr. So and So," the head of the neurosurgery department at a university medical center. Gayle then very politely said, "Wow, you know, that's something I've always wanted to do when *I* retire."

ACKNOWLEDGMENTS

There are many people who positively influence my life, and they deserve praise here. I can't list all of them because it would literally go on for pages.

First and foremost, a special thank-you is owed to Carla, my beloved wife of twenty-nine years. Here's to you, babe! I couldn't have done it without you.

Whatever success I've achieved as an author is also due in large part to my loving parents. My father, Paul Peterson, taught me the value of hard work and determination. In my world, there's just no substitute for them. As I mentioned in the author's note, writing novels is tedious, grueling, and time-consuming. My mother, Cindy Peterson, taught me creativity and patience, two vital traits in a novelist's personality. She encouraged me to pursue artistic projects during my childhood. Thanks, Mom and Dad; I owe you more than I can ever repay!

The team at Thomas & Mercer does an amazing job. A big thank-you to

Jessica Tribble, my editor

Gracie Doyle, editorial director

Laura Barrett, production manager

Gabrielle Guarnero, Adria Martin, and Laura Costantino, Marketing

Oisin O'Malley, art director, who helps the team work with the cover designer

Sarah Shaw, author relations manager

Mikyla Bruder, publisher, Amazon Publishing, Inc.

Galen Maynard, associate publisher, Amazon Publishing, Inc.

Clint Singley, senior product manager

Jeff Belle, vice president, Amazon Publishing, Inc.

All of these people are dedicated professionals who work behind the scenes to make Thomas & Mercer the best publisher in the literary industry. I'm honored to be in its family of authors!

A huge thank-you to Dick Hill, the voice of Nathan McBride. What can I say? Dick's narration is the driving force behind my writing style. I hear his voice when I'm crafting a manuscript.

My brother, Matthew, is an inspiration. A guy couldn't ask for a better sibling! I can always count on him for advice and guidance. Thank you for being who you are.

I can't leave out my Lord and Savior, Jesus Christ. I'm a Christian, and I'm not afraid to say so! In *Option to Kill*, Lauren asks Nathan if it's hard to be a Christian. Well, to get the answer, you'll just have to read *Option to Kill!* For those of you who've read it, you know the answer.

And finally, to you, the reader. Thank you for trusting your valuable time to me. Reading or listening to the Nathan McBride books takes many, many hours, and I appreciate your spending them with Nathan and Harvey. Cheers!

ABOUT THE AUTHOR

Photo © 2011 Mike Theiler

Andrew Peterson is the #1 Amazon international bestselling author of the Nathan McBride thriller series. An avid marksman who has won numerous high-powered rifle competitions, Peterson enjoys flying helicopters, camping, hiking, scuba diving, and questionable rounds of golf. He has donated more than three thousand books to troops serving overseas and to veterans recovering in military hospitals. A native of San Diego, California, he lives in Monterey County with his wife, Carla, and their three dogs: a giant schnauzer, an Irish wolfhound, and a Spinone Italiano. For more information about Peterson, visit him at www.andrewpeterson.com, on Facebook at andrew.peterson.author, on Twitter at @apetersonnovels, or on Instagram at andrewpetersonauthor.